EMERGENCE

EMERGENCE

BY
COURTNEY BEATON

ISBN 978-0-6488703-2-6

Published by Courtney Beaton
Cover design by Esther Maria
Edited by Kaitlyn Katsoupis and Dean Koorey
Typeset Minion Pro 10.7 / 14.7

For more information, visit:
www.courtneybeaton.com.au

To my family.
Who inspired the magic
and endured the madness.

ATHYRIA
SORYN
TERRAVETH
NERAVAEL
PYRAEN
N
W
E
S

At dawn, I am to prove my loyalty. To show I am my father's heir, his blade.

And the cost will be the one thing I cannot bear to lose.

I slam the door to my chamber so violently the foundations tremble, the sound ricocheting through the corridors like thunder. Good. Let them hear it. Let them feel the weight of what he has asked of me.

The fire snarls in the hearth, but it is the object on my bed that stops me where I stand—a tome bound in dark hide, its spine threaded with veins of light that pulse faintly.

In a rage, I pick it up and hurl it into the fire, but it does not burn, instead the flames recoil, hissing away from it as it hovers in the air above the hearth. Smoke coils toward the ceiling as the pages rip open and images form in the flames: wolves tearing free of fire; hawks screaming against a blackened sky; a blood-covered crown falling from a lifeless hand.

We all know this story. The High King and his Highborn, who bound their power into a single stone but when the king fell and the stone was lost, the balance shattered. Athyria turned on itself, and from its ruin rose a hunger that devoured everything.

I stare, jaw tight, fury rising fast as the visions of our undoing play out before me, knowing the worst is still to come. At my hand.

I throw out a force of power to end the visions and destroy the tome, but the moment my magic hits the leather, light erupts. It hits me hard enough that I stumble back a step. The pages snap shut, the visions die and the book just hovers there. I move closer as the heat claws at my skin, the air alive with a power I have never known before. As I get closer, I see a mark burned into the cover, the crest of the High King. The seal of the Corestone.

The flames still and the light steadies, daring me to reach for it.

I extend my hand. My fingers brush the cover, and the light leaps, racing up my arm, searing through my veins and I know, instantly, what this is.

The relic my bloodline has hunted for centuries. The weapon forged by the High King to bind the elements, the one power capable of saving us or destroying us entirely. The Corestone.

It is here in my hands and I know immediately what I must do.

I grab the tome from the fire and write quickly; words spill desperately across the page. Ink smears where my palm drags, but I keep writing until there is nothing left to say.

I tear the page free as a light flares, flooding the chamber in silver. I jerk back, instinctively reaching for my sword. The tome rises, twisting midair, pages snapping shut as the light folds inward. The glow condenses and hardens until a wolf of white stone drops soundlessly to the floor.

It stands there, still and perfect, its surface pulsing with the same light that burns beneath my skin.

I grab the stone and run. Every guard I pass pulls back, they know what has just happened with my father and none of them will meet my eye now. Cowards.

I reach her chamber. She wakes with a gasp, terror flashing across her face before she realizes who it is.

"Shh," I whisper as I gather her into my arms and tuck her beneath my cloak to shield her.

The air grows colder as we descend. By the time we reach the cells, the overwhelming smell of death hits like a fist. Against my chest she stirs and I look down to see her small fingers pinching her nose.

I use my magic to open the pen. Chains scrape against stone as a black wolf steps from the shadows, pelt darker than midnight, eyes burning with defiance. Freedom clings to it, but when I urge it forward, it does not move. A low growl rumbles from its chest, aimed at a silver shape chained in the corner.

Her small fingers dig into my arm. Her voice is soft and still sleepy. "Please don't leave that pretty wolf all alone."

I growl. I do not have time for this but the black wolf will not yield and neither will she.

I curse as I release the silver wolf from the shadows. Only then does the black one step back, pressing close at its side. "Don't make me regret this," I rasp. "Get us to Ivareth. Fail, and you will die a worse death than any Original before you."

I swing onto the black wolf's back, draw her tight against my chest beneath my cloak and pray its shadow will cloak us as we race to the passage.

When we arrive, I place her into the arms of the only woman I trust. I press the sealed page and the stone wolf into her small hands, kiss her brow, and vow that I will protect her, that I will bring her back when it is safe.

They move into the dark. I watch until their forms are gone and then I turn and shatter the last passage back so no Athyrian hand can ever touch her again.

The water moves beneath me in slow, deliberate pulses as I tighten my grip on the rails of the board, the wax soft beneath my fingers. Salt clings to my lips as dawn stretches across the horizon, bleeding gold into the dark ink of the ocean.

A breeze stirs through the morning stillness, cool against my damp skin, lifting a strand of hair across my eyes. I brush it back, gathering the loose ends and tightening the band around my ponytail for the third time since we made our way out, if only to quiet the restless energy in my hands.

Some moments have the power to stop everything. This is one of them. The sea lies calm, beautiful, so beautiful it almost feels harmless. But beauty hides its own kind of danger. Beneath the surface, a force like no other waits. That's what I love most about the ocean. Respect it, or it will show you why you should.

"Next wave's yours, Rae."

Ethan revs the jet ski, the low hum vibrating through my core as he edges us closer. I release a sharp breath as I shift my weight, trying, and failing, to settle the nerves twisting low in my stomach. My fingers flex on the edges of my board as my focus turns toward the horizon.

"You've got this," he calls. "Don't hesitate when I drop you in—"

I nod like I'm listening, but my focus is locked on the horizon where the shadow of the incoming wave begins to draw up from the surface.

Ethan circles the jet ski with steady precision, his eyes catching mine, holding for a beat before he gives a small nod. It's time.

His attention is immediately back to the water, reading the waves with the instinct only a lifetime of chasing them can teach. No one knows this break better than he does.

The wind tears at the damp strands of his blond hair, plastering them against his forehead, he shifts his stance, rising smoothly to his feet, his forearms flexing as he grips the handlebars. The sun cuts across his shoulders, carving out every line and shadow.

And for one reckless second, I'm not watching the ocean. I'm watching him.

"You sure you're ready for this?" His voice is teasing, but there's a current of fear beneath it. Possibly doubt.

I lift my chin. "You're seriously asking that now?"

He smiles, slow and crooked and I meet it with my middle finger. He huffs out a laugh and turns his attention back to the water. "Let's goooo," he yells.

The usually laid-back town of Rambler Bay is alive this morning. The unseasonably big swell has dragged them all out—surfers, photographers, locals. Along the cliffs, people stand shoulder to shoulder, cameras locked on the water. Kids run feral across the sand, collecting boards, or at least what's left of them as the debris washes up along the shore.

A white dog sits alone on the cliff, its fur bright against the background, head tipped in quiet curiosity, eyes meeting mine with a question only I seem to hear, like it's wondering if I'm ready for this too. A small, startled laugh escapes me.

"Rae! Did you hear me?" Ethan snaps. "This is it."

He swings the jet ski in a tight arc, lining me up with the precision of a professional. My stomach knots. He points toward the incoming swell. This is it.

The rope tightens in my grip, the tow line humming with tension as he guns the engine.

The swell rises beneath us, huge and dark, its edges brushed with molten light.

"Go!" he shouts, his voice ripped away by the wind as he vanishes over the tip. The wave surges up, a wall of water, fast and unrelenting. I release the line.

The drop hits like a free fall off the edge of the world, a near-vertical plunge that tears the breath from my lungs, my fears scattering like spray. For a suspended second, I'm weightless. The ocean screams around me, wind clawing at my wetsuit, salt water stinging my eyes, flooding my senses, blinding and sharp. The board bites into the wave, carving a hard, clean line down its face just as we practiced. Almost.

"Rae, you're too high!" Ethan's scream shreds through the roar. "Sh—"

Shit.

The board wobbles, the nose dips, and gravity takes hold. The wave's roar tears through me as I'm hurled like tangled seaweed into the churning chaos below.

The ocean rips me in every direction until I can't tell which way is up. Panic overcomes me as I kick blind, fighting toward a surface I can no longer find, my leash tangling tight around my legs. Salt floods my mouth; my throat burns; my lungs lock as darkness creeps into the edges of my vision.

Then a shape cuts through the deep. Not water. Not reef. Not debris. It surges toward me, white and fast and massive, cleaving through the dark.

It looks like a wolf. No, not looks. It is a wolf.

Everything slows as it nears, the familiar laws of water and weight peeling away in layers I can't begin to understand. Light bends across its shape and for a moment the world fractures and the chaos around me softens.

My body goes still.

This is it. The light. The end.

Just as it reaches me, I'm yanked upward. I gasp as I'm hauled out of the water onto the back of the jet ski, flopping and gasping like a fish on a dock.

Ethan's hand fists the back of my wetsuit, his breathing sharp and uneven. Tension rolls off him. "What the hell was that?" His voice is clipped, not angry, but close to it.

I cough hard, salt scraping up my throat. "Yeah, no, I'm good. Thanks for asking."

He exhales sharply, raking a hand through his wet hair, his eyes dark as they scan over me. His lips press into a tight line before he mumbles something and turns his attention back to the water.

He swings the jet ski toward my board. "Can you grab it? I'll take you in."

"No, I need to paddle."

"Rae—"

I don't wait for him to finish. I slide off the back, ignoring the way my legs shake beneath me, and swim toward my board. I throw an arm over and flip it as Annie paddles over, her strokes strong and purposeful.

The sunlight dances on her dark skin, highlighting her wild curls that tumble around her face in chaotic spirals. She looks like she belongs on the cover of a magazine, if not for the way her eyes, dark as fresh-brewed coffee, assault me.

"Rae!" she yells, splashing water hard in my direction.

I drag myself onto my board, clearing my throat to hide the waver in my voice. "Annie, I was so damn close."

"To the reef!" she barks.

"You were a damn ragdoll out there. Ethan practically broke the sound barrier to pull you out. The whole beach went still."

Behind her, Ethan watches from the jet ski. There's something in the way his shoulders are set, in the way his eyes track me that makes my chest ache and this time, I know it isn't from the wipeout. I slap the water in frustration before turning my board sharply and heading toward the shore.

I ride a small wave in on my stomach, my head pressed against the wax. The adrenaline is gone and my body burns. I reach out to grip the front of my board and feel the jagged edges of fiberglass and realize the tip is missing. Shit.

It's brand-new, and when I get home, Mum and Dad might finish what the notorious Outer Bommie of Rambler Bay only just failed to do…kill me.

When I reach the shore, Felix materializes out of nowhere, strolling toward me, his brown hair still tousled from his pillow. Of all the things he is, a morning person isn't one of them. He's Annie's mirror in so many ways, same rich brown skin, same effortless confidence, but where Annie is striking and sure, he's all easy charm and deliberate disorder.

"And we cross live to Rae Taylor, the newly crowned Kook of the Day…" He cups his hand like a microphone and thrusts it toward my face.

"Shut up, idiot," I grumble, shoving him out of the way with my board. Annie is unleashing a tirade of abuse from behind me, but I'm too exhausted to process her rapid-fire of words.

Felix throws his hands up in surrender at Annie. "Okay, okay, relax. I actually ran down here to make sure she was alive." He turns back to me. "You are, aren't you? You took an absolute beating."

He's not wrong. Every muscle aches as I drag myself further up the sand, collapsing onto my back.

Felix plops down beside me. "I thought you actually had it there, Rae."

I groan, tossing an arm over my eyes.

He settles in, elbows hooked around his knees, eyes locked on the action in the water, commentating every wave and wipeout like a running surf report.

"Ohhh, look at that set, clean lines for days and no one's on it. Still only half the size of the monster you paddled into. You're kidding me, he pulled off? Should've committed. Haven't seen the swell this good in years. Forecast says it's sticking around too. Is that Jay on the ski? Riding it like he stole it, he probably did. Oh, that guy just kissed the reef. Hopefully he collected your dignity while he was down there."

We sit here for a few minutes, him talking while I offer little more than the occasional grunt or groan.

"Anyway, I can't stick around." He lifts his arm and waves Ethan in from the water before looking back at me. "His dad's got us moving crates into the gallery today."

"Crates?" I ask.

Felix scoffs, double-tapping my shoulder as he bounces to his feet, stretching his arms so the sun hits his chest directly.

"Art. Antiques. Could be pirate gold for all I know. Myles has a knack for finding things no one else seems to know the value of, but whatever it's worth, it isn't enough to hire actual staff. So he's gone for beauty over brawn, and now we get to spend our Sunday afternoon hauling a bunch of old shit into his gallery."

I can't help but giggle as he whips Annie with his towel before jogging off. Over his shoulder, he calls out, "I'll try to steal one so we can afford some surf lessons for you, Rae!"

I release an unholy snort as he disappears into the dunes, his laughter following him across the sand.

Ethan's dad, Myles Astor, is a man of few words and the one person I'd never risk being late for. A world-renowned art dealer, he recently purchased a defunct waterfront warehouse and reshaped it into a gallery set to open within weeks; a project expected to draw tourists from everywhere. The whole town is waiting for it. He claimed he bought it to be closer to home, to Ethan, but the gallery now takes all his time. Which is why Ethan spends most of his days here instead, with us.

A sharp pang of guilt hits me as I glance out at the ocean, where Ethan is cutting through the waves back toward the Harbour.

"Come on, your boy's going to be fine, Rae," Annie says, reaching out her hand to pull me up. "Let's get you home."

"He's not my boy," I mutter.

"Tell that to your face," she says with a sly grin as she hauls me to my feet.

I wince. "Ow."

She hesitates. "You all right?"

"Yeah. Must've nicked my forearm on the reef where I've got that scar. It's just started stinging, that's all. I'm good."

She eyes me, concern flashing across her face, but says nothing. Instead, she loops her arm through mine and leads me off the beach, past the crowds already spilling onto the sand with their oversized cabanas.

Around us, Rambler Bay is waking up. Down the path at the surf club, early crews hose off boards and haul jet skis in from the water, laughing over coffee from dented thermoses. On the lawn, stalls are setting up for the monthly makers-and-growers market, while the smell of fresh coffee drifts from the café as we pass.

We walk in silence most of the way home, past weatherboard cottages with wide verandas and lawns where frangipanis and jacarandas drop purple blossoms onto cracked concrete paths.

My limbs ache, my skin feels tight with salt, and every step is heavier than the last. The morning's adrenaline has worn off, leaving only exhaustion and disappointment in its wake. I wanted that wave so badly.

After a few quiet minutes, I glance at Annie and see her staring straight ahead, shoulders rigid, mouth set in a thin line. The tension in her catches me off guard.

"You good?" I ask, nudging her lightly with my elbow.

"Yeah. Just thinking." She forces a smile, but it doesn't reach her eyes. Liar.

Annie and Felix moved to Rambler Bay when we were ten, but it feels like we've known each other much longer. She's been there for it all—the good, the bad, the regrettable. At my worst, her loyalty is as admirable as it is ridiculous, but it has never wavered.

And her twin brother Felix is the brother I never had. He walks the line between protector and instigator with infuriating ease. He's also best friends with Ethan, who's something else entirely. Next to Annie, he probably knows me better than anyone.

Ethan and I were raised on the sand together. His mum loved the water, she taught us both to surf, but died in a car accident when we were five. In her absence, the entire town of Rambler Bay stepped in to raise Ethan. Lately, though, something's shifted. Graduation looms, everyone is plotting new cities, new lives, falling in love, while we're stuck in this in-between, caught in the almosts and what-ifs.

The way he looks at me. The way I catch myself looking back. The space between us has never felt this loaded or this fragile. And once either of us makes a move, there's no undoing it. So we just don't. Haven't. Won't.

I shake the thought away as Annie sighs beside me, shifting her grip on the towel slung around her neck.

"You don't need to walk me home, you know," I say, trying for casual. "I'm a big girl, and I'm fine."

Annie lifts a shoulder in a half-hearted shrug.

"Something's up with you."

"I'm good," she says, too defensively, then quickly works to right it. "Felix is out, Mum and Dad are, um, out too, so I might as well hang out here for a bit and make sure you aren't suffering from concussion. Plus, your fridge is stocked better than mine and I'm starving!"

The mere mention of food makes my stomach groan. "Yeah, me too."

We cut through the front yard, my board still tucked under my arm, the snapped-off tip a painful reminder of everything that went wrong this morning. I dump it on the grass and grunt. As we walk through the front door, Annie beelines straight for the kitchen as I head to the upstairs bathroom, peeling off my wetsuit and adding a fresh layer of sand across the tiles in the process.

I catch my reflection in the mirror and laugh. I look like Beetlejuice.

My brown hair is a mess of wild clumps and shell grit. I wince, tracing a finger over the rash that's appeared above my right eyebrow. My olive skin is flushed pink, and my eyes look even darker than usual after the salt water burned them raw.

I step under the hot water, and my whole body sags as the heat penetrates my aching muscles. The wipeout replays in my head, but it's not the fall that haunts me, it's what I saw. The sound. It wasn't my first wipeout, but this one has followed me out of the water, and it isn't letting go.

By the time I'm dried off and dressed, I'm a little steadier but still far from great. In the kitchen, Annie is perched on the counter, spoon halfway to her mouth, peanut butter jar clutched in the other hand.

"Feel better?" she asks.

"Marginally." I grab an apple from the fruit bowl and lean against the counter across from her. "You know, of everything that unfolded this morning, the craziest part of it all wasn't the wave."

She tilts her head, watching me.

"It was right before Ethan pulled me out. I don't know, I was barely conscious, the water was everywhere, and then… there was this light. White. Moving. People talk about seeing that light, right? 'Follow the light' or whatever. Through the tunnel to a better place, higher purpose, all that." I pause, rolling the apple in my palm. "Man, for a second there, I saw that light… but instead of walking toward the tunnel, a wild dog came barreling out of it."

"Dog?" she asks, straightening slightly.

"I know it sounds insane. But even during the wipeout, I swear I heard—" I cut myself off, shaking my head. "Never mind. Doesn't matter."

She doesn't move, not really, but the set of her shoulders, the flick of her jaw, I see it.

"Hmm."

"Hmm?" I echo, raising a brow as I bite into the apple. "That's it? I nearly got mauled by the afterlife and all you've got is hmm?"

I take another bite, studying her. "You're acting weird," I say.

"You're acting like you copped a massive wave to the head and are now imagining things."

She hops off the counter abruptly, dropping the spoon into

the sink. "Actually, I should probably head home."

I blink. "What? You just got here."

"Yeah, I forgot I promised Mum I'd help her with something. While she's out. With Dad."

"Sounds convincing," I say, already watching her head for the door. "I'll see you later?"

Annie waves me off without looking back. "Yeah, sure," she calls over her shoulder but the lack of conviction in it stings, and now I need to figure out what she's not saying.

By the afternoon, the clouds have rolled in and the sun from the morning gives way to a heaviness that settles over everything.

I spend the rest of the day trying, and failing, to focus on anything other than Annie's abrupt exit. I even clean the house, moving from room to room with restless energy, hoping it might soften the blow when my parents see my board, or at least what's left of it.

Eventually, the aching in my body wins and I collapse onto the couch, scrolling mindlessly through my phone. A memory pops up of Ethan, Annie, Felix, and me at last year's swimming carnival. We made it to state as an under-seventeen mixed relay team and were the biggest bunch of misfits the sport had ever seen. Everyone else turned up in speed suits; we raced in boardies and bikinis and we didn't even come last. It was one of my favorite days ever. The realization of that hurts more than it should. I miss this. I miss us. And, as much as I fight it, I miss him.

I push off the couch with a groan, shaking off the weight of nostalgia and head for the kitchen. Throwing some noodles on the stove, I grab my phone to find out exactly what the boys are hauling into the gallery for Ethan's dad today.

I don't have to look far.

My feed is almost immediately flooded with international news headlines, and all I can do is shake my head, amused and a little exasperated, that Myles let those two anywhere near something so valuable. Maybe that man isn't as smart as I thought.

I turn down the heat on the stove, letting the bubbles subside as my thumb hovers over one headline:

"Astor Secures Famed 'Lost Collection' of Ancient Artifacts for Rambler Bay Exhibit."

I can't help myself, I tap it open.

"Internationally renowned curator Myles Astor has confirmed the acquisition of the fabled 'Lost Collection': a trove of ancient artifacts believed missing for centuries. The assemblage includes rare bronzes, fragmented manuscripts, and ceremonial objects of exceptional historical significance. Astor's team has spent years authenticating and securing the collection, which will make its public debut at a grand opening event at the Rambler Bay Gallery later this year."

I set the fork down, staring at the screen.

It's hard not to be impressed. I've always known Mr. Astor was important. He's rich, connected, influential even, but none of that makes him easy to talk to or any easier to actually like. And I'm not sure he likes us a whole lot either. He's the only reason our high school even has a sports program, though he's never shown up to a single game.

Now his name isn't just in local headlines. It's everywhere. And it's so much bigger than I realized. The thought makes my head ache. I stab my fork into the noodles, twirling absently, but the hunger I felt minutes ago is gone, replaced by a dull pressure behind my eyes.

I grab my phone and head out for a quick walk to get some fresh air. The offshore wind has hit, carrying with it the briny scent of salt and seaweed. It's my favorite smell in the world. It shouldn't be, it's sharp and messy, but it never fails to stir something deep in my soul.

Rambler Bay has always felt like a place time forgot. Just thirty minutes from the city but a world away. A town of weatherboard houses and peeling fences, with surfboards leaned against porches and wetsuits dripping from balcony rails that have seen better days. Shoes are optional and the days are dictated by the tides. It's small, tight-knit, sometimes a little too gossipy for its own good, but mostly always good.

You can talk your way out of a parking fine, outrun a rumor, but no one escapes the afternoon winds here. And they hit as soon as I reach the headland track, howling through the low scrub, rattling branches and sending sand scuttling across the path.

A chill winds up my spine and I shudder, suddenly caught off guard as my heart starts to race. I glance over my shoulder, but there's nothing there.

I shake my head in disbelief. Maybe Annie's right, maybe I did sustain a concussion. I steady my breath and glance back along the trail, just as a blur of white hurtles toward me. Before I can react, it slams into me and knocks me clean off my feet.

I feel like I've been hit by a meteor. I slam into the pavement, the impact knocking the wind from my lungs. My head spins and I blink up at the sky, trying to process what just happened. And there, hovering above me, is the dog from this morning.

I spit out a chunk of fur as I push myself up onto my elbow. "What on earth!"

The dog steps back. There's no tag or collar and this dog has absolutely no clue.

I dust myself off and continue walking, following the trail as it winds toward the edge of the headland. The dog follows. It bounces behind me, clumsy and excited, and I can't help but laugh at how dopey it is. I can't help but laugh at how absurd all of this is.

At the top, I climb down to one of the large rocks that juts out over the water. The sea opens beneath me, softened by the wind but still strong enough to draw a few late surfers carving lazy lines through the fading light. I tuck my knees to my chest and exhale slowly.

I've spent years training for the Big Wave Tour, chasing the dream of being one of the youngest and only girls to make it. This morning was it. My shot. The one chance to prove I actually belong out there, that I'm not just some kid chasing a baseless dream. One wave. That's all it would've taken. And I blew it.

The dog settles nearby, its tail thudding against the rock. I shake my head and huff out a laugh. At least it's distracting me from the weight of my disappointment. I just wish Annie were here to see it, so I pull out my phone and text her exactly that.

The dog doesn't bolt. It doesn't bark. It just watches me, but no matter how carefully I move, it won't let me get anywhere near it. A tinge of worry runs through me as I try to figure out what to do with it. I push off the rock and crouch down, stretching one hand out, palm open and waving my fingers.

"Come on," I murmur. "Please…"

The dog doesn't move. It just sits there watching, calm and curious, its green sea-glass eyes fixed on mine. I stay there for almost twenty minutes trying to bridge the space, but no matter what I do, it won't come.

With a grunt, I straighten, brushing my hands off on my thighs. "Alright, fine," I mutter, turning back toward the trail, more curious than hopeful.

It waits a moment. Then follows, a few steps behind me all the way home. I shake my head, laughing under my breath. "Unbelievable."

I round the corner and see Mum and Dad's car in the driveway, relief washes over me, as does the smell of dinner. I push through the front door, ready to call out for help with the dog, but instead, I walk straight into an argument.

"Kenny, violence isn't always the answer," Dad says across the kitchen bench, hands out wide as he tries to reason with my younger sister.

She scoffs, grabs the milk from the fridge, and takes a long swig straight from the carton. "It was today."

I pause, suddenly distracted by the exchange.

"What happened?"

"It was nothing," Kenny says flatly.

"Kennedy, you punched a guy in the nose and made it bleed."

I clamp my mouth shut to stop a laugh from escaping. Kenny only shrugs. "He deserved it."

Dad exhales, shaking his head. He's obligated to disapprove, but the gleam of pride in his eyes betrays him.

At thirteen, Kenny is all limbs and attitude. With long, beach-battered blonde hair, she's my height, maybe a fraction taller, but I won't get close enough to find out, with an enviable tan and a mouth that could do with a filter.

"Well, can I interrupt whatever this is and get a hand, please?"

They both look at me, finally breaking from the tension between them.

"A lost dog has been following me around for the last hour. Can you help me get it inside, or at least give it some water until I find the owner?"

"What dog?"

Kenny's already outside, scanning the street. I step out after her, and sure enough, the dog is gone. I take a few steps forward, glancing left and right. I try a whistle, but the only response I get is Kenny, who scrunches up her nose and stares at me.

"Yeah, all right, Ranger Rae," she deadpans.

"Dinner's ready," Mum calls from the kitchen. "Come in and we'll sort it out after you eat."

We take our seats at the table, one of the few rituals we have. Mum, a glass of red wine in hand, serves up a steaming lasagna, shaking her head as we pile food onto our plates like we haven't eaten in a week.

"Good Lord, you'd think you lot were raised by wolves."

Dinner rolls on in its usual rhythm, talking over each other, swapping stories, arguing about whose turn it is to stack the dishwasher. Word of my wipeout has clearly spread. The local shaper called Dad personally to say he'd fix my board for free because he was so impressed with the wave, which, of course, means I now have to explain what led to that call.

"Rae, you could have died!"

"Could have," I say, forking another bite of lasagna. "But didn't."

"That's a shame," Kenny mutters.

Mum slaps her arm, "Kenny!"

"And it wasn't even my only near-death experience today. I could've been attacked by a dog. Multiple times," I say, snorting softly through my nose.

"Honestly, it was so weird. One caught my eye on the cliffs this morning. After the wipeout, it was there again…"

I think back to the wave and scoff. "Pretty sure I saw it underwater during the wipeout. Then one followed me home this afternoon."

I shake my head, still trying to wrap my mind around the whole thing. I take another bite and when I glance up, the mood has shifted. The relaxed, chatty room from a few minutes ago is gone. Even Kenny senses it, her eyes darting between Mum, Dad, and me.

She lets out a low whistle and rises slowly from her chair. "On that note, I'm just gonna head upstairs and pretend I'm doing homework." She mock-salutes and disappears.

Across the table, my parents share a look, a silent exchange that makes my stomach twist.

"What?" I blurt, sharper than I intend. The accusation in my own voice startles me.

Mum clears her throat. "Nothing," she says. "You've had a big day, that's all."

She waves me off like I'm a fly buzzing too close to her face.

My jaw clenches. "I didn't—"

I stop mid-sentence, pressing my hand to my forearm as heat pulses under my skin, the burning sensation from this morning has returned.

Dad notices. The sharp inhale through his nose isn't concern. It's alarm.

He lifts his gaze, his voice low and wary. "Rae—"

"It's fine," I cut in quickly, forcing a shrug. "I wiped out on a monster wave this morning and scraped my arm on the reef, it's just irritated that scar. But you're right, it's been a day. I'm tired. I'm just going to get an early night. And I'll make sure I keep it clean so it doesn't get infected."

I push back from the table before either of them can respond. I take the stairs two at a time. I feel my phone vibrate in my pocket and look down to see a message from Ethan, but what really gets me is the message below it. My text to Annie. She never leaves messages unread.

I shove open my bedroom door and toss my phone onto the bed but because the universe has a sick sense of humor, it bounces off the edge and lands face-down on the floor with a sickening crack.

My jaw tightens as I pick it up, the screen fractured into an intricate spiderweb. I let out a low groan before slamming it down onto my bedside table.

I sweep a pile of clothes off the bed, pull on my pajamas, and crawl under the covers. After everything that happened today, sleep should come easy.

It doesn't.

When I open my eyes again, the room is dark.

I roll onto my side, reaching blindly for my phone. I squint through the shattered lines until the numbers come into focus. 11:47 p.m.

I roll back onto my back, yawn, and fluff the pillows, desperately trying to fall to sleep.

That's when I hear them. Voices drifting up from downstairs. For a moment I think I'm imagining it, but then I hear Mum.

"We can't wait anymore." Her words are hoarse, as if she's been crying.

"She's not ready," Dad says, his voice rougher than I've ever heard it. "Christ, Katie, neither are we."

Silence follows. Then another voice, familiar, but out of place here in the middle of the night. "She deserves to know."

A cold shiver races down my spine. I push the blanket off and swing my legs over the side of the bed. The floorboards creak beneath my feet as I move. I trail my hand along the dark timber banister, fingers catching on the little chip Dad's been promising to fix since we nicked it moving my bed upstairs last spring.

When I reach the bottom of the stairs, I pause.

They're all seated at the table. Mum and Dad... and Annie. Her elbows dig into the wood, hands gripping fistfuls of curls on either side of her head. She looks a mess, and almost instantly, the air feels like it's been sucked out of the room.

Mum's knuckles are white around the mug she's holding, her eyes rimmed red. She's always carried herself with a quiet authority that makes people look when she walks into a room and listen when she speaks. Her normally neat bob is disheveled, a signature stressed Mum look from her restless hands tearing through it.

And then there's Dad, he looks like he hasn't exhaled in minutes. Eyes that were once sharp with boundless energy hold something heavier now. He looks utterly exhausted.

Some of Dad's friends call me Dolly, his clone. We share the same dark features, olive skin, sharp expressions and dry sense of humor. But where he's tall and lean like Kenny, I'm shorter, curvier, impatient, like Mum.

"Rae," Mum whispers when she sees me.

I stop in the doorway. My voice comes out sharper than I intend. "What is going on?"

They all look at each other, but no one answers. Annie doesn't so much as flinch.

Mum's eyes fill. "Rae. Come sit."

But I don't move. I'm not even sure I can. My molars tighten.

"Please," Dad says.

I hesitate, then walk toward them. I pull out a chair and sink into it as Mum sets her mug down carefully.

"Oh, Rae, I don't even know how to start this."

"Maybe with why Annie is here, in the middle of the night?" My words sound sharp, tired, off-balance. "Has someone died?"

Mum offers Annie a soft smile and lays a reassuring hand on her arm as she draws in a long breath to steady herself. "No, Rae. No one has died."

"Do you remember the stories your grandma used to tell?" Mum asks, her voice unsteady.

A frown tugs at my brow. *That's* what this is about?

"The ones about magic, about wolves..."

Heat rises up my neck. "Seriously? She told us fairytales. She's a grandma, that's what grandmas do."

"Well, they were a little more than that. Those stories have been passed down for generations. Some believed, some didn't, but my mum did. She believed in them so fiercely, Rae. Magic and wolves and realms beyond this one. Even when I was growing up, we thought she was just a great storyteller, but to her..." She hesitates. "To her, it was all real."

"And as the years passed, her mind began to falter and I—" she swallows "—I guess I thought she'd made it up all along."

Dad rubs his jaw, staring at the table as she speaks. "By the end, her stories, what was real and what wasn't, blurred together. We couldn't tell where the truth ended and her dementia began. And when she died, it was easier to believe it was all in her head."

"Rae," Dad says quietly, "that scar on your arm... it's not what you think. You didn't burn it on a muffin tray. Your mum has never baked a thing in her life."

My fingers drift absently over the raised mark, the corner of my mouth lifting in a reluctant smile. "That's true."

Mum lets out a sound that's half sob, half laugh, swiping at her eyes with the back of her hand. "That's why it was so plausible you'd burned it so badly when I tried."

She nods toward my arm. "When you were born with that mark, Grandma knew what you were. She became relentless, trying to preserve what little knowledge was left. Studying, learning, spending time with you, anything to help prepare you."

"Prepare me for what?"

My parents exchange a look before turning back to me.

"It was never just a fairytale, Rae. Our family always believed this world was once bound to another, a place where magic is real. There were those among them called *Walkers*, the elite of their kind, chosen specifically because they could cross between realms, making sure nothing here threatened them, and nothing there endangered us."

"But something went wrong. A war erupted, a war so devastating that the crossings had to be sealed, completely and without warning, to keep whatever was tearing them apart from spilling into our world. And they've stayed closed ever since. It's believed our ancestor was caught on this side as the last gateway closed. The stories say she spent her life trying to find her way back, powerless to reach the battle she might have changed and haunted by what she left unfinished. Before she died, she made sure her fight wouldn't end with her. She believed her magic would know when the time was right, that it would choose the one strong enough to carry it forward. Rae, we believe it chose you."

I throw my head back, laughter bubbling up but it's brittle, humorless. "If this is some sort of j—"

"We wish it was," Dad cuts in. He doesn't even look at me as he reaches into his jacket and pulls out an old, faded envelope sealed with cracked black wax.

"This is for you."

I stare but I don't touch it.

Mum sniffles hard. "It's been in the family for generations, and it's remained unopened. It's the one thing that kept the story alive, even when no one really believed it anymore. Like a chain letter, an ancient one no one dared throw away for fear of the consequences. But Mum tracked it down. She said it would hold the answers you'd need when the time finally came."

"We hoped we'd never have to give it to you, Rae. We hoped the time wouldn't come. And right now, I hope we're wrong. But in case we're not... you should have it."

The room is still. I step back, staring at them like they're strangers.

"I think I've heard enough."

"Rae, please—" Annie's plea startles me

"When your parents asked me to watch out for you, I saw the worry in your mum's eyes. I didn't know what I was looking for, only that it was serious. When you wiped out today, I saw it too, Rae. That large white shape charging at you and then it was just gone. I told myself it was the morning light playing tricks on me. It was a frantic few minutes, and I didn't think much more of it until you said what you did. That's when I got worried. Either way, you wiped out on a massive wave today, and I wanted your parents to know."

I feel sick. My eyes sting, and my throat is too tight. "I'm sorry, this is... um... this is just a lot. All of it."

Mum's shoulders cave in on themselves. She covers her face with both hands and sobs, her voice muffled. "I'm so sorry."

Dad wraps an arm around her and pulls her in, holding her like it's the only thing left he knows how to do.

I don't say anything. I can't. I keep my eyes down because if I look at them, I'll fall apart too. Finally, I manage, "I just need some sleep."

I reach for the letter and without another word, turn and walk away. When I reach my room, I shut the door behind me with deliberate finality, collapse onto the bed and curl around the envelope, my finger tracing over the wax seal as the weight of everything just said ricochets through my head.

I must fall asleep, because when I next open my eyes, the atmosphere in my room has changed.

The ceiling swims above me, the ache in my head still pulsing. I pull the blanket up to my chin abruptly and hear the envelope hit the floor as I squeeze my eyes shut in an attempt to hide from the strange shift in the air. *Concussion. Concussion. Concussion.*

A breeze stirs at the edges of the room, gentle at first, like a draft under the door. I risk a glance as tendrils of silver swirl through the air, winding their way toward me before wisting around my arms and legs, delicately but firm. I try to move, but it's as if I'm paralyzed, pinned by something I can't see, can't fight.

Panic overwhelms me. I try to scream, but it dies in my throat.

Goosebumps rise across my skin as the sudden, unexpected scent of damp earth and pine threads through the air. Pressure builds, the atmosphere coiling tighter until it lifts me from the bed.

I try to resist, my hands grabbing blindly at the blankets, panic locking my body tight as the sheets slip away and I rise, weightless and helpless. The window eases open without a sound, letting in a flood of cold night air that chills the room.

The currents of wind tighten around me, then slowly loosen, guiding me forward until my feet find the floor, placed down carefully and upright.

Outside, the sky is a sea of black scattered with stars that watch in silence. The air that once lingered in my room now prowls along the grass in quiet, smoky ribbons.

And through them, a figure emerges. The dog.

But it no longer looks clumsy or uncertain.

Beside it, a hawk lands silently, wings folding with careful precision. Feathers glint as it settles, head tilting, eyes sharp and unblinking.

I swallow hard. I don't know what they want, but I know they want something.

I reach for my forearm, fingers grazing the scar. I've lived my whole life believing one version of the truth and tonight I was handed another. Screw it.

I yank open my closet and change into the first things I can grab—an old hoodie, a pair of worn jean shorts and two completely mismatched sneakers.

I race down the stairs, the dining room is now empty. I throw open the front door, grab my bike off the porch and when I look up, the dog is already moving as the hawk gives what looks like a nod before launching after it.

And I, against every shred of logic and every ounce of common sense, follow.

We race along the path that runs beside the beach, my gaze drifting upward to where the sky stretches endlessly, deeper than I've ever noticed before. I've spent my whole life under these stars, but tonight they feel different. Sharper. Like they're watching back.

Go right.

I startle. The words don't come from the dog. They don't come from the hawk. They don't come from anywhere at all and yet, I hear them. My hands tighten on the handlebars, my weight shifts, and I veer hard to the right. I turn late, almost too late. If not for the voice, I wouldn't have turned at all, but I make it. Just.

Ahead, the dog and hawk move like shadows, slipping effortlessly up the steep hill. This is a road I've ridden a thousand times before, but never like this. Never in the pitch black. Never like this.

I fumble through the gears like a rookie and curse under my breath as the dog lets out a sharp howl, half warning, and I get the impression it was half amused. I balance the bike with one hand, scrubbing at my face with the other. *Get it together, Rae.*

We weave through a row of parked cars, slipping into a

narrow alleyway behind a line of houses. Porch lights flicker on as we pass, setting off a chain reaction of barking dogs behind mismatched fences that blur at the edges of my vision.

Then, darkness. The last streetlight dies out, swallowing everything ahead in black. Or it should but just as quickly, the hawk's wings ignite, a white glow stretches just far enough to reveal the path ahead. Just enough to keep me moving forward.

I hit something hard, a root, maybe, and nearly launch over the handlebars. A strangled sound rips from my throat as I fight to regain control.

Both of them snap their heads back to make sure I'm still upright. Then, just as quickly, their focus locks onto what's ahead.

We're heading toward the forest, and in the reduced light and at the speed we're traveling, it looks like an impenetrable wall of trees. A solid mass of black swallowing the path ahead.

I know this place. I spent a lot of my childhood here pedaling bikes down rutted tracks, building jumps out of dirt and fallen branches. I even broke an arm on one. In the daylight, it's spectacular. Now, it feels like the forest doesn't want anyone finding a way in.

I stand on the pedals, pushing harder, forcing myself not to panic. The scent of damp earth sharpens in the cold, the air turns thick like the forest itself is breathing down my neck.

The wind lashes against me as the bike hurtles forward, gaining speed faster than I can control. The path narrows, swallowed by the dense thicket of bushes pressing in from either side. Branches claw at my arms, their jagged edges scratching my skin.

My handlebars clip a tree trunk and on instinct I yank the bars to the right. Too hard. The tires skid across loose bark, and the frame wobbles violently beneath me. I tighten my grip, every muscle straining as I fight to stay in control.

I scream.

The hawk jolts mid-flight, its glowing wings stuttering as it twists to look back and the light goes out.

I'm plunged into darkness. My stomach plummets as bushes whip at my legs. I tighten my grip on the handlebars, but the path is too steep, and I can't see a thing. My foot slips off the pedal and I scream again, frantically trying to steady myself. But it's too late.

The left side of my bike slams into something solid and I'm thrown over the front. The world goes black.

A violent jolt opens the airway into my lungs as I'm yanked onto something hard. No, *someone.*

Arms lock around me. I didn't die but I'm not sure I'm alive either. Muffled voices circle me. Talking. Maybe arguing. I can't make out the words. Then crying.

Mom. That's Mom. Her sobs cut through the fog, ragged and unrelenting. And Dad. He's not yelling, but someone's upset him. Probably me. I'm the one that's upset him. I snuck out in the dead of night without thinking, and he must have followed. Until I crashed.

The realization brings sharp awareness to my lungs, which burn. My body aches in places I can't name. I can't move. Pain ricochets through my skull, spreading like waves to every corner of my body.

I try to open my eyes, but they're heavy, and everything is wrong. Blurred shapes shift around me. Sound bleeds at the edges. My ears ring.

Someone's shouting. Another voice fires back. I think I hear my name. But I can't respond. I can't do anything as darkness swallows me again.

The first thing I feel is the throbbing in my skull, each pulse dragging me out of the dark. My eyelids peel open, heavy and raw. Light cuts across my vision. Shapes blur, then sharpen— timber beams above, stone walls washed in pale gold. The space is calm, serene, but unfamiliar. Relief settles over me, though I cannot explain why. I'm alive, that much is clear, but where I am, or how I got here, is not.

A woman enters the room, her silhouette framed by the soft light behind her. Her hair is a wild cascade of midnight black, tumbling past her shoulders. She pauses when she sees me tracking her and smiles brightly.

"Oh, Rae! You're awake!" she says in an unfamiliar accent. "I've healed plenty of injuries in my time, but not many mortals. Actually, come to think of it, you're my first. And, oh, what a state you were in when you arrived!"

I register her remark and let out a laugh, though it lands closer to a grimace. I must have misunderstood her, but before I can dwell on it, pain lances through my ribs. The woman tilts her head, one brow lifting in quiet confusion, as if she's trying to decide whether I'm amused or in agony. Honestly, I'm not sure I know either. I force a small, polite smile.

She glides across the room with a kind of effortless grace,

pausing in front of a wall lined with glass bottles and jars. They're filled with liquids in every color imaginable, stacked beside powders and herbs, each labeled in a language I can't read. Her hands move with practiced ease, plucking vials and mixing their contents in a small glass bowl with a wooden pestle. The air fills with the sharp-sweet scent of honey and chamomile. The aroma works its way into my senses, softening the pounding in my skull until it feels like I can breathe again. My shoulders relax, sinking further into the pillow.

I can't look away. She moves like the air itself is holding her up.. The happiness radiating off her is infectious, and I feel my own spirits lifting. There's a calm energy to her and despite everything, I feel a little less tense. When she glances at me, her smile shifts, like someone remembering an old friend, and I can't help but smile back.

She carries a bowl carefully in her hands, the vibrant mixture inside glowing faintly in the light. She moves toward the bed with quiet purpose, her skirt swaying gently as she walks.

It is in my throat before I can stop it.

The bile rises faster than my body can react. I twist my head to the side of the bed and vomit all over the floor. The woman is at my side in an instant, holding back my hair, her long skirt hovering just above the ground, swaying delicately in a phantom breeze that isn't there. Beneath it there's nothing. No shadow, no feet. I vomit again. And again.

When my stomach feels like it's turned itself inside out, she gently lowers my head back onto the pillow. Her touch is cool, soothing, and she presses a cold cloth to my clammy forehead. Her fingers graze my temple with a tenderness so surreal it makes me question if she's real at all. Her hands are ice, but her eyes, deep and dark like the night sky, shimmer like galaxies whirl within them.

"Sleep, Rae. You need to rest," she whispers, her voice like a lullaby. "You'll understand everything soon, I promise. We're so glad you're here. Now try and get some more sleep."

She fluffs the pillows around my head and tucks the blankets gently around me, I look closer at her. Her hair is wild, untamed, but her face is soft. When our eyes meet, my angst eases. Despite the confusion, despite everything else, I feel a deep, unspoken reassurance that I will be okay. I can no longer fight the pull of exhaustion, nor the lingering fear or pain, so I give in to the softness of her words. She adjusts my pillow one last time, and just as my eyelids grow too heavy to hold open, I watch, through half-lidded eyes, as she floats from the room—through the wall.

#

The memory of the woman lingers as I drift in and out of a restless haze, her cold hands and star-filled eyes burned into my mind. Every now and then, my awareness stirs, snippets of muted whispers, the faintest trace of sandalwood and pine, but I'm too weak to hold on to any of it.

Water crashes in my ears, weight dragging me down; the burn in my chest is fierce. I can't tell if I'm dreaming or drowning all over again.

The current twists, pulling me deeper, and it feels like the ocean is once again holding me in its grip. A low hum reverberates through the dark until my pulse beats in time with it. Then silence.

I wake gasping, the sharp intake of breath shocking my lungs as though I've just broken the surface. My hands clutch… soft silk. And stillness. The pounding in my head is gone.

Disoriented, I sit up, blinking hard as the world around me swims into focus. The sterile walls are gone, replaced by something so surreal, so utterly otherworldly, that I wonder if

I've slipped into another dream. I rub at my eyes in an effort to erase what I saw and start again. It doesn't work.

The room is magnificent. I glance around in awe. A massive fireplace stands at the far end, its mantel carved with intricate patterns that shimmer faintly in the dim light. The bed, grand and imposing, is draped in burnt-orange silk that ripples like water, and as I look down I realise I am no longer wearing the ripped and bloodied shirt from earlier. Instead, I'm in soft silk pajamas.

I swing my legs over the edge of the bed, my bare feet meeting the cool, polished timber floor.

My thoughts race, trying to make sense of it. I step toward the windows, each movement tentative and surreal. Beyond the floor to ceiling glass, snow-capped mountains stand in the distance, their peaks glistening in the sunlight like shards of glass.

"Oh, you're looking a lot brighter than the last time I saw you," a woman's voice slices through the silence. I spin around too fast, my left foot slipping, and I crash down on my butt with a jarring thud. Pain shoots up my spine, rattling my skull, and I groan.

"But still as clumsy," she adds.

"Wh… who are you?" I manage as I pull myself up to standing.

She steps into the room and my breath stills.

Her hair is a cascade of deep crimson, wild and unapologetic, falling in waves that catch the light like flames. Her cheekbones are sharp, her elegance fierce, but it's her eyes that hold me. They carry a spark that looks like it could ignite everything around her.

The healer's words from earlier play back in my mind.

Mortal.

I am. She definitely is not.

Dark leather hugs her frame, aged but finely worked, every strap and seam worn in. The cropped top reveals the muscle carved beneath her ribs, and her skirt falls uneven in layered browns and ochre, slit high along one side. A low bronze buckle fastens the belt at her hip, catching a dull gleam in the light. Armbands wrap both biceps, and her boots lace tight up her calves. She's taller than me by a few inches, but that's not what makes her imposing. It's the way she stands. The way she seems to burn.

"It's so great to have you here!" she says as she claps her hands together, bouncing once on the spot. An energy that is in total contrast to her appearance.

She gestures toward a timber dresser by the wall, then spins back with a quick shake of her head.

"Sorry, manners. I'm Ember. Hi. I'm here to help you get settled in." She nods toward the dresser again. "There's a change of clothes and everything else you might need over there. If nothing fits, we'll figure it out."

Settled. The way she says it catches me off guard, and she must see it flash across my face because her posture softens. "I'll try to explain everything once you've got changed. Take your time, Rae. Get comfortable. When you're ready, I'll be downstairs."

With that, she spins on her heel and heads for the door, a spring in her step that feels too light for the heaviness of the moment. Just before crossing the threshold, she stops, taps the wooden frame twice, then glances back at me like she's checking I'm not a figment of her imagination.

Her grin spreads wider. "I can't believe you're actually here. This is so great."

She lingers, smiling brightly, before clapping her hands and heading out the door.

Silence folds around me. The warmth Ember carried disappears as if it was never here, and what's left is the pounding in my ears and the hollow ache in my chest as guilt tightens beneath my ribs.

I press my fingers to my temples in a weak attempt to steady the noise in my head. I didn't believe the people who love me most, and now I'm standing in the middle of the truth they tried to prepare me for. Alone.

I drop onto the bench by the window. I don't know how long I stay there, only that when I finally look up, the snow-dusted mountains haven't shifted and neither has the panic.

On the dresser, a pair of denim jeans lies folded beside a plain black shirt. On the floor below, sneakers that appear to be my size wait, laces loose and ready. I drag on the clothes, my body moving on autopilot. I lace my shoes tight, sweep my hair back, and pause, drawing in a slow, steady breath. I wear a mask of confidence I don't fully feel, but it's going to have to do as I take a step toward the door, unsure if I'm walking into something new, or away from everything and everyone else.

#

The door swings open and the room beyond looks like something lifted straight from a fairytale.

My fingers brush against the cool glass of the towering windows that line the walls. Through them, the jagged mountain peaks loom in the distance, their sharp edges cut against the blue sky. Candles drift in the air, impossibly weightless, their flames throwing golden ripples across the walls, shifting and scattering like fireflies.

I stop at the top of the staircase, one hand tightening on the railing. Below me, the space opens in a way my brain struggles to process.

A massive tree grows in the centre, its branches stretching into the vaulted ceiling lined with intricately carved columns while murals of wolves, hawks, and creatures between the two run along the walls. My eyes drag up as my jaw drops.

I take one careful step down, my fingers skimming the banister. The craftsmanship is impeccable, carved with patterns that seem to shift beneath my touch.

I pause at the base of the stairs, hesitating. Then an instinct, a voice that isn't quite my own, urges me to follow.

Under the chandeliers, the light shifts as I move—brighter ahead, softer behind. I slow, watching it carefully as it draws me forward through the hall towards a set of tall timber doors.

A hawk with its wings outstretched is carved into the wood, each feather etched so finely it looks ready to stir with the slightest breeze. I reach out, my fingers grazing the surface, and at my touch, the door swings open on its own and I flinch back.

The space beyond is a masterpiece of elegance. Mahogany-red walls glow under the light of a fireplace, its flames pulsing like a slow heartbeat. Beneath me, a black-and-white checkerboard floor gleams, the polished surface catching the fire's light as shadows dance across the ceiling.

I take a cautionary step forward.

Two oversized lounge chairs sit at the heart of the space,

their deep cushions angled toward the fire. The scent of burning wood threads through the air. And standing just in front of it is Ember. She's even more magnificent in this dim, intimate glow, like she's drawing energy from the fire itself.

She smiles brightly, watching while I take it all in. "You're about to turn yourself inside out," she says, pouring a steaming cup of tea. "Come, sit."

She gestures toward a tray of fruits and pastries. "Would you like anything?"

I don't know how long it's been since I last ate. My stomach clenches at the thought, but I shake my head.

"I'm fine," I say as I sweep the room again, slower this time, trying to make sense of the impossible beauty in every carved line and delicate surface.

"What is this place?" I ask.

"This is The Academy," Ember says. I look to her for confirmation and she offers a warm, steady smile. "Welcome to Athyria, Rae."

I blink. "*Athyria*."

The name tugs at a loose thread in my memory. My grandmother used to talk about this place in her stories. Stories I brushed off. I clench my jaw.

"There's a lot to explain," she adds quietly, passing me a steaming cup of tea before settling into the chair across from me, crossing her legs with effortless grace.

"This realm was once tied to yours, though most people have forgotten that. Things have been broken here for a long time and—"

"Em." The deep rumble of a man's voice comes from behind me. "Sorry I'm late. Has she made it down yet?" I turn, instinctively.

A tall figure steps into the room, raven-dark hair falling

across his brow. He's handsome, in a rugged, untamed kind of way. For a second, silvery shadows curl behind him, but when I look again, they're gone.

His dark eyes land on me. "Oh, yes, she has."

"Hey, I'm Rae," I say, far too brightly. Seventeen years to master that, and today is the day I deliver it like a knock-knock joke to a six-foot demigod.

"Well, hey, Rae," he says, drawing out the vowel. I cringe as he lifts a brow, clearly amused by himself. "I'm Zye. Good to see you on your feet."

Ember rises and fills a third mug, shoving it at him. "Your timing is, as always, impeccable," she says, her tone sharp with sarcasm. Zye winks, unfazed, then drops into her vacated chair across the room.

"Rae only just walked in. But since you're here, you can bring her up to speed. I've got to get to the gym before those imbeciles tear a hole through the Rift." She rolls her eyes with dramatic flair.

She steps toward Zye, leaning in close enough their foreheads almost touch. She cups his face in her hands, her tone both teasing and firm. "This is new to her, all of it. Go slow and don't scare her." A playful slap punctuates her warning.

Straightening, she turns to me with a sugar-sweet smile. "He might run this place, but I will make sure he regrets it for the rest of his days if he does," she says with a stern nod. With her back turned to him, she winks but there's something in the way she moves that suggests she isn't playing.

Zye watches her go before turning his attention back to me with a defiance in his eyes that makes Ember's warning feel more like a challenge than a threat.

"Well, Rae," he says, spreading his arms in a dramatic gesture, "welcome to Athyria. Rather than sitting here and talking, how about I show you around and explain as we go?" He glances at my sneakers, a flicker of amusement crossing his face. "It looks like you've dressed for the occasion." He stands and offers me his hand.

I glance down at my outfit as a sudden wave of self-consciousness crashes over me. I'm painfully out of place. Zye, by contrast, wears a loose black shirt with the sleeves rolled to reveal muscular forearms, paired with pants tucked into laced boots. Striking but unlike anything I've seen anyone, especially our age, wear before. The boys back home live in board shorts and are almost always barefoot. Zye suddenly looks…dangerous.

My heart pounds in my chest, the drumbeat of panic rising. A soft but certain whisper threads through my mind:

You can trust him.

I startle at the sound. It isn't external, but it crashes through me all the same. Zye's posture shifts as I stiffen, his eyes cutting toward me, he's picked up on my unease.

His hand hovers midair, extended toward me, and I realize I've left it there a few seconds too long. "You heard her. Time isn't something we have a lot of right now. Let's go, new girl."

Reluctantly, I reach out. The moment our hands connect, his other hand slips beneath my elbow, steadying me. The closeness unsettles me; his sculpted chest hovers just in front of my face. There's an undeniable strength in him, a weight that feels older than his face suggests. He's taller than me by at least a foot, his arms solid and broad. The boys back home never looked like this. Not even Ethan.

Ethan.

The thought of him catches me off guard. Guilt, fear, sadness, all rise at once at the realization I may never see him again. That I may never see any of them again. My family, my friends… Annie. My throat tightens, and I pull my hand free, blinking furiously as tears well.

Zye steps back slightly, his sharp, cocky demeanor softening.

"I understand this is a lot," he says as he places a hand on my shoulder. "You're okay. Your family, your friends, they're all okay, too."

"Where are they?" I whisper, barely able to get the words out.

"Your home," he says simply, glancing away. "Where you left them."

Where I left them. He says it without conviction, yet it hits me like a slap. I wasn't taken, but I'm not sure I wanted to go either and then suddenly, the pieces snap together too quickly: the dog, the bird, the forest, the crash. My pulse kicks up as I fumble through the details, trying to piece together where logic should have stepped in, where I should have stopped myself, where I should have turned back. Or at least listened.

"The dog," I stammer. "I crashed. My bike—"

Zye turns to face me, his expression shifting. "Yeah, you did. And you did a damn good job on yourself." He snuffs out a laugh. "They've been waiting centuries for you, and you arrived so banged up they weren't sure you'd even make it. Broken collarbone, arm, ankle… your face was so busted up you looked like a cyclops." He snorts, shaking his head at the memory.

"As for that dog…" A sinister-looking smile works its way across his face. "I'll take you to see her later. But first"—he gestures down the hallway, his stride confident and dismissive— "let me show you your new home."

Home.

The word lodges in my throat as I stop dead in my tracks. Panic flares as I run a hand over my face, my arm, my shoulder. I noticed some stiffness when I jumped out of bed earlier this morning, but the pain had been drowned out by the sheer surreal rush of it all. I hadn't even stopped to look in a mirror, too caught up to care. Now, I hurriedly brush my hand down my face to confirm that I do, in fact, have both eyes intact. *Phew.*

The frustration builds, spilling over as I bark out, "What do you mean, *my* home?"

Zye flinches. "I—I, um—mean, well, home. Your real home is still there, just like it was a few days ago. You're just here. For now."

"But why—"

"I'll explain all shortly, I promise."

"Well, at least tell me, will I ever see them again?" The question burns in my chest as the tears reform, but his response is a wave of the hand and a clipped, "That's the plan, Rae." His strides resume, clearly telling me to shut up and keep up.

I swipe at my cheek to catch the rogue tear, clear my throat, and jog a few steps to catch up to him. Again, I hear the voice rattle through my head: *It will all be okay, Rae.*

I huff at the lingering effects of my concussion. I am anything but okay.

We finally reach what appears to be the dining room. Zye gestures toward a massive timber table that could easily seat twenty people, its surface bare save for a few candles. "You must be starving," he says.

Before I can respond, he waves his hand and the table transforms. Steaming meats, buttery potatoes, tiered platters of bread and vegetables appear in an instant. The air fills with the rich aroma of a feast.

I stumble back, catching my foot on a chair leg. The impact sends me to the floor, the thud rattling my teeth. Zye whirls back to look at me as licks of silver and white move around his wrists or maybe the impact has made my vision blur. I close my eyes to try to refocus.

"Oh, I am so sorry, I probably should've mentioned the magic," he says, coughing to disguise his laughter as he crouches to offer me a hand. His grip is strong, yet his touch is careful as he pulls me upright, the cool bite of his magic still curling at his skin.

He grins like a mischievous child caught red-handed. "Old habits…" He doesn't even try to suppress his amusement. "Please, take a seat Rae and eat." He guides me back to the chair, which has managed to right itself. *Magic.*

The smell of food hits me almost instantly and I'm ravenous in a way I wasn't five minutes ago. I'm shaken, but my body doesn't seem to care.

"Eat up. You'll need the strength."

I glance up sharply, but Zye doesn't elaborate. Instead, he just nods toward the food. I let out a quiet sigh, grabbing a pair of tongs as I reluctantly begin to load my plate but I barely have time to swallow the first mouthful before the doors crash against the stone walls and two men stride in, deep in a heated argument.

"I'm just saying," the taller one grumbles, swiping a potato straight off the table and popping it into his mouth, "if you'd listened to me, we wouldn't have been—"

The other slaps a hand against his chest. "If *I'd* listened to *you*—" He mumbles some expletives I can't make out as a plate materialises in his hand, and then he stops. Mid-bite, his entire body locked.

The other stiffens beside him, nostrils flaring. His head tilts slightly, a movement sharp and precise, like he's listening to something no one else can hear.

Their eyes snap to me at the same time.

"Well," the taller one says, "you're not what I expected."

He runs his tongue over his teeth, considering. The other doesn't blink.

"Gentlemen," Zye drawls, casually leaning back in his chair. "Meet Rae." He gestures lazily between them. "Rae, this is Kail"—he points toward the taller man—"and Thane. My most trusted commanders."

Kail snorts. Thane's brow lifts.

"What they lack in manners," Zye continues, "they make up for in—"

"Good looks," Kail interrupts with a lazy grin.

Zye barely suppresses a laugh. "Confidence."

Thane stands a few feet back, arms crossed. Everything about him feels closed off. He doesn't speak; he just studies me with narrow focus. And unlike Kail, who seems more interested in his food, Thane is almost reconfirming how I feel: I don't belong here.

The scar across his cheek doesn't soften him, and suddenly the room feels like it's closing in. *Breathe. Don't panic.*

This time, when I hear the voice, it knocks something loose. My body stills, but everything inside me starts to spiral. I panic.

"Will someone please just tell me what on earth or whatever glitch in the matrix this is, is going on?" I snap.

Kail and Thane exchange glances. Neither of them meets my eye. Zye does. His posture shifts. His jaw flexes as he takes a moment, choosing his next words carefully.

"You're here because the Corestone has reawakened," Zye says.

I blink. "The what?"

"The Corestone," he answers. "The Highborn poured their power into a single stone, binding the elements so Athyria couldn't tear itself apart, so no one element could rule over another. It held the realm together. But when the High King died, he hid it, so it could never fall into the wrong hands. No one's seen it in centuries but it's awakened, and it led us to you."

"What?" My voice cracks. "Why me?"

"Because," Thane cuts in, "despite being a girl, a human girl, untrained and completely unprepared, you're the one it chose to save us all." His eye roll is slow and deliberate, a dismissal that leaves absolutely no doubt about what he thinks of me.

Zye casts Thane a warning look. "He's blunt, but not wrong. This place has bled for years waiting for the Corestone to stir and when it finally does, it chooses someone who's never held a blade, never lived in this world and when the Corestone stirred, the echo carried through everything. Our enemy felt it too. And if they don't have it, they'll assume *we* do."

"But I don't," I say. "I don't even know what it is."

"And that's why we're moving things along Rae. We need to find it, before they find you."

The little food I just ate rises fast, but this time I react quickly, shoving my chair back and doubling over, retching onto the floor and all over my new sneakers.

Acid burns my throat. I squeeze my eyes shut, barely registering the silence around me as the door slams open, rattling against the wall as boots pound across the floor in quick strides.

A warm hand anchors my shoulder. "Easy."

Ember crouches beside me, sweeping my hair back with steady fingers. "Here, Rae, sip this," she says. She gathers my hair back with one hand, the other rubbing comforting circles on my back as she hands me a glass of water.

I glance up and meet Thane's stare. It's unnerving, and I look away quickly, focusing on slowing myself down, my breathing, my thoughts. It's fine. I'm fine. *It'll all be fiiiine.*

I repeat the desperate mantra over and over in my head, my head now hanging between my knees, and though Ember's touch is meant to comfort me, it's too warm, too overwhelming, and in this moment it's too much.

The panic claws its way back up, the lingering taste of vomit making it worse. I gulp down another mouthful of water, desperate to wash it away, but the throbbing in my head returns. And so does the voice: *It will all be okay.*

I drag the back of my hand across my mouth. "This is insane. I'm… I'm not whoever or whatever you think I am."

"No," Zye says simply. "You're not."

That stops me cold.

Ember turns sharply to Zye, fire flashing across her expression as they share a silent exchange.

Whatever message she sends with her glare, Zye doesn't back down.

"What you've set in motion has us bracing for something significant. If what stirs in you had awakened fully in the human realm, it would have torn it apart, not intentionally, but because you were in a world that doesn't know what it is. What you are."

"And what am I, exactly?"

Zye doesn't look away. "Our last chance."

I drop my head back between my knees and mutter, "Awesome."

"Athyria wasn't always split," he continues. "Once, this land was unified, governed by balance. Not perfect, but stable. Until one faction decided balance wasn't enough. They didn't want order; they wanted control. Vaulturia was born from that hunger. It wasn't a rebellion; it was a purge. Those loyal to the old ways fell; the rest submitted or were turned."

My head jerks up. "Turned?"

His jaw hardens. "Vaulturians believe power must be absolute. To keep it, they destroy anything that threatens it. That includes you. You're the greatest threat they've faced since the fracture. Your being here means the balance they shattered is fighting back. Magic that hasn't stirred in centuries is rising. Bonds are reforming. And the portal to the human realm they thought was sealed? It isn't. Which means you're not just proof their grip is failing, you're a bridge they can use to expand it. Your worth just doubled. So did the danger."

He pauses.

"That's why we don't have time to ease you in. Because when they come, and they will, we need to be ready. You will need to be ready. And hopefully wielding a little magic, or more."

"I…" My voice falters as I process what he just said. "I'm sorry, but this isn't… it can't be… You've got the wrong person." I shake my head, the panic building again.

The sharp scrape of Zye's chair cuts through the air as he pushes back from the table. Trails of silver curl around his hands, climbing his arms like living ink. This time, I don't imagine it. I see it and I gasp.

Zye rolls his shoulders as the silver peels from his skin, dissolving into the air like mist. He wipes his mouth with a napkin and drops it onto the table with slow, deliberate calm.

"Well, there is one way to find out," he says casually as he motions for me to follow. "There's someone, or something, you need to meet. And she's growing very tired of waiting."

Kail almost chokes on his mouthful of food. "She's what the Vaulturians warn their kids about if they don't eat their dinner."

"Kail," Ember groans through clenched teeth, cutting him off. "She's just arrived; she's petrified. Let's tone down the scare tactics, you knucklehead. Knuckleheads." The fire in her eyes flares as she turns to Thane before she narrows in on Zye. "I understand your logic, but now? Are you sure this is the best, the only, option? This is a lot for both of them. I think we need to—"

A thunderous roar rips through the room, the force of it causes the windows to rattle violently in their frames as vases topple from the mantel, shattering into a mess of jagged shards. Plates fly off the table, sending roast potatoes and thick gravy splattering across the floor as the ground beneath us quakes. A piercing, bone-deep scream rips from my throat, terror seizing every inch of my body.

"You think I don't know what's at stake here?" Zye's voice booms through the room, each word laced with fury. His chest rises once. "For what it's worth, Em-ber"—he breaks her name apart, each syllable deliberate—"I hate this as much as you do."

Zye jerks his head toward the source of the chaos. "But if there's anything in this place more impatient than me..." He exhales sharply as silver tendrils coil and shift, wrapping around him in fluid, restless arcs.. "It's her."

He takes a step closer as the scent of pine and leather washes over me, and my breath stalls as my head snaps toward him.

"You!" I stammer, realization hitting me like a lightning strike. "The shadows... in my room. The hawk. You... you were, you are... you—"

Zye's anger melts into a smile as he lifts his arms in an exaggerated gesture, showing off his very human, very featherless form.

Then, seamlessly, effortlessly, his shadows move. Not shadows. Air. Silvered currents gather at his back, shifting, twisting, forming wings, massive silver and white wings that stretch wide, their tips curling like smoke.

My mouth opens, then closes. I manage nothing but a choked sound; I just sit there, stunned.

"And now," he adds with a mischievous grin, "I think it's time we reintroduce you to that cute dog again."

Kail lets out a short, dry laugh. "Ha." From the corner of my eye, I catch Ember hurling what looks suspiciously like a small fireball in his direction, but I don't have time to process it as Zye steps closer, extending his hand toward me. "Hold tight," is all he says.

Before I can think, or protest, his hand closes around mine and the room vanishes and I land unsteadily on my feet, the oxygen is stolen by the crisp, biting cold of the snow.

"What. Was. That. Where. Are. We?" My words punch out, my vision tilting violently. A fresh wave of nausea rolls through me and I slap a hand against the nearest thing—a tree. My fingers dig into the rough bark as I brace. Cold air cuts my lungs, damp earth shifts beneath my boots, the ground still feels like it's moving.

I inhale trying to steady myself. Exhale, watching my breath curl in misty clouds, my pulse still feels a beat off from the world.

"That, Rae," his voice is laced with quiet amusement, "is what we like to call a rift walk. A teleport of sorts. A nifty trick reserved for a lucky few." He says it casually, like he didn't just drag me through the bones of the world itself.

With an effortless flick of his wrist, a thick black leather coat materializes in his hands. I watch wide eyed as he drapes it over my shoulders with surprising gentleness, the wool lining instantly warming my skin.

I blink. "Oh, um, wow. Thank you."

"That's just to make sure you don't freeze to death. I don't need the healer coming at me. Again."

"Again?" I quirk a brow, but he just shrugs.

"Elemental power isn't just common here," Zye says. "It's in everything. It shaped the land, divided rulers and decided wars.

It's the reason Athyria exists as it does and whether you want to accept it or not, it's the reason you're here."

A slow chill settles over my skin, even beneath the weight of the jacket.

"And if you weren't aware," he continues, "you'll possess your own in time too. Hopefully, for all our sake, sooner than later."

His words are a dagger to my chest. I wasn't unaware. Not entirely. They tried to tell me; I just chose to ignore it. To ignore them. The thought hollows something inside me. I turn away, blinking hard against the burn behind my eyes, my fingers curling deep into the coat.

Zye doesn't comment, doesn't pause, just keeps going, like none of this is new to him. Like none of it should be new to me.

"The Academy is more than stone walls and brilliant architecture." He gestures toward the structure rising in the distance. "It's woven with old magic, Terralyn craft, built to shield and sustain. Not invincible, not endless, but strong enough to keep us safe inside its walls, and clever enough to provide what we need. Out here, that strength thins and the further we travel, the weaker it gets. But within…" His gaze lingers on the distant spires. "Within, you'll feel it breathing beneath your feet."

A gust of wind cuts through the trees, and I glance out to where The Academy towers against the snow, its walls veined with silver and frost. The stone is weathered but unbroken, streaked with ivy that climbs the facade in thick, tangled ropes, curling around arched windows set deep into the structure. Balconies stack in uneven tiers, their balustrades heavy with snow, softening the geometry of the stone. A tall perimeter wall encircles it.

I pause to take it all in. Only then, when I finally move, do I shrug fully into the oversized coat. I glance down at it; it looks exactly as it should. Real. The fabric swallows me whole as I wrestle against its weight and hurry after him.

Ahead, a narrow track winds through towering pines, their branches heavy with frost. Zye cuts forward without hesitation. I falter, recalling what happened the last time I followed him blindly into a forest. A quiet laugh slips out at the irony, stupidity even. Fool me once…

The world around me is impossibly pristine. Each step crunches beneath my feet and despite the biting cold seeping through my ruined sneakers, I can't help but pause, awestruck. A small puff of air escapes my nose as I take it all in with a strange, creeping familiarity.

I shouldn't recognise this place, I don't recognise this place, and yet I can't help but feel something tugging at the edges of my mind. Like a half-recalled dream. I frown, lost in thought, scanning the trees, the mountains, the sky—

And then I slam straight into Zye's back.

"Ooft." His grunt is low, amused. I stumble backward, arms flailing like a newborn deer on ice.

He glances over his shoulder, eyebrow cocked. "They don't teach you to watch where you're going where you come from?" he teases, a loose chuckle slipping from his lips.

Before I can apologise, or explain, a deep, guttural growl rumbles through the ground beneath us.

My breath hitches sharply and Zye's posture shifts as he turns around fully to face me.

"She won't harm you," he says smoothly. The noise that just shook a building says otherwise, but I give him the courtesy of continuing. "If anyone's in danger, it's me." *That's a relief.*

"She's growing impatient that we took so long to reunite you," Zye continues. "She doesn't understand or care about the process or that you humans recover slower than the rest of us.

Especially her kind." His lips twitch. "So, if anyone's losing a limb today, it's me."

He shrugs, unconcerned, and turns his attention back toward the clearing ahead.

"There are a few things you need to know before we get to her," he says, his tone more measured now. "The dog you saw, that was just her juvenile form. A glimmer cloaked her, powerful magic that helped her blend into your world. Here, she is still, well… cute, as you called her. Young. And, as you just witnessed, testy."

As if in response, another roar rips through the air.

The sound rolls through the trees like a shockwave, shaking loose a cascade of snow from the branches above. Zye reacts instantly. He spins as silver tendrils rip through the air, his magic surges outward, creating a shield to protect us from the avalanche of snow.

He pulls me closer, my head pressing against his chest, the steady rhythm of his breathing grounding me against the chaos in my own.

"She's like a moody teenager," he murmurs into my hair, "but with impeccable hearing."

His breath is warm and the smoky scent of leather and pine seeps into the spaces between my own. The unexpected intimacy of it sends a shiver down my spine.

When the snow settles, Zye straightens, brushing off his leathers before shaking the powdery coating from my jacket. "Wolves are… complicated," he says. "We used to have more of them around here, but during the war…" He hesitates. I don't miss the way his fingers flex at his sides, the slight tightness in his jaw before he forces it away. "We lost a lot. Almost all of them."

A shadow of sorrow flashes across his face, but he blinks it away before it can settle.

"Wolves?" I repeat.

His eyes meet mine. "Wolves. But for now, let's start with yours… Alara."

Zye's expression darkens. "The Vaulturians weren't always like this," he says, "they were once protectors, guardians of Athyria's oldest places. Before they fractured. Before power turned preservation into control."

He looks beyond me, tracking the jagged ridgelines that frame the horizon. From where we stand, I can see the sweep of Athyria laid out in brutal, breathtaking contrast. Snow-capped peaks, dense pine forests stitched between them, and far below, a scattering of stone buildings clustered at the edge of a frozen lake. It doesn't look real; it looks ancient, with a stillness untouched by time. Nothing like anything I've ever known to exist anywhere else.

Zye takes a slow, measured breath, his eyes raking over me. I follow his gaze down to my feet, barely visible, buried ankle-deep in the snow. My sneakers are soaked, squelching with every shift of my weight. My long brown hair, once loosely tied, now clings to my face, rogue strands frozen against my jaw. The oversized coat drapes awkwardly over my frame, its snow-speckled fabric swallowing me whole. I can only imagine I'm looking more like a swamp donkey than a long-awaited savior.

I eye him warily as he rubs his jaw.

"You will be fine, just approach calmly. No sudden movements. Don't turn your back, don't run, and watch your tone. No yelling, no anger, and by the stars, don't call them something reckless like—" he leans in slightly, his voice dropping into a conspiratorial whisper, "testy."

A deep, guttural groan vibrates through the ground beneath us. Instinct overrides every rational thought in my head, and I do the exact opposite of what he just told me.

I turn to run. I am fast, but Zye is faster.

His arm snags around my waist in one fluid motion, yanking me back so hard my spine slams into the bark of a towering pine.

Zye's chest heaves. "That," he growls, his face inches from mine, "was your first test. And you failed."

I suck in a breath, still gasping for air, but then he delivers the final blow.

"Need I remind you," he murmurs, "wolves prey on the weak."

I clench my fists in an effort to contain the rising panic.

"She won't hurt you, in fact, her job now is to protect you, at all costs," he continues, his tone measured but firm. "But another one might. You've got thirty seconds to pull yourself together, or this ends badly for both of us."

Zye exhales sharply. "Through those trees is the clearing. Alara will be waiting for you." His hands remain firm on my arms. "I'll be there, but this is all on you now. And I need you not to collapse, vomit, or bolt."

His grip tightens. "Please."

The voice presses against the edges of my mind: *You're safe.* And this time, I almost believe it.

Pinned against the tree, I squeeze my eyes shut, forcing my breath to steady. *Breathe, Rae. Breathe.*

Zye slowly straightens, releasing me with a reluctance that suggests he doesn't entirely trust me not to bolt again. I lean back against the tree, tilting my head to the sky, I'm not sure I trust me either. Silently, I send a plea to whoever might be listening to give me the strength to face the beast waiting on the other side of these trees.

The icy air burns my lungs as I inhale deeply. It does nothing to quiet the storm raging inside me. I open my eyes, searching for some reserve of courage. Or stupidity.

"Rae." The sharp edge in his tone is gone. "I can hear your heart pounding like a drum."

He takes my hand, the rough texture of his calloused palm against my frozen fingers takes me by surprise. It doesn't feel right for someone so young.

He holds my gaze. "She won't hurt you. I promise."

And with that, we step through the final trees.

The world beyond shifts into focus. The clearing stretches ahead, bathed in a golden light, behind me, Zye lingers at the edge of the tree line.

"I won't let you out of my sight," he says, but his words are distant, muffled because my focus is now entirely on her.

Alara.

Alara stands at the center of the clearing, poised, shoulders squared and her head high. Despite the earlier chaos, she is calm but not idle, every part of her held in perfect readiness. The wind stirs, threading through her thick white fur like invisible fingers. The movement reveals the powerful ripple of muscle beneath her coat. She towers above me, larger than a horse, her sheer size a reminder that I am no longer bound by the rules, or the limits, of the human realm.

I exhale, willing my legs to move, one unsteady step after the other, my heart racing with a perfect storm of exhilaration and fear, as I move her tail gives a single, slow wag. I don't know why I smile. Only that I do.

Her fur is whiter than the snow drifting lazily around us, so pure it almost seems to glow. Her emerald eyes glint in the fading light as she tilts her massive head, assessing me with total, unhurried silence. I pause, taking it all in. The crisp air, the sound of wind stirring the trees, the sharp scent of sandalwood and untouched snow. I want to pinch myself to make sure this is real, but I don't want to risk waking up. Not yet.

Alara inhales, deep enough I swear it sucks the air right out of my lungs, and then blows. A blast of hot air swells around me. My hair flies back. Snow and half-melted sludge peel from my clothes in wet clumps, leaving me warm and almost dry. I gasp, stunned speechless.

She rumbles, her voice curling through my head, warm and dry with amusement. *"There. Now you don't look like a drowned rodent."*

My head jerks up, breath catching in my throat as her eyes lock onto mine.

I stumble back, blinking rapidly. "I… I can hear you." My voice breaks on the words. "You talk. To me."

A dull throb blooms behind my temples and I wince, pressing a hand to my head.

"The headache will pass," she assures. *"Your body's adjusting. The bond is new. It'll settle."*

I swallow hard. "That was you. That night, on my bike. I heard you. Your instruction. And today. You've been—"

Her ears twitch, eyes narrowing just slightly. *"So you can hear me."* She gives a slow, exasperated blink. *"Because from the way you've ignored every single thing I've said, I was starting to wonder if the bond was broken."*

A startled laugh escapes me before I can stop it.

She huffs, a deep sound that rolls through her chest and fogs the cold air between us. *"That's a much better look on you than panic. Or that jacket."*

Her gaze holds mine steady. *"You are not in danger here, Rae. Not with them. Not with me. I know this is a big change. But you're safe."*

My throat tightens as I nod, unable to look away. Her tail sweeps once through the snow. *"Trust that. Trust him,"* she adds, turning her gaze toward Zye perched silently on a nearby boulder. *"As insufferable as he is."*

I glance at Zye and back at her, a shy, disbelieving laugh slipping out of me.

"This is amazing, you, you are amazing, but I am not who you think I am."

"Not yet. But you will be," she says, matter-of-fact.

"And if I'm not?"

"Then I will protect you until you are."

"Now you're here, the bond is settled. I'll hear you if you speak, feel what you feel, know if you're lost or in danger. You'll feel me back. Over time, my strength becomes yours. My senses. My magic. This hasn't happened in generations, Rae. You're it. Don't waste time doubting or fighting it."

Slowly she lowers her head toward the snow, watching me with an expectant stillness.

With trembling fingers, I reach out, brushing my hand over the center of her forehead.

Her fur is impossibly soft, thick and warm beneath the dusting of snow. She exhales, a slow, gentle huff that tickles my skin. It draws me in. I feel it, my heartbeat slowing, my body syncing with hers, the wild hum of something electric wrapping around us.

My forehead presses gently against hers and as my eyes slip closed, a wave of warmth surges through me, washing away the last remnants of fear. My fingers trace the delicate contours of her face, each line, each strand of fur impossibly real beneath my touch.

This is the most incredible moment of my life.

"You're exhausted," she says. No judgment, just matter-of-fact.

She sniffs once, ears tilting.

"You need rest. Food. And a wash."

Her massive frame shifts as she rises, fur catching the pale light like frost. She holds her head high, not with arrogance but command.

"I have to return to my pack. He will take you back. Tomorrow, we'll do this properly." Her eyes hold mine one last time. *"Rae, this will all make more sense to you soon. I promise."*

Zye is suddenly beside me as Alara exhales a soft huff of air that stirs the snow at our feet. She turns toward the trees, where two dark figures linger in the shadows, waiting. As she approaches, she glances back at me, just once, before they slip into the forest and vanish into the darkness.

"Wow." I exhale sharply, my body thrumming with a restless energy I don't know how to contain. "Wow. Wow. Wow."

Zye watches me, one brow arching so high it practically merges with his hairline. "Well," he says with an undercurrent of relief, "that went significantly less catastrophic than I expected."

A breathy laugh escapes. "Glad to know I cleared your impressively low bar."

He gives an exaggerated shrug. "Hmmm… come on," he says, motioning toward the tall stone walls of The Academy in the distance. "It'll be nightfall soon, it's freezing, and you—" he leans in slightly and sniffs "—really need to bathe."

His nose scrunches, and I glance down, lifting my shirt for a second opinion. He's not wrong.

Behind him, the sun dips lower beyond the jagged mountain peaks, the sky shifting into a breathtaking blend of golds, pinks, and deep indigos. The view anchors me in place until Zye's voice breaks the quiet.

"Home time, Rae. I'm starving. Hold tight."

Before I can even register what's happening, he grips my arm; the world tilts and in a single, dizzying blink, we're back inside the house.

I stumble forward, disoriented, the warmth of the room slamming into my frozen skin like a wall. Ember catches me seconds before I stumble headfirst into the fire.

"Woah, that was close!" she says, holding me upright as I work to find my balance. "You're freezing, Rae! Stand here, I'll get you some tea to warm you up."

Her hair is pulled back tight, not a strand out of place. Her fitted leathers are well worn, marked by scuffs from what I assume, quietly hope, is training. Strapped against her thighs, twin daggers rest in holsters.

She moves with practiced ease, pouring the steaming liquid into a delicate porcelain cup painted with vibrant floral patterns. I can't help but smile at the stark contrast.

"I cannot wait to hear all about it!" she says, which snaps my attention back to her glowing features. There's an energy about Ember tonight, lighter than earlier. She beams, looking far more relaxed despite the weapons she wears strapped to her body.

She catches my gaze lingering on the blades and waves dismissively. "Oh, ignore those. I've been training. Just darted in here to grab this." She lifts a scroll of paper from the cart before adding, "And apparently to stop you from diving face-first into the fire!"

Her tone is playful, but there's a glint in her eye that tells me she's thoroughly enjoying my flustered state.

"I'm off to tidy up before dinner," she announces, tossing a casual wave over her shoulder. "We'll see you there soon. I want to hear everything about you, Rae!"

With that, she spins on her heel and disappears through the giant timber doors, skipping down the hall.

Zye watches her go, shaking his head with a sideways grin. "That's Ember after she's just beaten the ego out of the boys."

He pours himself a cup of tea, taking a slow sip.

"Would she actually hurt someone with those blades?"

Zye barks out a laugh. "She doesn't need a blade to inflict pain. She wears them purely for fashion."

I press my lips together, trying, and failing, to suppress a smile. I really like this woman.

Zye downs the rest of his tea, then sets his cup aside. "Dinner's soon. You need a bath. And probably a few minutes to decompress." His gaze lingers over me, assessing. "If you're up for one more rift walk, I can get you to your chamber."

He gestures toward the grand staircase. "Or you can make a start on the stairs and maybe make it back by breakfast tomorrow."

His eyes gleam with mischief as he extends his hand, the answer to his obviously rhetorical question.

I groan, rubbing my temples. "Honestly? I'm half tempted to take the stairs. I think my skull might implode with any more of these."

"You'll get used to it." His fingers close around my wrist. "Now, hold tight."

A sharp pull, not just on my body, but on every cell in it, and the next breath I'm stumbling into the hallway outside my room.

"Your landings are improving." I blink, still reeling from the rift walk as Zye chuckles.

"If you need anything, Ember's room is right there." Then toward the opposite side of the hall. "Kail, Thane, and I are just down there, past those windows."

I barely register his words. The architecture that had captivated me this morning is nothing after everything since. I let out a short, disbelieving snort.

Zye tilts his head, eyeing me curiously. "One hour," he warns. "That's enough rift walking for today. I'd hate to see what Alara would do to me if I made your head implode on day one."

"He'd be little more than an entrée."

I freeze. Alara's voice rings through my head, as clear as if she were standing beside me. Shock lurches through me.

Zye tenses instantly. "Rae, are you okay?" His fingers brush beneath my chin, lifting my face. His eyes search mine, intensely. "I, I didn't mean that," he murmurs. "I wouldn't... I didn't hurt you. I couldn't—" His touch is gentle, hesitant. Afraid.

I swallow hard and suddenly, I'm not sure who is more unsteady, him or me.

I can't meet his gaze. "I'm fine," I force the words out. "I think... I just need a hot shower."

I turn too quickly and nearly trip over my own feet. Without another word, I slam the door behind me, leaving Zye frozen in the doorway.

The moment the door shuts, a pulse of sharp heat flares across my signet. I press my palm against the scar and wince. "Alara?"

I grit the words through my teeth. "Are you here?"

"Well, not in your room," she responds smoothly, her words threading through my mind as easily as my own thoughts. *"You don't need to work so hard to talk to me. It's not your voice I hear, it's the thoughts you send to me. Unknot your face. I'm right here. Always."*

I stiffen. That's... unsettling.

"You'll get used to it."

I can feel her. Not just hear her, I can feel her. *"You... you can read my mind?"* I try through the bond.

"Not quite. But close. Emotions, instincts. Distance makes it harder, but you are proving quite predictable."

I let out a slow exhale through my nose, fingers blindly working at the tangled mess of hair at the nape of my neck.

"And can everyone talk to wolves?"

"*No. This is rare, Rae. No Athyrian has bonded like this in centuries.*"

Her presence doesn't just brush my mind; it roots deep and steady in my bones.

"*And you… you are the first human.*"

I stop fidgeting with my hair. "*I am the first of my kind in a long time too,*" she continues. "*An Original. The others were forged of the Corestone. I was born from what came after.*"

"*Athyria was never held by crowns or courts,*" she says. "*It was held by the Highborns—families whose strength came from the elements that shaped the four lands. Each region had several lines of wielders, but only the strongest among them rose to stand as Highborn. When the balance between the lands began to falter, the High King gathered the Highborns and together they made a choice that changed everything. They gave their power to the Corestone, they sacrificed the source of their magic so the realm would survive, and so no single element could ever rule the rest.*"

"*It was the greatest act of unity our world has ever seen and the Corestone answered their sacrifice with wolves—the Originals. To guard the Highborn lines and carry the strength they no longer could.*"

Her growl threads through me. "*When the High King died, he hid the Corestone as a means to keep Athyria safe. It's never been seen again, but your awakening proves it's no longer dormant. They'll keep hunting until they find you. But in their blind chase for power, they've failed to see the Corestone isn't the only power rising. We are.*"

#

I carefully peel my frozen feet from my ruined sneakers and step into the shower, dialing up the temperature to as hot as I can stand it. Steam rises around me instantly, curling against the tile.

I brace my hands against the wall, letting my hair fall over my shoulders as the heat soothes the tension wound tight across my back.

The water pounds against my skin, the sound filling my ears, drowning out the lingering noise of everything that has happened.

I absently reach down, tracing the signet etched across my forearm, my fingers skimming over the raised ridges of skin. I've known this mark my whole life. Or at least, I thought I did.

A few days ago, I was an inconsequential girl living an ordinary life, and now I'm… I don't even know. But something about it no longer feels inconsequential.

I turn my hands over, studying them like they belong to someone else. Curiosity has replaced the panic from earlier.

Steam swirls around me, clinging to my flushed skin as I step out of the shower. The cold that had seeped into my bones earlier is gone. I clutch the towel tightly around me, my gaze fixed on the fogged-up mirror.

Slowly, I reach out and swipe a hand across the glass, revealing my reflection. "You've got this, Dol," I whisper to myself, it's what my dad used to say before every big moment.

I inhale deeply, forcing the air to steady me as I turn around slowly, letting my eyes wander over my room. The scale of it still overwhelms me. I make my way over to the massive windows, where stars start to appear like specks of gold across the darkening sky. It's beautiful, but it feels distant, like I'm standing outside of my own life, watching it unfold from a place I don't belong.

"You've got this, Dol," I whisper again, catching my reflection in the glass. The uncertainty still clings, but the truth is harder to ignore—my world has shifted, and it will not shift back. I don't know if I'm meant to rise to meet it or claw my way through it, but either way, there's no turning back. A streak of light cuts across the sky like a shooting star, it's gone in a blink, but it's enough to feel like hope.

I square my shoulders, anchoring myself in the silence, and let the words settle like a vow. *You've got this, Dol.*

"Hey, Alara." A sound like a yawn hits me. *"Ah, um, sorry if I woke you, but do you know what I should wear to dinner in this place?"*

The hallway at the bottom of the staircase swallows me in shadow, chandeliers throwing long, uneven shapes across the walls. The windows are nothing but black glass, broken only by sharp pinpricks of starlight. Ahead, sconces flare to life as I move, pulsing brighter with each step, drawing me forward toward the dining room.

Then the smell hits me. It's rich, warm, and intoxicating. My stomach twists, a visceral reminder that I haven't eaten a proper meal in days.

"Rae!" Ember squeaks, the pitch unexpectedly high and still edged with leftover charge as she pats the empty chair next to her excitedly.

"I want to hear all about it!"

Across the table, Zye, Kail, and Thane trade a glance. Kail lets his head roll back, a long-suffering sigh escaping him, before his eyes do a slow, exasperated lap around their sockets.

Ember, completely unfazed, clasps her hands together, her entire face aglow with excitement. The warm flicker of candlelight reflects off her wild mane of red hair, which spills over one shoulder in loose, effortless waves almost to her waist.

I notice the way Kail watches her.

"It was…" I hesitate, searching for a word that will sufficiently capture everything that's happened today. There is none, so I settle on, "Incredible."

Ember's eyes sparkle, but she doesn't push. Instead, she gestures to the feast before us. "Eat," she says, pointing her fork toward a platter of roasted meats and vegetables. "You must be starving."

She's not wrong. This time, I don't hesitate. And, thankfully, the food stays where it belongs.

The conversation around the table is fast-paced, layered with sharp-edged humor and the effortless banter that reminds me of Felix and Ethan. A little too much ego, a lot of sarcasm, but beneath it, real respect. Real love. The atmosphere is warm, easy. For the first time since I arrived, I feel… comfortable.

"Are you seriously siding with her?" Kail asks, feigning disgust as he stabs a piece of meat off his plate.

Zye doesn't even look up. "No."

Kail's eyes flare toward Ember, already preparing his rebuttal.

Zye smirks. "Well… maybe."

"Wait. What?" Kail nearly chokes on the piece of steak.

Zye shrugs, unbothered. "Ember has a valid point. You have to admit, it's plausible."

"I will do no such thing."

Across the table, Thane exhales sharply, knuckles brushing his mouth. It takes me a second to realize he's laughing. I hadn't expected that.

"Let it go, Kail," Ember teases, wiggling her brows. "I'm smart, you're strong. We are who we are. And once again, I'm right, you're wrong."

Kail clutches at his chest like she's run a blade straight through him. The room erupts into laughter, Kail groaning as he slumps back in his chair.

Then, just as quickly, the mood shifts.

"So, are you ready for day two?"

The laughter stalls as every gaze shifts to me.

Thane's voice severs the moment. I glance over and find him leaning back in his chair, arms crossed, the jagged scar on his cheek catching in the low light. His eyes don't just watch, they pin me to my chair, stripping me down to something I don't want exposed. The longer they hold, the sharper the unease that crawls under my skin.

Ember sits upright, suddenly more measured. Zye had mentioned earlier the power she wields and now, watching her, I begin to understand. Like a wildfire waiting for the right wind.

Kail stays slouched, his focus on his food. He assembles his roll, his hands moving slowly, stacking crisp greens and seared meat onto a roll before taking an unhurried bite. His bright blue eyes cut to mine, one brow lifting in silent question.

I swallow hard, pushing back the knot of unease in my chest. "Ready is not the word I'd choose," I say, forcing a scoff. "Especially if today is the control of this experiment."

I shoot a pointed look at Zye. "But that didn't seem to bother anyone." A flicker of amusement passes over Zye's expression. He doesn't say anything, but a faint smile tugs at his lips.

Ember lifts her knife and taps it lightly against her glass. "To Rae, for surviving her first day and in celebration of the future. Our future. A future that looks a whole lot better with you in it."

She reaches out, wrapping her warm fingers around my wrist, giving it a firm, reassuring squeeze.

"These next few days, weeks, won't be easy, Rae," she continues, "but we are all here to support you."

Kail flashes a grin, sharp and playful, like a predator sizing up its prey. "Hopefully, your legs aren't too fatigued. Training starts tomorrow."

"What sort of training?" I ask, suddenly very curious.

Ember squeezes my arm again, heat radiating through her palm. "You'll learn to ignore those imbeciles," she says, her eyes flashing with a faint red glow as she levels her stare at Kail. He laughs, but the slight shift in his posture betrays him. For all his warrior bravado, something in her gaze unsettles him. I can't help but smile. I really like her.

She turns to me, all innocence, like she didn't just make a man twice her size squirm. "We need to build you up. Fast. Your body needs to keep pace with your power, or it'll burn through you before you ever get the chance to use it."

"Right, wow, and you threatened us to go easy." Zye's bottom lip folds down as he gives a single, deliberate nod.

"Sorry," Ember continues. "But we need to build up your strength. It will become part of your daily routine, anything from hand-to-hand combat so you're not defenseless up close, sparring and weapons practice so you don't stab yourself before the enemy can."

Kail snorts. "This is going well."

Ember doesn't flinch. "The Vaulturians are getting bolder. Every ambush, every raid, they edge closer to our borders. We cannot give them time to find you unprepared."

"We'll train with you every day. Your power is only one part of the equation, Rae. The rest is what we do with it." My jaw muscles clench, the comfort I felt a few minutes ago is now gone.

"Sounds great!" I force a smile.

She waves a hand in Kail's direction like he's an afterthought. "Their skills and expertise are second to none. You might have Alara, but she won't always be around."

"Yes I will."

Alara slides through my mind, her voice threaded with quiet amusement. I roll my lips together, using the napkin to conceal the chuckle bubbling up in my throat. Zye watches me, head tilted with a furrow in his brow. He says nothing.

Ember, oblivious, keeps talking. "—but more than that, we need to build your strength back up after that fall. Kail's the best we have on the ground. He'll take you tomorrow, nothing crazy, just a casual beating to gauge where you're at." She flashes a wicked grin. "We need to give you the best chance of being prepared, especially when, and if, magic fails you. It's the—"

"Who were you just talking to?" Zye asks.

"Derrr, her," Ember answers, throwing her hands up, clearly confused.

Zye shoots an equally confused look back at her. "Not you." His look nails me to the chair. "You."

From the corner of my eye, Kail and Thane straighten. The room is dead silent.

"It's, um, Alara. She's there. In my head. I hear her."
He doesn't react at first, just tilts his head slightly.
"You hear her?"
I nod. "I—" I hesitate, licking my lips, before forcing myself to say it. "It happened before. In the hallway when you, when I… slammed the door in your face."

Kail and Thane exchange a look as Ember grips my wrist in support and fills the silence.

"Zye, did you know?" she asks. "It's been centuries since a bond like that existed."

"I didn't know, but I had my suspicions after their meeting today."

I shift uncomfortably. "So… what does it mean?"

"This place is going to need a bigger kennel." Ember answers.

#

"Let's go, Rae! Up you get!"

No alarm. No pleasantries.

I wake with a start, the blinding morning sun streaming through the windows making my already reluctant eyes squeeze shut. Considering everything that unfolded yesterday, I slept incredibly well. And I could have slept for a few hours more.

"What… what time is it?" I croak, barely able to form words.

At the foot of my bed, Ember stands, arms crossed, a steaming mug in one hand. Whatever is in it doesn't even remotely smell like Mum's coffee. She's far too bubbly for this hour. "It's time to train."

I groan and drop my head back onto the pillow, pulling the silk sheets over me. "Nope."

The sheets rip away from me in a blur of movement, Ember's fingers flaring as she launches a set of clothes *at* me—not *to* me.

"No, nope, no," she snaps. "Kail's waiting for us. Move."

I blink at the clothes she just assaulted me with, my brain still catching up. "Wait… us?"

We discussed the plan at dinner last night. This wasn't it.

Ember sighs dramatically. "Plans change faster than the weather around here. Kail now has the pleasure of kicking both our butts. And if we're so much as a second late, whatever torture awaits us will be ten times worse." She levels me with a glare. "You may have a death wish, but I do not. MOVE."

She's already dressed, her hair tied back in a sleek ponytail, and she's back in her leathers. No visible weapons, but there's an edge to her today that suggests I'm moments away from seeing what she's really capable of. I choose life.

If I'm anything, I'm efficient; years of early morning surfs and sleeping to the absolute last second has at least prepared me for this. I pull on the black tights and crop top she brought, catching my reflection in the window.

My outfit looks nothing like theirs. Neither does my body.

I've always been strong, broader through the shoulders, built from hours in the water, but now, something's different. Maybe it's the accident. Maybe it's just me in comparison to them. Either way, a gnawing feeling of doubt creeps in. I'm nervous. Nervous I won't live up to their expectations. And we're mere seconds away from finding out.

I shove the thought away, tying my hair into a messy bun and slipping into a pair of boots that wait at the end of the bed.

"That'll do," Ember says, nodding in approval. Then, hesitating before she asks, "Are you ready to… rift walk? At this hour?"

I sigh. "I guess it beats the stairs."

She smiles as she throws out her hands.

I glance once more at the falling snow outside my window, a sight I know I'll never take for granted, before reluctantly taking her hand. I brace myself, pressing my other hand to my forehead.

She giggles just before the world disappears.

"Good afternoon, ladies!"

Kail's voice rings through the cavernous space. He stands in the center of the room, arms crossed, a Cheshire grin plastered across his face.

Wherever here is, it is nothing like The Academy.

Gone are the gilded embellishments, the grand chandeliers, the opulence. Instead, we are surrounded by raw, aged timber and weathered stone. This is a structure that has survived centuries. And it stinks.

Shelves carved from the rock line the walls, each stacked with different-looking weapons and hefty equipment that looks like it came straight out of the Stone Age. Sparrows flit through an open window that brings in a cool breeze, which does little to freshen the overpowering smell of sweat. Kail watches me take it all in, his piercing blue eyes flashing with amusement as if waiting for me to react.

"So," he drawls, "none of what you know or can do will do you much good here." His hand flicks toward the room, dismissive. "So tell me, little human, what useful skills do you think you have?"

"Well, I've never fought anyone in my life, but I'm fit, or at least I used to be. My parents say I'm a fierce competitor." I shrug. "I guess I'll find out." I widen my stance, crouching slightly, readying to spar.

Kail and Ember exchange a single glance before they burst into a fit of laughter. Kail shakes his head, still chuckling, as Ember bends down, pretending to tighten the laces on her already tied up boots to hide her laughter.

"No combat for you today, thankfully," Kail says, clearing his throat but unable to hide his amusement.

"Today is about testing what you do have," he continues, his brows lifting. "And letting me figure out what you don't. And the best way to do that is by exploring the hills and valleys of Athyria!" A crooked smile spreads across his face, clearly indicating that what comes next will not be pleasant.

His expression doesn't lie.

For the next few hours, we race through snow-blanketed forests, scale jagged boulders, and climb along precarious cliff-sides. Yesterday, I looked up at these peaks in awe; as of this moment, they'll forever haunt me.

Despite being fitter and stronger than me, there's a strange comfort in seeing Ember struggle too. Kail, on the other hand, bounds through the pseudo-obstacle course with such ease he looks more mountain goat than man. It's enough to make me want to shove him into the next tree.

Every part of my body burns. My legs scream in protest, sharp pain flaring with every movement. Scratches litter my arms and hands where I've misjudged the thorny underbrush or slipped against the rough stone. The cold air bites at my lungs, turning each inhale into a sharp, shallow gasp.

"Prove them wrong, Rae."

Alara's voice startles me, and I stumble.

"Pull it together. You're just about there."

I don't have the energy to respond and can muster little more than a nod of acknowledgment to no one in particular as I wipe the sweat and dirt from my face with the back of my hand. Kail calls over his shoulder, "This land is safe to travel. Don't venture out on your own. We'll give a rundown on the lands and who controls what, soon."

"'K," is all I can manage as I try to keep up and not impale myself on a rock edge. Safe to travel, my ass.

"Almost there," Ember promises, unable to hide the strain in her voice.

We crest a rise in the trail where the trees thin, and she slows, bracing her hands on her knees. I pull up next to her, chest heaving, as she collapses in a heap at the base of the rock where Kail is now perched like a gargoyle.

I blink up at him. "I'm starting to sense you enjoy watching people suffer."

He flashes a grin, teeth bright against his wind-chapped skin. "Oh, this isn't suffering. This was just a warmup."

Ember groans dramatically beside me. "When I get my breath back, I'm digging a grave at the base of that rock and burying you in it."

Kail drops from the rock in a single, easy movement, landing with one foot on either side of her. His laugh is low and rough around the edges. "Not with those noodle arms, you're not."

He nods toward where I'm sprawled in the snow. "But hey, that wasn't bad, not bad at all. You made it. Not all do."

I force out a sound between a laugh and a wheeze, sinking onto a rock. Kail turns and gestures with his chin. "Look."

Below us, the trees open into a wide bowl of land cradled between dark slopes. A village sprawls oute in layered terraces of stone and timber, chimneys puffing gentle smoke into the cold air. Winding paths thread between buildings, with people moving about. A woman balancing a sack on one shoulder while a child tugs at her cloak, a pair of merchants deep in conversation, laughter ringing in the clear air. Real people. A real village.

"You should see it at night. Lanterns lit up like stars on the ground," Ember says.

Kail steps back, arms folded across his chest, shoulders set like stone. His gaze stays fixed on the valley, steady but heavy. "They built this from ruin after the war, when everything fell apart. They didn't have much choice—lie down or rebuild."

I swallow, watching life moving through the narrow streets. "Rebuild from what?"

Kail's eyes narrow faintly. "From nothing. From ashes. This used to be ruins, abandoned, cursed ground. The people here made it livable again."

Ember picks up quietly. "Not everyone in Athyria has magic. Most don't, not anymore. But they still fight for a future no one promised them."

I blink at that. "No magic?"

Kail snorts, but it's not mocking. "Magic's not guaranteed. It's rare. Feared, even. Wars were fought over it. Still are, in ways."

A prickle runs down my spine.

Suddenly, Kail tenses. His head lifts slightly, nostrils flaring as he inhales, it's barely noticeable, but it's there. His body straightens, muscles bracing as a low groan rumbles from his chest.

He turns to Ember, a rare softness flickering through his expression as he looks at her. "What about it, fireball?" His voice dips, dangerously smooth. "Want to race back?"

He winks, but his focus is already gone, his gaze snapping back toward the tree line. His posture tightens, honed in, tracking something. Ember shifts beside me. "Absolutely not," she mutters.

Kail barks out a sharp laugh before he moves and gods, it's fast. He launches toward the first line of trees, his movements canine-like, his boots barely making a sound as he disappears into the forest.

I push my elbow into the snow, digging in, forcing myself upright despite the brutal ache in my limbs. Every inch of my body protests, but it's quickly forgotten.

Branches shift in the forest beside us, the sound crisp in the cold air.

They step out from the tree line one by one. Alara leads. Her white coat stands out against the dark forest, breath curling in slow, measured plumes.

They're massive. Not storybook wolves or overgrown dogs, they would dwarf a direwolf. Their size alone is enough to steal the air I just fought to get back into my lungs.

I push myself the rest of the way up, Ember doing the same beside me.

Ember's eyes burn bright as she eyes the wolves ahead. "I've never been this close to them before. I'm actually nervous," she whispers.

"She is fireborn. She has nothing to fear. Tell her to step forward. Soraya," she nods toward the silver wolf, *"and Aric,"* her gaze shifting to the largest black-coated wolf, *"are here to*

meet you both. It has been a long time since flame stood before the wolves without war between them."

"Ember," I say, forcing steadiness into my voice. "You're fireborn." I relay it without fully understanding what that even means. "They're asking to meet you."

"You really can talk to them." She tilts her head, studying me with new scrutiny.

"Alara. I can only communicate with Alara, I think." The words leave my mouth before I fully process them. I glance at her, seeking confirmation. She nods.

Ember turns back toward the wolves, squaring her shoulders. The air around her thickens, the temperature rising as fire curls around her arms, cascading like molten ribbons. Flames lick at her fingertips, dancing between her palms, moving with her. The fire doesn't burn her; it obeys her.

She hovers a foot above the ground as she tilts her body forward in a bow. I stand in stunned silence.

Steam rises as her fire-laden feet touch the ground, filling the air with the scent of burning wood. She straightens, looking at me, smiling. Her eyes are wild, alive, burning like an inferno. I knew she harbored a power from the way she glows at the height of her emotions, but this is something else entirely.

Ember exhales slowly, like she's trying to find words big enough for what this means. "They haven't been seen together like this in centuries, Rae." Her voice is completely awestruck. "And they have come together now, after all this time, thanks to you."

I stay still, unsure what to say.

"The Originals were wolves, forged from the Corestone and bound to the strongest wielders Athyria ever knew—the Highborns," she says. "They were created to protect, to carry the strength their bonded had given up when the Corestone was forged. The Highborn sacrificed power to save the realm. The wolves were the answer to that loss."

"But an Alpha?" She shakes her head. "That's different. Alphas weren't just protectors, they were the embodiment of the bond itself. They didn't guard the Highborn's power. They *became* it."

Her gaze shifts to Aric and Soraya. "Those two are more than legend. Aric was Alpha of the earthbound wolves, Soraya of the sea-bound. There was never only one Highborn per region, sometimes there were several, but only the strongest ever bore an Alpha. The Highborn didn't inherit crowns or wear them. They were power, and the Alphas were their ultimate defense."

"Highborns… that's what humans called the Walkers, isn't it?" I ask.

"That's them. They walked between worlds, bridging what no crown could. But like the wolves, they weren't always united. Even among the Highborn, rivalry ran deep. Yet in the end, they found uneasy ground with one another. Balance, of a kind. Until it broke."

Aric holds his head high, but his golden eyes remain locked on Ember. His black fur seems to drink the light around him, his massive form shifting in and out of the shadows like he belongs to them. The slow rise and fall of his chest is deliberate, controlled.

Beside him, Soraya stands slightly smaller but no less commanding. Her silver coat glistens in the low light, each strand catching like thousands of tiny mirrors. One blue eye, one brown, flicker between us.

And then there's Alara.

She looks even larger than yesterday; I barely reach her shoulder, her snow-white coat catching what little light slips through the canopy.

Ember swallows hard, her throat working, eyes shining with the effort to keep it together.

"When the Originals fell, hope fell with them. No one ever thought we'd see their kind again, let alone together. The only reason Aric and Soraya would return, would follow, is if they believed in the Alpha standing before them."

Ember lets out a quiet laugh, heat curling at her fingertips. "It explains why Kail took off the way he did. The big sook."

"He's scared of them?" I ask.

"Not scared," she says. "Just not ready, or willing, to... let's say submit. It's an ego thing."

She glances at Alara. "Wolves just know. It's instinct. Alara only follows one thing now." Her fiery gaze locks on me. "You."

I look at Alara who lifts her head and takes one step forward as they all watch her. Then her front legs fold, and she lowers her head.

The Alpha of Athyria is bowing.

To me.

"*And this position should help you climb on. We're here to take you home.*"

"Wait, what?" My head whips back, and I look to Ember for confirmation. She just beams at me, wide-eyed and clueless.

"*We. Are here. To take. You home.*" Alara enunciates each word, slow and deliberate. "*You need to learn to ride—and listen—Aric will take Ember, and—*"

"*I get to ride on you. Like a horse?*"

Her growl rumbles low, enough to vibrate in my bones. "*Deeply offensive.*" A pause. "*But... similar, I suppose.*"

A laugh bubbles out of me, exhausted and disbelieving all at once.

"They are here to take us home," I say, turning back to Ember.

"Us?" she squeals, clapping her hands together and a tiny ball of fire bursts from her palms into the air.

"Whoa," I say, jerking my head back, narrowly avoiding singed eyelashes. "Yes, I need to learn to ride. Aric will take you."

A deep, rumbling growl cuts through the cold air. Aric. The sound is edged with impatience and disdain. Ember doesn't flinch. She doesn't even acknowledge it, which makes me wonder if she's either fearless or entirely reckless. Possibly both.

She turns to me, eyes blazing, like we aren't standing next to a pack of wolves who could tear us apart in an instant. I shake my head at her and smile wide.

"Well, what are we waiting for?" She flicks her wrist, fire trailing lazily between her fingers. "Let's go."

This is no horse.

Alara towers over anything I've ever climbed, ridden, or even imagined riding.

There are no stirrups, no reins, there is absolutely nothing to hold onto.

"*Tell me how to do this, quickly,*" I say, noticing Ember suddenly looks just as panicked as I feel. "*Before she self-combusts and ignites us all.*"

"*You can't and won't hurt us. There's a small flat on my back. Sit there and hold on.*"

"*Right. Simple. What could possibly go wrong.*"

"*Tell her to approach slowly and carefully. This is significant for him, too. All she needs to worry about is holding on. Tight. Let's go. We don't want to be standing out here any longer than we need to.*"

My mouth goes dry.

Alara meets my gaze, her emerald eyes flashing with quiet reassurance. Sensing my hesitation, she rumbles low as she shifts her stance, lowering farther, one massive paw stretching forward in a deliberate, steadying motion.

I lift my hands to my hair, hiding the shake in my fingers, pretending to tighten my ponytail as I step forward. The moment feels monumental, but my legs feel like jelly.

I reach out, pressing a hesitant hand to her forehead first, then press my palms into her shoulder, feeling the muscle shift.

"*Use your arms to pull yourself up, or step onto my leg and climb.*"

I glance up. "I, I can't. I don't want to—"

"You weigh less than the mud I carry on my paws. Up. Now."

I tilt my head back; there is a mischievous glint in her eye.

I take a deep breath, grab a fistful of her fur with both hands, and haul myself up like I've seen them do with horses in the movies. Except this is no horse and I am no cowboy and I come crashing back to eat dirt.

"Again."

This time, she gets even lower. I tighten my grip; my apology is met with a growl, and I try again. Every muscle is screaming in protest after this morning's workout, but somehow, I make it. Barely.

I land without an ounce of grace, limbs flailing before I finally thud onto her back, draped over her like a drunk saddlebag. I can't help but notice the ground is a long way away.

"Ta-da," I gasp.

"That'll do. You're on. Stay there. The healer is not available today."

I press my forehead against her and before I can stop myself, I hug her. I close my eyes and inhale her in. I should feel terrified; instead, I feel exhilarated.

Aric bows low, allowing Ember to mount. Unlike me, she avoids humiliation entirely, using controlled magic to land gracefully in the hollow of his back. She braces effortlessly, leaning into his shoulders.

"I won't let you fall. Just hold tight and enjoy the ride," Alara says.

I swallow. *"I doubt that very much."*

A low chuckle rumbles through her chest, vibrating between my legs.

I have half a second to adjust my posture before she moves, and then we're gone.

My thighs and hands clamp down with full desperation, my fingers tangling into her fur as we tear through the trees like a rush of wind. Branches blur. Snow sprays upward in the wake of her paws. The forest is a blur of movement, the icy air sharp against my cheeks, but I can barely register anything past the sheer force of her speed. I feel the shift in her muscles before she leaps, before she lands again, her paws barely touching the ground as she surges forward even faster.

"I was prepared for more squealing," Alara muses, effortlessly sprinting between trees. *"Or have you fallen off?"*

A quick laugh escapes me, exhilaration crashing over fear. *"I'm still here, I'm just focused on all the trees—"* I duck suddenly as she darts under a branch that almost takes my head off *"—you're narrowly avoiding."*

Alara slows, the rush of wind fading as the world sharpens around me. *"Here we are, Rae. You made it."* What had taken hours to climb had taken mere seconds to descend.

"You say I don't listen, yet even I hear the underlying surprise in that statement," I say.

"I'm here to keep you safe, not hurt you; you do that on your own well enough."

"There's a common denominator here..."

Alara makes a sound that might be a laugh, a low huff that stirs the snow around us. A sharp gust billows up as she lowers her front leg, my legs are shaky, buzzing with exhaustion and adrenaline as I slide one over her back, gripping her fur to steady myself before dropping down.

My feet hit the ground and my knees threaten to buckle, my balance feeling all wrong now that I'm back on solid earth.

"Whoa there, wobbly legs."

I look up at Alara, her emerald eyes catching the light like polished glass as she watches me curiously.

I laugh, out of breath. My face is flushed, hair a mess, but I don't care. *"That was incredible."*

I reach out, fingers brushing the thick fur at her neck in a quick, grateful touch. "Thank you," I whisper, my voice still raw from the wind.

She doesn't blink. Doesn't move. Something passes between us and I sense she feels it too. But before I can say anything else, I'm crushed into a hug.

"HOLY WOW!" Ember blurts, laughter bursting from her like a fuse just snapped inside her.

She spins in place, hands out wide, little flames flickering from her fingertips as the smile on her face pulls so tight I think it might split.

Her hands clap against my shoulders, her fire warming my already burning skin.

But Alara isn't laughing.

"Rae, we have to go. Your people are gathering now. We can't stay out here."

Her tone turns my blood cold.

I follow her gaze to where people are emerging from the gym. Maybe twenty, thirty of them, mostly men, a few women, all wide-eyed and whispering.

Most of the men are shirtless, beads of sweat trailing down their torsos, damp hair sticking to their foreheads. The girls wear cropped shirts, each one standing rigid, staring. Not at me.

At Alara. At the wolves.

I realize then that Soraya never left the trees. She remained in the shadows and Aric had immediately returned to her side, his massive black form barely visible against the tree line.

Alara meets his gaze, then looks toward the growing crowd, toward Kail and Thane, who now stand at the front of them, arms crossed, bodies braced like they're holding a line.

This isn't at all the welcome party I was expecting.

Then Alara releases a sound. It isn't a growl; it's deeper, rougher. The hairs on my arms rise as I turn to find out what is happening, but I don't get the chance. The wolves are gone.

Almost as quickly, Kail and Thane close in on either side of me. It feels instinctive, protective, and it catches me off guard. I don't know whether to step back or lean in.

Kail mutters something, his eyes locked on the distant shadows where they disappeared.

I swallow. "What's all this about?"

Thane doesn't look at me. "History."

"Rae, meet me in the gym, same time tomorrow. We begin sparring," Kail adds. Then he turns, barking orders, rounding up the group, his tone clipped, his body rigid. His entire presence has changed.

That energy from before begins to pulse through my muscles again. Ember, oblivious or unfazed by the tension, links her elbow with mine. "Time for your briefing," she says brightly and, in the next heartbeat, we're back at the house by the fireplace.

With a flick of her wrist, a plate appears, stacked with a warm, crusty baguette. "I don't know about you, but I'm starving. Eat." Ember shoves the plate toward me, nodding at the lounge by the fire. "Zye was right, but if you tell him I said that, I'll torture you," she adds, eyes flashing. "You're stronger than I gave you credit for and you're ready to know more than I was prepared to tell you."

I pause mid-reach, narrowing my eyes. "You speak about me?"

Ember leans back on the arm of the chair opposite me. "Oh, constantly."

She's hooked me; I bite. "And what is said, exactly?"

She taps her chin, feigning deep thought. "Let's see...your strange fashion choices, the way you walk around with your eyes bulging at the sight of everything. How foreign it must all be. How brave you've been. How pretty all the boys think you are."

I nearly choke. "Excuse me?"

Ember grins, fire dancing at her fingertips. "I may have paraphrased."

I can't help but laugh, shaking my head.

"You're doing better than you think." Ember gestures toward the fire; the flames stretch toward her like they recognize their master. "You endured brutal training and rode a wolf like you were born for it."

"None of this feels real."

She exhales, tipping her head back slightly. "I bet it doesn't. It's not every day you're ripped from the only world you've ever known, dropped into a realm that makes no sense, surrounded by a group of misfits who casually gather around to yell, 'Hey, Rae, save the day.'"

A surprised laugh slips out before I can stop it. I turn to her, sensing the edge beneath the bravado.

She meets my gaze, and for a moment there's no fire, no teasing, just quiet certainty. "You're going to be okay, Rae." A pause. "I mean, probably. If Kail doesn't accidentally kill you in training tomorrow."

I groan, dragging a hand down the side of my face. "I'm still not sure he didn't do that today."

"Welcome to The Academy, and believe me when I say, he's done worse to stronger beings."

She pushes up from her chair. "Right, I need to grab a few things before we sit down for your history lesson."

Before I can ask what, she vanishes in a whisper of smoke, leaving only the faintest trace of heat in the air.

I sink into the large armchair, allowing the cushions to absorb the ache in my body. I had forgotten about the sheer brutality of this morning, but the ache, no longer dulled by adrenaline, returns with a vengeance. Just as I exhale, letting my head tip back, a strange sensation prickles at the edge of my awareness. Before the door even creaks open, I feel him and as if summoned, a heartbeat later Zye steps through.

Dim firelight catches on his silhouette, casting him in shifting shadows. He strides in confidently, every movement effortless as he makes his way to the armchair opposite me. He doesn't sit right away, he just watches me, leaning against the chair, his weight braced on one arm.

"I hear you had quite the morning," he says.

The firelight carves his face into shadow and flame, sharpening the cut of his jaw and the proud line of his cheekbones. Strands of dark hair fall loose across his brow, but it's his eyes that undo me, storm-dark and unapologetic, a gravity that drags you close before you realize you've already stepped into the fall.

I huff a laugh as I force my gaze to anywhere else in the room. "Turns out I ride a wolf better than a bike."

His mouth opens, his surprise breaking into a low, amused sound. He moves then, finally settling into the chair opposite mine, draping himself across it with a lazy confidence, one arm slung over the backrest. "Thank the stars for that," he murmurs, rubbing a hand along his jaw.

He watches me, not with the idle curiosity everyone else carries in this place, but with the quiet calculation of someone fitting pieces together. He looks at me like he's trying to solve a puzzle.

Without breaking eye contact, he flicks his wrist, and more food appears on my plate, piled with fresh fruit and a warm spinach-and-cheese muffin. My favorite. I hesitate. "How did you—"

Zye shrugs, looking almost bored as he picks up a grape from his own plate. "We had to learn what we could about you and—" he narrows in on the savory sensation "—and your elaborate tastes."

I blink. "That's kind of creepy."

He pops the grape into his mouth, chewing slowly before lifting a brow. "And yet, you're still eating."

I roll my eyes but don't argue, tearing into the muffin like I haven't eaten in days. It's still warm, soft, and perfectly seasoned, breaking apart in a satisfying crumble.

Just as he's about to speak again, Ember reappears in another puff of smoke, carrying a stack of leather-bound books and papers.

"Class is in session," she announces.

Zye barely has time to react before she drops the entire pile onto his stomach. His eyes widen as he jerks forward, barely managing to brace himself, his plate of fruit toppling onto the rug.

"Good," he mutters, shifting the pile off his ribs, "to see you, too, Em."

"Hey, boss."

Zye glares at her, but there's an ease to it, a familiarity that makes my heart ache. I don't know what it is that settles in my chest as I watch them; it feels too much like jealousy, and I immediately hate myself for it. I straighten and pull myself together.

Zye inclines his head toward the books. "All right, all right, let's get started."

Ember claps her hands, and a small flame appears in her palm.

"Oh, okay, we're here already," Zye mutters as she purses her lips and blows the flame into the fireplace, where it roars to life.

Ember wastes no time. "Firstly, your magic is rallying, Rae. I felt it when we mounted the wolves."

I freeze. The current. The rush. The way my body had felt alive in a way it never had before. It wasn't just adrenaline.

"How long have you felt it?" Ember presses.

I hesitate. "Yesterday at dinner. A few times today."

A faint hum stirs beneath my skin, like the echo of a heartbeat that isn't mine. I turn my hands in the dim light, half expecting a flicker, a spark, anything to prove it's real, but my very human hands stare back at me.

Ember nods, unfazed. "Good."

Zye doesn't echo her ease. His shoulders stay rigid, eyes fixed on something distant.

"You see, Rae," Ember says quietly, "from the moment you arrived, things have moved—escalated, even—rather quickly."

Zye exhales, sharp and controlled, dragging a hand across his face. "There was an attack last night."

Ember inhales deeply.

"Ivareth," he continues, voice flat. "Rogue Vaulturian footmen. They torched homes and fields. Total destruction. They're getting bolder, more frequent. Closer."

Silver currents stir at his fingertips, thin as smoke and just as restless. He clenches his fist, forcing them down. "They're testing the borders, pressing the wards, waiting to see how far they can push before we push back."

I frown. "Wards?"

"Terralyn magic," Zye says. "Invisible shields around The Academy. They run through the ground and into the sky, strong enough to hold, until they're not. If they're pressed, we know. If they're breached, we fight."

He rubs the back of his neck, gaze locking onto mine. "Ask Alara something for me."

I hesitate. "What?"

"What the wolves can bring to our forces," he says, voice low. "And whether it will be enough."

"Hold his hands. I will show him."

I frown. "What?"

"Hold. His. Hands."

A pulse of magic ripples through me. Zye tenses. "What's wrong?"

I swallow. "She says…I need to hold your hands."

A beat of silence.

Then he exhales and reaches for me.

Our fingers touch and a power flares. A current rips through me, crackling like a storm breaking over water. My skin pulses with warmth, an electric hum beneath my flesh. His hands are cold at first, soothing against the heat radiating from my palms, but as our fingers tighten, there is a sudden shift. Ember leans forward, eyes wide with intrigue.

"Well, this is new."

Then the vision strikes, and the room dissolves.

Mist hangs low over the cliffs and lakes, veiling the valley in silver. We move through it, through Alara's eyes. A valley untouched by war. Towers of carved stone rise between rivers, half swallowed by vines. Bridges spun from root and branch stretch between cliffs and lakes. And the wolves are everywhere. Zye's fingers tighten around mine.

#

This is the Wildlands. Our last stronghold. Warded by the last of the Originals, hidden by the last of our kind. Protected by elemental seals drawn into the land, into the bones of the mountains and rivers. Invisible. Impenetrable. No map dares mark it. No spell can breach it. The magic here is alive, and it answers only to us.

The Vaulturians have tried. They've sent scouts, spies, beasts. None have returned.

Vaulturia rose from greed, and they came for the wolves first. Break the bond and you break the power. Without their Originals, the Highborn fell. By every law of balance, the wolves should have fallen, too.

But Aric and Soraya did not fall. They should not have survived their Highborns' deaths, yet they did. Some say the

Corestone itself spared them, a mercy granted for bonds born of sacrifice, not greed. Others claim the land intervened, refusing to let its last protectors die. Whatever the truth, their survival broke every rule we thought we knew. And that is why they hid.

With the last of their power, Aric and Soraya raised the wards and carved the Wildlands, bringing as many of the wolves here as possible. Those they could not save were captured or killed. And some, we fear, were twisted into something else. What became of them, we do not know and it is better that we don't think too long about it.

For a long time, it was about surviving, not thriving. Waiting. Hoping. And for a long time, all hope was lost. Until I was born.

I was not forged like Aric or Soraya. At first, I was nothing more than a wolf among wolves. until the night I glowed beneath the rising moon. Aric saw it; Soraya felt it, and the others bowed. That night, I became Alpha of the Originals.

I am the first of a new kind—born, not made.

And you, Rae, are the first human in lifetimes to be chosen. With our bond renewed, the lands stir. So do the wolves. It has been centuries since a wolf tethered to a wielder, and longer still since that wielder was human.

But know this: my pack is done hiding.

They were born to protect, to run free, to fight.

#

The vision ends. The room is silent.

"Okkkayyy, then," Ember drawls, eyebrows raised as her gaze darts between our hands, still clasped together a beat too long.

I quickly pull mine away, brushing invisible dust from my lap. The heat that was in my hands now spreads across my cheeks. Wonderful.

"So…the wolves have a bigger contingent than we realized. That's good news, I guess," Ember says.

I shake my head, pulse still thudding beneath my skin. "It means the stakes are higher."

"Yes," I hear through the bond. She sounds like she's running, but before I can ask, a contemplative silence settles over the room.

Zye's gaze stays locked on mine, but I sense the shift in him. "And we must protect them at all costs," he says. "Because according to that, if Alara falls, Rae falls with her."

Ember frowns. "That can't be absolute. Can it?"

Zye's jaw tightens. "I'd rather not find out."

My mind snags, questions firing faster than I can catch them, each one landing harder than the last.

"*Rae,*" Alara says, calm as cut stone. "*Do not chase what hasn't happened.*"

"*You've brushed close to death more times than I care to count. If anyone should worry, it's me.*"

I huff a shaky laugh, the knot inside me loosening as she breaks into a low, rolling chuckle of her own.

Zye leans back against the chair, crossing his arms loosely behind his head. It's a lazy, effortless motion that only makes the muscles in his biceps look bigger, dragging my attention exactly where it shouldn't be, especially at this moment. I look away, clearing my throat, but that doesn't stop the slow, unwelcome heat creeping up my neck. If he notices, he doesn't show it.

"Em, go get Kail and Thane. Let's take this to the field. I think it's time we show Rae something."

Ember brightens instantly, fire dancing at her fingertips. "Eeeek!" And before I can blink, she vanishes, leaving behind only a wisp of smoke as Zye pushes up from the chair, the movement slow, deliberate. He extends his hand, palm open, fingers slightly curled, an invitation, not a demand.

"Do you trust me, Rae?"

I let my eyes trace the curve of his mouth. I reach for his hand but stop short, tilting my head slightly. I smile. "No."

His fingers flex, the muscles in his forearm shifting, weighing whether or not to take the choice away from me. "That's close enough."

And with that, he grabs my hands.

The air shifts.

The room vanishes.

And we're gone.

Zye and I land on the edge of a vast, snow-covered peak, The Academy rises from the mountains behind us, carved straight from the land itself. Its sprawling stone walls stretch across the ridge. Ivy, thick with frost, clings stubbornly to the walls, its tendrils encased in shimmering ice. Beyond the castle's protective reach, the land is wild and untamed. A dense forest of pines weighed down by thick snowfall, stretching toward the horizon like an endless frozen sea.

"This," Zye says smoothly, "is where we come to play."

I glance over at him, brows raised.

His smile is pure sin. "It's part of The Academy, protected by the wards that shield The Academy from Vaulturian attacks. You won't see them, but they're there. Unlike the wards on the Wilderlands, not unbreakable, but if they're breached, we know. And we will respond. But within the wards, we have plenty of space to—" he steps closer, his lips barely ghosting my ear "—be us."

Before I can respond, the air crackles.

Ember appears in a flare of heat and smoke, dragging Kail and Thane through with her. They land with far less grace than Zye and I, the snow crunching beneath their feet as they stumble forward. I notice Ember wince, a subtle giveaway that it took a toll on her, but just as quickly it's gone, tucked behind the usual spark in her eyes.

"What's so urgent we couldn't finish whooping a few more rookie asses?" Thane grumbles, running a hand through his messy, sweat-dampened hair.

Kail and Thane stand bare-chested, their bodies still slick with sweat from training, steam rising faintly from their heat-warmed skin against the icy air. Beads of sweat trail over hard-cut abs, catching the light like drops of honey sliding over lean, sculpted muscle. Raw masculinity.

I snap my gaze upward—too quickly, too guilty—right into the waiting eyes of Kail, who winks.

Zye chuckles beside me, low and knowing. Thane stretches, his muscles flexing lazily. On purpose. "Don't worry," he muses. "We'll give you something much better to focus on soon."

Zye laughs as I try to disguise my embarrassment. He flicks his wrist, summoning a thick black coat, tossing it to me with a little too much satisfaction. I pull it on quickly, realizing that, out of all of us, I'm the only one who feels the cold.

"Will you be joining us?" I ask Alara, the bond between us growing more familiar, more natural, each day.

"Give them their time to shine and show off, she replies almost hastily. I'm hunting with Aric and Soraya. Enjoy."

Something about the way she says it, like she doesn't want to be here, doesn't sit right. But before I can press, Zye steps closer, dragging my attention back to him.

"All right, Rae." His voice is steady, but there's a playful edge to it. "It's time to show you who we are, so you can understand all that you might be."

My pulse changes gears but before I can fully register the shift, Ember claps her hands together, seamlessly cutting through the tension. "Me first!"

Without hesitation, she lifts off the ground, floating effortlessly above the snow. A grin spreads across her face as fire curls and twists around her fingertips.

She spins midair, movements fluid and fearless, fire skimming along her skin like it was made for her. "I am fireborn," she declares.

Kail snorts loudly. "You are an inferno!"

She shoots him a sharp glare but mostly ignores the jab. "Born and raised in Pyraen, before they recruited me to unleash hellfire on these poor souls." She flashes a wicked grin, flames lapping at her fingertips.

She raises her hands, summoning a massive sphere of fire, tossing it back and forth between her palms, then, without looking, she tosses it straight at Kail's feet.

"Missed," he taunts. "You know, you're a lot of talk and empty threats, fireball. Yet, after all these years, here I stand."

"Only because I let you."

Thane nudges me, murmuring, "You're witnessing foreplay, Academy style."

I choke on a laugh. Kail arches a brow, clearly having heard, but doesn't deny it.

Ember, of course, takes the win. "Don't worry, Kail. You know I love a challenge." Her words are sickly sweet.

Kail grins back, slow and too damn confident. "Oh, sweetheart. You wouldn't survive me."

Ember throws another fireball. This time, Kail actually moves.

The flames vanish into the snow as Kail tenses, muscles coiling beneath his skin like a bowstring drawn taut, ready to snap. Ember lands lightly beside him, laughing, completely unbothered by the sharp contrast of fire and ice.

"Well," she says, "you might have noticed how effortlessly Kail moves, the ease at which he raced up that mountain earlier."

I barely nod, my stomach clenching as Kail's lips pull back into a snarl, the sharp glint of his canines catching the light.

"He and Thane," Ember continues, stepping back in anticipation, "are wolves."

I take a step back before I even realize I've moved.

And then Kail and Thane shift. Their bodies jerk, tearing through them from the inside out. Their spines arch, limbs buckle, and then contort, bones grinding as skin splits open and fur pushes free. Their fingers stretch and twist before disappearing into thick, clawed paws.

The sound alone is enough to make my stomach turn, but I can't look away. They hit the ground hard, shoulders rolling, muscles still flexing with the last of the change. No longer men, but wolves.

Kail's tawny coat of browns and grays bursts from his skin, bristling with each powerful step forward. He releases a low, rumbling growl. The sound reverberates through my chest, rattling deep into my core. I meet his gaze, and his eyes glow a brilliant shade of blue. My pulse quickens, my instincts caught between awe and primal warning. But then, just when the tension pulls too tight, Kail tilts his head and lowers himself.

His massive frame settles at my feet, ears forward, gaze still locked onto mine.

Thane's coat is jet black; his scar is even more pronounced now, cutting through his features. His brown eyes narrow on me before he takes one slow step forward. I don't move. Instinct tells me to fear him, but another part of me knows I don't need to.

Slowly, almost without thinking, I reach out, my fingertips brushing the rough, ridged scar along his face.

"This is where… or how you were hurt, isn't it?" I ask.

He simply nods and then bows his head.

A lump rises in my throat. Before I can stop myself, I move

closer, wrapping my arms around him. He rumbles low in his chest, but he doesn't pull away.

I turn to Zye.

"Alara…"

"Can't shapeshift," he says simply. "She's a wolf—an Alpha—but unlike Aric and Soraya, who were forged, she was born. We aren't sure what difference that will make yet. And if you sensed some tension between the boys and Alara, you weren't imagining things. They're not enemies, but they're probably not going to be best friends anytime soon."

"Why?"

"Because Kail and Thane's pack has guarded these lands since the Originals vanished. They want the same outcome we do, but wolves are still wolves. Packs live and die by dominance and order. Alphas hold the line; challengers test it, and every step inside their range is a question of who leads and who yields. Who's the top dog, so to speak."

A disapproving grunt echoes in my mind. *Alara.* I smile. "She's not thrilled with that explanation."

Zye's mouth curves, a quiet chuckle under his breath. "Didn't think she would be."

Kail lets out a sharp huff, standing to shake himself off, snow flurrying from his thick coat in protest. He prowls forward just enough to make a point, his massive form bristling with irritation as he releases a groan that makes the hairs on my arms stand.

I inhale slowly, forcing myself to keep my voice steady. "And you?"

"Saved the best for last." He winks, then spreads his arms in an easy stretch, shoulders rolling with deliberate grace. It looks casual, lazy even, but every movement is measured, a quiet display of strength held firmly in check. His head tilts back, exposing the strong column of his throat, his chest rising with a slow, deep inhale. Then he shifts.

Wings tear through his shirt in a brutal, effortless rip, fabric splitting apart like it was nothing more than paper. My breath catches in my throat as the sleeves shred and fall away, revealing the smooth, sculpted lines of his torso. A long, jagged scar slices across his ribs. This scar comes with a story. A story I suddenly want to hear.

The muscles across his stomach tighten with the movement, flexing as his wings fully unfurl—broad, magnificent, devastatingly beautiful.

A spiral of wind erupts around him, and then he's gone, soaring through the skies. His wings cut through the air like blades, his entire form a striking silhouette against the endless blue. He's much larger than he ever appeared on the night I… disappeared.

Streaks of rich, earthy hues blend into creamy bands that shimmer like gold when they catch the sunlight, every angle shifting, hypnotic, intoxicating.

"Show-off!" Ember calls up to him.

I turn to her, my thoughts still scrambled. She must see it in my face, because she just smiles.

"I know, I know," she says. "They're pretty awesome."

I glance at my hands, flipping them nervously, naively, like I might suddenly unlock some kind of magic just by willing it into existence and not sure what I'd do if it happened.

All at once, a wave of panic slams into me… because what if I don't? What if I never do? Or worse, what if I do, but it's too late?

Ember catches the flash of fear in my expression, because her grin softens just a little.

"Magic doesn't work like that, Rae," she says simply. "It's not instant. And it's not always kind, but it's coming. You don't need to worry about that."

Her focus turns toward Zye, Kail, and Thane, like she's deciding where to start.

"Our magic is elemental," she says finally. "It's a birthright, tied to the land you're born to, carried in the blood of the families who came before you."

She clicks her fingers, fire curling into slow, deliberate loops that burn gold.

"Once, magic flowed freely. It was part of life, common, though never equal. Some wielded it with ease, others barely at all. But when the war ended, everything changed. The Highborn fell and the bondlines shattered. Their families and the villages that once thrived beneath their protection survived, but only barely."

"Pyraen, Soryn, Terraveth, and Neravael each clung to what strength remained, desperate to preserve their names and their legacy. But no line could dictate who would awaken to magic, or when it would surface. Some families produced wielders every generation. Others waited a century for a single spark. Many saw their gift vanish entirely. That unpredictability became everything. The mere chance of a wielder turned magic into Athyria's rarest and most dangerous resource.

"And the Vaulturians preyed on that fear and vulnerability. They raided villages, tore families apart, hunting wielders wherever they appeared. If they couldn't claim them, they destroyed them."

She looks down at the flame in her palm. "I am from the south, Pyraen. A land of fire and flame. My family once carried that fire in full, but I am one of the last fireborn. Many still live there, but their power has thinned significantly."

She gestures at Kail and Thane. "The wolves? They are Terraveth's own, born of this very soil. Terraveth bloodlines are endurance made flesh: strength, instinct, resilience. When the Highborns fell and the war fractured the realm, it was Terraveth that held Athyria together. These wolves walk among us because of that legacy, shaped by Terralyn magic to guard what remains of the earth itself. That is Terraveth's legacy. And if Terraveth falls, the rest of Athyria will follow."

And then she nods up at Zye. "And Zye's just got wind." A beat, then a snort of laughter. "And when it's unleashed, when it's unchecked, it becomes the most dangerous of us all. The north is Soryn—storm and sky. Their land itself floats above Athyria, and their bloodlines have always been feared for it. A single Soryn heir can scatter armies, tear walls apart, bend the skies themselves. That's why their families guard their own so fiercely. Of all the regions, Soryn has always carried the power to shift the balance."

"And to the east… Neravael. Water. The most essential of all. They commanded tides, healed the wounded, and foresaw what others could not. But they were all but destroyed in the war. The seas were turned into battlefields, their rivers bled dry. Neravael was ruptured by greed until only fragments of their kind remained. Yet if their heirs were ever restored, if the tide can be turned, very few will withstand them. The force of water is relentless."

"Don't I know it," I mutter. The memory drags me back to the morning of the wipeout. I can almost taste the salt on my tongue, feel my lungs burning, the ocean crushing down, that split second I thought I wouldn't surface. Then Ethan, arms locked tight as he risked his own life to drag me free, his features carved with fear. Annie, Felix—gods, my family. The thought of them now almost knocks me off balance.

I shake my head, forcing focus. "So…" My voice wavers, then steadies. "If magic is elemental, if it's bound to who you're born to, what does that mean for me?"

Her expression shifts as she reaches out and places an arm around my shoulder, giving me a warm squeeze.

"You're different," she admits. "No one like you has ever walked through those halls before. No one knows what you're capable of."

"Zye was raised by Horo, you'll meet him tomorrow, and we hope he might be able to answer that." She pauses, a sideways smile tugging at her lips. "He's… an interesting old man. Guardian of the wild spaces, a man of secrets and spells." Her tone turns wry. "Let's just say he keeps things in some sort of order, in his own way. But growing up in the woods with him, yeah, Zye's early days were very different. He's spent his whole life here, rather than up there, not only sharpening his power, but shaping it."

I rub at the back of my neck, fighting to keep pace with what I'm hearing. "I've seen him do more than just fly. The food, the jackets, they all appeared, and—" I hesitate, the word sticking. "He, you, can rift walk?"

There is a sudden shift in the air. I spin, startled.

Zye stands just a few feet away, the Hawk gone, replaced by broad shoulders, defined muscle, and skin marked with jagged scars. My gaze catches on the largest one, the brutal slash cutting across his ribs.

"There are rules to magic, Rae. Elemental gifts come from the land. Some, like Ember's fire, are pure. Others, like mine, are layered."

I frown. "Layered?"

"In Soryn, our base element is wind. We can shift it, ride its currents; some can call a storm if they're lucky." His gaze sharpens. "But I don't just ride it, I shape it."

He lifts his hand, flexing his fingers, and the air around us shudders in response, twisting and pulling itself around him in sharp, controlled movements.

I barely hold my ground as a smoky mist unfurls. My breath stutters as massive, smoky wings spread from his back, sharp-edged and defined, built entirely from white winds that dance at the edges, shifting between solid and void.

He watches me watch them.

"Tempest Form," he says quietly. "Wind given form. A form that strikes. Shields." He pauses. "Destroys."

The air stirs. A ripple breaks around him, then he's gone.

"Rift walking," he continues from behind me, "is stepping into the Rift, a faultline in Athyria, and coming out the other side somewhere new."

"Oh, like teleportation," I say with absolute confidence, as Ember bites down on her lip, nose creasing in a sharp, almost sheepish wince.

"Not quite," Zye says with dry amusement. "Teleportation is instant; you vanish from one place and appear in another. Rift walking isn't that clean. The Rift is a break in the fabric of this world, a between-space. You step into it, navigate its currents, and exit somewhere else. But you move fast. Always. Because if you get caught in it, you may not come back."

"Oh, perfect. That's good to know. After the fact."

"I wasn't exactly going to tell you on day one, 'Welcome to Athyria, hold tight, we're taking a stroll through the afterlife.'"

I spin to face him. "You're actually serious."

Zye just shrugs. "There are things in the Rift," he says. "People. Echoes. Not dead, but not alive either. Anchored there because something in this world still holds them. Or they haven't been able to let go."

I look to the skies and blow out a puff of air.

Ember cuts in as she steps closer. "Zye is right, technically, but we keep it safe with you and anyone we take through. It's why we only use it for short trips, controlled distances. And the magic here on the grounds of The Academy stabilizes short entries."

"Only a few of us can rift walk. Ember uses fire to tear space. I use wind to move through it. But neither of us can do it endlessly."

"Magic isn't just energy," she adds. "It's instinct, command, and cost." She nods toward Zye. "His magic bends and controls. Mine burns. His shapes the world; mine consumes it."

She turns toward Kail and Thane, who are still watching from the edge of the training ground.

"The biggest difference between Zye and the boys comes down to conjuring. Zye can pull from The Academy. They can't. Essentials. He asks; it answers. Hence he can shift back and be standing in front of you with pants on. Those two can't."

I slap a hand over my mouth, stifling both a gasp and a traitorous giggle.

Zye just shrugs. "Truth. Fortunately for all of us, The Academy has learned to act, even if not summoned."

"Kail and Thane?" Ember jerks a thumb toward them, her grin sharpening. "As men, they're lethal. The best on the ground when it comes to traditional combat; their sharpened instinct, strength, and speed with blades or hand-to-hand is unmatched."

She twists a lock of hair around her finger, gaze flicking their way. "They don't need to shift to win a fight. That's the difference. Most wolves rely on instinct; shifters rely on control."

"They don't need a moon or a trigger. It's a choice. They use it when the fight or threat demands it," Zye adds.

Ember hums, amused. "Takes a dangerous level of discipline to hold that kind of power and still decide when to let it rip. Especially when they're angry."

Her grin fades to something more thoughtful. "And after everything that's happened, that control matters. A lot of villages fear magic. Sometimes the surest way to keep people safe is to show up as men with a blade and a steady hand. That is easier to trust than big claws and old power."

Then, with a conspiratorial whisper, she leans in. "This is all a very poetic way to say they're just feral dogs."

Kail reacts instantly, launching forward with a burst of energy so fast I barely track it. His muscles ripple beneath his sleek fur, his eyes locking onto his target. Ember.

In a blur of motion, he tackles her hard, sending her sprawling into the snow.

Kail pins her effortlessly, one massive paw pressing against her chest. A deep, rumbling growl rolls from him, feral, dominant, but not unkind. Then, with a wicked flash of teeth, he lowers his head and licks her.

Ember groans loudly, arms flailing as Kail stares down at her. Her fingers ruffle through the thick fur on either side of Kail's head, tugging just enough to be a menace. "Cute, feral dogs," she amends. "With incredibly sharp senses. And hearing. And claws." Her nose wrinkles. "And just gross." I can't help but laugh at them.

Kail huffs, clearly victorious as he steps back, releasing her. Ember pushes herself up, brushing wet snow from her knees, only for it to sizzle and vanish beneath her fingertips. Heat rolls off her in faint waves, melting frost wherever it clings to her. She shakes stray leaves from her hair.

Kail chuffs out a sound that is unmistakably laughter before turning to Thane.

Thane whips his head toward him, deadpan.

The tension holds for a single, charged second, then Kail bolts.

Thane launches after him, all muscle and vengeance, their heavy footfalls shaking the ground as he barrels forward, fully intending to tackle Kail into another realm.

"There are over fifty wolves within these walls," Ember says, a soft giggle curling at the edges of her words. She tips her head toward them. "Some are shapeshifters. Others…" She shrugs, her eyes locked on the line of trees where the boys have vanished. "Prefer the wild."

She nods toward Zye. "The wings don't have the same numbers. Their contingent is much smaller, which is why we focus heavily on ground combat. We don't have the power to attack from the skies, not yet."

"When the lands were split," Ember continues, "the Vaulturians didn't trust anything or anyone that wasn't human or that they couldn't fully control. They have even fewer allies now, and what they do have, we believe, are working under threat, coercion, or worse. Some of them probably don't even realize it."

I shudder.

"The rest of The Academy is made up of a mix of Athyrian warriors." She summons a ball of fire, spinning it lazily between her fingers. "Some are stronger than you, for now. Some are more skilled. But nowhere near as powerful as these idiots." She gestures at the wolves, at Zye. "They command respect for a reason."

She pauses. Then her gaze lands back on me.

"If what we believe is true?" She lets the fire burn out between her fingers. "You'll outpower us all."

Ember extends a hand to me, her warmth radiating even before I take it. "Feel like taking a walk through the afterlife?" she says with a wink as she purses her lips and blows gently, sending a ripple of heat over my skin.

I close my eyes as the familiar pressure builds behind my temples, the teleportation pulling me forward. This time, when my feet touch solid ground, I stumble only slightly, landing gingerly in the hallway outside our rooms.

#

"There you go!" she says, all sunshine.

I exhale hard. "I hated it when I didn't know where we were going. Turns out, knowing is worse."

She waves a hand dismissively. "Na, it's not that bad."

"Have you ever been there? The Rift?" I ask.

She hesitates. "Once, when I was first learning. It's… pretty wild." Then, like it's nothing, she turns and strolls ahead. "Anyway, did Zye show you around this wing?"

"Uh, sort of." I glance around, still reeling from what she just did, or didn't, admit.

I shake it off and try to turn my attention to the long corridor. A rich red carpet runs its length, and the warm glow of candlelight dances along the walls.

I glance toward Zye's door, staring at it longer than I mean to. Ember must notice, because when she turns to me, something in her tone changes.

"Zye wears the weight of this place and what's coming. We all have our stories, but his is right up there with the worst."

She rolls her shoulders but keeps walking. "When he needed somewhere to fight back, to take back what Vaulturia stole, Horo built The Academy. And when more kids like him showed up, kids with nowhere else to go, no one to fight for them, Zye stepped up. He leads because someone has to."

I chew the inside of my cheek, glancing toward his closed door.

"Zye's never gotten over losing his sister, Lyria," Ember

continues, with obvious emotion in her tone. "Or his parents, who sacrificed themselves to try and save them."

Her lips press together. "And now, he's ready to blow the whole realm apart to make Vaulturia pay, especially for Lyria."

Then, as if shaking off the weight of it, she tosses her hair off her shoulder, throws a beat into her step, and smiles brightly.

"And I, for one, can't wait to stand by his side when he does."

Then she waves a hand dismissively toward the other side of the building. "Anyway, most of the other rooms are shared, two or three per dorm. We try to match families or power types so training schedules line up."

"How many people are actually here?" I ask, still trying to gauge the sheer scale of this place.

"Around two hundred, maybe three," she says easily. "Sounds like a lot, but it works. Kail is usually quick to make sure everyone understands the rules, and if they don't—" she flashes a grin "—let's just say, he encourages them to think twice before breaking them again."

I laugh, nodding knowingly. I grew up with a swim coach who shared the same principle using a kickboard. "Ah. The old 'hit one, teach twenty' approach."

"Yeah! Something like that, ha."

I glance around, noting the relative silence. "Where is everyone?"

"We gave a big contingent some time off, let them go home, visit family, relax. As long as they stayed far from here while we got you settled in, they could do whatever they wanted." She shrugs. "And aside from the ones here, we've got hundreds more in the border villages. And then, of course, there are the wolves."

She hesitates for a fraction of a second, then spins back toward me, her eyes alight with mischief. "But enough about them, you fit in perfectly!" Before I can react, she lunges forward and pulls me into a tight hug. I laugh despite myself, unable to resist the warmth she radiates.

When she pulls back, she waves a hand toward my door. "I had your room protected, too, not from anything dangerous, don't worry, you're safe here. Just snoops and busybodies." She rolls her eyes dramatically. "The only person who can enter without permission is you."

"That's… reassuring," I admit.

"I have the same wards on mine, by the way, and you, Rae, are welcome anytime."

She pauses, then grabs my hands suddenly, holding them tight. "And I've given you one of my favorite helpers in the whole house."

I blink, confused. "Why would I need—"

"Rae, please don't vomit."

"Why would I vom—"

I don't have time to process that before she tightens her grip. "Come out, Nyxie."

The air shifts, a shimmer that hangs between form and light.

And then a girl, no, a fairy? A ghost? Appears like a glimmer. She's smaller than me, maybe shoulder height; she hovers at my eye level, her wings thrumming behind her like a fairywren.

Her wild blue hair is loosely braided at the sides, tiny jewels threaded through the strands, catching the flickering candlelight. Freckles fall across the bridge of her nose and cheeks, and her bright blue eyes glisten.

Her layered necklaces clink softly as she moves, the delicate gold chains dangling over a triangle-cut bralette of soft brown leather. The layers of soft fabric of her skirt ripple around her legs, floating just above the floor even though there's no wind. She is, without question, the most striking being I've ever seen.

"Hello, Rae." Her voice is light and melodic. "I've been so

eager to meet you."

I blink, staring at her. "Uh, hey… Ny—" I falter, realizing I've already forgotten her name.

"Nyxie," Ember fills in, finally easing her grip on my arm. "She's a Terralyn."

I tilt my head, the name familiar but never something I'd fully understood, just accepted.

"She's Fae," Ember explains, stepping forward to clasp Nyxie's hand. "One of the earth's own guardians. Unlike us, Terralyn magic isn't inherited as much as it's granted. They're born only during the seasonal rites, when the earth opens its power and consents to new life. Every Terralyn carries that covenant, and The Academy sits on one of the strongest convergences in Athyria. That's why these walls still stand when so much else fell."

Nyxie's wings flick, a small spark of pride glinting in her eyes.

"That same magic was Terraveth's greatest weapon in the war," Ember continues. "While other regions burned, the ground here refused to yield. The Terralyn vowed to guard it, and the land helps make sure they do. Cross them and you don't face a single Fae, you face a cataclysm."

She tips her chin toward Nyxie with a quick grin. "Don't let the pretty face fool you. She's a force."

Nyxie nods. "And I'm here for whatever you need, Rae."

"Oh, and she has impeccable taste," Ember adds. Then she tilts her head, teasing. "Maybe not as good as Alara's, but she's done all right so far."

A distinctly unimpressed huff echoes in the back of my mind. *Alara.*

I press my lips together, fighting back a laugh.

With a wink, Ember spins toward her room, her bright hair

bouncing as she tosses over her shoulder, "Dinner's at seven, Rae. Bathe, rest, whatever you need. We'll see you then," and then she vanishes. I turn back to Nyxie, still trying to process… all of it.

"Is that you who's been replenishing my clothes?"

Nyxie nods enthusiastically. "Yes! I hope it has been okay; you have quite a unique taste." She giggles softly, clearly amused by my current outfit.

I glance down at myself and shrug. "Fair."

"I am here to serve you," she continues, floating closer. "We all are." As she speaks, a rush of color swirls past us, a series of rainbow-hued shadows twirling through the hallway. Giggles follow them.

"Thank… you." The words slip out cautiously. It's all a little overwhelming, but in the best way.

Nyxie laughs, twirling midair. "The bath's ready, by the way," she says, gesturing toward the open doors of my room, where steam curls into the air, the scent of lavender filtering into the hall.

"The salts will ease the tension in your muscles instantly," Nyxie adds. "Enjoy it, you've earned it today."

I can't help but smile. I like her. And suddenly I realize I like all of this. A lot.

I step into my room, the warmth from the bath wraps around me, an immediate contrast to the cold still clinging to my skin. I strip down and sink into the water, letting it ease the sting in my muscles and the bruises blooming beneath my skin. But it's the ache in my chest that catches me off guard.

The more I find my place here, the more I want to stay.

And somehow, that makes me miss home even more.

I exhale sharply, eyes pressing shut, but it doesn't stop the memories from creeping in. My parents, Kenny, the stronghold that is, that was, Annie and Ethan. The feeling of belonging to a life that made sense. One that felt simple. Normal.

But now there's Zye. The way he commands a room without speaking. The way I shouldn't be drawn to him, but am anyway.

I bite my lip, staring at the rippling surface of the water, tracing my fingers along the surface.

Ethan is safe. He's familiar, steady. The one who has always been there. Zye is the opposite. Unpredictable. Unknown. All sharp edges and silvered winds. A force that makes my skin heat in ways that Ethan never has. And I don't know what to do with that.

I sink lower, until the water muffles everything. I stay there until my skin shrivels, until my thoughts slow, until I can pretend, for just a little longer, that I know who I am.

And what I am here to do.

I spend what is left of the day wandering The Academy with Nyxie as my restless, energetic, guide. She flits around like an excited dragonfly, weaving through the halls like mist curling in the wind.

The Academy is even more impressive than I realized. We walk through hallways of endless art and history, paintings that seem to watch as we pass. Nyxie leads me into the gardens, where flowers bloom in spectacular, impossible colors. She takes her time, explaining that many of them are cultivated for their magical properties, used in potions or as ingredients for spells and healing, and she goes into more detail about why I, or humans generally, heal slower than the rest of them.

"These," Nyxie says, gesturing to a cluster of violet-hued blossoms, "are Brimroot. You would already be familiar with them."

I wasn't, but I nodded anyway.

"They're used in healing elixirs, enhancing cell regeneration, speeding recovery." She moves to another patch, brushing her fingers over golden petals. "And these are for strength and stamina. Your mortal wounds close slowly, but you're not purely mortal anymore. When your power finally manifests, your body will answer differently. Cuts will knit faster, bruises fade in hours instead of days. And with Alara bonded to you, that healing will only sharpen. The Original's magic will steady your blood and lend you strength when your own starts to break."

She drifts to a low cluster of deep indigo blooms, trailing her fingertips across their velvet edges. A faint shimmer ripples through the petals at her touch ,the flowers seemingly react as if in recognition.

I huff a quiet laugh, unable to help myself. My version of medicine had always been a white pill in a plastic shell, sterile and lifeless. Not this. Never this.

We move deeper through the gardens, stepping over stone bridges that arch above narrow creeks, until we reach a larger body of water, a crystal-clear creek that seems to glow faintly under the afternoon sun. "There's someone I hope for you to meet before we head back."

Nyxie halts, her expression shifting to reverence. We wait. The breeze stills; everything around us seems to quiet in anticipation.

Suddenly, a creature emerges from the water, its long, sinuous body gliding through the current like a ripple of liquid silver. Her scales shift colors with every movement: pearl, sapphire, gold and shades I don't have names for.

Nyxie whispers, her tone filled with awe. "She's a Nymare. One of the few remaining guardians of our waters and the magic it holds."

The Nymare slows as she nears us, spyhopping, slow and deliberate, the water spilling off her skin like liquid starlight. Bioluminescent fractals gleam along her arms and collarbones. Her hair, sheets of silver and violet. floats in the current. A delicate ridge of spined fins arcs from her temples, fanning out like a crown, translucent and webbed with veins of violet and gold.

Her mouth curves slightly, almost a smile, before she dives again, disappearing beneath the surface and leaving behind a trail of glowing light that lingers before fading, like stardust dissolving into the water.

"She likes you."

I exhale, still mesmerized. "That's… wow."

"Yes," Nyxie agrees. "It is."

#

By the time the sun sets, the horizon is painted in fiery hues of burning oranges, deep purples and pinks all blending into endless twilight.

We cross the upper courtyard, and as we enter The Academy, gold spills over polished stone and climbs the timber wings framing the main hall. I've walked these paths before, but tonight the scale feels even grander.

The air hums, a subtle vibration pulsing from the mountain. Nyxie keeps pace beside me. "That's the outer ring," she says softly, gesturing toward the nearest peak. "Terralyn wards buried deep in the rock. They were forged to hold this place."

Her gaze lifts to the spires. "But the greater magic is inside. Every arch and pillar was shaped with Terralyn power. The stone carries the covenant, and it watches. It knows who enters, who lingers, who dares to take more than they've earned. The walls of The Academy protect… and every now and again, they might… play."

She lets out a soft, musical giggle, light and quick as wind through glass.

I arch a brow. "Play?"

Nyxie's wings flick with amusement. "You'll see soon enough."

She falls into step beside me as we wander deeper into

the hall, talking about life in Athyria—the good, the bad, the dangerous. Somewhere between all of that, she even helps me choose an outfit for dinner.

By the time I reach the dining room, I'm starving, and the lively buzz spilling down the corridor says I'm not the only one.

Zye, Kail, and Thane look completely at ease, each dressed in a loose white linen shirt, the laced-up chests slightly undone, exposing the hard lines of muscle beneath the soft fabric. Ember, on the other hand, looks effortlessly stunning in a one-shoulder white top paired with red wide-leg pants. Her wedge high-top sneakers look entirely out of place for this place, but she looks stunning.

"I thought of you when I put these on," she says with a wink, pointing her toe and twisting her ankle to show off her enviable kicks.

"I love them!" I reply enthusiastically, but Kail impatiently taps his fork against the table, cutting me off.

"Can the fashion parade wait until dessert? I'm starving!" he grumbles, nudging Zye with his elbow and nodding pointedly toward the table.

Zye rolls his eyes, snapping his fingers. Five bowls of steaming soup appear before us. Kail, wasting no time, grabs his fork like a weapon and digs in, only to scowl as the broth seeps straight through the prongs, dribbling down his shirt. The room erupts into laughter.

Kail points the fork at Zye, a playful glint in his eye. "I've killed for less," he warns dramatically, twirling the fork in front of his face like it's a weapon. "And with less," he adds, raising a brow.

Zye snaps his fingers again as plates of meats, breads, and vegetables run down the center of the table. Five silver spoons rest neatly by our bowls.

"Now, that's more like it, boss!" Kail cheers, as he and Thane dive straight in.

"Beasts," Ember snorts, blowing gently on her spoonful of soup before sipping. Her gaze sharpens over the rim of her spoon, narrowing as she casts a mock glare at the two of them.

Zye is watching me again.

I lift my eyes.

He doesn't look away.

Instead, he says, casually, "I hear you met Nyxie today."

I nod, grateful for the distraction. "And a Nymare."

He turns down his bottom lip and nods. "Wow. That's rare. They don't show themselves often."

"She was beautiful," I say honestly. "And Nyxie? She's… amazing. She took me for a full tour of the place. The library here is incredible."

"There's a library?" Kail asks, mid-bite into a bread roll. "Huh. Can't say I knew that."

"Oh, Lordy." Ember scoffs. "I guess between train, eat, sleep, repeat, there's not much time to read. Can you even read?"

"I doubt it; I've never tried!" he says, completely unbothered, while forking a massive slab of meat onto his plate. Zye and Thane just shake their heads, chuckling.

"Anyway," Zye starts, shaking his head as he tries to smother his laughter. "I spoke to Horo. We'll head to him at first light. Can you ask Alara to meet us in the courtyard? She'll need to take you; it's too far for me to rift walk us there. His cabin sits beyond the wards. It is not shielded like this area, so we won't have the same defenses. Kail, Thane and a few from their pack will secure the area before we travel."

I turn to Ember. "And you're not coming?"

"Someone's got to keep this place in order." She shrugs, casually. "That, and Horo and I have a … testy relationship. It's better for everyone if I stay here."

Thane points his fork at her, a slow grin cutting across his face. "Last time those two crossed paths, Athyria was almost reduced to a pile of ash." His words are half-muffled by food, but the way Ember rolls her eyes tells me it's not an exaggeration.

She levels a look at me that I can't quite gauge. "Horo is harmless."

Kail barks out a laugh, head tipping back. "And that kind of reckless underestimation is exactly why you two need to settle that score." He shakes his head. "For our sake. Rae, it's best you know, Horo is anything but harmless."

Ember lets out a dramatic sigh. "He talks a big game for a little guy."

Kail groans, dropping his head into his hands. "We're all doomed."

I glance around the table, watching their reactions. They're teasing, but there's an underlying tension.

Zye starts to speak, hesitates, then exhales. "Horo found me in a bad way when I was young. He took me in and raised me, but there've been a lot more over the years. Most just needed a little guidance." He stares pointedly at Ember.

"But mostly wolves. Pups who needed protection. A new pack. That's why you're seeing a little more respect from one side of the table than the other."

Ember lifts her glass and takes a slow, deliberate sip.

"Nobody really knows where Horo came from," Zye continues. "If you ask, he'll give you a different answer every time." A hint of a smile crosses his face. "I know him better than anyone and still know next to nothing."

"Because there's not much to him," Ember cuts in, but her words hold an edge.

Kail presses his hands together in mock prayer, muttering

something to the heavens, but I'm surprised to see a nod from Zye in agreement.

Kail exhales, shaking his head. "Horo has been the father most of us never had. It started with Zye. Then there was another. And another. And another." There is a small pause; the weight of memory settles in his shoulders. "And suddenly, there was a whole damn school."

Thane crosses his arms, leaning back in his chair. "That's why The Academy exists in the first place. To train and prepare and to keep us hidden enough until we're strong enough to stop hiding."

Kail's eyes find mine. "The Vaulturians have spent decades breeding monsters. Magic-warped weapons. Soldiers raised to tear through us without a thought."

Thane jerks his chin. "So we train so they can't touch us. In dirt, with blood and broken bones. Magic, blades, bare hands, whatever keeps us alive. They have more numbers. More power. More people. But we have more to lose, and that makes us more dangerous than they'll ever be."

His words feel like a punch to the ribs, the realization sinking fast and hard. Different powers. Similar stories. Each of them pulled from the wreckage of war, torn from homes, from families, from lives that should have been their own.

I look around the table, my gaze catching on each of them.

Every person in this room has lost something. Been abandoned. Torn from the life they knew, or left behind by the people who should have fought to keep them. And I see The Academy for what it truly is. Not a kingdom. Not a school. A sanctuary, born from loss, a last chance for those who had nowhere else to go.

I glance at Zye and force my voice steady. "If Horo built all this, why does he live in the woods?"

Zye's lips press together as he considers his response. "Because The Academy was never for him."

He leans forward, elbows on the table, rolling his glass between his fingers. "Horo doesn't believe in walls, or keeping power trapped in one place. He built this because we needed it, because too many kids were getting lost, taken, hunted. But he doesn't belong here." He exhales slowly. "Some people need structure. A place to be safe, to train, to learn. Others? They belong to the wild."

"But isn't that dangerous?" I ask.

Zye's lips twitch. There is a joke behind them, but he thinks better of it and just shrugs.

"For an old guy, he's got skills."

Ember pours me another glass of water, then refills her own. She opens her mouth to speak again but suddenly snaps it shut. Her expression shifts, fear flashing across her face like a lightning strike.

Suddenly, heat surges through me and it's all consuming. The fork slips from my fingers and clatters against the plate, the sound splintering through the now silent room.

I shove my chair back, too hard and too fast, the force toppling the entire table.

The boys lurch to their feet in unison, their eyes wide. "Rae, what—"

"Brace yourself, Rae. NOW."

Alara's voice cuts through as a warning just as a surge of energy tears through me, and a bolt of light explodes into the room. The force is so powerful it launches me backward into the wall, shattering a painting and spraying shards of glass everywhere. As I struggle to regain my bearings, a metallic taste fills my mouth. Blood.

"Rae!" Zye's voice is the first I hear as he's suddenly at my side. The shards of glass surrounding me vanish in an instant. He kneels before me, his hands gripping my shoulders tightly, his brow furrowed in concern as he scans my body. "Are you okay?"

I lick my lips and wince. I try to raise my hand to it, but a sharp pain shoots through me. I look down to blood running down my arm, pooling between my fingers.

"You've got a decent gash on your arm," Zye adds, carefully lifting my arm by the elbow, checking for breaks. It doesn't seem broken, but everything else in me feels wrecked.

He rests a hand on my cheek, but before he can say more, the heat in my veins rises again.

"STEP BACK!" I scream, shoving him away instinctively. The force sends him across the room. Ember races to his side as my vision blurs. Another surge rips through me, more powerful than the first. I collapse onto all fours. The pain is instant. Every nerve flaring like I've been set alight from the inside out. I can barely breathe.

"You're almost through it," Alara says. *"This is your magic, Rae. Let it claim you."*

I press my hands and knees harder into the floor, bracing against the overwhelming energy coursing through me. My skin tingles, alive with an irrepressible power punching through muscle and bone.

Finally, the pain begins to ebb, but the power lingers, pulsing through my veins like molten lava. I try to push myself up from all fours. There is a weight in my arms that makes the movement impossible, as Zye and Ember arrive at my side to help me up. I take another pained breath, the agony and power now humming through me in equal measure. I try again to right myself but my legs feel like they no longer have bones.

"Slowly, Rae," Zye says. Our noses are almost touching as I attempt to thank him, but my mouth is dry and it comes out rough and husky. My senses feel alive. And much like the ribbons of wind had when we first met, I feel my body take comfort in his proximity. Ember rights a chair, and together they guide me into it.

Amid the destruction, I notice the rainbow shadows swirling through the room. Nyxie and the Terralyns have arrived, already working to mend what I've destroyed. Ember hands me a glass of water, and I sip it, allowing the icy liquid to cool the fire that simmers inside me. I glance at Ember, my vision still blurry, and attempt to smile, but it comes out as nothing more than a grimace.

"Easy, Rae. Take it easy," she says gently.

I scan the room. The table we'd been sitting at minutes ago lies in three jagged pieces, splinters scattered like shrapnel. Pumpkin soup streaks the walls in dripping orange arcs, black scorch marks spider across the stone, and the chandelier dangles by a single chain, swaying in slow, dangerous circles. It resembles a war zone.

"I… I am so sor—"

"What the hell was that? What shakes the foundations like that? Did anyone else see bolts of lightning rip out of the sky?" Kail's voice booms through the room.

"*Rae!*"

"*I'm okay, Alara. I'm okay,*" I manage, though my arm is bleeding heavily and my body feels like it's been turned inside out.

"*You need the healer,*" Alara insists, her tone sharp.

I grit my teeth to try to lessen the pain. "Alara said I need the—"

"She's already on her way," Ember says, grabbing a cloth to apply pressure to my arm. She brushes a strand of hair from my face. "This will be fixed in no time. As for the room, close your eyes."

I don't have the energy to fight her, so I do as she instructs.

"No protest? You are in pain," Zye says, his teasing threaded with a hint of concern. A sharp smack echoes, followed by his grunt.

"Ignore him. Open," Ember says.

I do, and the room is whole again, as if nothing happened. The sight undoes me, and I fall against her, trying to hide the tears that spill down my cheeks.

"You're all right, Rae. I'm here."

"Yooo hooo!" A familiar voice cuts through the silence in the room. She doesn't use the door. She doesn't need to. I instantly recognize who it is from her accent and her wild black hair, pulled in a half-up, half-down style. It's the woman from the hospital. The healer. And no longer am I surprised that she floats.

"I'm okay." I flinch as the pain flares again.

"Okay?" Kail challenges, his nostrils flaring. "The room might look better, but I can still smell the blood that was spilled, and did you see what just…" He doesn't finish.

The healer turns to him, eyes narrowing as she sniffs the air once, sharply.

Kail stills. A muscle jumps in his jaw.

She doesn't speak; she doesn't need to. The look she gives him is enough. Kail shifts back a fraction, sensing it's not the time to push.

"It's a wolf thing," he mutters, easing a step away. "I'm sure it's fine. Probably."

The healer turns back to me. "I wasn't expecting to see you so soon. You humans really are a fragile breed." She smiles. The galaxies in her eyes seem to dance even more brightly than the last time I saw her. As she fusses over me, a silver shadow, whisper-light, swirls around her feet.

"Well, the good news is your injuries have healed nicely, much better than I expected, to be honest. I wasn't sure how your human blood would respond, but it looks like the magic did the heavy lifting. Tell me, Rae, have you always been a fast healer?"

I pause, thinking back to my injuries, how severe they were and how relatively fast they seem to have mended. "I mean, I guess so. Maybe. Broken bones were fixed on time, if not earlier. Cuts and bruises cleared pretty quickly, I think. I've never really paid much attention to it, if I'm honest."

"Ah, interesting," she murmurs. "When things settle, I'd love to learn more. But for now, Rae, can you close your fists for me?"

I nod, straining to curl my fingers into my palms. It feels as though the force inside me is protesting being contained.

"Good. That's not as much for your benefit as it is their safety." She gestures toward where Zye, Kail, Thane, and Ember stand. The weight of what just happened is clearly sinking in. Kail and Thane look tense. Zye massages the back of his neck, streaks of my blood still on him, while Ember fidgets nervously with her fingers.

"Your powers are new and very unpredictable. Here, let me help you." She places my closed palms into her hands and blows softly. A ripple of magic passes through me and the heat seems to lessen.

"I must stress, Rae, that these hands now have the ability to inflict an incredible amount of power. I don't want to alarm you, but I need you to understand."

I inhale slowly and stare down at the apparent weapons at my fingertips, nodding even though all I want to do is cry.

"There's no need to panic," she reassures me gently. "I felt the mountains shake from three valleys away. You are unlike anything this place has seen in a very long time. You'll learn to harness that power and wield it when you need to. Trust yourself. You'll figure it out."

She offers me the same warm energy she had at the infirmary, and I manage to smile right back at her. If I could move my muscles without fear of hurting her, I would have reached out to hug her.

"All right, hold tight," she says. "This might tingle, but after what you just endured, it's just as likely you won't feel a thing."

She places her palms on my injured arm as a soothing, cooling sensation washes through my skin, chasing away the heat and tension that had been threatening to suffocate me. I feel the scar on my arm pulse. My signet.

"That's that fixed," she announces as she removes her hands. My wound is now a faint pink line, barely noticeable. The pain is gone. "I've taken the edge off everything else, too."

The nebulas within her eyes swirl like a cosmic dance. Gently, she brushes a loose strand of hair from my face, tucking it behind my ear. Her hand lingers on my cheek, her gaze locking onto mine with an intensity that makes my breath catch.

"I understand this is a lot and, what happened tonight aside, this is all probably feeling like a strange dream. But this is what you were born for, Rae. They—" she tips her head to the others "—are extraordinary souls. Trust them with your life. And don't doubt for a second that they won't put theirs on the line for you. Any of them."

She turns and looks at Zye.

"Housekeeping…" she says, matter-of-factly, as she glides to a far corner, motioning for Zye to follow. There's a shift in him, a commanding presence I hadn't noticed before. What I'd mistaken for arrogance now reveals itself as leadership. It's clear Zye is the one they turn to when it matters.

The healer and Zye exchange words. He nods, gesturing as

he speaks, his shirt torn from where I blasted him across the room. Minutes ago, I tore through this room without meaning to, without control, knocking them off their feet and shattering whatever sense of safety they had. And now, as I stand here watching them recover from the chaos I caused, one truth settles heavy in my chest, undeniable and cold. I am the threat.

"Calm your beating heart, young one, before you cause any more damage. There's no need to panic. This kind of manifestation usually takes months, even years, to mature. With you, it's happened in days. Tremendous power is at play here, Rae, more than any of us truly understand. But you'll find your way. The healer is wise; she'll help you."

The healer returns, gliding effortlessly across the room. She uses her cool hands to cup my cheeks once more. "Go do great things, Rae," she says. She smells of oils and spices as she leans in, her lips brushing my forehead like a feather as she whispers something too quiet for me to catch.

Just as I'm about to tell her as much, she's gone.

Zye is back with Ember, Kail, and Thane. Whatever they're discussing is much more heated and animated than anything he discussed with the healer. Kail wipes his hands down either side of his cheeks, while Thane looks at him, hands tightly gripping his hip, his sheer strength evident, the scar across his cheek pulsing.

I try to take another sip of water, and as I do, I notice through the glass that the water behaves differently. I watch it carefully, slowly tipping the glass back and forth as it appears to dance, not in sync with my movements but wherever my eyes track. I start to play with it and the water responds. I pour it from the glass but focus on holding it in the air. It floats, like a jellyfish bouncing through the ocean.

"This won't end well for you, Rae."

I ignore Alara's words of warning. Concentrating even harder, I lower the cup, the water floating before me as it had before. I work on moving it up and down, side to side, and then take aim, shooting it across the room. *Bullseye!*

Zye startles as the water bomb hits his face, soaking his hair and dripping off his jawline. Ember and Kail go wide-eyed, then throw their heads back in a fit of laughter. Thane doesn't. He stays still, watching me, his jaw clenched.

Then Zye turns. His eyes lock onto mine and the grin that curves his mouth isn't playful, it's wicked. Heat sparks low in my stomach, a slow, treacherous pull that dares me to keep looking even as every instinct warns me not to.

A towel materializes in his hand, and he drags it down his face. His eyes flick between Ember and Kail, who are still working to compose themselves, but his focus doesn't linger.

Because he's already moving. Prowling. Each step is deliberate, predatory, and suddenly he is right in front of me, and there is no space for anything at all.

I have to lean back as he places a strong arm on either side of my head, caging me in, bracing himself against the chair. His face hovers dangerously close, close enough for the last bead of water to slide from his jaw and catch the light, close enough for the warmth of his breath to brush across my lips.

"Glad to see that after nearly tearing us apart from the inside, you're in such good spirits," he murmurs, the words a low drag of heat against my skin.

I sink further into the chair, trying and failing to reclaim any semblance of composure. My arms fall limply to my sides as a half-laugh escapes me. "You're brave, getting this close."

Zye hums, the sound laced with amusement.

"Keep your acquaintances close," he murmurs, and his lips tilt, "and your enemies closer."

My skin prickles. Not from the words. From the sudden, searing heat that burns along my arm.

I tense, inhaling sharply, my hand flying to my forearm as the signet reacts.

Zye pushes back instantly, his eyes darkening as he tracks the movement, as I trace the lines of my skin and finally, finally, see it for what it is.

A wolf and a woman.

One single, elegant line carving the shape of a howling wolf, seamlessly blending into the silhouette of a woman at its base. Their forms are intertwined, indivisible.

"As it was always meant to be, wolf and wielder, bound as one," Alara says, with a new clarity.

"So, what's for dessert?" Kail says, shattering the silence that had settled on the room, his tone light and teasing as he glances around.

Thane groans and shoves him in the chest. "Come on, man!"

"Rae," Zye says. "I'll be there at first light to get you."

"You need rest. Get someone to take you up to your room," Alara echoes.

Ember kneels before me, steady hands resting on my knees. "Rae, if you're up for it, I'll take you upstairs. Or, if you'd rather walk, I'll come with you and make sure you make it without combusting." She raises her brows, her playful smile nudging a glint of amusement in me.

Somehow, I find the strength to stand, but my legs betray me. I stumble forward, nearly collapsing onto her. A silver tendril catches me before I fall. I glance up and see Zye, a subtle smile at the corner of his mouth.

I clench my fists so tight my nails bite into my palms. "Maybe just hold onto my waist," I murmur, with a tinge of weary humor. "And I'll try not to ignite us both."

Ember's laughter is soft and bright as she wraps her arms around me in a brief, reassuring hug. "A little fire won't scare me."

When we arrive at my room, there is a tub of ice, a cloth, and a note:

Good night, Rae,

Try and sleep. You need it. Tomorrow, everything shifts, and whether you feel ready or not, I want you to know you are.

I'll keep watch tonight, just in case things stir while you sleep. Your powers will be unpredictable and possibly a little destructive. It's all normal. The next few days might feel heavy. Strange. If you need space, I'll give it, but if not, I'll be here with fresh ice and calm hands, ready to help however you need.

You'll save the day, Rae.
With love, N x

When my eyes blink open the next morning, the faintest rays of dawn spill across the room. My chest tightens as I take in the aftermath. A hole gapes in the wall, my dresser lies on its side, my clothes are scattered in disarray, and my duvet is charred, scorched with the unmistakable mark of flames.

The pulsing sensation has subsided, but every inch of my skin tingles. I place my palms gently over my eyes, rubbing them as I slowly rise, stretching out my body. Despite all it has endured, I feel remarkably refreshed.

A flash of color catches my eye as a rainbow blur moves at the edge of my vision.

"Good morning, Nyxie."

"Good morning, Rae! You're looking bright and ready for the day."

"I don't feel particularly bright and not sure I'm ready, but sure, let's go with your version." I stretch again and push myself into a sitting position, throwing my legs off the side of the bed.

Nyxie glides effortlessly across the room, her movements fluid, and I can't help but notice she glows a brighter shade of blue. "You are intriguing," she says. "The magic in you, it's elemental, raw, but there's more... forms I've never seen before. At least not all at once. That little five-foot-five frame of yours sure can pack a punch!"

I exhale sharply, running a tired hand through the mess of my tangled hair. My body still feels like it hasn't quite settled, the aftershocks of whatever happened last night lingering beneath my skin, pulsing softly.

"Well," I mutter dryly, "at least I didn't destroy the place entirely. That's got to count for something."

Nyxie laughs as she settles at the foot of my bed. She stretches out on her stomach, propping her chin on her hands. Her beauty is still radiant, but this morning she looks different— so young, so unguarded.

"Ember threatened to burn down this entire place when her powers manifested. And trust me, you haven't seen it yet, but when she's in a mood, whatever you do, do not, no matter what it takes, get caught in her line of fire."

Nyxie extends her arm. A crystal-like stone rests in her palm. "Here, this is for you. It'll help siphon off some of that raw energy and release the pressure until things settle."

"Just keep turning it over in your palms like this," she says, closing her fingers around it and demonstrating a slow, deliberate motion, flipping it between her fingers. "It'll help you control the currents."

"Oh... like a fidget spinner," I say with a grin.

Her brows knit. "A what?"

"A fidg—never mind." I laugh, shaking my head. Her expression softens slightly as she continues.

"You need to get moving, or you'll be late. Be careful today. So far, all you've seen has been fun and friendly, but Rae, not everything beyond these walls is. Stay close to Alara and Zye."

"And remember, you aren't the girl you were yesterday. That version of you was brave, but this one is about to rewrite what is possible."

I start flipping the stone over in my hands, the cool surface already easing the nervous energy that buzzes in my fingertips. "I will," I promise, my voice steady despite the current of uncertainty running through me.

#

The courtyard glows in the soft golden light of early morning as I arrive, the morning air cuts cool against my skin. I inhale and the world sharpens, the sights, the smells, even the faint shift of wings overhead, each detail flooding in with incredible clarity. My senses are sharp. Really sharp.

"I'm one minute away."

"Don't rush," I reply to Alara, my gaze drifting upward to where Zye is circling in the sky. *"I'm enjoying the view."*

"Ten points if you throw your hands up and hit him!"

"As tempting as that is..." I giggle, shaking my head, but my gaze lingers as he loops into another impossible roll, the sunlight catching on his dark wings before he disappears into the trees.

Show-off.

I hear the soft crunch of paws behind me and turn just as Alara approaches. Her presence still takes my breath away. Every day, she seems more magnificent, more commanding than the one before. Zye was right, wolves grow fast but I wasn't expecting this. My experience is only a few days old, a part of me senses Alara is becoming a force this land has never known.

The ground almost yields to her as she moves and I can't help but smile, yet my hands instinctively tuck behind my back, a futile attempt to keep from striking out as she approaches.

But she doesn't slow. She closes the space between us quickly. I barely have time to react before I have to reach out to brace myself against her, steadying my footing as her powerful frame presses into me.

"You won't hurt me," she murmurs, the deep timbre of her voice vibrating through my bones. *"Don't hide your hands. You're going to need them."*

I press my face into the thick silk of her coat, inhaling the grounding scent of wild earth. The tension in my muscles loosens, if only slightly. My grip tightens on the crystal Nyxie gave me, rolling its cool surface between my fingers.

"You don't need to fear the power," Alara murmurs. *"Feel its ebbs and flow. Learn what makes it surge. If you don't release it, Rae, it will destroy you."*

"Oh, that's reassuring," I muse, rolling the crystal even faster.

"What exactly are you doing with your hands?" Alara tilts her head at me, the same awkward kink she had the first time I saw her. So big, so ferocious, and still, somehow, so impossibly cute.

"Nyxie gave it to me," I admit. *"She said it'll help siphon off some of the power and—"*

"Siphon?" Alara huffs, her eyes glinting with amusement. *"That? No, she pulled it out of the creek. She told you that so you'd focus your energy better. Clever little fairy."*

I glance down at the crystal. *"Well, I haven't destroyed anything or anyone since she gave it to me, so as far as I'm concerned, it's working."*

"Or maybe," Alara counters, her gaze sharp, *"you're better than you realize."*

I stick out my tongue like a defiant toddler, earning a low growl. That's when I hear the rush of wings.

The instant he lands, my body reacts before my mind does. I step back, the shift so subtle, but he catches it.

"Whoa, Rae," he says, throwing his hands up in mock surrender. "Don't shoot." His laugh is warm, disarming.

"If only you had a rock to throw at him," Alara quips.

I whip my head toward her, catching the mischievous glint in her eyes. Her tail wags, a rare and genuine happiness radiating from her. It's infectious, and I realize her lightness has somehow tamed the tornado churning inside me. *Clever little wolf.*

Zye takes a step closer, deliberate, slow, daring me to back away again. I hold my ground, but the air crackles between us and for one dangerous heartbeat, I wonder what would happen if I didn't move at all.

His black hair is wind-ruffled from flight, strands curling at his temples, the mess doing nothing to diminish the controlled sharpness of his expression. Shining strands of wind coil subtly around his shoulders, sliding over hard muscle, alive and keyed to every shift in his mood. He isn't hiding them when I'm around anymore—pure, unfiltered power on display, effortless and unapologetic. He's never looked more dangerous. Or more impossible to look away from.

He's dressed in plated armor I haven't seen before, blackened steel molded cleanly into dark leather, the chest piece marked with the faint outline of wings, subtle but unmistakable. A single sword is strapped to his back, its hilt wrapped in weathered leather, the metal engraved with symbols I can't decipher. Two daggers are secured at his thighs.

"All that you've got going on," I nod toward his arsenal, fists still clenched at my sides, "is that to protect you from me or us from something out there?"

He pauses, gaze fixed on me, biting down on his bottom lip. "Both." Then he turns to Alara, giving a brief incline of his head.

"Kail and Thane are out there. There've been signs of activity, but so far, the forest is clear. We need to move quickly. Horo sent word that Lord Erian's men know she's here."

A sharp jolt shoots through me, heat blooming in my chest and climbing to my neck. My hands tremble despite the crystal pressed tightly between them. Sensing my sudden panic, Alara blows a soothing current of chilled air that swirls around my feet. Reassurance.

"Breathe, Rae," Zye says. "Close your eyes. Keep flipping that... What is that? Did you take it from the creek?"

Another billow of cold air swirls around me.

I sigh in defeat. "I didn't. No."

His brow lifts slightly, but he continues. "Don't combust in the next few hours," he adds dryly. "We'll deal with the surges when we're back. Until then, Horo will have something to help. Are you good to ride?"

"I think so."

Zye glances at Alara.

"*Get on,*" she says.

I hesitate, then step forward.

Alara growls low in her chest as she dips into a bow, extending one foreleg to help me clamber up, and as I swing myself onto her back, the movement feels so instinctive, so natural, so easy, I almost throw myself over the other side. I realize I no longer need her assistance.

"*It's your power. The bond between us. You were born to ride, believe it or not.*" A rough huff of amusement ripples through her words. "*Trust it. Trust yourself.*"

And before I can process that or overthink what will be in harm's way if I unfurl my fingers from the stone, Alara takes off toward the forest. I bite down on a squeal and throw both hands into her ruff. Her fur is coarse, and the moment I grip, something races up my arms like a live current, and I sense she feels it too. The bond thrums between us. I sink lower against her, trusting it. Trusting her.

Her shoulders roll like boulders beneath my thighs, muscle and bone driving forward with relentless power. My knees clamp tighter, but I realize I'm no longer fighting to keep my seat. Maybe I am a rider after all.

The woods blur past us in a rush of browns and greens, the wind biting at my face as Alara's pace only quickens. "*Keep your head down,*" she warns.

She moves like a river unleashed—swift and fluid, carving

her way through the forest with unforgiving grace—and I can do little more than cling to her and hope this bond she speaks of is extra adhesive.

I crack my eyes open just enough to see him above us, Zye, massive in his hawk form, wings driving the air in a steady, commanding rhythm. Each stroke cuts clean and sure, holding his altitude with effortless strength. The sheer span of his wings dominates the sky. Then he looks down, our eyes meet for a heartbeat, and he gives the slightest nod before slicing forward into the wind.

Finally, we begin to slow. *"We are here,"* Alara confirms.

The birdsong is the first thing I notice, a delicate melody that weaves through the trees, perfectly in rhythm with the crunch of leaves beneath Alara's paws. It's like a welcome anthem.

I peel my eyes open slowly and shift my position to sit straighter as Zye lands nearby, transforming mid-motion with an ease that still makes my stomach flip.

Smoke drifts lazily across the tops of the pines, and nestled deep among the green is a cabin. I feel the magic that flows from it move over my skin almost immediately.

"Let's take you to meet Horo," Zye says, now standing beside Alara.

He reaches out to help me down, but I hold my hands firm. "I'm good. I have to learn to do this on my own," I say, unconvincingly.

"You won't hurt me, Rae," he says, holding his hand up higher.

I sigh as I reach out cautiously and he whisks me down. I stumble the landing, falling forward into the armored chest.

I don't need to look up to know he's laughing. I feel it.

"Alara, if you don't mind waiting here, we won't be long," he says, patting her with an unexpected amount of affection. She nods in acknowledgment and turns to me.

"I'll keep myself busy. You're safe here, but if you need me, I will know."

"Okay, Mom."

She huffs and before I blink, she's running through the first line of trees and out of sight.

"She must be hungry," Zye adds as he gestures for me to follow him toward Horo's cabin.

We climb the steps and I pause to glance at him, a hazy memory of my grandmother's stories stirring.

Zye meets my look with quiet curiosity just as the cabin door flies open and a small, wiry figure launches at him, wrapping him in an embrace so fierce it almost lifts him off the ground. Almost. Zye doesn't budge, he's got at least a foot and a half on him.

The man steps back, patting Zye's arm in a way that's somewhere between affection and absentminded reassurance. I catch the flicker of warmth in Zye's eyes, the kind reserved for only a handful of people in a lifetime, I know exactly who this is.

Horo.

He stands no taller than my shoulder, his wild silver hair a tangled crown above robes of midnight blue. His beard falls in a long, smoke-like cascade that nearly brushes his toes, threaded with tiny orbs of light that glimmer as he moves. His eyes, the color of amber resin, are bright and youthful, a stark contrast to the deep lines on his face that look like they've been carved with a blade. But his hands are what truly capture my attention.

His knuckles are like twisted roots, but there is something in them, in him, that suggests the slightest gesture from one of his crooked fingers could unravel the horizon like a loose seam.

A surge of power moves through my body but this time it doesn't feel like it might rip forth at any given moment.

This time, it's waiting almost patiently beneath the surface of my skin, harnessed and awaiting instruction—an instruction I don't know how to give. I flip the stone feverishly again through my palms as I see Zye look at me sideways through narrow eyes.

"Come in, come in! Make yourselves at home," Horo announces. "It's so nice to finally meet you, Rae."

We step inside, the air carrying the unmistakable scent of cookies fresh from the oven—warm, sweet, and completely unexpected. The smell settles around me, disarming in its familiarity, enough to pull a small smile to my lips. I relax, and the sensation in my body settles.

The space is as eclectic as Horo himself. Shelves climb every wall, packed to the edges with curling scrolls, bundles of dried herbs, and odd metal instruments whose purposes I can only guess. Glass jars glisten beside rough-hewn bowls, stacked and scattered in a riot of disorder that could only exist here.

The hearth glows low in the corner, washing everything in flickering, honeyed light.

"Anyway, Rae, what do you know of our world, your world? Good versus evil. It's not all unfamiliar, is it?"

I take a deep breath and look at Horo. "My grandma, mostly, but sometimes my mom told me bedtime stories, or had songs…"

Horo tilts his head and begins to hum; the tune is unmistakable. It's the same melody my grandma used to put me to sleep. I gasp as it pulls me back to her and the nights we spent wrapped in stories I thought were just that. A tear slips free before I can stop it.

"That's it. That's the song," I whisper. "How did you know?"

"Because not all stories are just stories, Rae," Horo says gently. "Some are left behind on purpose, waiting for the right ears to remember them when the time comes."

The room settles into quiet. I swipe at my cheek, embarrassed by the tear, but he says nothing; instead, he turns away.

"How's that power bubbling in you?" Horo muses, changing the subject in an instant. "Well, bubbling might be generous. Raging, perhaps."

He rifles through a stack of papers, muttering to himself, then lifts a small glass jar. "Ah! Here it is. Drink this. It'll help with the burn."

I smile shyly as I take the vial and swirl it. The purple liquid rocking from side to side against the glass makes me instantly queasy.

"Thank you," I say, my attention still locked on the potion.

Horo chuckles heartily. "And you, Zye, what a guy! Come here and give the old man another hug. It's been forever and a day since I've seen you. You've gotten so big!" Horo holds him at arm's length once more before embracing him.

"It's been a week, Horo. Relax."

I chuckle as they have their moment and stomach my fear, popping the lid off the vial. As soon as the smell hits my nose, I gag. It's sharp, like my dad's whiskey. I snap the lid back on and tuck it into my jacket pocket, hoping Horo doesn't notice.

And if he does, he doesn't acknowledge it, diving straight into his monologue. "Zye grew up here, causing absolute chaos with all the potions and spells. He'd be flying around, knocking things off shelves, creating all sorts of concoctions, half of which usually blew the roof off. This guy"—he pats him proudly on the forearm—"is why I got so gray." He winks and lets out a chuckle.

"Once his parents..." He pauses, glancing up at Zye, who stays silent, his jaw tight. "Well, that's his story to tell."

He clears his throat and shifts tone. "But I will say this, Zye, your boys"—he gestures toward the forest with his head—"they are doing great things, but they need a better handle on their pack. Some nights, their howls go on all night. Hunt, sure, but do so respecting the fact that there is an old man within the trees who needs his beauty sleep!"

He pauses. "And how's that little ball of fire going? Flame? Fyre? Ash?"

"Ember, Horo. Ember."

"Oh, yes, that's her. The powers sure knew what they were doing when they got their hands on that feisty little thing, didn't they." He chuckles as his focus skitters elsewhere yet again. "Can I get you anything to drink, kids? Some hot cocoa to warm you up?" He starts fussing around again, this time in a little kitchenette.

While Horo is busy, Zye takes the opportunity to let me know he knows I still have the vial in my pocket. I mouth, "No. Yuck," hoping my desperation is apparent, but he just purses his lips and shakes his head.

"You see, power can do incredible things to a person," Horo says as he turns to us. "You'll learn that sooner than you realize." He reaches out to hold my hands, I oblige begrudgingly. His touch is soothing as the sensation spreads up through my arms.

"It's what you do with that power that matters," he says as his amber eyes lock onto mine and the now-familiar hum rises through my cells. "Some people might think their intentions are good, but their execution is bad. And it's bad, really bad, for a lot of really good people."

Horo exhales, shaking his head as he adjusts his robe. "Erian, our own antihero, hasn't been seen in years, but his grip on these lands hasn't loosened. Not even a little." His hand drifts toward the giant timber table in the center of the cabin. "Let me show you."

As I step closer, the table transforms into a map, the chart's ancient contours coming to life in front of us. As my gaze fixes upon a specific region, the map stirs, its borders rippling with energy that animates the lands.

Horo jumps up onto a small timber stool and swipes a rickety hand across the map, and suddenly the lands shift and twist, rearranging themselves.

"Once, Athyria was four great lands," Horo says, his hand sweeping across the map as it glows beneath his touch. "Vast and untamed, divided not by walls or crowns, but by ridges and rivers, forests and stone. Each land was made up of villages and communities, shaped by the element that ruled it, and led by its Highborn."

He points north. "Soryn. A kingdom of peaks that touched the clouds, where hawks and riders ruled the skies. Their wolves were born with wings, soaring above the land as guardians."

His hand shifts south. "Pyraen. A land of endless flame and heat, where volcanic ridges split the earth, their wolves rose from fire."

He traces east. "Neravael. Rivers that never sleep, an ocean that swallows the horizon. Their wolves ruled the tides, fast as a breaking wave, striking with the sudden force of a rising flood."

Finally, his hand presses west. "Terraveth. Where we stand today. Stone and soil. Forests stretching farther than sight, mountains rooted deep into the marrow of the land. Their wolves were endurance given form, guardians that would—that will—never break."

The glow sharpens at the map's center. "And here, at the heart of it all, stood the High King. Not of one region, but of all. He alone could wield the four elements together, not to conquer, but to keep the balance between them. Under his rule, magic and humankind thrived. And for a time... Athyria thrived with them."

Then Horo's tone shifts, the warmth draining from it. "But

when the High King fell, everything he held together cracked. His two sons each believed themselves the rightful heir. And the youngest, Solir, made certain his brother would never stand in his way."

The map fractures. Rivers bleed outward. Shadows pour across the borders.

"Solir was never meant to rule," Horo says. "It is believed his father did everything in his power to prevent that, but it wasn't enough. Solir believed the wolves were just the beginning and that Athyria was his to rule. He wanted to unlock the very thing that tied the seams of the worlds together and was powerful enough to bind all four elements into himself."

His gaze flicks to me. "The Corestone."

The map ignites from the center outward, the four lands of Athyria glowing bright before crumbling in flame and shadow.

"And Solir would stop at nothing to claim it," Horo says. "He crowned himself ruler of all and demanded the regions bow to him. When they refused, he turned good magic bad. He smothered Pyraen until the mountains bled ash and the forges went dark. He choked Soryn's skies with shadow so thick the hawks fell from the sky and the winds screamed with poison. Neravael was either dried up or used to flood villages until its people fled out of fear. And Terraveth, he sought to poison the very earth beneath us. He thought if the land itself could be broken, nothing here would stand again. It was the first time we learned that magic could be corrupted, that what gave us life could be turned against us."

"Then, when the lands were crippled, he hunted their Highborn and the Originals who guarded them. One by one, they fell. And with them, the world we knew."

The map fades to black as Horo jumps down from the stool. "Balance shattered. And from that ruin, the biggest threat our lands had ever known rose—Vaulturia. Solir's rule spread like rot, twisting what had been the King's palace into darkness."

He sighs. "The wolves that survived scattered. Some fled. Most fell. We thought their bloodlines were lost."

Then his gaze lifts, a glint sparking in his amber eyes. "And then Alara was born. And not long after, she came crashing through that forest like a storm given teeth, demanding answers, tearing through every rule we thought we understood. And the next thing I know"—he throws his hands up, grinning wide—"poof. A human walks among us for the first time ever. Talking to wolves. Wielding magic. Waking old power we thought buried with the dead."

At that, I hear my name.

At first, it is just a soft whisper, but it grows louder with every repetition. I freeze as I feel Zye take a step closer to me, his demeanor changing instantly.

"Oh, jeepers, I almost forgot. You can stand down, Zye, no threats here. Well, at least not for her. It's you and I who aren't as safe." He chuckles as he starts shuffling piles of papers and books before grabbing one off the shelves. "This is for you," he says as he holds out a large book. The leather is warm in my hands, dark brown and worn smooth at the edges. Creases mark the spine, the gold detailing along the border dulled but still intact. I lift it slightly, the parchment smells of charred oak, a dry bite that catches in the back of my throat.

"Well, I assume it is. This Tome has been calling your name since you arrived. I have tried to understand or open it several times, but I've been refused. Whatever magic binds it, I have seldom seen."

I squint at it. "Wow. This is an old book."

The book hisses, as though I've just insulted it.

I stumble back a step, instinctively thrusting it forward.

"Did it just—"

Horo chuckles, not even trying to hide his amusement. "You'll find it takes great offense at being called a book. One is paper. The other"—he taps the cover lightly—"is power."

And then I hear it again, a soft whisper. "I have waited a long time for you, Rae."

Horo clicks his tongue in contemplation. "Its whereabouts, or how it made it to me in the first place, is a total mystery, but it's far from coincidence that you and it arrived almost at the same time."

A trill of magic races up my arms as I gently undo the leather bow that binds it and carefully open the cover. The first page bears the marks of its age, with delicate creases and faded ink that dances across it. The words are illegible.

As I turn to the second page, the Tome takes on a life of its own. It lifts gently into the air, drawn upward by invisible threads. I watch as Horo and Zye exchange an intrigued glance. The pages start to flick at an incredible pace before stopping at one. A chill seeps into the air, scratching across my skin like blades of ice. A face appears in dark, inky shadows, and I instinctively recoil.

My mind is moving at a million miles an hour. I whip my head toward them. "I know—" I halt on the word. I need to think this through.

I know this man, but it's not the man I know. There is a sinister edge to him, a cruel awareness, as though he's watching me. Shadows crawl over his features, casting his face in an unnatural, ominous light, and I feel the room itself tense around me.

Each breath is like swallowing glass.

I know him, and I know him well.

It is Myles Astor. Ethan's dad.

"You recognize him?" Horo asks as his gaze shifts between me and the image that contorts on the page. It's a valid question considering the circumstance, but there is a curiosity written on his face that is unmistakable; he's not only studying the image, but my reaction to it.

I look at it again in case I let my imagination run wild and this was a case of mistaken identity. But there's no mistaking him. The shadows dance and twist over his familiar features: sharp cheekbones, a slightly crooked nose, the line of his jaw. And yet something is wrong. Myles is stern, but this face is menacing.

"I... I do. Well, kind of, but, um, I don't know what to make of this. Any of this."

"Are you a chess player?"

"Not at all, no..."

"It's a game of strategy, skill, and patience."

I internally chuckle at that. Felix has recited that exact line to me at least a thousand times, but it was always followed by, "None of which you possess, Rae."

Horo has conjured a chessboard, hovering midair, pieces arranged in the middle of a match. "The Vaulturians made the first move when they declared war. They are prepared to sacrifice their pawns for power, but we replied with a king"—he nods toward Zye—"to send a clear message we will do whatever it takes to protect the queen"—he extends his palms, face up, toward me.

"But I, I..."

"Once upon a time, the queen was just another chess piece, but over the centuries she's risen in power and rank as the game has evolved. Much like I expect you to, Rae. In today's game, the queen is a powerful player on the board, but even then, she is only one of sixteen pieces that make up the game; she can't win it alone. You must trust that each piece will do its part to protect you, if we have any chance of winning this.

"She needs her king."

Zye doesn't move, doesn't blink, but as I look to him, I see his jaw pulsing.

Horo exhales. "She can fight. She can burn through the board if she has to. But she won't win this war alone. She can't." His gaze settles on Zye.

And just as he says that, the book's pages start to flip again, this time to the beginning. Words flow across the page, settling quickly, but most of it is illegible.

Then lines and more names begin to appear.

"Is that... a family tree?" I ask, almost dumbfounded, as random names flare to life across the page.

Horo strokes absently at the frayed ends of his beard, the motion absentminded, as a chuckle slips out. "It would appear so."

At the very top of the chart, one name glows softly—High King.

Beneath him, two names branch downward, though only one sharpens enough to read: Solir.

The branches spread wider from there, splitting again and again, dozens of names, but all of them are little more than smudges, shadows of letters that never quite form. I watch the blurred names flicker and fade, then eventually one of them forms—Ira.

Horo hums in contemplation for a brief moment. "Solir opened the floodgates to tyranny. What followed wasn't war. It was worse. Centuries of control, with each Vaulturian heir more twisted than the last. And in time, three children were born: two sons, one of which was Ira, and a daughter. The girl was cast aside before her power ever had the chance to rise."

Zye's jaw clenches. "Her mother died giving her life. Her father saw that life as a curse. Born without magic, she was marked mortal."

"And so, as tyrants do, he ordered his eldest—" Horo taps the name on the page. At his touch, the ink hisses, glowing faintly. "Ira. He ordered him to kill her."

I go still. My throat tightens.

"But he defied his father. He defied everyone. He took her and ran to where the Vaulturian guard could never find her. What happens next is a great tale, but the more consistent and viable believe they didn't leave empty-handed."

"The Corestone," Zye says quietly.

Horo nods.

I stare at the pulsing ink. "So Ira gave it to her?"

"Maybe. Or maybe she found it. Either way, the Corestone is the most powerful artifact ever forged, and that is its last known whereabouts."

Zye doesn't move, but I feel the tension rolling off him.

"Ira carried more power than any of them. Killing him wasn't an option, so they did whatever else they could. They erased him. Branded him a traitor. Stripped his name from history. Buried the truth with his memory. You won't find his name in any tome."

Horo adjusts the rope at his waist with slow, deliberate hands. "With Ira abandoning his claim to the throne, it meant there remained only one heir, and he was nothing like his brother. He was ruthless, cruel, and before long, history began repeating itself. Over and over. Each heir raised in the ashes of a kingdom their bloodline burned."

His gaze drops as more branches start to appear, before settling. Horo taps the single name seared into the bottom edge of the page. "And Erian, is no exception."

"And this Erian, he leads the Vaulturians now?" I ask.

"Not so much leads as rules. Erian is as old as the mountain's spine, but that's made him worse, not weaker. He's the last Vaulturian king, and he knows it," Horo explains. "And with no heir, no successor, the Vaulturian stronghold ends with him, and he knows that too. No dynasty has held power as Vaulturia has. Ira was proof of how strong it could be, but when he vanished, everything started to unravel. Erian has been clawing to hold what's left ever since. And without someone to carry it forward, it ends. So now Erian is trying to forge what he can't father. Right now, that's through trial and error and, I can only assume, torture."

Horo pauses to catch his breath. "But the Corestone is what he needs. Its power could create what he couldn't, and now it's awake, he'll raze whatever's left of this realm to get it."

The book trembles in my hands as shadows slither across the leather edges.

"And what happened to him," I hesitate. "Ira?"

"His whereabouts remain a mystery. It's assumed he died long ago, a casualty of the war, but there are whispers." He leans in closer. "Whispers that he still wanders these lands, protecting them until we are ready to defend it ourselves."

"But that would make him... old. Very old."

The thought catches me off guard. I never considered that time might pass differently here, that maybe they don't age the same way we do. My mind races, trying to piece together what that could mean. "How long do your people even live? How old are you?"

I blurt the last part out before I can stop myself. My eyes flare wide as my own words register. I slap a hand over my mouth, too late.

Horo throws his head back with a full, delighted laugh, his eyes twinkling like I've just walked straight into one of his favorite games.

He pats my arm, winking. "Some men count their years in seasons, some in battles. I prefer to count mine in stories, and, much to Zye's horror, I've got plenty left to tell."

I lower my hand slowly, still watching him. "I'm sorry, that was rude. I just hadn't considered that maybe, that maybe here, in this realm, immortality was possible."

Horo hums thoughtfully, clearly sensing my hesitation. "Where there is magic, there are always... exceptions."

He flicks a hand toward the Tome. "Solir is proof of that. He believed the forged Originals held the key to unlocking true immortality, to make sure his rule never ended. He tried to take their power for himself."

A pause. His expression darkens, but there's relief in the way he exhales. "Thankfully, he failed."

A slow shiver creeps up my spine. "But Ira...?"

I don't even know what I'm asking.

Horo lifts a brow, with a stare that reveals little yet implies much. "Ah. Now, that is an entirely different question."

He leans back, fingers tapping against the table. "Perhaps he found the cure. Or perhaps"—his grin turns sly—"he found the curse."

"A curse?" I ask.

"Immortality isn't a gift, Rae. It's a sentence. It's watching everyone and everything you love wither and vanish while you remain. It's being chained to a world that forgets you, carrying memories no one else recalls. And that"—he pauses as if in contemplation—"that is the cruelest curse of all."

And just like the Tome, Horo makes it known that storytime has ended with a dry, deliberate clearing of his throat.

"Now," he says, more serious this time, "there's something you need to understand."

He leans forward. "There was a time when the human realm and ours weren't separate. The Highborn crossed freely, but to protect the powerless, the humans, from Vaulturia, the passages were sealed shut. Which is why it was rather surprising when the twins, you'll meet them soon enough, Puk and Eko, those two are a story in themselves, started sticking their knuckleheads where they shouldn't, and they came across something," he says with a wiggle of his brow. "Something deemed destroyed long ago."

He pauses and says, barely above a whisper, "At first, they only used it to skip through lands, but then they got bored and started to test where else they could go. And, well, once you meet them, then you will understand all the places those two have been, but never beyond the realm."

His fingers tap once against the table. "At least not until Alara crossed over. And you came back with her." My face clenches as I try to process everything at once.

"No one knows how or why, after all this time, someone like you, a human, managed to stir the dust from the bones of this world. The portal was sealed to keep what was left of our world from falling and taking yours with it. And it has stayed closed since. Or so we thought."

His fingers tap once against the table. "But you, Alara, the Corestone, the Tome, it all tells me one thing. You're not an accident, and whatever thread you were cut from, it wasn't a common one."

I exhale slowly as heat creeps into my cheeks and the memory rises. The letter I left behind on my bed, still sealed, still unread. It had been passed down through my family for generations. And if I'd believed them, if I'd taken even a moment to read it, maybe I wouldn't be standing here so unprepared.

"When I left," I admit, "my parents... they tried to tell me. They gave me a sealed letter. They said it was proof, proof that our line was bound to something greater, that I was destined for more. But I didn't open it. I didn't believe them. I didn't believe any of it. And before I had the chance... I was gone."

The shame of it stings. I lower my gaze, blinking hard, wishing I could take it back.

Horo's fingers trail through his beard. "Then perhaps fate will grant you the chance to read it. Letters guarded for centuries are never idle things. But until then, dwelling on what you left behind won't serve you. What matters now is what lies ahead."

He turns to Zye. "And it is imperative that you stay sharp. The mere rumor of her being here has reignited Erian's desire to finish what his ancestors began—to rule not only our lands, but hers as well."

His eyes settle on me again. "If you don't like chess, then you'd better like reading. Go lock yourself away and see what that Tome is trying to tell you."

He clasps his forearm with a firm, affectionate squeeze. "Get her and the Tome out of here safely. Do not stop. For anything. The woods are riddled with Vaulturians and Veilkins. I caught two in a snare just yesterday, thieving, malicious creatures. They know she's here, and they will sell her out to anyone for a price. You are no longer safe."

"Veilkin?" The question scrapes out of me. Suddenly it all caves in. Ira. Erian. The Tome. The letter I never opened. All the warnings have stopped being warnings. This is real. The people, the dangers. I look at my hands, my powers. All of it.

A metallic taste sits at the back of my tongue, and I start rolling the stone frantically in my palm.

"Be calm." Alara's voice slips into my mind and I startle.

Horo is speaking, but his words blur, distorted beneath the rapid rhythm of my own breathing... "Pesky creatures... be on alert."

My pulse pounds, hammering against my skull, my throat, my fingertips.

"Vaulturians are readying for an attack."

The walls press closer. I swear the room just got smaller.

My fingers curl into my palms, nails biting into my skin, but the shaking won't stop. My heart races ahead of me, like it, too, is trying to escape from all of this.

"Watchers. Informants."

I need to move. I need to run. But my legs won't listen, won't respond. "Things that move through the trees unseen."

I gasp, choking on the inhale, dragging air back into my lungs like I'm surfacing from deep water. "Things that will trade her like currency."

The words hit like a strike of flint against stone.

"Settle it, Rae. You must settle it." Alara senses the panic flare, but her words do little to control the heat that surges through my veins, climbing fast, too fast. The magic swells, too big for my skin, pressing against my ribs, demanding to be let out.

Zye moves before the magic can explode, throwing up a shield, a curved arc of shimmering white light as sparks crackle from my fingertips, white-hot veins of lightning carving through the air, slamming against the barrier, bending under the force.

My chest seizes. "Zye—" He's controlling the shield. From the inside.

"Get. Out." I struggle as the magic pulses harder and I struggle to contain it. And I won't for much longer. If I don't release it now, it will consume me. But if I do, it could consume him.

Zye doesn't flinch. "You're okay."

I release a desperate groan. I am not. The magic won't let up. It's pushing, burning, trying to claw free. Another bolt splinters up my arm, burning through my signet before lashing against the shield. The glow wavers.

"You. Aren't. Go." I grit out.

Zye doesn't move.

"You control it, Rae. Not the other way around. Pull. It. Back."

I shake my head. "I can't—"

"Yes, you can."

Another bolt. The shield buckles again. My vision narrows. The magic presses outward, clawing at the edges of me, frenzied and ravenous.

"Not like that. Feel where it's spilling over. You have to find its center and ease it back. Find the center of the storm, Rae. Listen to it," he commands.

"TO WHAT?!" I scream.

"Let it settle where it belongs," he says.

"Settle?" I scoff as a bead of sweat races down my cheek.. "I am about to explode. Get. Out," I grind through gritted teeth.

His hands grasp my face, firm but careful. The contact startles me. My eyes snap open, meeting his.

"Rae." His voice is softer, but no less commanding. "Find the center. Not the chaos. Not the edges. The center."

I shake my head frantically. "I can't. I don't know how—"

"Yes, you do."

His thumbs brush over my skin and I latch onto the touch, grasping for control.

"Close your eyes, Rae. You have to find it."

I barely hear him over the roaring inside my skull. The power is everywhere, splitting through my nerves, searing down my spine, pressing at my ribs like it's seconds from ripping through my skin.

Another surge builds. I can feel it clawing up my throat, ready to explode—

"Focus. You can do this," he says, calmly.

I close my eyes, but it's everywhere—too much, too wild. I suck in a breath, gasping, searching, and then I feel it. A pull from deep inside me.

"It's in you. It is you. You don't command a storm from outside. The power is in the eye. Find the center."

I squeeze my eyes harder. The magic hesitates.

Slowly, agonizingly slowly, the power begins to fold inward, curling back into my ribs, retreating like a tide.

The shield lowers. The air settles. But the moment the storm disappears, so does my strength.

The weight of it crashes over me, my body folding forward, knees buckling. I collide against Zye's chest as his grip tightens, holding me up as my fingers clutch weakly at his armor.

"I've got you."

I squeeze my eyes shut, exhaling a shaky breath as a roar splits the night, raw and urgent. Alara.

"I'm okay, Alara. I'm okay."

"And you thought that pebble was going to control that." I sense her huff.

Horo exhales, shaking his head as he looks around at the

scattered remnants of his cabin, the charred edges of his desk, the singed papers still floating to the ground, the lingering hum of magic in the air. Then, to my surprise, he laughs. It bubbles out of him, pure joy.

"Well, that was something."

I stare at him. "Something," I repeat with a scoff.

"Something incredible." Horo exhales, shaking his head, but there's no mistaking the gleam of pride. "And I'm glad I won't be on the wrong side of it—or you."

He tilts his head as he takes me in. "Do you feel better now? The release of all that pent-up power surely helped? Clearly, that tonic worked." He looks at me, winks, and chuckles as he busies himself around the hut.

"I can assure you, Rae, when Zye lived here, explosions like that were a daily event!"

That's when I realize I'm still leaning against his chest.

Heat rushes to my face as I push off him too quickly, nearly stumbling in my hurry to stand on my own. I straighten, awkward and flustered, clear my throat, and for some reason tap him on the chest. Awkwardly.

"Uh. Thanks. And sorry."

Zye doesn't react at first, he just watches me. Then his lips twitch, amusement flashing behind his eyes.

My gaze catches on a singe mark across his armor—a dark streak against the silver plating, dangerously close to his ribs. My stomach twists. Zye follows my gaze, then shrugs like it's nothing. "Just a nick."

"Kids, it's time you got going. Alara's frantic pacing out front is doing little to keep your presence here a secret for much longer."

"There is a lot of movement in the forest. Let's get out of here before nightfall."

Without thinking, I drop down and wrap my arms around Horo. "Are you safe here, alone?"

He stiffens briefly, caught off guard, before a deep chuckle rumbles through his chest.

"Yes, my dear, you need not worry about me."

When I pull away, his hands find my wrists, his grip firm but reassuring.

"Rae," he says. "You are not here by chance. Athyria may feel wild, unfamiliar, but it knows you, just as you, in time, will come to know it. The blade is only a tool. You are the weapon."

His fingers squeeze lightly, just once.

"I see it in you. Trust it."

#

The hum of power lingers beneath my skin long after we leave the cabin. I can feel it curling at the edges as we walk through the forest. It hasn't fully settled, and neither have I.

I shift slightly on Alara's back, my fingers curling into her fur, the weight of exhaustion pressing against me.

"Stop fidgeting."

"I'm trying," I mutter, shifting again.

Alara huffs, ears flicking back. *"Try harder."*

I grunt, which earns me a strange side-eye from Zye.

"All good up there?"

"I'm fine," I bite out, sharper than I mean to. "I just need to move my legs."

Before either of them can protest like I know they will, I swing myself down from Alara's back, landing heavier than intended. I wobble but straighten quickly.

Zye and Alara lock eyes in silent exchange. No bond required.

I'm ready to argue back as Alara stops abruptly. Her entire

body goes rigid, ears flat, a deep, vibrating growl rolling through her chest. A shiver skates down my spine.

Zye doesn't hesitate. His sword is already in his hand as the forest shifts around us.

Figures begin to emerge, slowly stepping out from the trees. Metal catches the light. The crunch of boots grinds into the earth. A man steps forward, broad and unshaven, reeking of sweat and stale ale. He spits into the dirt between us, his eyes dragging over Alara, then settling on me.

"Well, well, well...what an interesting find we have here." His grin splits wide. The others chuckle, shifting closer.

His attention flicks lazily to Zye, "I tell you what, boy. No need for blood today. Just step aside, and we'll take these two off your hands."

His words slur, his stance unsteady. He takes one slow, heavy step forward, then another.

Zye doesn't move. Alara snarls.

Despite their weapons, the men look ragged and disheveled. They wear aged leathers with frayed linen that appears to be hastily knotted together—signs of years, if not decades, of wear with very little washing. Their feet are bare and calloused, their hair unkempt and wild, with leaves and dirt matted through the wiry mess. The man who spoke has a deep, jagged scar that cuts down the left side of his face, splitting through what should have been an ear.

Alara's growl starts low, rumbling through her chest. Her lips peel back, baring long, lethal teeth, sharper than I've ever noticed before. I'm stunned, caught off guard by the sight of her like this.

She takes a calculated step forward. I feel the frequency of her warning vibrating through the ground beneath me. Another step. Her body shifts closer to mine. A protective stance, as Zye moves with her, blade unsheathed, his presence a force of its own.

There are four men in front of us. At least six more under the shadows of the trees.

The leader tilts his head, watching me with the slow, hypnotic sway of a serpent, rising and drifting side to side. His lips pull into a slow, rotting smile. "So, the girl does exist."

"What's your name, new girl?" one of them asks, casually.

"She's none of your concern." Zye's words cut sharp and clipped, a warning in every syllable. "Back to the forest. Back to the hole you dragged those corpses up from."

The man in front of me laughs, the sound jagged, teetering on the edge of amusement.

He exhales through his teeth, his lips curling in pure malice. "Give us the girl, and you can keep your little wolf."

Zye's grip tightens on his sword. "Tempting. She's unpredictable, stubborn, she's torn through my routine, shredded my patience, and I'm fairly sure she just busted a rib or two."

He steps forward, sword drawn.

"But she's under my protection now, which means she's untouchable to you." His jaw tightens, the heat in his voice finally breaking through.

"Finders, keepers."

The leader lunges. Zye meets him mid-strike, stepping back fluidly, sword flashing up to block.

"GET ON ALARA NOW!"

I move, but as I do, the second man lunges for me as Alara rears onto her hind legs, slamming down with a force that ripples outward, sending them stumbling.

Zye is already on the next one; his opponent swings wildly, thrashing like an animal caught in a trap. Zye remains poised.

Calculated. One strike, clean and deliberate, slashing across the man's arm.

A scream tears through the trees. The man grabs at the wound, blood spilling between his fingers. Zye could have ended him right then, but he doesn't. The man staggers back, grabs his sword, and bolts into the forest, leaving a trail of blood behind him.

Another one pulls two daggers from his chest holster, slashing toward Alara. Rookie.

Her snarl splits the air, deep and vibrating with fury. Before he can strike, she lunges. Her massive paw catches him mid-step, sending him flying backward, daggers scattering into the dirt. Unlike Zye, Alara doesn't hold back. She pounces, claws unsheathed, jaws clamping down in a single, merciless motion. The man doesn't even scream. I go still.

"RAE, BEHIND YOU!"

I spin just as a blade flashes toward my shoulder.

I dodge left, narrowly avoiding the dagger that buries itself in the trunk of the tree beside me. The attacker snarls, ripping his weapon free, already swinging again. I move. I dodge the first swipe, block the second, but the third knocks me backward, slamming me against the dirt as his blade swings downward.

I barely have time to react, raising my forearm to block the strike.

"FIGHT, RAE!" Alara's voice is sheer desperation. *"UNLEASH YOUR DAMN POWER!"*

Alara's words land hard, I don't know what happens next, but suddenly I am burning.

The man crashes into me, the weight of him pinning me to the earth, blade poised, every line of him radiating the certainty of a kill. But he won't get the chance.

The power inside me ignites—white-hot and furious,

surging through my limbs before I even think to stop it. I barely register Zye shouting my name.

The man reeks of death and decay as he rears back for the final blow, but he doesn't have time to take it. I slam my palm into his chin, and at the contact, heat erupts from my core.

His face twists with shock and then he is gone. His body turns to falling ash that rains down on the ground around me.

"That's one way to do it."

Alara's voice drags me back, but the ground tilts beneath me as I roll onto my side, gasping.

Through the blur, I see another attacker lunge, but Zye is already moving. A blade slashes once, twice, forcing Zye back a step. On the third swing, he ducks, then slams into the man in one smooth motion. Zye knocks him to the ground, sword pressing against his throat, his boot braced firm against the man's chest.

Zye tilts his head. "Leave."

The attacker wheezes beneath the weight of him as Zye presses his blade just a fraction closer. "This was your warning. The only one you'll get." The man gasps, struggling for air. "And tell whoever sent you that we're ready."

Zye eases his boot from the man's ribs, but the blade never lowers.

The attacker scrambles to his feet, coughing hard, using a tree to steady himself. Then he looks at me and snarls.

"Power to command the forces, but no clue how to wield it." He sneers, coughing as air makes its way back to his lungs. "Interesting." He dusts the leaves and dirt from his already filthy leathers, laughing as the remnants scatter into the wind. "You'd better learn fast, human. They're coming for you."

He spits in my direction just as Alara roars, the sound tearing through the clearing like a shockwave. The man's grin vanishes. His body stiffens, and then he bolts. His laughter follows him into the trees, eerie and splintered.

Zye is immediately by my side. He's panting, his chest rising and falling in quick, uneven bursts. There's blood spattered across his forearm but no apparent cuts.

One hand grips my shoulder, the other cups my trembling hands, prying my fingers open gently, his thumb smoothing over my knuckles in slow, steady strokes.

"Rae. It's over. You're okay. Everything is okay."

I close my eyes. I am not okay. None of this is okay.

Alara paces nearby, ready to launch at the first sign of movement.

I try to pull air into my lungs, but my chest is too tight; my skin is too tight. My magic thrumming beneath the surface. My body shakes at the realization.

Zye exhales sharply and shifts closer, his forehead nearly brushing mine. "We need to go, Rae. Now."

His fingers tighten around mine. I swallow hard, blinking through the haze, but my legs won't move. His grip shifts, one arm coming around my waist, pulling me into him, holding me upright. "I've got you."

I open my mouth, but my voice is sandpaper. "Tome."

"It's safe, Rae. And so are you. Alara is going to get you home."

Alara crouches low as Zye helps me climb onto her back. I collapse against her, warmth unfurls around me. My heart rate slows. My body stops fighting.

I feel him step back. Hear the shift of wind as he launches into the sky.

Alara surges forward, racing through the trees, her speed faster than I've ever felt. The wind rushes past, but I don't feel like I'll fall. Something holds me in place.

"This is the reality we face. Believe me when I say there's worse out there. Don't give guilt a chance to take hold. You did what you had to do, Rae. And you'll have to do it again."

#

The Academy rises in the distance, its walls dark against the twilight.

Zye descends from the sky, talons out, silver tendrils of air trailing behind him like ribbons of smoke.

Ember is already there, pacing furiously, her eyes glowing with barely contained fire. Moments later, Kail and Thane emerge from the tree line, flanked by a pack of wolves moving as one fluid unit.

As they sprint toward us, Kail shifts, his form snapping back into human as he closes the distance.

He's shirtless, breath ragged, blood streaking down his shoulder. Also not his.

He glances back at the pack, giving a single nod. Without hesitation, they turn and disappear into the forest in a rage. Their howls echo through the trees. They aren't retreating. They're hunting.

"Alara... is that man dead?"

"Better him than you," she says, matter-of-factly. A shudder rolls through me, and I don't know if it's from the cold or from the weight of what she's just said. Of what I already know is true. It was me. Or him.

The same unseen force that steadied me on Alara's back wraps around me again, barely there, but certain, almost tender in the way it gathers me. Zye.

He kept me from falling then; he's keeping me from falling now. Not just the weight of my body, but the parts of me splintering beneath it. The realization presses into something raw and bruised deep inside me, but before I can fully reach for it, the current of air shifts again, and I'm lowered carefully into Ember's waiting arms.

If I had the strength, I'd thank him. Or maybe I wouldn't. How do you thank someone for holding you steady when they're also the one who pulled you into freefall in the first place?

The same magic that tore me from my life, the same power that shattered everything I thought was safe, isn't enough to protect me here. It was never going to be enough.

"It wasn't his fault."

Alara's growl cuts through me, rattling down to my bones. She feels it, the shift, but because I've found it now, the place where her presence threads through mine, I find it and shut it off. Not in anger. Not in rebellion. Just silence.

Because right now, I need space. I need to be my only thoughts.

She pushes back, slamming against the wall I've built in my mind, testing it, searching for a crack—for a way back in. But I don't let her. Not yet.

I feel her turn. Feel her watching me. But I won't meet her eyes. If I do, I'll unravel.

So I look anywhere else, and my gaze lands on Kail as he crosses the space toward Zye, his movements clipped and focused. Zye stays silent, but the fury in his stare finds me anyway.

Before I can unravel it, Thane steps to my side, steadying me. Ember's grip tightens around my waist, warm and reassuring. Above us, Zye launches into the sky, wings cutting through the fading light, back into the forest. A hollow ache settles in my chest.

"You're home now, Rae," Thane says.

Ember exhales. "Let's make you right."

Before I can respond, the world dissolves.

The bath is already waiting when we arrive, warm steam curling through the air, wrapping the room in a soft, calming haze. Ember steadies me as I sway, but I barely feel it. I barely feel anything.

She doesn't say much; she looks at Nyxie, and in that glance, they say everything they can't bring themselves to speak aloud.

Ember squeezes my arm once, then she lets go.

Nyxie starts to reach for me. Stops. Her hand hovers in the air before she folds it into a fist and lets it fall to her side. "If you need anything, Rae... you know how to find me." She lingers for a beat before she turns away.

They both do. And the second they are gone, I break.

I collapse onto the floor, tuck my knees tight to my chest, and cry. Not the silent kind. Not delicate or pretty. I cry until my throat aches.

I cry because I was ripped out of my world and thrown into this one without warning, without choice. I cry because I don't understand this magic clawing at my insides; I cry because my body doesn't feel like mine anymore. Because what I want is my mother's arms around me, holding me tight the way she used to until I am strong enough to stand again. To bury my face against her, inhale the scent of her and feel her fingers comb through my hair.

I don't know how long I stay there, how long the storm inside me lasts, but when it fades, I'm hollow. Bruised. Shattered. And I realize, in the silence that follows...

I'm not ready for any of this.

Not even close.

Beyond the walls of The Academy, Athyria is under attack.

Villages burn, entire towns have been reduced to ash. Doors bolted, windows shuttered, the market square abandoned. On occasion Kail, Thane, and Zye vanish for hours, sometimes days, defending the vulnerable. When they return, their shoulders are tight, their blades are still within easy reach, and they wear the signs of battle. Mud and blood. They don't speak of what they've seen, but the silence says enough.

And I am useless against it.

Since the attack in the forest, I haven't found my footing. Sleep didn't come the first night. Or the next. Or the nights since. And when it does, it is a mercy I wish hadn't been given. Because the nightmares don't stop.

Every one begins the same. I am standing on the sand at a calm, moonlit cove. Someone I love is out in the surf, waist-deep, laughing, smiling as if nothing in the world could touch them. But when I step toward the water, the tide shifts. The current drags back, the ocean splits, and a trench yawns open in the dark. A voice I feel in my bones speaks a single word—choose.

The dream always forks. Another figure is pulled into the undertow while the first cries out for me. And I run, I fight, I choose. But no matter which path I take—toward one, the other, or even if I throw myself into the trench—I lose. One, both, or myself.

Then there is the face I can't forget. Blood I can still feel on my hands. Over and over, I watch the way he looked at me just before he was erased. The moment he saw me for what I was and what I was capable of.

But it wasn't just the nightmares that haunted me. It was the waking hours. Because in the silence of my room, with nothing left to fight but my own mind, I was forced to face the truth of it. Not just what I did. But what I am.

Because when the time came, when death was inches from my throat, my power didn't hesitate. It didn't beg to be contained. It roared.

And the thought of losing control again, of being outnumbered, outmatched, of not being enough when it matters most terrifies me. So I learned to fight back.

I spent the next few weeks absorbing everything I can from Kail and Thane, combat, self-defense, weaponry. Daggers, swords, anything that gives me an edge over my opponent. Their lessons are thorough, patient, and brutal.

They don't go easy on me. Not when I stumble. Not when my arms shake with exhaustion. Not when I hit the dirt so hard the air is ripped from my lungs. Kail hauls me back to my feet with a growl. Thane just watches until I force myself to stand on my own.

Alara hasn't let me forget what the bond means either and the strength it has. Every strike I land in training, I feel her pulse with it. Every time Kail knocks me flat, she snarls through me until I stand again. When Thane drives me to the dirt and demands more, she lends me the strength to answer. My limits are no longer mine alone; they are hers, and she will not let me stop short of them.

But slowly, something shifts. Thane stops looking at me like I don't belong and starts meeting me strike for strike, his corrections sharp, his approval wordless but there. He doesn't say I've earned it. He doesn't need to. The weight of his blows tells me I have.

"Enough napping, Rae. Rise up and fight." Kail stands over me, arms crossed, sweat glistening on his bare shoulders.

I groan, rolling onto my side. "Give me a second—"

"Your enemy won't," Thane chimes in.

"I hate you both."

"Good." Thane tosses me a dagger. "Now, prove it."

I absorb everything. Every strike, every block, every detail. Daggers, swords, close combat, footwork. I train until my fingers are raw, until bruises bloom beneath my skin like war paint, until exhaustion claws at my ribs, and still, I don't stop.

The extra time spent in the gym also gives me a chance to meet the other students of The Academy who have returned to camp. Training and recruitment intensified following the attack, and now The Academy is alive with activity as everyone, human or otherwise, moves about with urgent purpose.

The Vaulturians are closing in. And with every strike and every bruise, I'm less afraid of them.

In the gym, the sound of fists connecting with flesh and the clanging of swords and daggers reverberate off the rock walls as the Athyrians spar with one another. Outside, the wolves and hawks engage in rigorous and fierce training. This is my favorite part of the day. It is mesmerizing to watch them move with such fluid and deadly precision, but it also serves as a stark reminder of where I am and what this is. War camp.

The wolves, at their best, are wild and just incredible to watch. I often sit back with Ember as we look on in awe at their power and skill. Mud clings to their fur, painting them in shades of the earth as they maneuver through obstacle courses of decaying logs and gnarled roots with unmatched agility and near silence. Each movement is a ballet of raw strength and unbroken focus.

High above in the sky, the hawks cut through the air in sharp, purposeful arcs. They are newer and fewer, but Zye leads them with the knowledge and leadership of a seasoned warrior. They move as one, their silhouettes dark against the twilight sky, each movement a display. Their wings flick and snap, twisting through air currents with deadly focus, testing their limits, anticipating every shift, every gust. Each calculated dive is faster and more threatening than the one before. Their talons gleam like sharpened steel. They are weapons of war, threatening to rip apart anything, or anyone, in their way.

When I'm not in the gym, I'm outside with Alara and Ember, practicing to wield my powers, which proves harder than the worst days with Kail and Thane.

The bond is the first thing Vaulturia will try to sever. That is our weak spot. The Originals weren't always killed by blade or violence; the Vaulturians found something far worse. They learned to strike at the bond itself, dragging Highborns from the back of a wolf until both fell, choking, clawing at air that no longer filled their lungs. Once the bond was gone, the battle was already over.

The only two wolves to survive the loss of their bonded Highborn were Aric and Soraya. They endured the break and lived, a miracle no wolf has managed since.

That is the weapon our enemy will use. So Alara and I work tirelessly. Not just to fight together, but to lock every fracture in place so it can never be exploited. To strengthen the thread between us until no power, no blade, could ever sever it.

This is where Aric and Soraya take over.

They press me through drills designed to split my focus. Kail's blade at my throat while Soraya hammers Alara with her weight. Orders shouted in my ear, steel striking too close, dirt in my eyes. I'm forced to hold the bond steady while everything in me screams to break.

Pain. Exhaustion. Distraction. That's what they're after, because that's how Vaulturia will come. And Alara doesn't stand apart from it. She takes the hits beside me, forcing herself to hold the thread just as tightly, learning when to shield and when to drive forward. Her instincts sharpen against mine until we're pushing back and pulling forward as one. For all her power, even she admits the truth: the bond is her weakest point. Not because she lacks strength, but because it leaves her open to me. And there is no one who understands that better than Aric and Soraya. What they unleash on Alara is nothing short of brutal.

In those moments, I force a wall up in the bond, sealing her from me. The first time we tried this, I nearly collapsed under the pressure of it, her pain ripping through me like it was my own. Now, in training, it's safer this way. I can't feel her. I can only watch. And sometimes, I can't bear to do that.

I stand back, chest heaving, dirt clinging to my palms as Soraya circles like a predator, her hackles high, eyes locked. She slams into Alara with her full weight, claws raking, teeth snapping at her throat. The impact rattles through the ground. Alara stumbles, skids in the dirt, then surges back up before Soraya can pin her. The bond thrums faintly against my wall, pressing, but I hold it shut.

Alara doesn't yield. She roars, the sound so raw it shakes my ribs, and throws Soraya off. Her shoulders roll, muscle on muscle, as she charges again. They collide, white against silver, dust rising in thick clouds around them.

Aric waits on the fringe, silent, patient, like a hammer ready to fall. He lets Soraya drive Alara to breaking, lets her test every weak spot—ribs, flanks, hindquarters—before he steps in. When he does, it's brutal. He doesn't circle. He hits head-on, teeth bared, slamming her to the ground with a force that makes me flinch.

And still, she rises. Blood streaks her muzzle, her sides heave, but her stance never falters. She is Alpha, but here she's stripped bare, a soldier being broken down and built up again. Every strike she takes, every time she forces herself back to her feet, it becomes clearer why the wolves follow her.

It's mesmerizing and terrifying. Watching her endure them both, refusing to back down, I finally see the scale of her power. But it also makes the truth hit harder. While Alara hones herself sharper with every strike, my own powers remain unpredictable. The bond, I've learned to hold. I'm a stronger warrior, thanks to the wolves, but my magic remains unruly and, right now, useless.

"Again," Ember orders, flicking a ball of fire at me. I barely block the flame she hurls, and once again, my magic falters. The heat scorches the edge of my armor, curling smoke into the air, the sharp tang of burned steel stings my nose.

Alara circles me, her presence heavy, expectant. *"You're holding back."*

"I'm not."

Alara moves in a flash of white fur and muscle. Before I can react, she's on me, knocking me to the ground with a force that rattles my bones. *"Then why am I still standing?"*

I gasp as I push up onto my elbows, my muscles shaking. *"Because I don't want to kill you."*

"But they do. Fight back, Rae. You have to."

I tighten my grip, flex my fingers, but my magic refuses to rise.

"Again."

I move quickly, but the force knocks me back a step, frustration curling beneath my skin like a trapped storm.

"You're hesitating."

"I am not."

Ember circles, slow and deliberate this time, like a lioness toying with a lamb. She's enjoying this.

I clench my fists, trying to shove down the frustration curling in my chest. My magic hums beneath my skin.

"Again."

I barely escape the flame this time. The heat grazes too close, searing my arm. My pulse spikes, the power inside me raging against its leash.

"Hesitation is a very consequential game, Rae. You of all people should know that. Out here, it's a matter of life and death, but with Zye, it could be love or loss..."

I snap to attention. She smirks. "I see the way he looks at you..."

I force my breath to steady, but it doesn't work.

"But you won't even acknowledge it, will you? You shut it out. You shut him out. Just like your power."

Heat surges. My vision narrows.

Ember tilts her head, watching me—watching the way my hands tighten, the way my magic shudders. And then she twists the knife.

"I don't know if you've noticed, Rae, but there are a lot of other girls walking the halls now. A lot of very pretty girls. He's got options."

My lungs lock.

"And needs."

My magic claws to the surface.

She steps closer, too close.

"You hesitate too long, and someone else is bound to—"

She sighs, tossing back her hair.

"Come to think of it, I've been kinda lonely lately—"

And just like that, I detonate.

The onslaught is relentless, a storm of element and fury crashing down without pause. The ground fractures beneath us, veins of molten heat tearing through the stone as fire erupts from the cracks, scorching everything in its path. Overhead, the sky splits open, water spilling from the heavens in sheets, colliding with the flames below in a deafening hiss of steam that cloaks the world in mist.

Wind howls through the clearing, sharp and furious, ripping branches from their roots, tearing ancient trees from the earth, sending shards of bark and ash spinning through the air like shrapnel. Fire. Water. Earth. Air. All at once, untamed and unforgiving, tearing the world apart at the seams.

And when it's over, the clearing is unrecognizable, a wasteland of scorched earth and smoldering ruin.

Silence.

Then, a slow, satisfied laugh.

Ember lowers her shield, her grin curling like smoke.

"There she is."

I collapse to the ground, gasping. Every muscle wrung out, every nerve alight. I can't breathe, but I've never felt more alive.

Across from me, Ember watches, hands on her hips, her expression carefully measured. Then, after a beat, "I didn't mean all those things I said."

I lift my head, brow arching.

She shrugs, then grimaces. "At least the part about him anywhere near my bed. Gross."

She winks, hands lifting to tighten the ponytail at the crown of her head, her entire face alight with something between exhilaration and mischief.

She looks out over the clearing, or what's left of it. "Damn, Rae." She exhales.

"But I do have to tell that man of yours that someone harbors the power of all four courts." She laughs, full of something electric, something dangerous. "And suddenly, this fight just got really interesting."

I push up onto my elbows, legs shaking, magic still flaring through me, uncontained.

"Ember—"

She simply blows me a kiss, then vanishes in a flicker.

Alara appears to survey the clearing, then exhales through her nose. "Well, that was immense."

I groan, rolling out onto the only patch of ground I haven't obliterated. *Tell anyone what just happened, and I'll have you skinned. Alive.*

She huffs out a laugh, then nudges my ribs, not gently.

"Come on, Rae, let's go. I'm hungry. Want me to fetch Zye to scoop you up in his tornado to take you home?"

I don't dignify that with a response.

She snorts and flicks her tail as she stalks off.

#

I fill my rest breaks with reading, forging a reluctant bond with the ill-tempered, petulant little book that holds more secrets than answers.

Nyxie and I pore over its pages, unraveling riddles, piecing together fragments of a past no one bothered to record properly. The library's ancient texts are scarce, unreliable at best, deliberately erased at worst. But every so often, the Tome offers glimpses, visions of Athyria before Solir and Lord Erian, before their family's reign of terror.

Nyxie tells stories of a world that thrived, of power balanced, of Athyria pulsing with life, of the portal standing open, binding realms together in harmony. Until it wasn't.

Later that night, I climb wearily into bed, sore from training and heavier from everything I still don't understand.

"The past is a dangerous place to visit, Rae... but you must. You must understand the past to protect the future."

My body jolts. Exhaustion gone. I sit upright.

The past. The past that holds the answers no one seems to have.

I reach for the Tome, but the second my fingers touch its cover, lightning snaps across my palm. "Ow! What was that for?" I hiss, shaking my hand.

"Master the power, Rae," says the voice, and I startle.

"My power?" I snap. "I'm trying. Every damn day. And I'm exhausted. I don't even sleep, and you speak in riddles. I don't know what you want from me."

Pages flip violently, like the book itself is searching, frantic. Then, just as quickly it stops.

A woman appears.

Not drawn.

Not ink.

A vision.

She watches me. Just long enough for me to wonder if she knows me. Then she vanishes, swallowed by smoke that twists and shifts, forming a shape. A wolf and a woman. My signet. I gasp.

And the battlefield appears.

The sky is thick with wings, birds and beasts clashing midair, talons tearing, shadows diving. Below, wolves tear through trenches, bodies strewn like shattered flags, blood soaking into ash and mud. Screams echo across the battlefield. In the center of it all is a man. He's kneeling, suddenly a surge erupts, golden, violent, final. It throws bodies and beasts back in a wave of light. A scream tears the air, and then he's gone.

"Rae, when they tell you your blood is a threat, remember what ours cost. Don't let them fear what's buried beneath a name."

My signet flares, heat tearing through my bones like recognition.

"You are who they need to do what we could not."

The Tome snaps shut.

And the world goes still.

I am exhausted. My body aches, yet as I lie alone in bed, staring at the ceiling, Ira's vision sears behind my eyelids. The instant I drift, the nightmares come, hard and fast. And unforgiving. It is always the same cove, the same calm sea turned cruel.

Every few hours I wake gasping, thrashing, my pulse wild. And every time, Nyxie is there, her cool hands steady on my skin. On those nights when sleep won't return, she curls beside me, fingers idly threading through my hair as she talks, sometimes in fragments, sometimes whole stories, until my eyes grow heavy.

"I served the High King," she tells me that night, her words settling into the silence like a lullaby. "He was a wonderful man. Not flawless, but good in a way kings rarely are. He told the worst jokes, laughed harder than anyone else at them, and despite a castle full of us fluttering around him, he insisted on cooking. He loved it. He wasn't very good, but he loved spending time with his eldest son in the kitchen. Usually burning everything."

Her laughter is warm, but it fades quickly. "He could be fierce when he needed to be, but most days, he was gentle. He wasn't blind to his sons. He saw the cruelty in the youngest, Solir. He once told me he didn't know what went wrong. He hoped he'd change. But Solir was bad through to his core."

As she speaks, light catches in the strands of her hair, that striking shade of blue that ripples like water under moonlight. Tiny beads and threads of gold woven through it glint when she tilts her head. She is both impossibly fragile and devastatingly beautiful.

"When Vaulturia rose, they came for us. We thought the High King's men would intervene, that someone would hold the line. But the truth is, by then the power was already broken. His death fractured everything. Those who remained were either too afraid, too scattered, or too intent on saving their own to save anyone else. And even if they had come, I wonder now if it would have mattered."

Her hands still in her lap. "They took my people, twisted them into things they were never meant to be. I was captured once. I don't remember for how long. Long enough to watch friends turned into enemies, their wills shredded until they wielded their magic against their own. Long enough to learn what despair tastes like." She draws a long deep breath. "I escaped because one of them chose me over their orders. Just a flicker of who they used to be, and in that flicker, I flew. Others weren't given that chance. I still wake with their screams in my ears."

I close my eyes, letting her voice carry me. "When the King fell, most of this land fell with him. For years this building, as you now know it, stood in ruin, silent and broken. But with Horo, we rebuilt it. Brick by brick. Memory by memory. Because if we didn't, there would be nothing left worth fighting for."

Her fingers drift through my hair. "I have lived centuries. I have seen more cruelty than I can count. But you…" She exhales, more wonder than sorrow. "You are the greatest thing I have ever seen walk these lands."

The next morning, I wake tired and hollow-eyed, but steadier. Beneath the exhaustion is something else, something pushing me toward answers, toward truth.

Nyxie has breakfast sent to my room, giving me time to recount everything the Tome revealed. She listens, quiet but intent, fingers tapping absently against her teacup.

I pause. "You good?"

She nods, the loose strands of her blue hair shimmering like waves under moonlight. Tiny jewels woven through the braids like scattered stardust. "Yes, yes, keep going."

I frown but don't press. After a quick shower, I twist my damp hair into a messy bun and make a direct line for the library.

The Academy's library towers around me, shelves stacked to the rafters, spiraling ladders that creak with age, scrolls and tomes tucked into every corner and spare space. I move between them in silence, dragging my finger over the aged leather covers, looking for anything on the Corestone. On the High King. Or a man in the war. Anything that can make sense of any of this.

The library should have answers. But today, it feels like it's hiding them.

Hours pass. I sift through dusty tomes, torn parchments, half-deciphered texts, legends that contradict themselves. Nothing. Frustration boils over. I shove back from the desk, throwing an arm over my head with a groan. "Gah! This is useless."

Nyxie hums, flipping through another book.

I glare at her. "Zye's smug, you're sweet. So explain the face you're pulling before I lose my mind."

She finally looks up, a slow, knowing smile forming. "You're looking at this wrong."

My eyes narrow.

"You keep asking what. What happened? What does it mean? But you're missing the most important part."

A pause.

"The who," she says, matter-of-factly.

I sit up straighter. "What do you mean?"

"The Tome isn't just showing you the past, Rae. Someone is showing you." She nods toward the Tome. "So ask it."

I blink at her. Then at the book. Then back at her.

I cross my arms. "That just seems too... obvious."

She shrugs. "And yet, it's the only thing you haven't tried."

I huff, shaking my head. She's right.

Nyxie tilts her head, watching me carefully. Then, casually, like she's just thinking out loud, she says, "You know, Tomes like this... they're rare, but they were used long ago to keep histories and stories of each of the lands. Life before it all went bad. And then, along with anything that stood to be true and good, the Vaulturians had them destroyed because these books harbored one of the biggest threats of all—the truth. The written language has a way of preserving power long after their authors are gone."

My fingers drum against the table. Before I can decide how to test this theory, what to ask, how to phrase it, if it even matters, Nyxie stretches, rolling her shoulders, the delicate gold chains of her layered necklaces catching the light as they shift against her skin. As she tilts her head, the freckles across her nose crinkle with realization. "Ah, didn't you promise Kail and Thane you'd meet them to train this morning?"

Panic slams into me. "Oh, shiiiit." My chair scrapes against the floor as I bolt upright. "The time. They'll kill me. Actually kill me."

She shoos me off. "Go. An hour of training might actually clear your head."

Flustered, confused, and now late, I mumble a hurried thanks and race out into the hallway, lost in thought, until I feel him.

Zye.

I spin back to see him walking down the hallway. Dark hair falls across his forehead, unruly in a way that feels deliberate.

Black combat leathers cling to him, a blade sheathed on each thigh, his stride all power and control. The air stirs at his shoulders, the ghost of wings trailing as he closes the distance between us.

I've barely seen him in the weeks since the attack. He's been on the front lines, fortifying villages and training with the Hawks, or working with Horo and the Terralyns to strengthen the wards that keep The Academy standing. And when he's not fighting or shoring up defenses, I've heard he's been with the Healer, scouring abandoned homes and villages, making sure no one gets left behind or is injured. Not just soldiers—families. Children. Anyone.

His eyes drag over me with quiet interest.

"Well, hello, stranger," he says.

I arch a brow, clearing my throat. "Well, hello, savior," I correct.

He laughs as he closes the distance.

"Oh, you have been spending too much time with Kail. What are you doing?"

"Right now? Losing my mind." I deadpan, the weight of everything slipping into my tone before I can rein it in.

Zye stops mid-step, caught off guard. His lips part, but no words come out.

I sigh, softening. "Sorry, my mind is mush. I'm heading to training with the boys. Apparently, I've still got a lot to learn in hand-to-hand combat. But..." I pause, adjusting my bun, my fingers tugging at a loose strand. "I had a late night with the Tome, and I need to figure it out. And I can't."

"Sounds fun. I'll come."

I blink. "Huh?"

"I'll help you."

"With the Tome or the training?" I ask, narrowing my gaze.

His eyes lower, the corner of his mouth barely moving, but the intent is clear.

I follow where he's looking. Socks and slides. My sister's ultimate fashion crime and of course, nothing slips past hawk eyes.

"I'll train with you," he says.

"Not necessary," I say quickly, shaking my head.

"Oh, I think it's very necessary. Sounds like you need a sparring partner."

"The boys take care of that."

"I insist," he says with a grin that tells me this is more for his entertainment than my education.

I glare. "I hate that smug thing you're doing."

"Perfect. That's the right energy for a fight."

I sigh, throwing up my hands in mock defeat. "Fine. First one there takes the first round."

I turn to run, and he grabs my hand.

The world lurches as my feet slam onto hard ground. The scent of sweat and old leather fills my lungs, as does the dust. We're in the gym.

I stumble, blinking hard. "You could've warned me."

"And miss that reaction? Not a chance."

He gestures toward a spare mat in the corner of the gym. "Ladies befo—"

I press a finger against his lips, cutting him off. "You're enjoying the fact that you're about to whip my ass. Please don't finish that sentence with 'gentlemen.'"

He smiles against my finger before stepping back, dipping into an overly dramatic bow. "Ladies first." He winks, gesturing grandly to the mat.

I shove him lightly in the chest, laughing as I move past him.

"And you're wrong, Rae," he says, his expression shameless.

"I'm here to watch that ass."

That stops me in my tracks. I laugh, short and sharp. Then I spin, magic crackling at my fingertips as I fire a bolt straight at his head.

Zye jerks to the side just in time as it hisses past his ear, close enough to ruffle his hair. It slams into the wall behind him with a sharp crack, knocking a rack of equipment to the floor, leaving a fresh scorch mark seared into the stone.

"Hey!" Kail shouts as I throw up my hands in apology. "Rule one. No magic in the gym! Death by a hundred hill sprints up Widowmaker's Peak is not a nice way to go out. You wouldn't be the first, and you sure as hell won't be the last. Rules are rules, even for the golden ones."

Zye waves a hand, all lazy ease, magic rippling out as the equipment rights itself and the scorch mark fades like it was never there. He winks.

Kail scoffs and, with a parting flick of his middle finger, turns back to where he and Thane are demonstrating wrestling techniques to a group of recruits.

Unbothered by the exchange, Thane catches my eye, lifts a hand—five minutes.

Zye waves him off and I realize then that I haven't seen him this at ease since the ambush. I've barely seen him at all, and when I have, he was never like this.

"See? Lucky I came after all." He nudges me with his elbow. "Now, let's see what those boys have taught you about self-defense and daggers."

I grunt, pulling off my slides and stripping down to my training gear. "Looks like we're really doing this."

"Oh, we're really doing this."

For two hours, Zye doesn't let up.

His movements are fluid. Lethal. Calculated.

Every strike is a lesson. Every shift in weight, every silent correction, a demand to keep up. The fabric of his shirt clings to his back, damp with sweat, outlining every flex and twist of muscle as he moves. Veins cut down his forearms, his grip sure and unrelenting. His hand finds my wrist, steadying it. The other brushes my hip, correcting the angle. Heat flares low in my stomach, but I lock it down. He adjusts my stance without a word, and I follow the pressure of his palm like instinct. We don't speak. We don't need to.

His body guides, mine learns. Strike. Block. Step. Again. Again. Until I'm drenched and breathless, until every muscle in my body burns but the movements start to click. Start to sharpen.

By the time he finally steps back, I'm no longer chasing him; I'm holding my own.

"Closer," he instructs, adjusting the way I grip my dagger. His fingers brush mine and I swallow hard, refocusing. "With shorter blades or no weapon at all, you have to get in close," he adds, stepping toward me. I shift my stance.

"Closer."

I roll my shoulders, ignoring the way his chest shifts with the movement, muscles flexing with effortless precision.

"Will you two stop circling each other like dance partners and actually engage?" Kail shouts from across the gym, waving half a sandwich like a weapon.

Zye, clearly toying with me, extends a hand, palm up, fingers flicking in a lazy challenge.

"Come on, Rae. Make me work for it."

I lunge, my dagger aimed at his ribs, but he anticipates it and pivots. Before I can counter, his arm hooks around my waist. The world tilts. My back hits the mat, hard, with Zye's weight pressing down, his body braced over mine. His knee slots between my legs, pinning me, his breath warm against my jaw.

Everything shifts.

I feel every inch of him—the slow rise and fall of his chest, the tension locking us in place.

"Better," he murmurs. "But still not good enough." His dagger is across my throat.

I don't move. Neither does he.

"Are you going to let me up?" I breathe.

His grip tightens. Just slightly.

"Do you want me to?"

I swallow hard.

Somewhere across the gym, Kail groans. "Spare us the torture and kiss already!"

Zye laughs, winks and rolls off me in one fluid motion, offering his hand. I ignore it.

I get up on my own. His mouth barely shifts, but the look he gives me hits almost harder than anything that came before it.

#

"Let's get cleaned up. It's a beautiful afternoon. I'll walk you back, and you can fill me in on the past few weeks of work you've clearly been putting in," Zye says, one brow raised.

My cheeks flush. I don't know why.

As we head for the door, he holds it open, stepping aside just enough for me to slip past. His hand brushes mine.

The contact is fleeting, inconsequential. Except it isn't. A jolt of warmth shoots up my arm, my pulse stumbling over itself. His presence fills the space, and for one dangerous beat I want to stall in it. But I don't. I won't. I can't.

Outside, the air is crisp. The sky melts into soft streaks of pink as the sun sinks toward the mountains, casting long shadows over the snow-capped peaks. The scent of damp earth lingers from the morning's storm, the world calm despite the war brewing beneath its surface.

"So, now you've had a chance to clear your head, talk to me," Zye says, his voice steady but curious. "What has, or had, you losing your sanity?"

I exhale, dragging a hand through my hair. "Well, I've grown close to the Tome. In a weird, noncommittal, barely verbal, and not-at-all warm or friendly way."

Zye tilts his head, nodding mockingly. "Sounds healthy."

"Nyxie uncovered a heap of history, but it's fragmented. There are diary entries from the war, letters but even those feel vague, like pieces are missing."

Zye hums. "Because they are."

Suddenly, he stops walking and shifts gears entirely. "I've got an idea," he says.

I narrow in on him. "Hmm…"

"Ask Alara to meet us in the courtyard in an hour."

And that's all he says before disappearing into the rift.

Smooth pavings stretch in even lines through the courtyard, their pale surface shimmering with hints of quartz that catch the late afternoon sun.

Alara waits at the heart of it, her white form even more imposing in a space clearly not built for her kind and I can't help but smile. I cross the courtyard to where she stands and bury my hand in the thick fur at her chest, rubbing in slow circles.

"Thanks for meeting us, even though I still have no idea why."

"We're about to find out," she replies, as the air splits open and Zye steps through.

"Alara, if we move quickly, we can make it to Hanging Rock in a few minutes," Zye says, addressing her directly without so much as a hello. "I'll fly overhead and keep an eye on everything, but we'll need to make this fast."

"Climb on, Rae."

"Is anyone going to explain what we're doing?" I mutter.

"You'll see," Zye says as we make our way to the gate. "Now, up you go and hold on tight."

I shoot Alara a pointed look, but she simply nudges me forward with her nose.

His tone is anything but serious, which only stokes my curiosity. I swing onto Alara's back, fingers sinking into her thick fur as I grip tight. A flash of silver, and Zye shifts into hawk form. In the next heartbeat we're moving, Alara surging forward at a breakneck pace.

The rush of wind tears through my hair as the courtyard falls away behind us. Towers and arches shrink to specks, swallowed by the sweep of forest rolling out in every direction, deep green broken by flashes of rivers. Mountains rise in the distance, sharp against the fading sky, and I can't help but laugh.

By the time we reach what I assume is Hanging Rock, Zye's back at my side. I will never get used to the way he looks after flight—his hair tousled and untamed, the luminous ribbons of wind that cling to him, the way his steps hit the ground with unwavering confidence. But it's his eyes. The intensity in them, shifting, flashing between hawk and human. One moment they gleam with the sharpness of a predator, ruthless, calculating. But in the blink, that fierceness softens, and his eyes are human again.

Ahead, the peaks rise in clean, commanding lines, their slopes tumbling into green valleys thick with wildflowers. Color spills toward the lake below, its surface so still it mirrors the mountains and clouds above until it's hard to tell where the land ends and the reflection begins. The water stretches out as far as the eye can see, meeting the base of the mountains and flowing through inlets and coves into the valleys below.

I stand in awe. Every color richer, every shadow sharper. When I finally glance at Zye, his expression is softer than I've seen in weeks. "This is incredible," I whisper. "It's beautiful."

Zye steps closer, and my heart betrays me by racing a little faster.

"Sure is," he says. I glance up, expecting him to be watching the view, only to catch him watching me instead. Heat rushes to my cheeks, and I quickly look away, shy under the weight of his gaze. He clears his throat to hide what sounds suspiciously like a laugh.

"I come here a bit," he says, "when I need to think, or just breathe. Sometimes… just, to forget. To, I don't know, to just…"

"Not be a warrior?"

His hand drags over the back of his neck, his expression torn between confusion and reluctant confession. "Yeah, I guess so…" He bends to pick up a rock and launches it into the sky. We watch in silence as it lands a few seconds later in the water below.

I study him then. It's easy to forget the pressure he's under, the toll it must take on someone his age. Ethan and Felix, beyond the odd surf rescue, weren't out saving lives. If anything, they were doing their best to make their lives shorter. But Zye carries a weight that doesn't belong to someone so young.

"How old are you?" I ask, tentatively.

He shrugs.

"Honestly? I'm not sure. We think about nineteen, maybe twenty. Maybe not. But that kind of thing, keeping track of ages, only started when you arrived." His lips form a faint, wry smile. "None of us ever kept records. No birthdays, no milestones. It's just… not something we do. If anything, it's a reminder of how long it's been since we lost the ones we love, so we'd rather not think, let alone know."

I catch the hint of pain in his expression and scramble to recover.

"So, what you're saying is… you've never had a birthday party?"

He raises an eyebrow. "A what?"

I gasp in mock horror. "Cake? Candles? People singing out of tune while you sit awkwardly at the center of attention?"

His lips twitch. "That sounds awful."

"That last part is, sure." I nod firmly. "But we're doing it. From now on. I'll get Nyxie to make a calendar, and we're celebrating each and every one!"

"Even yours, Alara. Hip, hip, hooray!"

She doesn't dignify that with a response. *"Stop distracting us from what we've come here to do, Rae."*

Before I can question what that even is, he takes my hand and leads me closer to the edge. I look at him quizzically, then stop short, my stomach plummeting as I take in the drop, it is at least a three-story plunge into crystal-clear water.

He tilts his head toward the water.

"Oh, like hell I'm doing that!" I blurt, pulling back sharply.

Zye's laughter erupts, rolling across the valley. "How about I go first? When you see I don't die, you—"

"Nope. Not happening."

But my eyes betray me, drawn back to the water below and I'm reminded of home.

Even on the coldest winter days, when I was frustrated, restless, drowning in my own thoughts, I'd go straight to the ocean. No one ever leaves an ocean swim sad, my dad would always say. The thought of him makes my heart ache. But damn it, he had a point. And if there was ever a time I am all of those things, it's now.

"I might live to regret this, or not," I mutter, swallowing hard, "but will you do it with me?"

He nods. Once.

"You're going to be pulling me, because there's no chance my body is willingly stepping off that edge." I peer over again, exhaling sharply. "And you're sure you've done this before?"

"No rocks. No submerged boats. No krakens waiting to be unleashed." His tone is teasing, but the glint in his eyes is a challenge.

I shoot him a hard glare. "A kraken? I hadn't even considered that, but now—"

"It's safe, Rae. And just one step."

"The water—"

"Freezing," he admits easily. "But I'll dry us off quickly. Your choice."

I grunt. Choice. This will be held over me for the rest of my days if I don't do it. And I sense he knows I'm too stubborn for that.

"Take off your jacket and shoes," he says, nodding toward my boots.

I exhale through my nose, not quite a sigh, not quite surrender, and crouch to unlace my boots as he mirrors the motion.

From the cliff's edge, Alara watches, completely unfazed.

"Why aren't you doing this?" I ask suspiciously.

She snorts, flicking her tail lazily. *"I can think of a thousand ways to get an adrenaline rush—or die—that don't involve plummeting off a cliff. That, and I don't like water."*

I arch a brow. *"Really? I've seen you swim for me before."*

Her head tilts, eyes narrowing with mock severity. *"I went in because you left me no choice. You heard him, this is your choice. And it's a dumb one."*

I can't help but laugh, the memory of the wipeout flashing through my mind—me thrashing, half-drowning, her charging in through the carnage like she was charging into a war. At the time I didn't understand, but now it feels like the most Alara thing in the world.

I ruffle her fur as I let out a deep breath and rip off my jacket, setting my daggers carefully beside it. I've started carrying them everywhere since the ambush, training has drilled that much into me. They're not a natural extension of me yet, not the way they are for the others, but the weight at my hips has become a strange kind of reassurance.

Alara peers over the edge.

"It's not too late," I muse.

"I'll be lying in the sun until you return. If. If you return."

I shake out my hands, trying to loosen the nervous energy threatening to choke me. My pulse is everywhere—loud in my ears, hot in my throat. I turn back to where Zye is standing. "You have ten seconds before common sense kicks in and I change my mind."

That's all he needs. He grabs my hand and drags me to the edge. He has ten seconds. Five now. And he's going to make every one of them count.

The wind whips around us, the rush of adrenaline sparking under my skin. I know he feels it too because his grip tightens, his knuckles flexing over mine. I look up and curse him.

"On three. One… two—" He doesn't wait for three. We drop.

The wind rips past my ears, my scream shattering the quiet. Zye's grip is steel, his body solid beside mine as we plummet, the rush of air pulling at us, the cliff vanishing into streaks of color.

We hit the water and I am immediately overwhelmed by a rush of bubbles and darkness. The only thing I can see is the white blur of surging water around me with no sense of direction or ability to find the surface, until I'm there and gasping.

A second later, Zye emerges beside me, shaking water from his face. I throw my head back and let out a scream, unrestrained, unfiltered, pure joy. "Wooooooo!"

The sound echoes across the water. Tossing my arms back, I let my body drift, floating weightlessly on the surface. Then I flip upright, spinning toward him.

"Thank you." My voice is shaky. "For everything."

Zye drifts closer, soaked hair clinging to his face; his grin is contagious. The water ripples around him, the space between us disappearing, inch by inch.

"That wasn't so bad, was it?" he teases.

The way it rumbles through the air, through me, is entirely unfair.

"And that isn't even the best part."

I blink, immediately suspicious. "Wait, what?"

Zye tilts his head toward the cliffs as we start to swim toward shore.

"What goes down must go up, Rae."

"Surely you aren't planning to hike when you can rift walk that distance?"

Zye snorts. "And where's the fun in that?"

We clamber onto the rocks, dripping wet and shivering, the air offering no relief from the cold. My limbs are numb, my teeth feel like they're rattling in my skull.

"Let's test your powers here," Zye says, watching me carefully. I wrap my arms around myself, shuddering. Despite standing like a figure carved from ice, Zye appears unmoved by the chill, his body rigid, his gaze sharp.

"You're cold, Rae. Wet. I can fix that, but I want to see if you can, too."

I swallow hard. "How? I can't—"

"You can. Channel it. Let it rise."

The cold is unbearable as it seeps further into my bones. My body shakes violently, my breath is unsteady but then, I find the sun. I lift my chin, let my mind grasp for that warmth, for that lick of fire. It starts deep in my core, slow and unsure, then spreads down through my legs, through my toes and then up, into my chest and out to my fingertips. Heat licks at my skin, wrapping around my shoulders, unfurling like wildfire. I exhale softly, tilting my palms outward.

Zye watches, unmoving, but the look on his face is unmistakably pride.

I turn to him, stretching out my hands, and exhale. The heat surges forward, a wave of warmth wrapping around him, curling over his skin like fire meeting ice. Zye stands rigid, his body now trembling from the cold. His muscles are tight, his breaths shallow. Then the heat takes hold. It rolls over his chest, spreading across his shoulders, licking up the curve of his neck. His skin shifts from a shade of blue to flushed as the color returns. Droplets of water rise and evaporate instantly, trailing along the sharp ridges of his abdomen, his arms, his collarbone. His hair dries in an instant, strands falling effortlessly back into place.

His lips part slightly, his chest expanding as warmth floods through him. He smiles. "Impressive."

I shake out my shoulders as Zye exhales, raking a hand through his newly dried hair. "And now to get back to the peak, there are two options: your way or mine."

I scoff, rolling my eyes. "Don't pretend my way is even an option. So, tell me, what does your way look like?"

Hot. His wings snap open, and every thought in my head evaporates. I gasp.

His wings spread wide, bronzed feathers streaked with deep russet, the edges fading into a darker hue, almost gold. Air currents whip through the feathers, making them ripple and dance.

But it's not just the wings. It's him. Bare-chested, firelit, standing in the wind like he was born to rule it. Every inch of him is carved and I should not be looking at him the way I am, but I am, and it's too late to stop myself.

"How. What. Wow…" I spit out, words failing. "Does that hurt?"

Zye rolls his shoulders, stretching his wings as if testing their weight.

"Not really," he muses. "Feels a bit… naked, though." He glances down at himself and his shirtless torso. I swallow hard, unable to breathe properly.

He steps forward. His gaze lowers, tracing my lips. Heat flares in my chest and I clench my fists, desperate to keep it in, to hold any part of it still.

Zye's eyes widen slightly, and before I can react, his arm hooks under my knees, the other locking around my waist. I yelp, clutching at his neck. "Zye—" The ground vanishes beneath us, the world blurring into streaks of green and blue.

My scream shakes the mountains, echoing through the valley. Zye laughs, the sound rumbling against my chest. The air rushes past us, whipping my hair into wild ribbons, but the panic fades almost instantly, because we're soaring.

The motion shifts, our ascent leveling into a smooth, effortless glide over the water.

I risk looking up and instantly regret it. Because his face is too close, his smile too knowing, and my heart is entirely too treacherous.

"Enjoying yourself?" he teases, his voice like gravel. I scowl, ignoring the way my pulse refuses to slow.

I glance away, desperate for a distraction, and find one in his wings. Each mighty beat cuts through the air with effortless precision, shifting between power and grace so seamlessly it feels impossible.

We circle wide, descending in a slow, controlled sweep and instinctively my arms tighten around his neck.

Zye's grip on me tightens in response. "I won't drop you."

I manage a small laugh. "I'd appreciate that."

He chuckles, the sound vibrating through me.

I dare to look up again. His wings beat strong and sure against the sky; I catch a glimpse of his eyes. They have transformed, just like his wings.

No longer just human, a predator's gaze, and yet, as they lock onto mine, they soften, just enough to remind me that beneath all that power, beneath the wings and raw strength, he's still him. And I am entirely at his mercy.

Zye angles us back, wings slicing through the air as he guides us toward the grassy rise where Alara waits, pacing, her ears flicking back as she tracks our descent. Ever the protector.

We touch down in a rush of air and beating wings, his feet slamming against the earth with controlled force. His wings vanish almost instantly as he sets me gently on the grass beside her. My legs give out, and I fall into her, breathless and laughing.

"That was the most incredible moment of my life."

"Oh, I heard," she says, flicking her tail. *"And it might just be the last thing I ever hear."*

I push my hair from my face, still grinning, while Zye crouches a few steps away to tug at the laces of his boots.

I sprawl out on the grass; the sun is warm on my face, the earth solid again beneath me. "Thanks for that," I say, glancing over at him. That's when I notice the way his shoulders have drawn tight, a stillness settling into him like stone.

"Zye," I ask softly as I prop up on an elbow, "is everything okay?"

His jaw works once before he answers. "Rae… I wanted to tell you earlier, but I wasn't sure how. We've got a theory. A wild one. But it's the only thing that makes sense."

"What kind of theory?" I ask as a roll to my side to face him.

"That you're not the only thing that ended up in the human realm."

My pulse skips, and I push off the grass, shooting upright. "What?"

Zye finishes with his boots, then rises. He crosses the space between us and offers his hand, pulling me to my feet.

"We think the Corestone's there."

"What do you mean there? As in… my world?"

Zye nods once. "I've searched every corner of this realm. It's not here. Not buried, not broken, not locked away. It's gone."

"But… how?" My voice cracks. "You said the portal was sealed. That no one—"

"I know." He cuts in gently. "But we just proved it's possible."

"Rae, if the Corestone is in your world, it won't look like anything you'd expect. It could be a weapon. A book. A piece of fruit, for all we know. Something forgotten… ancient."

Almost immediately my pulse starts to race as the pieces start to fall into place. I blink. "A relic," I murmur.

Zye's gaze sharpens. "Exactly."

I stagger forward, catching myself against his forearms. His hands come up instinctively, steadying me.

No. No, no, no.

A sick feeling churns low in my gut. I stagger back a step, pressing my fingers to my temple, trying to think. I need to think. "Rae?"

"The artifacts. The gallery. Ethan's dad, Myles, acquired a collection of ancient relics. They were unloading them into the gallery the day I…um, I left. Rare. They're said to be worth millions, apparently."

I look up and find Zye already looking back. "What if that collection included the Corestone?"

I can't finish. I don't need to. The nausea hits fast and sharp. Myles has it. Or worse, the Corestone has him.

I step back.

"He wouldn't know what it was. He wouldn't understand—"

"He wouldn't need to," Zye says. "The Corestone needs to be found by you. It would get wherever it had to, however it had to, to make sure that happens. And if he was touched by—"

"They're all in danger," I whisper, the names clawing their way up. Ethan. Felix. Mum. Dad. Annie.

Zye rubs a hand over the back of his neck. He nods. "So we better get you back to stop it before it starts."

I open my mouth to argue, but the words stall. My brain trips, stutters and then slams to a halt.

"Wait. What?"

I go to speak, then freeze, realization hits.

"Are you saying we have to go back?"

"Unless you'd rather stay here and pick the sparkleflowers in the garden."

I stare at him.

He smiles, bright and infuriatingly calm. "Yes, Rae. It's time to go home."

The Tome is heavy in my hands, heavier than usual.

Whether it is the weight of the book or everything it carries—Myles, my family, Ira, the Corestone, or the thought of home waiting like a reckoning I am not sure I'm ready to face—I don't know.

I hesitate at the door, my knuckles hovering over the wood. This is stupid. I should turn around, walk away, go back to Nyxie, go anywhere but here, but my feet do not move.

So, before I can think myself out of it, I knock.

There is a beat of silence. Then another, until the door finally opens, and whatever resolve I thought I had disintegrates.

Zye stands before me, a towel slung around his neck, steam still clinging to his skin. His dark hair is damp, curling slightly, a few strands falling into his eyes. He is barefoot and shirtless.

He does not speak right away. He just leans against the doorframe, watching me. "Is everything all right?"

"Oh, I am so sor— I, um, did not mean to interrupt. I just… didn't." I sound like a mumbling idiot. I shift on my feet, suddenly unsure. I should leave, turn around, and pretend I never came. "This was probably a mistake."

I shift back a step, already retreating, the embarrassment clawing up my throat.

But then his gaze lowers to the Tome clutched tight in my hands. Understanding dawns in his expression.

He steps aside. A silent invitation.

I swallow hard and step past him.

When I enter I realize immediately the room is nothing like I expected. Not that I knew what to expect, but it was not this. Or, as I take in the details, maybe it was.

The air inside is cool and quiet. Dark walls, etched with silver filigree, stretch high, disappearing into the vaulted ceilings. The bed is massive, the windows even more so, floor-to-ceiling panes of glass overlooking the western cliffs and the distant spires of The Academy. A sword rests beside a stack of books on the desk. A single candle flickers near the hearth.

It is every bit Zye. Beautiful. Humble. Dangerous.

I do not go far, just hover near the chair closest to the fire, almost waiting for permission to fall apart.

"I need to ask it something." I shove the Tome toward his chest, and he leans back.

"Whoa, be careful with that thing. It's angry."

"Ha, you are not wrong." I exhale sharply. "Nyxie says I need to ask it something, and I… I do not know how. Or what to do. And I just… I—"

I lose the ability to form a coherent sentence and internally curse myself. Squeezing my eyes shut, I blurt it out. "I did not want to be alone. And I did not know where else to go. There."

Zye closes the door behind us and turns, drying the back of his neck with the towel. "Give me a minute to not look like I just got dragged out of a river," he says. "Sit. I will be right back."

I do not know what has come over me. I am a wreck. A few weeks ago, I was blaming this man for untethering my entire life, and now I am practically begging him to save me from it. Get a grip, Rae.

By the time he returns, dressed in black, sleeves rolled, jaw set, he looks exactly like himself again. But he does not ask what is wrong, or come anywhere near the chair. Without hesitation, he walks to the end of his bed and pulls on his boots.

I frown. "Oh, am I interrupting?"

He throws me a dry look as he buttons his cuffs. "My bath, yes. My night, no." He reaches out his hand. "Come."

With a flick of his fingers, a controlled current of wind slips the Tome from my hands. It hisses in protest as he tucks it into a satchel, the fabric crackling with leftover static. He shudders at the contact. "This one is a little farther through the Rift," he warns. "Stay close."

I exhale, shaking my head. "Zye, I—"

Too late. He is already reaching for me.

Wind curls around us, pulling tight. The room vanishes.

Almost instantly my feet hit solid ground with an unceremonious thud. My stomach flips, my balance sways, and before I can even blink, the smell makes me gag.

Dust. Rot. Something distinctly moldy.

I wrinkle my nose, glancing around. "I think I preferred cliff jumping." I gesture at the mess of collapsed shelves, piles of crumbling parchment, and the squish beneath my shoe.

"But if your plan was to bring me somewhere more depressing than my mood, you nailed it. Take me back now. Please."

He is unbothered, hands in his pockets as he leans against what is left of a crumbling wall. "Give it a chance."

I arch a brow. "A chance for the black mold to eat away at my lungs? I can feel it happening. Time to go."

His lips twitch. "Just shut up and look up, please."

I huff but do as he says, stepping deeper into the space. My boots crunch over broken glass, and my fingertips graze a splintered table as I scan my surroundings. Stone walls rise high around us, cracked with vines curling through the breaks. Heavy wooden beams stretch overhead, blackened by time and fire.

"This was once the heart of the realm, a thriving village," Zye says.

I freeze mid-step.

He gestures around us, toward the ruined archways, the blackened hearths, the once-vaulted ceilings now shattered open to the gray sky.

"This was the last remaining piece of who we were, what we are. Where the Highborn of each land came to share history, to trade knowledge. Athyrians met here, before the wars, before the betrayal, before the doors to your world were sealed shut."

A chill slides down my spine.

"It looks like an old bookstore," I say cautiously.

"Not just a traditional bookstore. A living archive of all of Athyria."

He swallows. "These were not just books. They were proof. Of who we were. What we could be. That scared Vaulturia more than any weapon or magic."

His jaw clenches. "So they burned it. It was destroyed out of fear. It held too much truth, stories of joy, unity, what the realm used to be before they upended it all. They needed to destroy any memory of what was possible."

The wind shifts through the broken ceiling, scattering a flurry of torn pages across the floor. A single page lands in front of my foot. I crouch, brushing away the grime until the edges of parchment peek through. It is not a book this time, but a poster, cracked and curling, its colors faded but still clinging to the paper.

I lift it carefully, shaking loose the debris. Then I freeze. *Children.*

Dozens of them, hand-drawn in a joyful chaos of color and motion. Some are mid-laugh, others mid-leap, riding wolves, playing with them. One kid is being dragged through the mud by a grinning pup twice their size. Another balances on the back of a gray-furred beast mid-bound, arms out like wings.

It is magic in its purest form, wild, messy, uncontained joy. I do not realize I am smiling until my cheeks hurt.

"This was real?" I ask, barely above a whisper.

Zye does not answer right away.

"It was more than real," he says finally. "It was normal. Before the war, kids used to grow up with magic like this. Learning it. Playing in it. No fear. No limits." Then he reaches into his pocket and pulls out a small, folded scrap of parchment, its edges frayed. He holds it out to me, just a few words, scrawled in uneven, childish ink:

> *Today I made a flame float.*
> *It was fun.*
> *- Horo*

I stare at the note, heartbeat slowing to a crawl.

"He was a kid here," I whisper. Zye nods once. "He was."

"He never talks about it," Zye adds. "What this place meant. What he lost. But this is why he built The Academy. Not for soldiers. For hope."

"Why there and not here?" I ask.

Zye's jaw hardens. "The Vaulturians laced the walls with dark magic after the fall. Drained the place dry. Stripped it of every trace of elemental power. They knew if they killed the roots, nothing would grow again."

I look back at the note, my fingers trembling slightly.

"I do not know how to fix any of this," I whisper. "Every time I think I am getting closer, it slips away again. The Tome will not talk unless it wants to. Apparently Myles is the keeper of a very dangerous stone. My family—"

"You are scared," he says quietly. "You should be."

There is no judgment in his voice, only truth. "None of this is easy, Rae. Not for you. Not for any of us. But you are not alone in this fight."

He steps closer, slow but sure, until the air shifts between us. I can feel the buzz of his magic just beneath his skin, like a storm on the verge of breaking.

"Do not underestimate what this means, what you mean," Zye says. "You are not just surviving, Rae. You are making others believe they can too. This"—he gestures to the broken stone, the wreckage around us—"cannot be rebuilt the way it was. But with you here, with Alara, there is finally reason to believe that what was lost could be rewritten."

My breath hitches.

His eyes stay locked on mine as the Tome jolts violently in the satchel and we both flinch.

Zye reacts fast, swearing under his breath. "I hate that thing."

A laugh slips out before I can stop it as he shoves it toward me like it is on fire and nods toward a timber beam half buried in dust. With a flick of his fingers, a gentle breeze moves through the air, sweeping the space clean.

"Take a seat," he says dryly. "Looks like story time is about to begin."

#

I move to the bench, lower myself slowly, and slide the Tome from the satchel.

The Tome shudders. A pulse throbs beneath my palms.

Then the ink bleeds.

And then, just two words:

Hello, Rae.

I freeze.

My name is Ira.
And I have waited a very long time to speak to you.

The world stills.

I have been watching over your path to make sure
it led you here. To where truth can finally find you.

Firstly, not all who bear the Vaulturian name are monsters.
My sister was proof of that. She was light where we were dark,
compassion where we were cruelty.

Agatha was everything we were not—kind, powerful in ways we
did not understand. I was meant to protect her. I swore I would.
But when our father marked her for death, by my blade, I did
the only thing left to save her. I ran. I got her to where they could
never find her, where no one would ever find her.

I knew someone who could become the mother my sister never
had, to hide her and raise her as her own, far from our name
and its curse. I told myself it was the only way.
That among humans, and as far as possible from our father,
she might finally be safe, free.

And once they crossed into the human lands,
I did the only thing left to keep them that way.
I destroyed the last passage between realms.

The Corestone is stirring again, and it is calling for you.
That is why you must go back. Find it before it is too late.

You are the last true bearer of the Vaulturian line worth saving. You carry what they feared most, the power of all four lands. Like our High King, like Agatha, but unlike Erian and the heirs before him. Only you can fix this. You must go back, find it, and restore what has been lost.

But unlike Agatha, you are not alone. You have the truth. You have time, and the choice to wield it well. If the stars are kind, you will succeed where we never could.

Ira.

I lower the Tome, hands trembling. My mind does somersaults trying to make sense of it, and when I look up, Zye is already watching me.

But it is not the way he usually does.

There is no warmth in it. No teasing. No spark.

"Zye?" My voice comes out too quiet.

His expression does not shift. "You are Vaulturian."

Three words. No inflection. No pause.

But everything inside me lurches.

"No, wait, I am not, I mean, maybe, but that does not make me them. Ira said he has protected me, this whole time—"

"Rae." His voice slices through me like glass. "You are born of the line that burned this. This exact place."

He waves his arm around the ruined bookstore, the splintered beams, the blackened stone, the sagging shelves stripped of meaning. Silver air surges around him, feeding on the fury bleeding through his control.

"Vaulturia did this," he says. "And they did not just destroy buildings. They destroyed anything and everything in their way."

His eyes drop to the note beside me, Horo's handwriting, small and scrawled, full of hope. "They destroyed everyone in their way."

I shake my head, stepping toward him. "I am not them. I am not—"

He steps back, dragging a hand through his hair, pacing, his breath sharp and restless, the space between us suddenly too small to contain him.

I move to reach for him. "Zye, please—"

He reaches out, hesitates, and grabs my hand anyway, the wind whips and I land hard on the carpeted floor of The Academy hallway.

Alone.

A soft knock raps against the door.

I startle, my mind caught somewhere between fury and ruin. The full moon hangs high, casting a blade of silver through the window.

Once upon a time, this would be my favorite kind of quiet, but tonight it feels like a spotlight of shame pinned directly on me.

The knock comes again. Softer this time. Almost hesitant. I drag myself toward the door and open it, just a crack.

Ember stands there, two oversized mugs balanced in her hands. She doesn't speak, she just holds one out to me.

"Can I come in?" she asks softly.

I hesitate, but only for a second, then step back.

She moves quietly, setting her mug on the edge of the desk. "I figured you might not want to be alone." Her eyes land on the duffel at the end of the bed and she freezes. "Oh," she says. "You're packing. To leave."

I don't respond. My throat is too tight to try.

"Rae," she says gently, nodding toward the bag. "Before you go making decisions that might get us all killed… will you sit? Just five minutes. Then you can do whatever hellfire plan you've cooked up. But five minutes first. Please."

I cross my arms, not to shut her out, but to keep myself from unraveling. "Did Zye send you?" I ask, trying to sound neutral, but it lands somewhere closer to broken.

"No." Her eyes soften. "But I heard what happened."

I bite the inside of my cheek.

She shifts her weight, expression pinched. "It also explains why Alara is currently outside The Academy, seconds from tearing down the front gates. Or Zye. Honestly, it's hard to tell which one she'll go for first."

The smallest sound escapes me, a half laugh, half sob that barely makes it out. My knees give way and I sit back on the edge of the bed, like the air's been pulled from the room.

When we landed—when I landed—Alara was already spiraling. But I didn't need to tell her what was said. She already knew. She'd known all along. Aric and Soraya knew too.

Do not fear your blood, she said. The Vaulturians were not born monsters. They became them. You are the reckoning Athyria has long awaited.

She hadn't seen the way Zye looked at me. Like he didn't know whether to reach for me or draw his blade. And she knew all along.

Every turning point in my life, every moment that shaped who I am, was built on someone else's silence. Every single one of them chose to decide for me. What I should know. And when I was ready to hear it. And every time, it has cost me the people I love.

So I shut her out. If I'm to do this, I'll do it my way.

Ember watches me but doesn't move. "She's still out there," she says after a while.

My fingers dig into the edge of the mattress.

I look at the duffel. Then at the window. Then anywhere but Ember's eyes. "I can't stay here while they're in danger. My family. Annie. Felix. Mum. You. Everyone. Ember, everyone I love is in danger."

"I know," she says gently.

"And once they find out who I really am…"

"They might have questions," Ember finishes. "They might flinch. They might whisper. But, Rae, if you think for one second that changes who you are, you're wrong."

She steps closer, crouching in front of me. "We are not where we come from. We are who we fight to be."

Tears blur my vision, unspooling before I can stop them.

She reaches for the mug she set down earlier and places it in my hands. "Here. Take a sip." The cinnamon spice floats up, warm and sharp.

"This one was my favorite growing up," she murmurs. "My dad used to make it when I was getting a little 'hot to handle' and sit with me to tell stories as I drank it and calmed down."

"It was the only nice thing he ever did. And only if he was sober. Or there at all." She looks down into the hot liquid and swallows heavily. "I'm not even sure he didn't lace it with something that would knock me out for a few hours. Maybe days at a time."

My breath stutters. The tears are silent now, just steady streaks down my cheeks, carving through the numbness like rivers through stone.

She shrugs. "I didn't come from love. Not like Zye. My family wasn't kind. Wasn't gentle. It was survival. And hate. I was an only child, and I guess I ruined whatever grand plans they had because they made it known, every damn day, that I was the worst thing that ever happened to them. The Academy's the closest thing to family I've ever had."

Ember reaches up and swipes at a tear on my cheek, the droplet sizzling softly against her skin.

We both flinch, then burst into a watery giggle, a blubbering mess of sound that somehow eases the ache.

She exhales. "Rae, Zye reacted the way he did tonight because you're the first woman that boy has let in since Lyria. His sister was everything to him, and I see it—gods, I feel it—in the way he looks at you. He's already terrified of losing you too."

The instant those words leave her lips, they sever the only thread I had left holding me together. Ember reaches for me, without hesitation, and pulls me into her arms to catch me as I break.

I collapse into her. Every last fraying thread of resolve unspooling. My chest heaves with the force of it, sobs racking through me like tremors. There's no clever deflection, no iron mask or false calm, just the ugly kind of grief that rips from the center and takes everything with it.

Ember doesn't flinch. She just holds me tighter. One hand firm on my back, the other threads through my hair.

"I don't want to hurt anyone," I manage, voice shredded and broken against her collarbone. "That's the last thing I ever wanted."

"I know," she whispers.

"I didn't ask for any of this. I didn't want to be… whatever I am. I just want to get home. Back to how things were. Before. Before all of this."

I pull back just enough to see her face, blurred through tears, barely more than a shape in the glow of moonlight.

"But I don't want to leave either. This. This place, you, Alara, Zye…what if I don't make it back?" My voice cracks hard. "What if this is the last time I ever—"

I can't finish.

Ember cups my face between her palms. "Then we make damn sure that's not the case."

I try to speak, but all that comes out is a thin, helpless squeak.

"I know you feel pulled in a thousand directions," she says. "Torn between who you were and who you're supposed to become and I can only imagine that weight feels impossible."

"It is impossible," I croak.

I close my eyes, and she presses her forehead to mine.

"Downstairs, Kail and Thane are already trying to figure this out," she says. "Alara is still outside, ready to fight whoever she has to, including Zye, if he doesn't get his shit together. And he will. Horo's got him locked in a wind-silenced corner, dousing him with enough calm to soothe a hurricane."

A broken laugh escapes me.

"We'll get through this, Rae. Together."

For the next hour, we sit and talk about everything—her family, mine, life before all of this. She lies beside me, her head lulled to the side, her red hair fanned out to frame her young features. I knew from the moment we met that I liked this woman and that has only deepened in the weeks since.

I tell her everything. My family. My friends. Who Myles was. Who Ethan is. What he meant, what he means, and what that even means now. I'm not sure I even know anymore.

I tell her what the Tome said. About Ira. About Agatha. I tell her about the way Zye looked at me like I'd betrayed him, worse, like it was me who inflicted the hurt that started all of this.

She listens. Not once does she interrupt.

It's only when I reach the part about Alara, how I shut her out, how I hurt her too, that she reaches over.

Then, with a shimmer of glitter in the air and the scent of wild mint and lavender, Nyxie appears.

Her blue hair tumbles down her back in silken waves, rings catching in the light as she moves. And then I'm in her arms, wrapped up in a hug that's soft and fierce and absolute, like she's physically trying to keep me from falling apart.

I sniff and laugh, and then cry a little more.

Nyxie smiles brightly. "Don't shut us out, Rae. We know who you are. And if you're ready, there's a group gathering downstairs to show you that nothing the Tome said has changed what they think about you, none more so than Alara, who is currently pacing trenches in the outer courtyard."

Alara.

I bring down the walls of our bond immediately.

Her growl doesn't come loud, it comes like thunder curling through a dark sky, coiling around the edges of my thoughts. She never stopped trying to claw down the barrier I'd put up.

"Welcome back, Rae."

It's dry. Sarcastic. But careful. Just sharp enough to sting but underneath it, I feel the relief pouring in.

"I'm sorry, I—"

"Panicked," she cuts in, matter-of-fact. *"Next time you panic, remember who you're tethered to."*

Her presence flares hot. *"A predator. A protector."*

"And a liar," I bite back.

"I didn't lie," she growls. *"I told you what I could."*

My pulse kicks. *"You should've told me everything."*

Her snarl cuts through the air. *"The only thing knowing earlier would've done is mark you as prey, before you were ready to bite back. Now they've rallied here, waiting for you to step forward. To lead them. It was the only way I could protect you when I couldn't be there to do it myself."*

Tears sting, and I hate that they do. She's still protecting me, even now.

"I didn't want you to feel it," I whisper. *"The panic. The shame."*

"You have nothing to be ashamed of."

A roar splits the room, thunderous enough to rattle the stone walls. Ember's mug crashes to the floor and shatters, porcelain scattering. She blinks at it, then at me, before breaking into a laugh.

"So, if you'd like to avoid witnessing exactly what I'm capable of… you have two minutes to get to me."

I exhale the air from my cheeks. "Two minutes."

A pause.

"And Rae…"

I brace.

"Don't shut me out again. I was born to protect you. Let me."

#

I grab the Tome as Ember grabs my hand and the rift grabs the air from my lungs.

The world rips sideways. When it rights itself, I stumble, catching myself on the wall just as Ember straightens beside me, already solid again. Her grin is wicked.

"Oh, whoops," she says, entirely unconvincing. "Missed that landing. My bad."

And just like that, she disappears into a puff of smoke and a giggle.

I blink, eyes adjusting and freeze.

I'm not in the courtyard like I was meant to be. I'm in a dimly lit corridor just inside the glass doors, the familiar stone walls of The Academy stretching ahead. The sconces burn low, casting flickering shadows along the walls. Warm light bleeds across the floor, and standing at the center of it is Zye.

Shoulders tense. Fingers twitching. Gods, he looks wrecked.

"Zye—" My voice is careful.

"Rae," he counters.

"This doesn't change what we've come to do," I say, softer

now. "Agatha was good, Zye. I am too. I'm like her. I'm not, I will not be them."

His eyes drag over my face. "I know," he says eventually. "I know that. But I keep thinking about what they took from this world. What they took from me and now I look at you, and I—"

He doesn't finish. He doesn't have to.

"You're scared of me." The words feel foreign in my mouth.

"No," he says instantly. "I'm scared for you. That's not the same."

A sharp sting pricks the back of my eyes but I refuse to let the tears fall.

"I trust you, Rae. But it terrifies me. Because it means every force I've been fighting against my entire life… it's now in you."

"But it's not me," I whisper. "You know that. You know it."

The silence stretches, brittle as glass. His breathing is rough, his hands curling into fists at his sides.

"Don't you get it, Rae? You're the only one left."

His voice breaks, a fracture in his control, and I feel Alara release a low rumbling growl—a warning.

"You don't know that," I say, but the denial sounds thin, even to me.

Zye lets out a rough, humorless laugh, his hands landing on his hips as he looks away, then back to me. He drags a hand through his hair, eyes burning. "Yes, I do. Every Vaulturian line, every bloodline that held a claim to the throne, they're gone. You're all that's left of them. The heir to the dynasty. To the High King himself."

I close my eyes for a second, forcing the pieces to shift, to settle. When I open them again, I meet his stare head-on.

"Well, I don't care."

His brows furrow.

"You think this changes everything? Fine. It changes what

we know. It changes what we thought. But it doesn't change who I am. And it sure as hell doesn't change what I'm here to do." My throat tightens, but I keep going. "And damn it, Zye, it doesn't change what I'm willing to do. To protect you, Ember, Alara—every single one of those wolves. I don't care about some stupid ancient rule, not when my family or those I love more than anything are in danger. And—" I stop to steady myself. "And I expected you, of all people, to know. To trust that. Damn it, Zye, at the very least—trust me."

His jaw clenches. He still doesn't speak, but he takes a step closer as I back into the wall behind me.

"I expected you to trust me," I say, tears forming. "To know me. Not my name. Not my blood. Me."

Still nothing.

"So go ahead," I murmur, blinking hard. "Be pissed. Shut down. Throw your little pity party. But tomorrow? I'm going after answers and this damn stone. With or without you."

I press a hand to his chest, right where his heartbeat slams beneath my palm.

He flinches but he doesn't pull away.

His breath stutters. His jaw tightens.

"Put down the Tome."

I blink. "What? Why?"

"Just put it down, Rae."

His words come rough and cracked, cutting straight through my bravado. I hesitate, then gently set the Tome beside me.

The heat from his body wraps around me. Veins pulsing. Chest heaving.

"Because it already ruined my night once," Zye leans in closer. "I'm not letting it ruin it twice."

His mouth crashes into mine without hesitation—hungry. Teeth and lips and desperation. I gasp against him, hands fisting in his shirt, dragging him closer as he angles his head and deepens the kiss. His tongue brushes mine and I meet him with everything I have left. The ache. The fire. The need to feel something real.

He groans low in his throat, the sound sending lightning through my spine. His hand finds my waist, anchoring me, pulling me flush against him. My back hits the wall with a soft thud, but I barely register it. All I feel is him.

His mouth tears from mine only to blaze a path of fire along my jaw, down the line of my throat.

"I was an idiot," he whispers against my skin.

I hum my agreement, a broken sound caught between laughter and breathlessness.

He pulls back just far enough to see my face. "And I am so sorry."

And just like that, I shatter.

The tears hit fast. Quiet, endless tears that slip free as every wall inside me buckles. Zye pulls me in and lets me collapse into him.

At the end of the hallway, the courtyard comes into focus through the glass doors. Dim and silver-washed, the moon hangs low, skimming the horizon. I didn't realize how late—or early—it was until now.

I stop just short of the door at the gathering of shadows and silhouettes on the other side. They're all out there. Zye looks at me and gives my hand a reassuring squeeze.

Horo leans against the stone wall, arms crossed, his robes a mismatched weave of worn leather, faded linen, and charms that glint with quiet magic. His gray hair is a storm in its own right, wind-tossed and disheveled. The silver flecks that once shimmered like starlight now look like they're clinging on for dear life.

Whatever chaos Zye unleashed on him was a ride. Gods, I wish I'd seen it.

Ember stands beside Nyxie, their shoulders brushing next to Kail and Thane, who sit at a weathered wooden table, their bare feet propped on the bench, their loose shirts hanging off their frames. Despite everything, I'm surprised—relieved, even—to see them looking so relaxed.

But it's Alara who undoes me. She stands in the moonlight, too big for this space, her power visible in her stillness. Her white fur is a stark contrast against the dark, her eyes locked on me through the glass. She doesn't move, not until I do.

Then she's crossing the space, fast and quiet as smoke.

I open the door and the moment I do, her head buries against my ribs, and the sound that rumbles from her chest shakes the glass. Not quite a growl, but a sound born of fury restrained and relief finally exhaled.

"I'm sorry," I whisper into her coat.

"Don't apologize, but don't ever do that again."

Alara steps aside, and I take a deep, steadying breath before I move forward to finally face everything that's changed.

Kail moves first, dropping from the table with easy grace, shoulders loose, a hint of a smirk curving his mouth. He slows, nostrils flaring as he pointedly sniffs the air.

Twice.

He looks at Zye. "Aha, about damn time, you two."

Heat flares in my cheeks as quiet laughter ripples through the group. I shoot Zye a glare.

He throws up both hands, all mock innocence, as Thane joins Kail at his side, already laughing. "He didn't kiss and tell. Heightened senses tell us what he never would have. We can smell him on you." He winks at Zye. "And vice versa."

Zye just arches a brow, *apology accepted*, it says without a word, as I bite down on my lip and quietly pray for the stone tiles beneath my feet to crack open and swallow me whole.

But then Thane sobers. The grin fades, but not the warmth in his eyes as he steps forward and places one heavy hand on my shoulder.

"Nothing said tonight changes who you are," he says. "You're one of us, Rae. We've seen who you are. We don't care where that came from."

He pauses. "And anyone who does? They answer to us."

My throat tightens as Kail claps a firm hand on my back. "We've seen what you can do," he says. "And I'm no fool. I know who I want to be standing behind when you release."

I manage a nod, barely, locking my jaw down tight to keep the emotion from cracking through. When I glance at Zye, he's already watching me. His eyes don't waver, and something in them softens. A small smile touches his lips, not smug, not playful. Just real. And just for me.

Horo steps forward, clapping twice, the noise echoing across the stone.

"Right, it is decided. Rae, we fear not who you are nor where you come from. But all of you should fear who I will become if I don't get some sleep soon."

A few chuckles rise. "Let's get on with it, shall we?"

I settle beside Zye on the edge of the weathered timber table, the Tome tight in my arms. I don't know why I'm holding it like this, like it's a lifeline. But for all that Zye heard, my version felt different. For the first time since I arrived, I feel like the odds are in my favor.

Over the next few hours, we tear the plan apart and rebuild it, over and over until it's watertight. Every risk, every angle, nothing is left untested. Because one misstep will cost us everything.

Kail, Thane and their pack will move first, they will head to the borders and form the line and to buy us time. The wards are holding, for now, but they're flickering more each day, the cracks spreading faster than the Terralyns can mend them. If they fall before we reach the Twins, there won't be anything left to return to.

And we're not alone out there. The Terralyns intercepted whispers that Vaulturian spies were circling the outer perimeter, looking for weaknesses. If they confirm we're gone, they'll strike.

Which means we can't just leave—we have to disappear.

Aric and Soraya are already en route with the wolves from the valley. Alara and Horo will leave soon to meet them, where Horo will cloak the entire pack in a glimmer, one powerful enough to disguise their arrival at The Academy. With the exception of Alara, they'll take our place, fortifying the grounds. Then Alara will join me and Zye, and we'll travel through the night toward Puk and Eko, stopping at the cabin beyond the ravine, a Terralyn-built safe house carved into the rock, shielded by old wardlines, while Ember, alongside the Terralyns, will protect The Academy.

The second Kail and Thane move and the enemy realizes the frontlines are shifting, they'll come. If our deception doesn't hold, if the wards fracture before I make it to the portal, none of this will matter.

The Twins are the only ones with the power to open a portal, but bringing them here would risk everything. Every Vaulturian spy in the realm is tracking distortion magic, and The Academy's wards would repel their entry before they ever crossed. We must get to them.

As the final pieces lock into place, a strange hush falls over the courtyard.

The air is slick with dew, the stones beneath our boots still dark with the remnants of night. First light creeps over the tallest spires of The Academy, washing everything in rose-gold and bone-white glow. The flowers along the southern wall catch it, petals gleaming like they've been dipped in molten silver.

This is the kind of morning that would feel sacred if not for what's coming.

Somewhere behind us, birds stir, their soft calls threading through the stillness as I stop and take it all in. The people, this place, this moment. Even if it's fleeting.

Before the sun fully rises, Horo and Alara move out toward the wolves. Kail and Thane disappear toward the gym to prepare. The others scatter, melting into the soft hush of morning. I make my way upstairs to rest, to try and get a few hours of sleep before we begin the trek to the cabin, but as soon as I fall back onto my bed, the floodgates open. Thoughts pour in, realization crashing through my chest like a dam has cracked somewhere deep inside.

For weeks now, I've ached for home, for the comfort of the familiar. For my family. The steady rhythm of a life I can barely remember how to live. And now it's here, within reach, the way back. But what if the one place I've been fighting to return to isn't where I belong anymore?

I should feel ready. Relieved. Hopeful. Instead, I feel off balance, like my feet are planted on ground that's no longer solid.

I end up sitting at the window, arms wrapped around myself, watching the sunlight stretch across the floor. It spills over the sheets, over the corners of my room—a room that not so long ago felt foreign, a figment of my imagination. Now it feels like something else entirely. It feels like mine.

I am not ready to say goodbye. Not yet.

The thought that it might be, that maybe this is the last time I'll stand in this space sits like lead in my soul.

I dress slowly, zipping my jacket all the way up to stop the cold air that clings to the morning. The snow is melting, but the air still carries winter's edge.

I pack with care, fingers brushing over every item. I was warned to pack light, but I have no idea what to pack at all. The Tome comes last. I cradle it, clinging to hope it holds all the answers.

And then I take the stairs for what I hope won't be the last time. I want to savor it, memorize all the sounds and scents of this place. Just in case.

As I make my way through the halls, passing the now-familiar artworks and doorways, the dining room, the room where I first met Ember and Zye, memories rise with every step. When I first walked these halls, I was terrified. Now I'm terrified of leaving.

As the glass doors that lead out to the courtyard come into view, I notice the sun has crested the ridgeline, painting the courtyard in pale gold and long shadows. I walk slowly, letting this place imprint itself on me.

I cross to the same weathered timber table where I sat only a few hours earlier and take a slow breath, savoring the crisp morning air. Then, from behind me, I hear the glass door creak open. His presence sends an unexpected thrill through me.

"How'd you sleep?" Zye's voice is a little rough around the edges.

I glance at him over my shoulder.

I didn't. "Terribly. You?"

His mouth curves into the smallest smile. "Yeah. Sounds about right." I sense a hint of nervousness in him as he walks to my side, scanning the duffel I've dropped at my feet. His brow lifts.

"Rae. What is that? How much have you packed?"

"Just the essentials," I defend.

He turns, already shaking his head. "Rae, this is all for one night before we get you home."

"We've got one night in a cabin that has everything we need. I made sure of that. The priority is getting there," Zye says, finally meeting my eyes. "We'll set off for Puk and Eko first light tomorrow."

Then he lifts a finger. "One more thing."

I arch a brow as he steps closer, holding out a folded pile of leathers.

"The clothes you're wearing won't cut it."

I glance down, feigning offense. "What's wrong with what I'm wearing?"

"You look like you're about to go on a hike around your hometown."

"We *are* going on a hike!"

He huffs a laugh, shaking his head. "This is not Rambler Bay, Rae, trust me." He nods to the leathers. "Nyx helped. I hope they fit."

I reach for the leathers, fingers brushing his. When I finally meet his eyes, a flush creeps across his cheeks, and I look away quickly.

"You can try it on in there," he says, gesturing toward a room just inside the glass doors. "Be quick, we need to move."

We both go to step forward and awkwardly collide.

I freeze. So does he. Then, clearing my throat, I step around him, disappearing inside before I can embarrass myself further.

The leather molds to me like a second skin. The top fits snug across my chest and waist, perfectly tailored but giving me enough room to breathe. The material is softer than I expected, supple and flexible, allowing full range of movement.

The pants sit high on my waist, reinforced at the thighs and knees for protection, the stitching intricate and sturdy. My fingers trail over a slot for weapons at my hip. There's even a strap across the back to hold the Tome tight.

As I step out of the room, my reflection catches in the window and I stop. The person staring back at me is stronger. Different. But not different in the same way I was when I arrived. This is a good different. Stronger. Capable.

I barely recognize the girl anymore.

And judging by the expressions on Zye and Ember's faces, they see it, too. Even from this distance, I hear her sharp inhale.

Zye's expression is harder to read, but the intensity in his stare makes my pulse race.

Then Ember claps her hands together, practically vibrating with excitement. "Now that's what I call an emergence! Warrior Rae! Would you look at you?"

As I make my way out to them, she lets out a sharp wolf whistle, circling me like a craftsman admiring their own work. "Damn, girl, this look suits you! Are we absolutely sure I can't come with you, Zye?" She arches a brow dramatically, mischief curling at the edges of her lips. "I'd make a great backup. She can bait them with her good looks, and I'll burn them."

She throws a small fireball into the air for emphasis, the flames crackling before winking out.

I shake my head, laughing despite myself.

"As tempting as… whatever that was," Zye replies, his lips twitching, "I need you here keeping everything and everyone in line. That includes those two."

He gestures toward Kail and Thane, barreling up the hill from the gym, locked in a sweaty, mud-covered wrestling match.

Ember pouts. "Be safe." She clasps my shoulder briefly, her grip warm and grounding. I swallow hard, pushing down the lump forming in my throat

Kail and Thane skid to a stop near us, sweat glistening on their foreheads, grinning wide.

"You don't need to worry about us, boss!" Thane shouts, chest puffed out. "We've got it covered. This pack will be ready when you give the word!" Then, without hesitation, he tilts his head back and lets out a triumphant howl.

Kail claps him once on the shoulder and joins in, their call carrying across The Academy.

Zye shakes his head, but smiles proudly.

Seeing him like this, at ease, surrounded by his pack, his people, makes something deep inside me shift. Something I don't have time to think about. Not now.

"The plan is set," Zye says, addressing the group. "We'll head to the cabin today. The forecast is clear, so we should make it by afternoon. Ember, I'll send word with Ravi when we arrive.

Tomorrow, we move for the Twins. From there…"

His voice falters slightly, but he clears his throat. "We don't know how long it will take, but we'll return as soon as we can.

Before anyone can respond, Ember pulls us both into a bone-crushing hug. "You'd better," she whispers.

Thane clears his throat. "One last thing, Rae," he says. "We hope you don't need them, but if you do…"

Kail steps forward, a dark bundle cradled in his hand. "Designed for small hands that move fast and are going to need to strike faster."

He sets the blades in my palms, one by one. The metal isn't just silver; it glints with a subtle ripple, like light passing over water. Each hilt is wrapped in dark leather, etched with the mark of a wave. The grip molds to my fingers like they were made for me. They *were* made for me.

"They're yours," Kail says simply. "Custom-forged. They'll hold their edge no matter what you hit, and they'll never miss unless you mean them to."

My fingers curl tighter around the leather. The weight is featherlight. Perfect. And I smile, big.

Thane steps up beside me, his hand landing solid between my shoulders, with his usual no-nonsense strength. "You're stronger than you think," he says. "But just in case someone out there's dumb enough to test it…"

Kail bares his teeth. "Show them, Stingray!"

A rush of emotion surges through me and before I can

stop myself, I launch forward, wrapping them both in a fierce hug. Kail's quick reflexes keep me from impaling myself on the blades, his soft chuckle vibrating against my shoulder. Thane lets out a laugh so loud it echoes through the courtyard, ending in a low, wolfish howl. Then, the sound of paws on stone.

We all turn as Alara and the wolves stride into view, their powerful forms gleaming in the morning light. The sight of them against the backdrop of Athyria makes my chest tighten. There is something final in this moment.

Thane and Kail straighten instinctively, but this time there's no bristle at the backs of their necks. I catch Thane's wrist, meeting his gaze. He hesitates, then gives a small, reluctant nod.

Alara tilts her head, assessing me. *"Well, well, well,"* she muses. *"Don't you look the part of a born warrior."*

It hits me all at once, all too fast.

A few weeks ago, this place and these people didn't exist in my world and I didn't exist in theirs. Now, I can't imagine one without the other. And as I look around at the faces surrounding me, I know one thing with absolute certainty: I will do whatever it takes to protect them.

More hugs. More quiet words of luck and wisdom. More promises to return safely. I swipe at a few rogue tears, trying to hold it together even as my throat tightens. Of all the impossible things that have happened since I arrived in Athyria, the act of leaving feels the most unreal.

I struggle to say farewell and hope, with every cell in my being, that this isn't forever.

As Alara, Zye, and I make our way to the outer edge of The Academy, the echoes of our goodbyes still linger in the air, and I do my best to lighten it. "Nervous?"

Zye's answer is immediate. "No." But the tightness in his jaw betrays him.

"Me too," I admit. He glances at me then, a sidelong look that makes my smile grow.

At the edge of The Academy, where the outer gardens dissolve into wild terrain, there's a wall of stone, overrun with vines and cracked by roots, all but destroyed by time and I can only assume war. Except for one thing. Near the base, half-hidden beneath moss and shadow, a small crest is etched into the stone. The markings of a wolf and wings shimmer faintly with age or magic, it's hard to tell. I wouldn't have seen it at all if Zye hadn't slowed beside it.

"Most of the realm's magic runs aboveground now," he says. "But there are old paths, ones created by the Terralyns that run through the core. This is the mark of the Corestone."

The stone hums. Then it splits down the middle with a low, hissing sigh.

I step back as a wave of magic burst outward. curling against my skin. Beyond, a narrow tunnel opens up, descending in a tight, dark, spiral of carved stone veined with crystals, their light shifting in tones of silver, green, and gold.

"This," Zye says, glancing back at me, "is a Hollowrun. It's how we disappear."

Alara inhales, long and deep, and I feel her unease thrum across the bond.

"Not built for small spaces?" I ask gently.

She growls low in response as I reach out, brushing her shoulder in silent reassurance. She steps forward, reluctantly.

"Here goes," Zye adds as he starts the descent.

I move after him, the Tome pressed tight to my back. Alara follows at my side.

The air changes almost instantly. It's cooler, but despite the damp earth, there's a sweetness that floats around us. Power hums beneath our feet. The further we descend, the stronger it grows. My chest vibrates with it. Even the Tome rustles slightly, like it can feel the shift in magic.

The deeper we go, the light steadies to a slow pulse, and the ground stirs beneath my boots. A soft vibration hums through the stone, rising through my bones as the crystalline veins flicker before bursting into motion. Light ripples along the walls in playful streams, chasing itself through the rock like it's laughing. Alara's ears flick forward, eyes bright. The tunnel seems to be happy as if the Hollowrun itself is excited by our presence.

The path narrows, then widens, opening into a longer corridor where the energy changes, it buzzes through the stone like wind funneled through a blade. The air tastes metallic, sharp against the back of my tongue.

Then the ground shifts. Not violently, just enough to jolt my balance. I instinctively brace, the walls rough under my touch.

"That's normal," Zye says, his voice echoing off the walls. "It's closing one path to open another."

The tunnel shifts again. A ripple moves through the stone, and just ahead, the wall begins to split, not like a door, but like silk tearing in slow motion. A seam parts, pulling back into light. A re-entry.

We step into the light and emerge onto an open field. The air smells like rain, the grass is so long it tickles the back of my legs. In the distance, remnants of old villages emerge—stone chimneys standing stubborn against time, their homes long gone. The land reclaiming what was lost long ago.

The Hollowrun behind us seals without a whisper, leaving no sign it ever existed.

I open my mouth to ask Zye a thousand questions—about the Hollowruns, who built them, why they were buried—but he's already moving.

"We need cover," he says, scanning the horizon. "We're too exposed out here. And Alara's not exactly subtle."

I swallow my questions and walk.

The afternoon sky darkens to muted gray, heavy with gathering clouds. Wind cuts through us, carrying the smell of rain as the first drops begin to fall lightly over our heads.

Before leaving The Academy, we agreed that there was no unnecessary magic. Once we crossed through the Hollowrun, we had to stay hidden. The enemy was watching, waiting and the smallest hint of power could give them something to track.

We move swiftly, stopping only to drink from rushing creeks and refill our canisters. The further we travel, the more the terrain shifts. The path weaves through a dense canopy of tall trees, their roots curling over the damp earth. The scent of rain lingers masking any trace of our presence.

Zye walks with us for the most part, but every so often, he takes to the sky, disappearing into the clouds to scout ahead. When he's on the ground, we make the most of the long walk ahead.

"So… what's your favorite color?"

He glares at me like I just slapped him with a fish. "What?"

I grin, undeterred. "Color. What. Is. Your. Favorite. Color?" I drag out each word with exaggerated clarity, just to annoy him.

His brow furrows. He actually considers it.

"Black."

"Shocking. So morbid, so dark. I had you pegged as a lime-green kind of guy, personally."

He studies me like he's trying to decide if I'm serious.

"You're acting weird. And black isn't morbid. It's strong. Nothing works with black unless it agrees to the terms. Mess with black, and boom, everything becomes black. Work with it, and you get depth and perspective."

I snort at his considered answer. "That was… unexpectedly deep."

He shrugs. "You asked."

I laugh, the sound light and easy, echoing through the narrow weave of trunks and fern. The forest answers in soft percussion, raindrops loosening from branches, a chorus of unseen life stirring in the undergrowth.

Zye glares at me.

"Sweet or sour?" I ask, shooting off another question before he can fill the silence.

He just scoffs and shakes his head. "Sweet. Seriously, what's with the questions?"

I shrug. "Just killing time. Getting to know you. Leveling the playing field."

His eyes narrow. "Fine. But on one condition."

I pause. "What?"

"You stop fussing over those daggers."

My hands freeze mid-fidget. I hadn't even realized I was doing it. Quickly, I release my grip and wiggle my fingers innocently. "Fine, fine. Your turn. What do—"

Alara stops abruptly, ears twitching.

Zye's sword is out in an instant.

Before I can react, he steps in front of me, backing us both into Alara's protective bulk. Her fur bristles beneath my hand, a low, guttural growl rumbles deep in her chest.

"Something's watching us. It's been following for a while now."

The trees shift in my vision, thin, bent figures slipping between the branches, quick and unnervingly quiet.

My fingers instinctively move back to my daggers, but Zye catches the motion and sends me a sharp warning glance. Then, the whispers begin:

> *Silent as night, swift as the breeze,*
> *We move unseen among the trees.*

The voices are shrill and sing-song—high-pitched as children—but they scrape like glass across my skin.

"On Alara. Now."

Zye's voice is barely above a whisper, but the urgency sends me scrambling onto her back as his hand whips out, snaring something mid-flight. He slams it to the ground. I barely make it onto her back before Alara pounces, her teeth bared as she pins the wriggling creature beneath her massive paw.

It writhes, snarling, its body no bigger than a child's; limbs twitching like snapped branches, skin stretched too thin over spindly bones. Filthy tufts of fur cling in patches, and its wings are lined like wet parchment. And its face, gods, its mouth splits too wide in a grin lined with needle teeth, eyes huge and glassy, reflecting back my own horrified stare.

Zye exhales sharply, unimpressed. "A Veilkin."

"A what?" I ask, still staring at the awful thing.

"Trickster fae," he says flatly. "Parasites. They get inside your head, twist it. Drive whole villages to madness for the fun of it." His sword presses closer to the creature's throat. "Who sent you?"

The thing wheezes, then begins to laugh, a ragged, hiccupping cackle that makes bile rise in my throat.

Through mountains high and valleys deep,
a quest for something secrets keep.
Not made by hands, yet shapes our fate,
our stars fall dark if you arrive too late.

Alara presses down harder, claws dimpling flesh as she snarls.

The Veilkin's head jerks unnaturally, twitching side to side before it snaps its attention to Zye. Its grin widens, jaw stretching far too low, and then it sings again:

In shadows deep, their powers grow,
With a golden crown atop her head,
History can kill both friend and foe,
Be wary, Zye, of the devil you know.

Its voice fractures into a shriek as its body convulses. Light sears through the cracks of its skin, and before Alara can tear it apart, the creature combusts into ash, leaving only the stench of burnt iron as dozens of eyes ignite in the treeline, glowing pale and hungry. The whispers return, louder this time, layered over one another in a frenzy of rhymes and laughter. And then, silence.

Zye's face pales, his composure cracking momentarily. I open my mouth to speak but stop myself, because I don't know what to say. And neither does he.

"We need to keep walking," he says. Five words that carry us through the next few hours of silence.

The humor that usually lingers in Zye's eyes is gone. His jaw flexes, his fingers rake through his hair. Every movement is sharp and frustrated. The Veilkin's riddle is torturing him, and there's nothing I can do but watch it eat him alive.

"We're almost there," Zye says, hours into our trek through the densest stretch of forest yet. The trees here are taller, older, their bark split and crowded with moss, with thin rows of mushrooms edging up the trunk.

We navigate down a rocky incline, the ground unstable beneath our boots. Then he stops.

His gaze locks ahead. "This is it."

I follow his line of sight. But there's nothing. No cabin. No shelter. Just a deep ravine, its jagged walls cutting through the land like an open wound. The river below churns violently, dark water frothing against the rock.

The drop is steep. The raging river is impossible to cross without a bridge. And, of course, there isn't one.

"This is it?" I repeat flatly.

Zye nods, like the problem is my hearing. It's not.

Alara huffs beside me, unbothered.

I glare at Zye. "This… looks like a dead end. Or death trap."

His lips twitch just slightly. Then, without a word, he

steps forward and the water moves. One by one, eight massive stepping stones rise from the depths, slick with spray, forming a precarious path across the current. Zye doesn't wait.

He leaps to the first stone, then the next and within seconds, he's on the other side, turning back to face me. "Your turn."

I glance at Alara, silently pleading for guidance. She offers none.

Instead, her eyes glint with amusement. This is a challenge.

"If I fall in and either of you laugh, I swear I'll make your lives miserable. Both of you."

Zye chuckles, a momentary relief from the tension clinging to the air. "Just hurry up. If you can't cross a few stones without tripping, we're doomed anyway."

I scowl but leap forward onto the first stone, then the second. They hold firm. I make the mistake of glancing at Zye, who gives me a slow, sarcastic clap.

"Shut up," I mutter, gritting my teeth and picking up the pace. With a final leap, I clear the last stone, landing solidly on the far bank. Alara, naturally, bounds across in one effortless arc.

I throw up my hands. "You couldn't have just done that for me?"

"Not when her money was on you swimming," Zye says, deadpan.

My head snaps toward him. "You two made a bet?"

He doesn't even try to hide his silent laugh and Alara's smug expression seals the betrayal.

I feign outrage, throwing my hands up. "Un-be-lievable. Both of you."

The moment the last word leaves my mouth, the stones vanish beneath the water. The river swells, a calm trickle seconds ago now a raging torrent, surging over the path we just crossed. I flinch back instinctively, but Zye's already moving.

"Get on Alara. We've got a climb to make."

He jerks his chin toward the slope ahead where the trees thin and the ground kicks up hard enough that I'd be scrambling on hands and knees to make the ascent alone. Near the top, the forest breaks open into a narrow glade cut into the rise. Beyond it, a cliff towers over the clearing, tall and sheer, its surface marked with bands of crystal like stone. The face curves inward just enough to form a rough, natural amphitheater at the crest.

I swing onto Alara's back, and she takes the slope in long, sure strides, the ground steep enough that my thighs start to burn just watching her work.

When we crest the rise, she stops beneath the cliff, and I stay seated, staring up at the sheer face towering over the glade.

"Unless your magic is about to conjure a cabin, or we're actually lost, there's no 'fully equipped' anything here."

He strides forward, plucks the duffel from Alara's back, then with an exaggerated wave over the stone, murmurs, "Abracadabra."

A massive section of the cliff withdraws, sinking back into itself before sliding aside in one seamless motion. A dark entryway yawns open, carved cleanly into the heart of the cliff.

Beyond isn't a rugged survivalist bunker, it's a cliff-face chalet seamlessly carved into the face, the entrance almost imperceptible, while.the interior has been lifted straight out of a magazine.

"You're joking."

We step inside and golden light dances against the walls, thrown by a crackling fireplace that fills the space with the scent of burning wood.

Hand-carved beams stretch across the ceiling, cozy nooks are piled with thick blankets and vintage fabrics, and at the center of the room a brown leather chair sits draped in fur throws.

To the left, a kitchenette occupies a corner, cabinets crafted from the same timber as the walls, a cast-iron stove rests between the counters. Above it, open shelves hold neatly stacked crockery, pots, and pans. A queen-sized bed, dressed in thick linens and layered blankets, rests against the right wall.

"This…" I whisper, trailing my fingers over the worn leather and the rough grain of the beams. My heart swells as my eyes dart from one detail to the next. "Wow. Just… wow."

Zye watches me with a subtle smile that doesn't quite mask the tension drawn behind it.

"It's also warded," he adds. "The lines run with the river. Anything on this side is safe."

"Good luck to anyone who gets across that," I scoff.

"You can train here. Release your fire and lightning and no one will know. Alara's safe here, too."

I hesitate. "Zye?"

He sighs. "If this is another question about colors or fav—"

"Are you all right?" I cut in. "You haven't said anything since it happened."

"I'm fine, Rae." Sharp. Final.

I nod slowly. "Okay. Well, I'm going to check on Alara and I'll let you stay here for a minute and… be fine."

As I pass him, I pause and squeeze his forearm. The strength beneath my fingers surprises me; when I glance up I catch the tick of his jaw.

"Just don't go beyond the water," he says. "I'll get some food ready and meet you out there soon."

I grab the Tome from the bag and head for the rocky entrance. It slides open effortlessly as I approach.

Outside, Alara is nowhere in sight.

"Alara?" I call, scanning the tree line.

"I'm right here."

Her voice comes from the shadows as she steps out from between the trees. *"Just checking the perimeter."* She studies me, then tilts her head. *"How's he doing?"*

I exhale. *"Quiet. That Veilkin rattled him. How reliable are they, really?"*

She shakes out her fur, expression darkening. *"They don't lie. But they rarely say what you want them to. Veilkin are bone-deep ugly things, half fae, half something fouler. They've been here since Athyria was first formed, why or where from, no one knows. Tricksters, scavengers, they thrive on torment."*

A cold sensation twists down my spine.

"They're not dangerous," she adds after a beat. *"But they're not gentle either."*

She flicks her ears, watching the distant trees. *"This will have Zye second-guessing what he knows and who he trusts, right when he can't afford it. Give him time. And for what it's worth, I never trust magic or wards entirely. Under pressure, they weaken. Remember that."*

I nod, tightening my grip on the Tome. *"Okay."*

The book shudders in my hands. Alara huffs, fur bristling. I settle onto the grass, the sun warm on my skin, and flip it open and, to my surprise, Alara doesn't leave.

She settles behind me.

"I need to understand more about Agatha and this Coresto—"

The ink curls like smoke across the page. "Oh," I mutter. Behind me as Alara growls, despite revealing himself, Zye and Alara still haven't warmed to the Tome the way I have. And from the way it hisses at their touch, it doesn't appear to like them much either.

Let me tell you about my sister.

Agatha and I grew up in the same castle but lived in different worlds. I was nine when she was born, old enough to understand what was coming for her, especially after our mother died. She was a beautiful woman, trapped in a cruel world.

I used to watch Agatha from the towers, her joy unburdened by duty, running through the outer fields with wildflowers tangled in her hair. She was everything I wasn't allowed to be.

My fate had been sealed before I could speak.
I was born to rule. Agatha was born to run.

When our father ordered me to end her, I had to act. I took her and vanished, far beyond reach, into a place even he couldn't follow. The human realm. That was the night everything changed. The night I swore before the Corestone that I would do anything to protect her, no matter the cost. It was also the night I met Aric and Soraya and together we began to rebuild what little hope remained, making sure that if the Corestone ever stirred again, someone would still be here to answer.

I was the strongest wielder in the realm but I wasn't strong enough to face my father. Not then. Not until much later. When it mattered most, I was a coward. And that cost me everything. But I made a promise: protect Agatha and the Corestone. I've kept it. I shattered legacies, burned bloodlines, buried truths so deep they became myth.
All to keep one thread alive. One chance.

And now... here you are.

The ink fades. Silence settles. I let the Tome fall gently shut and lean back into Alara's warmth, into the steady rise and fall of her chest. My head finds its place against her shoulder, and I tip my face toward the sky.

He gave everything to protect her and I have to assume Agatha risked it all to save what he couldn't. Now it's my turn to carry their love, their loss, their legacy and write the ending they were never given.

When I return to the cabin, Alara heads out to hunt. Zye is in the kitchen chopping vegetables, filling the space with a feeling that's strangely… domestic.

"What are you making?" I ask, stepping closer. "That smells incredible."

Zye flips the meat, watching it brown along the edges. "Honestly? No idea. I just needed a distraction to clear my head. If it's terrible, I'll conjure something better." He tosses a handful of herbs into the pan. "But I think I could get used to this cooking thing."

"The novelty wears off, trust me." He arches a brow; I wave it away with a giggle. "Hopefully it tastes as good as it smells."

He plates two bowls, and we take them outside, settling onto a blanket beneath the stars.

I twirl my spoon before taking a bite. "This isn't half bad."

Zye snorts. "I made enough to feed an army—force of habit. Kail and Thane eat like starved bears. I'll let Alara know there are leftovers when she's back."

The mention of her absence makes me pause. "Is it safe for her alone?"

Zye doesn't answer right away, but then a familiar *pfft* echoes faintly in my mind.

"She's fine. Alara is hardly prey, and the shield around this place is strong. It cloaks the entire area from unwanted eyes.

Only a handful of people even know it exists." He glances toward the rock. "It was built as a Terralyn stronghold, somewhere the Terraveth Highborn could protect their bloodlines, their families. But no one stayed for long. Not while the rest of Athyria was at war."

Before I can ask more, Zye stands.

"Here he comes."

I blink, following his gaze toward the darkness beyond the clearing. I expect Alara, but there's nothing. I glance back at him, confused, until I notice his arm raised, bent at the elbow like he is waiting for something to perch there. Then, from the shadows, a bird emerges.

At first, I mistake it for an owl, but as it cuts through the night, its wings shimmer in deep purples, shifting from amethyst to plum with each powerful beat. Gold threads its feathers, intricate lines pulsing like liquid light.

"Rae, meet Ravi," Zye says, quiet pride in his voice. "Hardest worker in Athyria."

I stare, stunned. "He's… a pigeon?"

Zye chuckles. "I don't know what that is, so, in your world, sure. Ravi's a messenger. It's how we communicate when we're apart."

I sit up so fast my bowl tips, dinner lost to the grass, but I barely notice. I'm locked in awe as Ravi descends, wings stretched wide.

"Hey, boy," Zye greets as the bird lands with pinpoint accuracy on his forearm, inclining his head in a subtle nod. "Ravi's no ordinary bird or pigeon. He's from Soryn, one of, if not the last of his kind. They're raised alongside their families, trained to find them anywhere, mainly messengers, good spies if you need one. Near impossible to track. Ravi's been with me since before I could fly."

With his free hand, Zye unfastens the parchment from Ravi's leg and unfolds it, a quiet laugh slipping out.

"What does it say?" I ask.

"It's from Horo." He wipes his brow with the back of his hand. "He says, 'Be safe, young adventurers. And remember that there are some things that feed on the dark. Don't let them dine on you. Use her light to burn them, the stars know she's bright enough for both of you.'"

He looks at me, the corner of his mouth twitching as he closes his fist. The parchment disintegrates, ash lifting into the still air. His attention returns to Ravi.

"Thank you, buddy. There's plenty of food if you're hungry."

Ravi doesn't linger. He unfurls his wings and takes flight, a streak of iridescent purple and gold vanishing into the night.

"For someone so vital to your communication, he's not much of a talker," I tease.

Zye's gaze stays on the sky. "He's very special. Ravi can carry messages across Athyria and into your world undetected. He's the only one who can traverse the most dangerous paths and pass through the portals seamlessly. And fast."

"Amazing."

"He's another secret we have to protect from the Vaulturians."

I hum thoughtfully. "Where I'm from, pigeons are just pests."

Zye side-eyes me. "Takes one to know one, I guess."

I scoff. "You heard the note, I am light," I say, shoving his arm before leaning back on the blanket, staring up at stars scattered like glittering confetti.

"Hey, Zye," I say after a pause, turning my head toward him. "That thing from the forest? I… I don't think it was talking about Kail, Thane, or Ember if that helps clear your head."

He goes still, the silence stretching. "Oh, I know it wasn't them."

He lies back beside me, folding an arm behind his head. "I just can't wrap my head around what or why. Those things are notoriously accurate but have a way of twisting truths."

He takes a slow inhale and lifts a hand, pointing to the stars. A subject change.

"That's a wolf," he says, tracing a constellation. "See the head, legs, tail?"

I squint. "Maybe? Sort of? No, not really. Um… no."

Zye laughs. "All right, how about that one? That's the Cup."

I nod, tracing the stars the way he does. "I think… there?"

The ghost of a smile curves his mouth. "You've got it. On the best nights, that one's dominant. But with this war brewing, its light has weakened. Still, it's not extinguished. Legend says if the Cup's light ever goes out, we'll be plunged into eternal darkness. The nights before you arrived were the dimmest I've ever seen."

"Are the stars the same in your world as they are in mine?"

"They are and they aren't. Same sky, same constellations. But here, the stars are alive. They draw power from the Corestone, each one a fragment of its first fire. They rise and fall with the land, respond to magic and even pain. When Athyria falters, the stars dim. When balance steadies, they burn bright again."

He glances at me. "What you see from your world is only the reflection. The light reaches you, but not the power behind it. You see beauty. We feel consequence."

I look up, searching for proof in the dark. "So when I make a wish on one…"

He smiles faintly. "Then those stars hear it first."

For a long while, he says nothing. Then he points again, leaning closer until our shoulders touch.

"And there," he murmurs, gesturing toward a small cluster just beyond the milky band. I glance at him, taken aback by the rawness in his expression. "That's my family."

My stomach twists.

"I was eight," he begins, swallowing. "Erian had seized territories around my home, demanding we bow to him as High Lord of Athyria. My family, like many, refused."

Dread rises..

"One morning his army marched into our village. They seized everything, our homes, our people. When they reached our house…" He falters; a tear slips down his cheek.

I squeeze his hand.

He grips back.

"I hid in a cupboard," he says hoarsely. "My parents were in the kitchen. They knew what was coming and surrendered to give my sister and I a chance to hide. They made us promise not to move, not to make a sound, and to run when the soldiers left. Lyria was twelve. She thought she knew better."

"Lyria was bold. Too bold. Always pushing limits, testing our powers. We drove our parents insane." He lets out a breath that almost sounds like a laugh, without humor. "We'd sneak out to test magic in the fields. Oh, we did some damage."

His gaze turns glassy. "She could cast better than me. She was older, but so much stronger. Magic came easy to her."

His knuckles press white. "She should've run. I should've made her run. Or been as brave as she was and put up a fight."

His voice cracks. "They grabbed my mother, she'd surrendered and was walking out, but one of them took her by the hair and threw her to the ground and Lyria snapped. She killed three before they overpowered her. It took four men to bring her down."

Tears spill down my cheeks. Zye wipes at his face. "I don't know how long I stayed in that cupboard. Hours, maybe days. When I finally ran, it was those three stars that guided me through the forest. They shone brighter than anything else. Horo found me by the river, half-dead. He raised me. Taught me. And now… here I am."

I sit with his words and let them settle.

Then, gently, I brush a stray tear from his cheek. "We'll make them pay, Zye."

His jaw tightens. "Yes," he murmurs. "Yes, we will."

"Come on. Let's get inside. We've got another big day tomorrow," he says.

His gaze lingers on the stars a second longer. Then, wordlessly, we turn toward the cabin.

#

The sand is cool beneath my feet, damp where the tide has rolled back. The bay is washed in moonlight; the water laps softly along the shore. The air is warm against my skin, and I can't believe there aren't others here to share it. It's perfect.

Zye is out in the water, waist-deep, hair slicked back, smiling wide as he waves me toward him. I can't remember the last time he looked so at ease, so unguarded. "I see why you love this," he calls. "Come on, get out here already."

I laugh, light and giddy and step into the water. It curls around my calves, pulling me in. There's no war, no Corestone, no fear. Just us. Just him.

I dive beneath the first wave. When I break the surface, everything has changed. The calm has churned to dark, heaving folds. I look around frantically for Zye.

"Rae!" My name tears across the surf but it isn't Zye. Ethan is there, only a few feet away, thrashing in a current that hadn't existed a heartbeat before. His eyes lock on mine, wide with panic, as he shouts again, reaching for me.

My heart lurches. Instinct drives me toward him, arms cutting through the surge.

Zye cries out.

I twist back. Water has lashed up like tendrils, coiling around his chest, his throat, dragging him under. His hand breaks the surface, reaching for me, and terror splits me in two. Ethan is fighting for breath while Zye is fighting for his life.

"No!" Power ignites. Silver light surges across my skin, racing to my fingertips until the whole bay glows. The waves bend as I drive the magic forward with everything I have. For a heartbeat, it works. The trench quakes and then the light falters as my magic sputters.

"Rae!"

"Rae, wake up!" Zye's hands grip my shoulders.

It's not real, Rae. Wake up. Listen to him. Alara.

I jolt upright, a choked gasp tearing from my throat. The world is a blur of shifting shadows; my vision is wild and unfocused, the remnants of fear and fire still crackling under my skin.

Zye is there. Right in front of me.

"Look at me, Rae," he says. "You're safe. You're here. I'm here."

I blink hard, forcing my vision to clear, my mind to catch up. His face is inches from mine, close enough to see the exhaustion in his eyes. The panic dulls as the heat burning beneath my skin fades.

Tears prickle as I take in the wreckage around me. The sheets are scorched; the air smells singed. The room is intact, but only just.

"Zye," I rasp, my throat so dry the word barely forms. "I'm so sorry. I didn't mean to—"

"It was just a nightmare, Rae. That's all."

A glass of water appears in his hand. "Here. Drink." His other palm rests warm against my back, rubbing slow circles.

I reach for the glass, but as my fingers brush it, the heat returns and my panic surges. I flinch. "I...I'll break it."

Zye wraps his hand around mine, steadying the tremor. "Here," he says, guiding the glass to my lips. "Drink."

The cool water is a relief, but the shame burning in my chest is harder to swallow.

"I... I'm so sor—"

"Rae, stop."

He exhales, scrubbing a hand down his face, exhaustion lining his features.

"I should be the one apologizing. Nyxie told me you were having nightmares; I didn't realize they were this bad. I should've helped."

"There's nothing you can do," I whisper. "Trust me, she's tried. And they're not always this bad." I rub my hands over my face, trying to shake off the haze. My gaze drifts around the room. I see the damage. "Oh, hell."

Tears spill before I can stop them. "Look what I've done." I swipe at my cheeks. "I'll fix it, I swear—"

"I don't care about the damage," he interrupts. "I'll have it fixed before sunrise."

Overwhelmed, I drop my face into my hands. Embarrassment and exhaustion crash over me in equal measure.

"I'm here. Alara's outside," he says, gently.. "It's still. It's safe."

He flicks his wrist, and a swirl of mist gathers around the bed. The shredded sheets dissolve, replaced by fresh, impossibly soft linens. A thick duvet drifts down from the rafters, settling over me like a feather.

"I'm so sorry," I murmur. The regret hangs heavy.

"Stop apologizing and try to get back to sleep."

He turns back to the lounge and before I can think better of it, the words slip out. "Will you lie with me? Just for a while?"

He hesitates mid-step, then nods once and crosses back to the bed.

I roll onto my side to make room, the mattress dipping as he lies down carefully, leaving a stretch of space. His magic hums low in the dark, silver threads shifting lazily. For a while he stays rigid, then gradually he shifts. His hand brushes my hip, tentative. When I don't move, he exhales and closes the distance. His arm slides around my waist, drawing me gently in. His chest meets my back, the rise and fall slow and steady until mine syncs to match. His thumb traces a quiet path along my ribs as I settle into him.

The fear doesn't vanish, it just… fades, softened by the certainty of his hold. The last thing I remember is the quiet, impossible thought that for the first time in a long while I'm not afraid to close my eyes.

#

When I wake, the space beside me is empty, but the sheets are still warm, and the smell of freshly brewed coffee fills the room.

"Well, good afternoon, sunshine."

I groan, stretching like a lazy cat, a small sound escaping my lips.

Zye leans against the counter, one arm braced casually, the other lifting a steaming mug to his lips. The lower half of his face is hidden behind ceramic, but the amusement in his eyes is unmistakable—so is the fact he's shirtless. Hard lines trace the sharp ridges of his abdomen and the cut of his shoulders. I want to ask about the jagged scar across his ribs, but he's relaxed in a way I rarely see. I can wait.

"It's been a while since I shared a room with someone who snores like a smoke-choked dragon."

I freeze mid-stretch, blinking at him, the mug doing a terrible job of protecting his smile or the pillow I hurl at his head.

"Come on," he says, setting the cup down with a chuckle. "Up you get. Let's get you home."

The road to home is shorter than it's ever been, and somehow it feels the longest.

Excitement thrums through me like an exposed wire, buzzing beneath my skin. I know it. Alara knows it. And despite the Veilkin's ominous words and the wreckage I caused last night, Zye knows it too. For the first time in days, he looks almost happy.

And yet, beneath the surface of my joy, there's an ache I can't shake. A quiet whisper of finality. Of farewell. When the feeling creeps in, I do whatever I can to shove it aside.

We leave for the ravine after breakfast, food born of magic, not effort. The memory of last night feels distant as we reach the edge, the wind sharp and cool against my skin. The rocks jut high above the water. I take a breath and leap, landing sure-footed on the first stone, then the next. Each bound comes easier than the last, confidence blooming where fear once lived.

"Do you want to talk about your nightmares?" Zye asks as we clear the stones to the other side.

I don't hesitate. "Do you want to talk about what that Veilkin said?"

Zye throws me a sharp glare over his shoulder before he turns back to the trail. His steps are steady, sure. Mine are… less so, as I stumble over roots and slick rock. Alara follows behind, her occasional huff an unmistakable sign of growing impatience.

"Damn it, Rae," Zye mutters. "I'm serious. If they're that bad, if it's about what happened that day, that was a lot. But it's not your guilt to carry. You did what you had to, and you might have to again. That doesn't mean it won't haunt you."

I pause mid-step, his words hitting harder than I expect.

"Honestly, I've dealt with that," I say, though my voice wavers. "What wakes me now is… different. It's always the same dream. Someone I love is in danger, and I can't save them. Last night, after everything we talked about, the emotion of going home, maybe it just… escalated."

I exhale. "The hardest part isn't even what happened that day," I admit. "It's realizing what I'm capable of. Zye, a few weeks ago, I was just a kid. I blinked, and suddenly I was capable of killing."

The word catches in my throat. *"Better him than you. Watch your—"*

I lose my footing on a slick stone and stumble forward, wincing as my palms scrape dirt. *"Yes, yes, I know,"* I mutter, brushing grit from my hands. *"I'm trying."*

Zye stops abruptly and faces me, gaze dark. "I wish I could tell you that was the worst you'll face," he says quietly. "But I won't lie to you. This, what we are, who you are now, isn't something to fear, Rae. You have to accept it. Own it."

He turns to the forest ahead. What was green and bright has become an eerie shade of black.

"And you might need to be ready to fight sooner than you realize."

"Hey?"

Alara slows at my side, posture tightening, ears flicking at the slightest sound. I look between them, momentarily confused.

Zye nods toward the looming treeline. "Welcome to the Black Forest."

"I can see how it got its name."

"This next part isn't nice, but it's our only way through. Decades ago, it was a battlefield. They say the souls of the dead still haunt it, bound here by vengeance. If you speak, engage, or acknowledge the shadows or worse, step off the track." His gaze slices to mine. "You don't step back."

"Oh, good," I mutter.

"You must keep your head straight and your stride steady. Do not stop. Do not step off the track. And above all, do not look at the shadows."

Alara's warning rumble is enough to send a shiver down my spine.

The trees close in, trunks crowding together. Whispers reach us before we even step under the canopy, too soft to understand, enough to raise the hairs on my neck. Even Alara releases a low grumble.

We pass beneath the first boughs, the world shifts. Light disappears. The ground turns uneven. The air stinks of damp rot. Shadows slide along the trunks, weaving just out of reach, moving when I move, pausing when I pause.

"Just walk," Zye whispers. "Don't look. Don't flinch."

Alara moves lower, fluid, controlled, a predator walking as prey. The air carries a metallic tang beneath the rot. At least I hope that's what it is.

Ice splinters through me. My pulse hammers. "At what point can I run?" I whisper.

"Patience," Zye says without looking back. "Almost there."

Heat rises under my skin, fire sparking too close to the surface. Alara's voice steadies me. *"Combusting will do you no good in here. Cool down."*

I exhale hard and match Zye's pace for what feels like hours, despite it being mere minutes, until two glowing orbs flare ahead, bobbing and weaving through the dark.

"Puk and Eko," Zye whispers. "They'll get us through. Stay close. Keep walking."

The orbs skirt faster, darting across the path, disappearing and looping back again. Where they pass, the shadows shrink away, receding deeper into the trees.

Zye glances at me, tension easing. "We made it."

At the forest's edge, the orbs peel away, darting into the dark.

Something else crashes through the trees. Two figures trip out of the underbrush, branches snapping beneath them, their entrance anything but graceful.

"Zye! That look of fear on your face was legit," one crows. "Don't tell us those shadows made you nervous?"

"And Alara," the other chimes, skipping toward us, "aren't you looking all razzle-dazzle!"

He claps Zye into a rib-bruising embrace as Alara releases a low, unimpressed gruff. Then their attention snaps to me.

"And you," the first says, tilting his head as he sizes me up. "Rae, you're looking a lot better since the last time we saw you!"

I look to Zye for confirmation on when we met.

"These two brought you back—" he starts.

"From the dead," one chimes.

"From—" Zye cuts them a warning glance "—your world. To here. And they'll get you home."

They step closer, stopping right in front of me, forcing me to pull up short. Arms crossing in perfect sync, heads tilt left, then right. Their gazes rake over me with unhidden curiosity. That's when I really take them in. The twins. Identical.

Rugged faces, unshaven. Hair a haphazard mess across their foreheads: one a rich navy blue, the other a deep ember-orange. But it's not the hair, or the grins, or the way they move in tandem or even their sharp, too-perceptive eyes, that catches me off guard.

It's the horns. Twisting, curved, rising from their heads like figures pulled from myth.

Apparently no one thought to mention that Puk and Eko were part man, part goat.

Puk and Eko's outfits are as bold as their personalities.

Cream shirts, collars popped and half-unbuttoned, revealing just enough of their chests to feel deliberately careless. Heavy silver and gold chains clink with every move, an effortless display of wealth or unfiltered confidence. Given the setting, I'm betting on the latter. At the center of it all, against bare skin, a light-pink crystal glows faintly, pulsing with arcane energy. Their pants are fitted, tailored, a sharp contrast to their bare, entirely human, feet.

I open my mouth, then shut it. Then open it again.

I'd been warned about their wit, their charm, their abilities. Even Nyxie spoke highly of their power. Not once did anyone mention that Puk and Eko were… faun. Of sorts.

"Well, don't you look like you've just seen a… goat!" they say in unison, knocking horns and laughing.

"I'm Puk," says the one with navy-blue hair.

"And I'm Eko," chimes the one with burnt-orange.

Before I can muster a response, Puk waves a hand toward the trees. "Formalities later."

Eko throws an arm over Zye's shoulder, practically bouncing. "Let's get you treasure hunters out of these woods before something decides to hunt you back."

I hesitate. Alara leans in, dry as dust. *"They might share a single brain cell, but while they're around, the shadows won't be. They keep their grotto here for safety, they're the only ones more powerful than the dark magic that lurks around us."*

"I'm not sure if that's comforting or horrifying."

"Both." She flicks an ear. *"Now walk, Rae. I'd rather not do this in the dark."*

Eko takes the lead with an effortless, theatrical skip. Despite myself, his energy is contagious. Even the air seems to play, its cold touch tickling my nose.

Then, almost without warning, the woods break open and reshape around us. The darkness behind us vanishes like it never existed. The trees, once twisted and ominous, breathe with life, trunks thick and weathered, branches stretching wide, heavy with emerald and gold. Sunlight filters through the canopy, scattering beams across moss-covered ground. Clusters of wildflowers burst in bright hues, their fragrance replacing the damp heaviness of decay.

Eko stops abruptly and throws his arms wide. "Welcome to our grotto!"

He pulls back a curtain of cascading willow leaves, bowing dramatically. The tree responds, branches parting to reveal a hidden cave entrance cloaked in leaves. The archway is carved into the cliffside, its weathered face etched with runes.

Puk gestures us inside. "No need to remove your shoes."

Floating candles drift lazily overhead, casting warm light against stone walls, waking the engraved runes. A large round table anchors the center, ringed by six intricately carved stools. Two staircases curve along the cavern walls, spiraling into unseen corridors. Eko plops into a chair and kicks his feet onto the table.

"Right, welcome, welcome!"

Puk claps. "Drinks, anyone?"

Zye glances at me. I lift my full canteen, give it a little shake. "We're good. And as much as we wish we did, we don't have time to waste."

In unison, the twins tip their heads. "Let's get this going, then!"

Zye doesn't hesitate. "The plan hasn't changed. We need to get her home. There's someone there we believe holds the key to ending this. It's time to pay him a visit and ask a few questions."

Eko leans back, brows lifting as he studies us. "There's a lot of fear in Athyria right now. But twice as much hope knowing you two are here to right those wrongs." He turns to Alara, dipping his head. "Three. My apologies, Alara. Don't take my head off."

She answers with a low growl.

"These lands haven't been the same since Lord Erian started barking orders from his castle," Eko says, flipping a coin between his fingers. "Honestly, the guy's as thick as the throne he sits on. And the fools who follow him? I can't decide if I pity them or want to see them suffer for being that stupid."

"Anyway!" Puk claps again, already moving on. "Business."

Eko lifts his hand, letting a pink crystal drop from its gold chain. It dangles between his fingers, smaller than the ones they wear but just as mesmerizing. The surface catches the light, glowing faintly like it's alive.

"This is cut from the same crystal as ours," Eko explains.

As they bring the crystals close, a crackle of static jumps between them.

"Funny story," Puk cuts in, grinning. "We were out in the woods, minding our own business—"

"Trying to see if you could outrun a hawk," Eko says.

Puk waves him off.

"Point is, I did… and then we spotted this little spark

knotted in a tangle of roots like it was waiting for us."

Eko shrugs, unbothered. "Never turn down new bling."

"Obviously," Puk adds, dangling the shard. "We picked it up, unraveled it, and realized there were two. In our excitement, we clinked them together, toast to new treasures, and boom. A vortex."

I stare. "And you just… jumped in?"

They trade a look.

"Well, yeah," Eko says, like it's obvious. "Then it got weird. We were floating in this middle ground of nowhere, it was pretty trippy."

Puk nods. "Eko starts panicking—"

"I did not panic!"

"—and says, 'Man, how do we get home?' The second it had a destination—home—poof." He snaps his fingers. "We were home."

Beat.

"And then things got really interesting," they finish together, smirking before bursting into laughter.

Zye pinches the bridge of his nose, exhaling. "You two are actually insane."

"Anyway!" They chorus. Puk holds the glowing shard between thumb and forefinger. "Turns out it's not just pretty. We discovered, thanks to Horo's endless lectures and warnings, that these are pieces of an old Basalith. Back in Highborn days, they used the full crystal to travel between realms. Needed it, actually. No crystal, no passage."

"Once," Eko says, lifting his shard so pink light spills across his palm, "there were four Basalith crystals, one for each region. They were the only way the Highborn could jump between worlds. When the wars came, every crystal was destroyed. All but one… though they had a good go."

The Tome stirs at my side, recognition threading through me. Eko tilts his shard toward Puk's. A tiny spark hisses across the gap. "We can get where we need to go if we keep the halves close and play it safe. Which is no fun, so we've been on some wild adventures." He slaps Puk's shoulder.

His grin fades a notch. "Then Alara threatened to turn us into chew toys if we didn't get her to you."

Eko snorts. "We got her there in one piece, but realized she was stranded with no way back. So we sent Zye in with a half which was barely enough to carry him through."

"Getting all three of you out again was—"

"Wild," they echo, shaking their horns like they can clear the memory.

"You were half-dead, looking like you'd been mauled by a beast," Puk says. "Alara was raging, and the Basalith was burning hot."

Eko steps forward and holds his shard out to me. "And now it's time to do it again."

He presses the crystal into my palm. The glow flares where their hands meet, lighting the grotto.

"Grip it, close your eyes, and call for us," Eko says. "Go on, try it."

I take the crystal. It's warm against my skin.

I hesitate, glancing between them and the softly glowing stone. Then I curl my fingers, the edges biting into my palm. "Puk… and Eko."

Puk groans, flopping into a chair. "You're going to need a little more oomph than that, Rae, dear."

"Say it with heart! With theatrics! Say it like you mean it: PUK, EKOOOOO!" Eko belts, arm raised like an opera finale.

I roll my eyes but humor them. "Puk and Eko!" Louder. Still more street-busker than soprano.

"That'll do it!"

The crystals flare and in a blink, the twins vanish.

I glance at Zye. He leans back with a knowing smile. He's seen this trick before. A strange tap-tap tugs at my palm. I uncurl my fist and there, inside the crystal, are Puk and Eko, tiny and waving energetically.

I blink. Then laugh.

Across the room, a portal stirs to life. From nowhere, a swirling vortex of color and light appears, twisting in hypnotic patterns, stretching into infinity.

"Don't enter that," Zye warns. "Who knows where those two will send you. Probably across the room. Maybe upstairs. Or, knowing them, straight to the foot of Lord Erian's throne."

I sputter. "What—"

"Close your hand, tell them to hurry up and get back here. Remind them we need to move."

I do as he says, clenching the amulet and muttering as enthusiastically as possible for them to stop screwing around.

The portal hums. A second later, Puk and Eko pop back in a flash of light, knocking over their stools. Puk brushes himself off like nothing happened.

"Now it's your turn!"

Zye exhales, already rising.

"You know the drill," Puk says, twirling his shard. "Gather up, kids! Rae, you step in and badda-bing, badda-boom the portal takes you straight to your childhood room!"

"We hope," Eko adds.

I snap my head toward him. He only shrugs.

"We're really doing this?" I ask Zye.

"We're doing this," he says. He gives Alara a quick nod. "Sorry for this. Don't hate me."

With a snap of his fingers, a brilliant flash fills the room.

When my vision clears, Alara is gone.

I spin to Zye. He gestures at the floor. I look down and there she is.

Exactly as I remember.

"Oh, you're so cute!" I crouch and rub her cheeks between my hands.

Alara bares her teeth, a growl rumbling in her tiny chest.

"Even when you're angry," I coo, scooping her up.

Zye offers his elbow. I loop mine through his, steadying my nerves as we approach the portal.

Home.

I'm going home.

"Fortune favors the brave! Go get 'em!" Puk and Eko cheer as the vortex pulses, parting like liquid glass.

"Oh, and Zye, you'll need this." Eko tosses him a small satchel. He catches it, barely glances just gives a curt nod.

Then, without warning, Zye steps forward giving my arm a not-so-subtle yank so I do too as the portal swallows us whole.

The sensation is instant, crushing. It threads us through the eye of a needle, force pressing against every inch of me.

I lose my grip on Alara almost immediately.

Panic spikes but before I can react, the pressure vanishes and we land with a jolt.

"Well," Zye says, dry as bone, "this is as plain and boring as I remember it."

Everything is as I left it.

Which is to say, as plain and boring as I remember it too, at least in comparison to Athyrian standards and I've never been more excited to stand among my humble, far-less-extravagant belongings. I inhale deep through my nose; my body instantly reacts to the fresh, familiar smells of my room. *I'm home.*

I drop to my knees, my hands instinctively finding Alara, clasping her fluffy little face.

"Small but still violent."

Her words thrum through my mind, and I let out a shaky laugh, pressing my forehead to hers.

Across the room, Zye is testing his magic. Wind stirs between his fingers. It's diluted, but still there. Still him.

The sound of voices and movement from downstairs startles me. Zye slumps into my chair. "You gonna stand there all day, or…?"

I whirl toward him. "Cover your eyes. Now."

His brow lifts before realization dawns. "Riiiight." He huffs a laugh and drops his head, hands clamping over his face.

I strip off my leathers with a speed that could only be described as frantic. In seconds, I'm pulling on my old clothes, my old, much softer, much less battle-ready clothes. The material feels unexpectedly light and cool on my skin, and I can't help but wipe my hands down the cotton and smile.

Zye lets out a low, amused chuckle. "Yeah, I definitely don't miss those."

Ignoring him, I bolt for the door, throwing it open just as the sweet sounds of blues float through the house. Mum's favourite. I'm home. And so is she.

For the first time in what feels like an eternity, I pause at the top of the stairs, taking a moment to appreciate the simplicity of it all. The chipped paint on the walls. The familiar, manageable climb. Piled on the side of the bottom three steps is folded laundry, ready for its owner to collect on their way past. Which won't be any day soon. Ordinary, and in its own way, perfect. It's home.

When I turn the corner at the bottom of the stairs, Mum is at the kitchen table, eyes fixed on her laptop, utterly unaware. Dad is here too; he stands by the stove making tea, phone pinched between shoulder and ear, deep in conversation.

"So, what's for lunch?" I ask.

Mum's head snaps up. She blinks. Once. Twice. "Rae. Rae. RAE."

The laptop slams shut. The teacup Dad was holding shatters on the tiles, along with his phone.

Before I can take another breath, I'm swallowed whole. Mum's arms crash around me, her hold desperate. My face is crushed against her shoulder, and her whole body trembles against mine.

Dad is there a second later, hands gripping my arms, my name breaking out on a strangled sob.

Mum shakes her head, swiping at the tears still slipping down her cheeks.

"It's you. It's really you."

"Yup, it's really me," I say as I'm swallowed into another group hug.

"Come," she murmurs, voice unsteady. "Sit. Are you hungry? How did you even—" She waves a hand, trying to gather her thoughts. "I'll make—" she glances at her watch, then back at me, "lunch… food… whatever meal fits whatever time zone you're running on. Wait, are you even hungry?"

But just as she turns toward the kitchen, a sound from upstairs startles us. In the excitement of the reunion, I've almost forgotten they were there.

"Wait. There's someone, and… something else you need to meet, or re-meet. I don't even know" I say with a shake of my head.

Mum clasps her hands together, barely restraining a squeal.

"Oh, wow." I glance at Dad, who just shrugs, grinning. "Someone's happy to have their baby girl back!"

A laugh escapes me, loud and freeing, as I turn toward the stairs. "Come on down."

Alara steps into view first, Zye a stride behind her. And in that instant, everything else seems to still.

I stop breathing.

Gone are the battle-worn leathers, the weathered armor, the hardened warrior stance. Instead, he's wearing a simple tee and jeans. He looks plain. Human. And completely uncomfortable with the attention, his fingers twitch at his jeans where his daggers should be.

After weeks on the back foot, there's a sharp, almost wicked satisfaction in watching him squirm. But deep down, I know this wasn't an accident.

Zye wasn't about to show my family that I needed a warrior to survive. What I needed was someone.

Dad steps forward first. "Thank you."

Zye blinks in surprise but recovers fast, gripping Dad's hand in a firm shake.

Without missing a beat, Dad crouches, running a hand through Alara's thick fur. "For keeping her safe. We owe you both more than words could ever say."

Zye glances at Alara, shifting on his feet. "It was my, our… honor," he says, stumbling slightly over the words, uncharacteristically nervous. And that makes me smile even brighter.

Mum, however, does the unthinkable. She pulls them both into a hug.

Zye stiffens as if frozen in time, then he exhales and returns the hug. Mum holds on a second longer before stepping back and wiping at her face with a shaky laugh.

"Now, sit, all of you." She waves us toward the dining table like she's herding cattle, dabbing at tears that just won't stop falling. "There's a lot to catch up on."

She yanks open the fridge, sighing dramatically. "And unless anyone wants leftovers or expired yoghurt, I'll order something."

Just then, the front gate clangs outside. A heartbeat later, the front door swings open with such force it rattles the house. Zye and I freeze, instinctively tensing, his hand reaching for daggers that aren't there.

Before I can react, Annie is running for me, throwing her arms around me in a hug that knocks the air out of my lungs. I can barely breathe, let alone speak.

"Annie, you're crushing me!" I laugh through the tears streaming down my face.

"I don't care," she chokes out. "I've missed you so damn much!"

She pulls back just enough to look at me and then, without warning, squeezes me again, nearly knocking me over.

"Felix apologizes for not being here," she says. "He's with…" she hesitates, it's faint, but it's there, "Ethan."

Her fingers tighten slightly, and I'm caught off guard.

"How did you know we'd be—?" I turn back to Zye, who looks smug as he shrugs.

Annie's smile threatens to split her face. "A bird came, Rae. It was the coolest thing I have ever seen."

"And it's nice to finally meet you," she adds, playful, turning to Zye. "I think I was picturing someone more, I don't know… older. More hero-looking."

I throw my head back and laugh. God, I've missed her.

I've missed this. I've missed them.

We talk for a while, catching up on everything and nothing, until a knock sounds at the door. The smell of freshly baked bread and pastries fills the room as Mum sweeps in, arms full of paper bags. She empties them onto the table in a glorious mess of golden crusts and flaky layers, then spreads her arms wide like she's unveiling a royal feast.

"Eat," she declares.

I glance at Zye, who is staring wide-eyed at the chaotic pile of paper and pastries with barely-concealed amusement.

"Dig in!" I chime.

Through a mouthful of bread, Annie speaks. "The rumors about you have been wild."

"Felix is telling everyone you've been headhunted, traveling the world on a renegade surf tour. Another said you were in the hospital hiding a massive scar across your face. My personal favourite: you were sent to the country to live with your cousins because you were failing school and needed to focus more on studying than surfing."

Dad tilts his glass toward me. "That last one might have some merit."

Annie takes a slow sip of water, then casually tacks on, "Oh, and also that you've had plastic surgery and may or may not be ridiculously hot now."

I toss my hair dramatically. "So does that one!"

Mum takes a sip of coffee, watching me over the rim. "So," she says lightly, her voice carrying a thread of unease as she finally addresses the one question we've all been avoiding, "what brings you home, Rae?" She eyes Zye and Alara, cautiously. "Is it… over?"

Zye shifts beside me, the air tightening, but I find my voice first. "It's Myles. Ethan's dad, he—"

Dad stills, his glass frozen halfway to his lips.

"We believe he has the Corestone. The same relic that Agatha—" I look to Mum. "That our ancestor carried across realms, all. Those. Years…ago."

The words die in my throat. My stomach hollows, a cold ache spreading through me.

The letter.

I shove back from the table, the chair screeching across the floorboards as I bolt for the stairs.

Another clang at the gate. I freeze mid-step, hand gripping the banister.

"Shit, it's Kenny," says Dad. "I didn't realize the time. Rae, she doesn't need to know this. Not about… him, anyway, at least."

The door bursts open. I suck in a sharp breath, barely able to compose myself, but the moment she sees me, even perpetually unimpressed Kenny looks happy.

"Ah, the prodigal child has returned!" she announces, raising both hands in exaggerated worship before bowing theatrically.

I laugh as I race to her, pulling her into a hug. "Hello, Kennedy. I've missed you, too."

She wrinkles her nose. "Ew, you need a shower."

I snort, releasing her as she brushes past and heads to the table to grab a pastry. Her eyes flick over Zye and Alara, then back to me.

Mum clears her throat. "She knows about you, Rae."

"And so does Felix," Annie says, nose scrunching, the admission tight with guilt. Mum's hand finds hers across the table.

"The day you left… there was no hiding it," Mum continues. "We fell apart, and they saw every bit of it. We'd already learned the hard way what secrets can cost." Her gaze drops, fingers fidgeting at the paper bag. "So we sat her down and had the second-hardest conversation of our lives. All in the space of a few hours."

I introduce Zye and Alara, and to my surprise, Kenny beams brightly in a way that almost catches me off guard. She even bends to pat Alara, who sits tall and to my shock, leans into her touch. Kenny's smile widens, lighting her whole face. She's changed so much since I've been gone, and I quickly swipe away a tear before anyone notices.

Kenny straightens, glances between me and Zye, and with mock gravity says, "You can't marry a man you just met."

Zye freezes mid-reach for a pastry, his brow pulling tight. Heat rushes up my neck, and a graceless laugh bursts out. No, she hasn't changed at all.

"There is no way you're Elsa in this story," I manage, still laughing.

Kenny just shrugs, totally unbothered, and rips into some bread. And just like that, the house is alive again with familiar noise and easy insults as we catch up on all that has happened since I've been gone.

For the most part, Mum is happy, bustling as she always did, but her movements are more deliberate. Every so often, I catch her staring at me, eyes brimming with joy and fear, like she's trying to hold on while piecing together everything all at once.

#

Through the window, a fairy floss sky stretches toward the horizon, long clouds tinted rose and gold. Before the sun disappears completely, I offer to take Zye and Alara up to the beach.

We walk in silence toward the water. Sand dusts the pavement, carried up by the afternoon wind. The air tastes of salt, and I draw it deep into my lungs. A neighbour's dog barrels toward the fence, barking at Alara, who doesn't so much as glance its way. I can't help but laugh.

Over the rise, the ocean stretches wide and dark. Behind us, the sun dips into the mountains, leaving a thin band of pink across their ridges. It's not Athyria, but it's still beautiful.

I realize then how quiet Zye has gone. "What is it?" I ask. "You've barely said a word."

He exhales. "Your family... they're incredible. It was good to meet them. To see how much you all mean to each other." His voice roughens. "And I'm sorry. For the way we took you. If I'd understood what you were leaving behind... I would've done it differently."

"You don't have to—"

"I do." His eyes stay on the ocean. "Your sister reminds me of my own, Lyria. Same fire, same sass. I looked up to her the way Kenny looks up to you."

"With pure disgust?"

His laugh is short, but real. "No. I mean... when my family were taken, I had nothing to return to. You do. And when this is done, I'll make sure you get back here. To them."

There's silence. Only the sea and the sound of seagulls

somewhere above. Zye steps closer. I stay where I am.

His gaze holds mine as his hand lifts. He brushes a strand of hair from my face, tucking it behind my ear. His fingers graze my skin, leaving a trail of heat that makes it hard to think.

Then he finds my hand, his fingers sliding through mine. "I know Athyria's not your home," he says. "And I won't ask you to make it one. But I'll find a way to keep the portal open for you. Whenever you need it."

His grip tightens, just enough for me to feel the tremor he won't show.

"You shouldn't have to choose between who you are and who you were."

His jaw tightens, but he doesn't move away. He tilts his head slightly; his eyes drop to my lips, his thumb grazing absently along my skin.

"Not for us and not because of—"

"Oh, what a beautiful—"

A deafening squeal splits the air as Alara's teeth snap together, missing an elderly couple's fingers by millimetres.

Zye rips his hand away, his body instantly shifting, ready to strike.

"Stand down!" I hiss, grabbing his arm before this escalates any further. "Sorry," I say through gritted teeth, eyes boring into Alara. "She's, um, she's not used to strangers!"

"Used to strangers? That little thing almost took my hand off" one of the women shouts, the other clutching her handbag like a weapon.

"Oh, she's more than capable of that," Zye mutters toward the ocean, and I have to cover my mouth to stifle a laugh.

"Sorry, again!" I call as they hobble off, glaring over their shoulders and cursing under their breath. Zye crosses his arms, glaring at me with nothing but humour in his eyes.

"You need to work on her people skills."

"Apparently. Come on, let's get you both out of here before someone loses a limb," I snap, then huff a half a laugh, shaking my head.

#

By the time we step through the front door, the smell of melted cheese and garlic fills the house. Long after dinner is gone, we stay at the table, caught in the quiet magic of it all. Even Alara seems at ease, curled up by the door.

For a brief, precious while, I let myself forget the reasons and the weight of them and just exist here, in this small, perfect now, knowing it can't last.

Eventually, it's the three of them still at the table—Dad with his usual enthusiasm; Zye, increasingly lost; and Kenny laughing so hard she can barely breathe as Dad tries to teach him the basics of technology and the incredible power of a mobile phone. It's like watching the blind lead the blind, and her laughter fills the home as I slip away to the lounge to curl up with Mum.

I tuck myself against her side, resting my head on her shoulder as she pulls the blanket across us both, her hand finding mine.

"Oh, Rae, you have no idea how good it is to have you, all of you, home," Mum says.

"It's great to be home," I say, but my voice falters, a small frown pulling at my lips. "It does feel weird, though. Like I was never gone. Like I just… woke up from some weird dream."

Mum exhales and pulls me in. "I've been living a nightmare."

"What's it been like? These last few months, for you?" I ask.

For a short moment she doesn't answer. Then, quietly: "Like holding our breath and never finding air. I thought it would get easier. We tried to be strong for Kenny, but the house was too quiet, Rae. Too empty." She swallows hard. "We just wanted you home. Safe. Zye made sure we knew you were, it helped more than you can imagine. But if there was ever a delay, even just a day, we panicked. Sometimes it felt easier not knowing, just believing you were okay." Another swallow. "But nothing compares to having you here."

I lean back at that, stunned. I had no idea. The thought of Zye, quietly making sure they never felt as lost as I did, that they knew I was okay, as I did them, despite everything else he had going on. I look up to see tears in her eyes and my heart aches seeing her this vulnerable and fragile. I pull her into a tight embrace. She holds on like she's afraid I'll slip away again, arms shaking as she buries her face in my shoulder.

"Mum," I whisper softly into her hair. "I'm okay. And soon enough, all of this will be okay too."

She nods, a small gesture that tells me she wants to believe it.

That's she's trying.

Maybe she does.

Maybe I will.

For now, that will have to do.

The next morning, I walk alone past the beach shacks, toward the beach, the sky still pale with dawn. The air is cool and threaded with salt and I breathe it in deeply, letting the quiet settle through me.

Zye and Alara had left well before sun-up to go to the forest where he could release the glimmer hold that is keeping her small. It's the only place where they can exist as they truly are, even if only briefly, before the world wakes around us.

The local cafe, Billy's, is already open. One of the boys drags chairs across the timber decking while the smell of coffee drifts through the open French windows. A blender whirs and muffled laughter spills from the kitchen. Behind the counter, a girl I used to sit next to in science class wipes down the bench. She glances up, surprised, then smiles and waves. I return the warm gesture.

The world goes on. Running groups trace the shoreline, someone's dog tears through the shallows chasing a ball, a few locals out for their morning walk toss me a casual "hey", but most are wrapped in their own worlds, earbuds in, eyes fixed forward, offering nothing more than a lazy wave or passing smile. It's just another day in Rambler Bay.

I take a seat on the backrest of a timber bench, balancing my feet on the seat below. The wood is sun-warmed, the white paint peeled back almost bare to reveal the weathered wood beneath.

I watch the tide fold over itself, the same rhythm that's always ruled this town, pretending that I still belong to it. Then a flash of light catches at the edge of my vision. I follow it across the bay to the far headland, where the glass burns gold in the morning sun.

The gallery. Myles built it to save this town, to put Rambler Bay on the map. Maybe he did. But whatever waits behind those walls could just as easily wipe it off.

The Corestone is close. I can't explain it, but I can feel it.

"Well, well, well. Would you look who it is." I startle, spinning to see Felix, grin wide, eyes gleaming with mischief.

"Whoa there, tiger." He laughs, fingers snapping into a ridiculous gun shape to shoot me. "It's all good, it's just me. My pathetic human powers are no match for you anymore, although my good looks have been known to make the girls go weak in the knees..."

Without hesitation, I race into his embrace. "Oh, I've missed you, you and your terrible one-liners!"

His laugh rumbles through his chest as he pulls me tight. "It's great to have you back, Rae!"

I smile into the rubber of his wetsuit. Even that nostalgic smell of that blindsides me, and I have to choke back the sudden wave of emotion.

Felix pulls back just enough to study me. "Are you all right, Rae?"

I haven't been asked that in a while. The question hangs.

"Yeah. All things considered, I am," I say at last, forcing a lightness I don't fully feel. "I'm just enjoying the view."

Felix chuckles. "I bet! Can't believe you didn't even bring a board, you have changed." He says as he shifts his own board under his arm. "I'm about to meet Ethan. Oh, by the way, he thinks you've been overseas—"

At Ethan's name, my stomach lurches. It feels like something is ripped out of me, leaving raw emptiness. I try to focus on Felix, but his voice blurs.

Despite everything that's happened and everything unfolding, it's Ethan who makes my heart beat too fast. Truth be told, I've been scanning the water watching for the familiar figure cutting through waves, my chest tightening each time I think I've found him. Not out of fear, exactly, but because I don't know what I'll feel when I do.

Whatever teenage crush I once had is long gone. It's not that I want it back, it's that I can't even remember what it felt like. Too much has happened since I last saw him and now I am home, Ethan feels like a thread I haven't figured out how to untangle.

And then there's Myles. Every thought of him leaves me uneasy. I don't know if any of this is a choice or consequence... if he's a monster or a man caught in something bigger than he is. And I can't stop wondering what that's done to Ethan. Whether Myles has kept the truth from him or if Ethan's known all along and just stayed silent.

The thought barely forms before I see him walking down the path.

Blond hair caught in the wind, sun-bronzed skin, warm brown eyes. For a second, everything stops. He's laughing with two boys from school, then he looks up and sees me.

The shift is instant, like the world clicks into focus. A genuine smile lights his face. He crosses the distance in three strides, and then he's here—and I'm airborne.

"Rae!"

Without a word, he drops his board and sweeps me into a bear hug that pulls a startled laugh from my throat and spins me around. I go limp as the world blurs into a dizzy kaleidoscope of colour and motion. He holds me there, suspended in a moment that feels both infinite and fleeting, my mind and double-crossing heart waging a silent battle.

When he sets me down, my feet are steady, but the rest of me isn't.

"Rae," he says again.

"Ethan," I reply, trying to match his energy. I don't want to feel this, whatever it is, but I do.

"You're back."

"Yeah. I… sure am. It's… good. To be back," I say, my voice pitching higher than usual.

Ethan laughs, warm and effortless. "You almost made that sound believable." For a beat, his eyes linger on mine, like he wants to say something but doesn't. Or can't.

"I haven't had a chance to talk to you since the other week." He rubs the back of his neck nervously. "Since the wipeout. I just wanted to say I'm really sorry." The words spill out, like he's been holding them since it happened. "I shouldn't have pushed you into that, and then all the stuff with Dad's exhibition and the gallery happened, and I tried to reach out a few times, but Felix said you didn't put on international roaming, so you wouldn't have service overseas, and that's why you hadn't returned my messages, but I've missed you. And—"

I glance at Felix. He shrugs as if to say, 'I did my best to protect you…both.'

Guilt hits like a blow. The last time I saw Ethan was the morning of the wipeout; we haven't spoken since. Before that, we talked every day.

"Yeah, no, I didn't—" I manage. "I'm sorry. But… yeah, I really missed you too." That part isn't a lie, but the rest of me unravels right there in front of him.

"Hey, anyway, I've gotta run, meeting Annie," I blurt, glancing at my wrist like I'm wearing a watch. I slap bare skin, realising I haven't worn one since I left. "Yeah. Five minutes ago."

Ethan steps closer, his hand landing on my shoulder with a gentle squeeze that shoots straight through me. "Let's catch up later? Tonight? Tomorrow? It'd be good to see you and hear about your trip. Maybe a burger at Billy's?"

Before I can respond, he's already turning away, flashing a smile over his shoulder. "It's good to have you home, Dolly."

Dolly. It undoes me entirely. I watch him go, eyes following every step to the water.

"You good?" Felix teases, nudging me with his elbow but his eyes say he means it.

I groan, dragging a hand down my face and collapsing onto the bench. "Yep. Peachy."

Felix props his board and leans a hip against the bench, watching me with that familiar glint. For a second his expression shifts, like he'll say more, then he reconsiders.

"I mean it, Rae and so does he. It's good to have you back," he says. "He's bloody missed you. Bad. I'll stop by later to meet the others and catch up." He turns, hesitates, glances back. "And Rae, what I do know? Ethan doesn't know a thing."

His gaze softens as he nods to himself, then he lifts a hand and waves before following the same path Ethan just took.

I drop my head into my hands and claw my fingers through my hair, hoping to erase the last four minutes of my life.

For almost my whole life, Ethan knew me best. Now he doesn't know me at all. He doesn't know what I've seen, what I've become or what I will have to do to save everyone I love. And I don't know at what cost.

Nausea rises. I spin hard and fast, almost taking out an innocent runner as I sprint home, rush through the front gate, tear down the hall and into the downstairs bathroom. I barely make it before I collapse to my knees, stomach heaving until there's nothing left.

#

"Rae?" Mum knocks softly.

"I'm good, I'm coming," I say, and stumble out to find a glass of water waiting.

"Do you think it was the pizza? Your stomach might not be used to it?"

I look into her eyes and realise even she doesn't truly know me anymore. Not really. Something fractures at the edges of my heart but I do the only thing I can to keep her fragile bliss intact. I press my lips together and nod.

"Yep. Could've been," I say quietly. "I might just lie down for a bit, if that's okay?"

"Of course. Yell if you need anything."

I turn for the stairs and hear soft paws behind me.

"How was the forest?"

"Better than your morning, apparently."

In my room I collapse onto the bed and stare up at the ceiling. Everything looks the same. It's all mine. But it's changed, or more the point, I have. Every now and then I almost believe I'm still her, the girl who lived for the next wave, the next sunrise but too much has happened since. Too much for anyone here to ever understand.

That life, that girl, is gone.

I wanted to come home, I wanted it more than anything but now that I'm here I realise that maybe this is no longer where I belong. So much has changed since that night at the kitchen table when my parents told me about the signet, about Agatha, about...

I sit up, my pulse already racing. I rip open my bedside drawer, empty. I ruffle and shake my sheets out, nothing. I race to my cupboard, ripping clothes out and searching shelves high and low as panic claws its way up my throat. I spin trying to remember my movements, what happened and how and then I drop to my knees, checking beneath the bed, pushing aside boxes and old notebooks until something catches my eye. There it is.

The letter.

I pick it up and just stare. Everything from this morning is too much to carry. Alara jumps onto the bed and curls beside me.

"Nothing in there, not now, will surprise you, Rae. You can read it."

I lean back against the headboard, knees drawn up, and trace a thumb over the black wax seal before tapping it once. Carefully, I peel it open so I don't tear the paper beneath. The ink has bled and smudged; the writing is almost illegible.

My Dearest Agatha,

Athyria is rotting from the inside. You are no longer safe. The crown sworn to guard us is now the sword held to your throat.

And so, I make the choice I pray you will one day forgive. I have taken you through the last working passage, into a realm untouched by magic or war. There, you will bear a name that is not your own, but Athyria will never forget you. I will make certain of that.

I do not believe in miracles. But I believe in you. And if there is one thing you carried that they feared most, it was hope.

Now you carry something greater. The Corestone. The wolf will watch over you when I cannot. It will keep you safe. Trust it, Agatha. And when the time is right, it will lead you home.

I do not know if I will survive what's coming.
I have made too many enemies, and this world is bleeding faster than I can mend it. I can only pray I have done enough.

I hope I am there if you do return, but if I am not… know this: nothing in this world or the next will be able to stop it.
Or you.

—Ira

The letter trembles in my hands long after I finish.

My pulse pounds so hard I barely notice the faint hum rising from the Tome on my nightstand. A single page lifts, then another. Every hair on my arms stands.

The Tome peels open, and silver spills across the room. Alara surges to her feet with a growl as the walls dissolve. The bed, the house, everything, falls away until I'm standing in a vast chamber lit by fire and moonlight.

A door slams hard enough to shake the floor. I flinch and see him.

Ira. Golden hair unbound, sword drawn, fury alive in every line of him. He crosses the room in three strides and hurls the Tome into the fire.

The flames leap and do nothing. The book floats above the blaze, pages snapping open with a sound like breaking bone.

Visions pour out—wolves ripping free of flame; hawks screaming through a sky split black; a king collapsing beneath a crown cleaved in blood. Ira reaches for it, tearing a page free as magic flares so bright it's blinding and I throw up an arm as the tome twists in midair, folding in on itself and reforming into a wolf of pure white stone that lands soundlessly on the floor.

The Corestone.

Ira doesn't hesitate. He seals the page, tucks it into his cloak, and seizes the stone wolf before racing into the night. The vision follows.

Corridors blur. Guards stand watch. To Agatha. Tiny and fearless, she reaches for Ira as he sweeps her into his arms and runs into the cells where a chained black wolf rises, eyes burning. I gasp. Aric. A silver shadow stirs behind him. Soraya.

Moonlight erupts as they break into the night, racing through forests and over mountains. A crystal bounces against Ira's chest, the Basalith thrumming with raw power. They stop in a clearing; he wields it and a vortex opens. A woman cloaked in green waits by the gate. Agatha wriggles toward her, laughing, trusting. They recognize each other. Ira presses the sealed page into Agatha's waiting hand before she spins and skips away. He turns, draws the Basalith from his cloak, and slams it onto a rock. The crystal screams as it cracks in two.

Ira remains. Sword raised. Jaw set with grief as he stares at the space where Agatha disappeared.

Darkness rushes back. I'm on my bed again. The Tome rests on the side table, its pages flicking softer now. The letter still trembles in my grip.

"Ira…" I whisper, looking to the Tome as a faint silhouette blooms across the page.

Blue eyes pierce through the haze, glowing like glittering fragments in the dark. Golden hair tumbles around his face.

"I was bound to protect Agatha. That was the vow I made the night the Corestone found me, found her. The Corestone didn't give

me death. It gave me duty. It bound me between worlds, where I have waited for the one who could bring it back. Where I have waited for you. The Corestone wants to come home now, Rae."

His form begins to unravel, threads of gold pulling from his edges. "*I've done what I can from afar. Cleared the path where I could. But my reach is ending. It is now up to you.*"

A final thought. "*You remind me of her, you know. Same smile, same fire and when you do find the stone, I pray I'll finally be free to find her in the afterlife.*"

The Tome closes, and I sink back onto the bed, eyes on the ceiling as the tears fall.

I came home to remember who I was.

Instead, I found who I'm meant to be.

And now I know what I must do.

I peel myself off the bed and drift to the porch, drawn by the smell of rain.

I've always loved an afternoon storm. Thick, heavy clouds rolling in, swallowing everything in their path. The way the air shifts with pressure, the hush that follows like the world is bracing for impact.

As kids, we'd sit out here with Mum and Dad, huddled up, counting the seconds between lightning and thunder. Now that same energy is barely contained under my skin, a storm building from the inside out. I can't focus. I can't think. I can't function.

"Up you get. Let's go."

I blink up at Zye, arms crossed tight across my chest.

"Go where?" I scowl, unmoving, then realize he's soaked. "And why are you so wet?"

His forearms flex as he folds them. Wind tugs at his rain-slick hair. "You're about to find out. Get up, get ready, let's go."

"Go. Where?" I ask again, sharper.

He steps closer, "your mood dragged this storm in. You need to let it out."

I squint at him. "What?"

"You're about to explode, Rae," he says, bluntly. "If you don't release it, someone's going to get hurt. And it won't be the one who deserves it. We'll use the storm. We'll hide you in the noise and wind. You can unleash your fury there."

A sarcastic laugh bubbles up as I roll my eyes. "Where is Alara?"

"Already in the forest. She's waiting." He holds out his hand. I take it, grunting as he hauls me up.

The storm hits us the second we step outside, rain sheeting sideways, soaking everything. I stand beneath the roof's feeble shelter, arms folded, drenched and fuming. Zye, of course, looks annoyingly energized, the rain only sharpening the mischief in him.

"Okay," he says. "Rules are simple—get them before they get you." He winks, snaps a silver whip at my feet, and I stumble forward as he takes off, nothing but a blur against the rain.

"Wait, what?" I shout, bolting after him. His laugh floats back, swallowed by thunder.

I'm gasping by the time we reach the beach track. "Zye, will you slow down!"

"Keep up, Rae," he calls out over his shoulder. "Or this will be a very unfair fight."

"Smug bastard," I mutter, lungs burning.

He's already at the forest waiting, by the time I arrive, the rain is hammering through the canopy. His shirt clings to his chest, hair plastered to his forehead, water streaming down his face.

"Hi," he says, mouth twitching.

"Hi," I manage, out of breath. "Dare to explain what's going on?"

"I already did. Get them before they get you." He flicks his hand. The ground bucks. I hit face-first in the mud.

"What the hell?" I spit grit, shove up, fury flashing hot. "You—"

Wind howls. It knocks me sideways. I slam into the earth again. "Zye!" I gasp, wiping mud from my eyes. He just smiles, no remorse. I want to strike it off his face.

"Fight back, Rae," he taunts, thunder cracking overhead.

He vanishes. His voice threads the trees, close and nowhere.

"I was expecting more from you."

"From me?" I pivot, searching for any hint of him. "Step out and face me, then tell me I'm not enough."

Heat licks my palms; power claws at my ribs.

"You're a feisty thing, aren't you?" His voice is a sneer and a lesson. "None of it matters if you don't channel it. Release it before it consumes you."

"This is reckless and stupid."

"This is training," he growls. "You're no good in a battle if you can't wield your power. Release it."

The air folds. Silver shadows peel from the trees, swirling into warriors—dark, faceless and closing in. I reach for my daggers and find nothing.

Zye's laugh slices through the rain. "Unarmed in a battle? Now that's reckless, Rae."

A wind-warrior strikes, pain blooms as I stagger back. The figures press in and my power rises. A blast rips out. Shadows catapult upward, crashing into the canopy. Bark rains down. Lightning tears the sky; the thunder shakes my bones.

"That's more like it," he calls. "But you'll need more."

The air snaps again, this time into wolves with glowing eyes and bared teeth.

"Where's your puppy-dog friend now, Rae?" Zye sings, somewhere in the storm.

A roar answers, ripping the sky in two.

"Where are you?" I shout down the bond.

"Focus. Don't let him in your head. He's testing you. Fight back."

The wolves lunge. Fear and fury blur. Twin bursts of light slam into them, flinging bodies into trunks with a crack.

"Oh, close," Zye says, maddeningly mild, "but not close enough."

"I don't want to hurt you."

He laughs, low. "You won't. Not with shots like that."

I inhale, deep, and try to ground myself as I call the storm.

I pull from rain and earth and everything I've been. Will be.

The downpour twists into a whirling column around me. Wind and water obey. I move, fast, threading trees by instinct and memory, betting I know this ground better than he does.

"Come out, come out, wherever you are," he lilts.

I pivot and fire. A bolt spears into a silver shield, flaring hard. Found you. I strike again and the shield shudders. I fling a gust, a trunk groans. Zye shifts. I fire and miss by a hair.

Alara roars.

Not just sound, a pure force that rolls through me. Her power floods my veins, igniting every nerve. The world sharpens, it slows, and now all I feel is the storm and Alara's power braided with my own.

I plant my feet and release everything.

The blast leaves me like a thrown spear, white-hot and laced with wind and lightning. It hits Zye square in the chest. The sound alone is violence. He doesn't stumble, he flies.

He slams into a tree, the trunk splitting with a scream as the roots tear free and wood shrapnel slices through the rain.

"Zye." My voice breaks as I race to him. "I'm sorry. I didn't mean…Alara…everything just—" I drop to my knees. "Are you okay?"

He winces. "Alara?" Confusion tightens his features.

"I think it was her, I felt her roar through me and then everything—Zye, I'm sorry. I didn't mean to hurt you. I—"

"It's fine," he grunts. "I'll be fine. Hopefully I still heal fast here without the healer."

He reaches up to take my hand as I pull him up, Alara's power still pulses through me and I do it with such force that we both stumble back, his hand grabbing my waist. His lips are close, they brush against my temple, and suddenly, I'm too aware of everything. I freeze. And so does he.

The air reacts, curling like liquid silver, alive with a mind of its own. It twines around my body, slipping along my skin with a heat that shouldn't belong to the breeze. Silver tendrils slide across my skin, wrapping low at my back, grazing the slope of my ribs, caressing places his hands haven't dared reach. I suck in a breath. Zye does, too.

His eyes lock with mine, wide, dark and stunned. His fingers tighten, not out of force but restraint, I can see it in his face, the confusion, the crack in his usual control. He doesn't know what's happening, but he feels it, just like I do. And neither of us knows how to stop it.

I don't know who moves first. Maybe it's both of us. But carefully, slowly, almost reluctantly, the ribbons of white recede, dragging like it doesn't want to let go. His fingers linger for a moment more before they too leave my waist.

"I—" he starts, jaw flexing. He swallows, looks away, scrubs a hand through wet hair. "I don't know what just happened. I, um…"

I clear my throat. "I think you're trying to say I win."

A beat. His mouth twitches. "You cheated."

"That's definitely something a loser would say." I grin, the adrenaline finally breaking into laughter. "Come on, there's only one thing that is going to fix this."

His eyes narrow, curious. "Yeah? What's that?"

I glance over my shoulder. "A hot shower."

"Would you watch it! You're going to stab me in the eye."

"Then stop flinching," Annie hisses, steadying my chin with one hand while the other wields the mascara wand like a blade.

Alara paces the room like a caged beast, frustration spiking through our bond in electric bursts. I crouch beside her, pressing a hand into the soft white fur along her shoulder. She growls and turns her back on me, the sound echoing like thunder beneath my ribs as she disappears down the stairs.

I face the mirror and barely recognize the girl staring back.

Annie sets the mascara down and moves behind me to adjust the bodice of my dress. It's black, elegant and unlike anything I've ever worn. The bodice hugs close, boning sculpted to my shape. Between each seam, sheer panels dip in precise curves, tracing down to a waist drawn tight; from there, the skirt falls in layered folds that move like smoke. A slit slices high up my thigh, freedom to walk, to run, to fight if I have to, but not high enough to reveal what waits beneath. Kail and Thane's daggers lie hidden against my leg, sheathed behind silk.

Annie does a final check and nods at my reflection. "Well, Rae," she says proudly, "you look absolutely beautiful."

It hits harder than it should. I blink, then pull her into a hug.

She looks devastating herself, dark hair swept back, a cream satin slip clinging like paint. We giggle and do our best not to cry. "If you ruin your mascara, I swear to you, Rae..."

I laugh, but it snags in my throat.

Because beneath the makeup and silk and sisterhood, we both know this isn't dress-up. This is it.

The plan was finalized this morning. Every face around the table was drawn tight, eyes glassy, pretending this wasn't the hinge. Pretending we weren't already halfway to goodbye.

I've done everything I can to make this time matter. Soaked in the normal, the quiet, the pieces of home I can't carry with me. Tried to burn them into memory—every voice, every touch, every stupid joke. Hoping it will anchor me when the world slips again. Hoping I'll remember who I am when it does.

And what I'm fighting for.

Everyone was involved, even the Tome, open and waiting in case Ira had more to give.

Felix delivered the intel. Myles has unravelled. Paranoia is chewing through him, and the gallery is now crawling with armed security. Ethan says he hasn't slept in days. And there's the hero piece, which we can only assume will be under armed guard, and what we've come for. The Corestone.

Zye and Felix will arrive first, right on time. Their job: slip through the crowd, read the room, make sure we're not already too late.

Mum and Dad are staying behind with Alara. They were given the choice, but with everything on the line, we couldn't afford to have them fall apart mid-plan. And Mum hasn't stopped crying since the day started, so that decision made itself.

If the Corestone reacts, if *I* do, there won't be time to pull anyone back. And I won't risk putting them in any further danger. Alara is fury wrapped in fur, her power trapped in a form too small to fight. She hates it. I feel every beat of that rage pounding through our bond. But there was no other way. Not tonight.

That leaves Annie and I. We'll arrive last. We don't know how the Corestone will respond when I walk through that door. We don't know how Myles will respond or if he will respond at all. All we know is we need to get in, get the Corestone and get the hell out of there before anyone gets hurt.

#

The gallery is in full swing by the time we arrive. It's a grand affair that's drawn almost everyone in Rambler Bay. Everyone except my parents. As we make our way up the stairs, a wall of sound crashes into us. Laughter. Music. Sharply dressed waiters glide through the crowd with trays of drinks and canapés in hand as a small orchestra plays, the soft melody painting a perfect image of grandeur and an illusion of normalcy.

We reach the entrance and almost immediately my eyes find him.

Zye stands in the far corner, deep in conversation with Felix, but his head lifts the second I hit the landing, a slow, deliberate turn like he felt me arrive before he saw me. His gaze holds and for a precious second, it's just him and me.

He looks sharp. No tie, top button undone, navy suit tailored within a millimeter of precision. He's never looked more like the weapon no one here realizes he is.

He bites back the rest of the smile, says something to Felix, and starts toward me—

"Rae, wow. You look—"

Ethan.

He's at my side before I can turn. A hand at my waist; a brush of lips at my cheek with a closeness that used to mean everything. His touch lingers. So does his look.

A few steps away, Zye goes still. His shoulders set. Hands flex once at his sides. The restraint in him is absolute but a subtle tendril of air curls around his wrist, barely visible.

"Annie," Ethan says, nodding politely. "You both look incredible."

"You say that like you're surprised," Annie muses, arching a brow as she smooths her dress.

Ethan laughs as he slowly drops his hand from my waist.

"I'm going to head on in and pretend I know anything about art," Annie says, tossing a hand in the air before sauntering toward Zye, who's already turned his back to us.

Ethan turns to face me directly. "I'm so glad you could make it."

"I wouldn't have missed it." Not a lie. Entirely.

Ethan takes a step closer, his hand reaching out. The back of his fingers brush mine before he curls his hand around it. A spark zips up my spine and I feel like I've been hit with a live current.

"You..." he starts, but the word dies. His gaze drops to my dress, jaw tightening. His fingers flex in mine. "You almost get yourself killed, disappear for months and then show up looking *like this?*"

He swallows hard. "Rae, I—"

"How about we go inside," I cut in, too fast. I try to soften it, but I know he hears it, the shift, the shutdown.

"Yeah, right. Um, sure." His fingers tighten around mine for a second, before he lets go and gestures toward the door.

It's impossible not to be impressed. The gallery was always going to be a draw card for Rambler Bay, but standing here now is immense. Myles has turned the old waterfront warehouse into something fit for a city far larger than this one. Concrete floors cradle plinths of intricate work; dark timber and steel climb the walls with giant canvas and works placed precariously in between. Pools of light fall across sculpture and glass, every angle and artwork curated to perfection.

I take a single step past the main doors, and the instant I do, I feel a deep punch through my ribs that knocks the air out of my lungs. My knees buckle, one arm shooting out instinctively, the other clutching my chest like I've been struck.

"Rae!" Ethan's beside me, one hand at my back, the other on my arm. "What's wrong? What happened?"

I shake my head. "It's nothing." It's not nothing. My signet is on fire.

Zye is suddenly there, his grip clamps around my arm, his eyes sweeping the room with lethal precision. Power hums under his skin, restrained but ready, every line of him coiled to move if I so much as sway.

Ethan stays where he is. "You don't look okay," he says, "Let me take y—"

"I'm fine." The words scrape out. I hate how it sounds.

The burn licks up the length of my forearm, white-hot and wild beneath the skin. I shove the pain down, straighten. Smile. I pull my arm in tight, tucking it against my side before Ethan can see anything I don't know how to explain to him, especially not right now.

"*Rae.*" Alara's concern weaves through me.

"*I'm good,*" I say, steading my breathing, pushing the thought away. "*I'm holding it.*" Barely.

Then I feel her. The pain ebbs as her strength pours through, stripping away the pain until all that's left is her presence, threaded through mine.

Zye's gaze doesn't leave me. When he speaks, his voice is low and smooth. "Here, let me take you."

Ethan's head turns, his expression shifts. "And you are?"

Zye finally looks at him, slow and intentional. "Zye." No handshake. No smile. Just his name as a statement.

"I'm Ethan." He straightens, just enough to assert something, there's a quiet defiance in the way he stays close.

Zye's mouth lifts at the corner, barely. "I know."

My heart pounds in the split second I have to diffuse the situation as Annie slides in with a practiced smile, her arm looping casually over my shoulders. "Okay, gentlemen, Rae's fine. I'll go get her some water so you two have a chance to meet and greet." She waves theatrically as she leads me away, quickly.

"That is not how I needed" I wince, as my signet flares again "those two to meet."

"What the hell just happened?" she whispers through gritted teeth.

"Ego-"

"Not them, you Rae, what happened, what is happening. To you."

"I'm okay now, maybe it was my power, the Corestone, who kno…"

"Rae!" It's Zye.

I turn as he closes the distance, his hands gripping my shoulders, eyes sharp and searching. "That was one way to make an entrance. Are you hurt? What happened?"

"What the hell was that for?" I whisper, sharply, stepping in close enough to keep my voice from carrying. "You didn't need to act like that."

"Act like what?" Zye's brows lift, innocent on the surface but his stance doesn't soften.

"Like whatever that gun show was. He's a friend Zye, not a threat." Zye tilts his head, he's definitely amused now. "Oh, I know that." His mouth curves, slow and wicked. "I'm the threat."

I scrunch my face up in confusion.

He leans in just enough that I catch the quiet heat in his voice. "Oh, come on, you have to see it, Rae."

"See what?" I ask.

"That there's a guy standing next to his *friend* and that guy ain't him?"

I choke.

"I'm not worried about that, him, are you—" suddenly he's cut off by the clink of glass. The lights dim. A hush rolls over the crowd as a tall, polished man steps into view at the far end of the gallery. Myles.

"Are you okay to wait here?" Zye leans in and whispers.

"I'll make sure of it." Ethan is back by my side.

This can't be happening.

I inhale deeply as I spin to Zye "Where are you going?" I hiss.

He leans in even closer, the room has fallen silent, so I can only imagine it's to further grind Ethan, but the proximity of his lip to my ear sends an unexpected bolt of lighting up my spine.

"I don't have time for speeches, there is no wolf here, Felix gave me a key. While Myles is out here, I'll go check in there."

"I'll come."

He straightens. "Stay here, with your" his jaw ticks "friend" he makes eye contact with Ethan, "I'll be right back."

"Good evening, everyone." Myles starts and I immediately turn to where he stands in the centre of the room as Zye turns into the crowd.

"On behalf of the Rambler Bay Gallery and our extraordinary team of researchers and collectors, I want to thank you for joining us tonight. It's a rare thing, to bring together a crowd so rich in curiosity, in culture, and in belief that the past still matters." He looks straight at me and I straighten as I feel Ethan eye me curiously.

"For the past six years, my team and I have worked to recover, restore, and most importantly, protect the pieces you see tonight. These works span continents. Dynasties. Myths. Some predate modern recordkeeping altogether. But as you are all aware, there's one piece that's drawn more speculation than the rest. A sculpture with no confirmed origin, no known signature, and no exact match in any archive. It's the reason we're all here. Other than the free bubbles and canapes..."

That draws a laugh from the crowd.

Suddenly Myles coughs, his eyes blink and he tries to mask it with a laugh. He takes a sip of his champagne.

"Without further delay—on behalf of the Gallery and our international curatorial partners—it is my absolute honour to unveil the centrepiece of the *Lost Collection*."

Something's wrong.

It's not what he's saying. It's how.

There's something off in his cadence. The way the syllables fall like commands, not words.

"Let it remind us that even the oldest power, buried, broken, forgotten, can be reborn."

Applause rises, I shift my weight, trying to focus, but my pulse is spiking. The pain behind my ribs tightens. A spotlight shines behind him as a white silk cover is pulled back and the sculpture is revealed. A wolf. I gasp.

Myles' voice cuts off entirely. A muscle in his jaw twitches. And his eyes, when they shift to me, are not Myles' anymore. Zye spins, his gaze finds mine across the gallery, his calm fracturing as smoke rolls off his wrists in slow, warning curls.

The floor beneath me trembles, a subtle vibration that sends my heart racing as the Corestone flares. Ethan steps forward, his body angles closer to mine, a subtle shift that has him pressing protectively against me. His eyes move between me and the source of the shift, his jaw clenched, the muscles in his neck taut. His chest rises and falls faster.

"Rae?" Ethan's eyes are wide as he stares at me, then at the center of the room to the source of the light.

The Wolf. It's glowing.

The light builds from within the sculpture, seeping through the cracks of the carved wolf until it's impossible to ignore. The room stills. Faces tilt. Conversations die. Every gaze locks onto the sculpture, all eyes but Ethan, he stares in confusion at me as light bursts from the glass plinth like a sunrise splitting stone. Glass explodes outward in a violent shockwave, shards slicing through the air like thrown blades. Screams erupt as the crowd surges back. Armed guards reach for weapons, confusion written across their faces as the chaos swallows the room.

"Rae!" Zye's growl slices through the madness. He moves fast, stepping in front of me with a sharp intensity. "We need to get you out of here."

Before I can respond, Ethan's hand lands on my arm, his grip tight, urgent, but instinctual. "What's happening?" he demands, eyes now glued to the Corestone as its glow intensifies.

Felix's voice cuts through the chaos like a whip. "Everyone out. Now!" His tone is razor-sharp, commanding, it's the first time I've heard him sound serious. "Security breach. Fire. Emergency. Just get out the doors, now. Go, go, go…"

"Ethan." I step in front of him, placing my hand on his cheek to pull his focus back to me. His eyes lock on mine, wide, searching. "Help Felix get everyone out. I'll explain."

Without waiting for confirmation, Zye grabs my hand and yanks me into the sea of panicked bodies, all running in the opposite direction. But my eyes never leave the Corestone. The glow falters, the pulse of energy quivering in the air before it suddenly stops. And that's when I see him. Myles.

His hand shoots out, grabbing the Corestone, his eyes wild as he sprints toward the back of the gallery.

"There" I point urgently, Zye sees it too and without a word, we both race after him, cutting through the last of the crowd towards the back of the building.

We race into the back gallery, where shattered works of art litter the floor, jagged fragments of glass and splintered wood strewn in every direction. Frames lie discarded in piles, their once-proud contents now ripped and defiled, slashed beyond recognition. It's a mess.

And at the center of it all, he waits. Not Myles. Not anymore.

He stands motionless, his presence commanding the space like the eye of a storm. His head is slightly bowed, eyes dark and menacing as they lock on us. The fractured light catches on his form, outlining him in jagged shadows, every inch of him brimming with barely restrained power. Every inch of him is wrong.

The door slams shut behind us, the sound reverberating like a gunshot. My heart leaps to my throat as cold fingers of fear curl around my spine.

Zye doesn't flinch. His power, visibly ripples and twists, creeping outward like a tide. Myles tilts his head, the motion slow, deliberate, and calculating. His gaze tracks Zye's silver tendrils, now twisting and writhing in the dim light, sharp and dangerous, yet oddly beautiful.

Myles is panting. His hands twitch at his sides, fingers curling as if he's holding on to something no one else can see. "You need to leave, Rae." His voice is tight. "Now. Please. Before—"

The words choke off. His jaw clenches like he's forcing them through locked teeth.

Zye steps forward, intentionally, putting his frame between

Myles and me, every muscle in his body locked, his eyes never leaving Myles. "Not without that."

The faint tremor in his hands stills, his shoulders squaring with unnatural precision. His lips curl into a smile that isn't Myles' at all.

"You woke it," his voice slithers, but "I want it." His jaw tightens, eyes flashing with cold, desperate resolve.

My breath comes fast as my body reacts before my mind can catch up. My hands tremble, the electricity in the room spiking as my magic surges to life, reacting to the threat before me. The Corestone's pull is undeniable now, feeding the storm inside me.

Myles' gaze locks on mine, and for a heartbeat, something in his features falters—confusion, almost recognition—before it hardens into something far darker.

"When the Corestone woke, I felt it," he says, the words rasping like they are clawing their way through his throat. "Its magic tore through both realms and through me. But our magic found me. The relics we had forged centuries ago. Vaulturian artifacts imbued with Vaulturian power." He barks out a laugh. "And you. You are as much as a surprise as this was."

"It's Erian," Zye whispers.

My stomach knots.

"We got them into the human realm before the portal closed. Waiting for a moment we could arrive. Those artifacts carried my magic. Enough for me to ride the surge into this body. I thought in death, I had woken the Corestone...."

His hands twitch, veins darkening. "But not enough to wield it." His gaze snaps to mine as a humourless laugh rips from his throat, sharp as breaking bone. "But it was you."

His voice dips his body contouring unnaturally. "But I can't take it from you like this, can I, little storm? No. I need you to give it to me. Or better yet, I get rid of you entirely."

Before I can react, his right hand cuts through the air and the room shifts. The pressure slams into me, but Zye takes the brunt of it, thrown backwards so violently he crashes into the wall, the sickening crack of impact swallowed by the rain of shattered glass.

"No!" The word rips from me as the Corestone's pulse tears through my veins.

"Do you know what it took to claw my way back here?" Myles stumbles, a hiss of pain cutting between his teeth, the Corestone slipping from his grip and striking the floor. His body jerks violently. His spine arches, his head snaps back, and the veins in his temples surge black. A light bursts from his chest, a blinding white-hot intensity flooding the room like a nova, burning everything it touches.

Zye's arm is around my waist before I can blink, yanking me back with a force that knocks me off my feet. We stumble, Zye's breath is harsh against my hair as he pulls me into the shelter of his shield just seconds before the room erupts.

A violent blast of energy rips through the air, a shockwave that hits with the force of a storm. The shield Zye throws up cracks and flares with light, pushing back against what Myles has unleashed. I press closer to him, my hands gripping his shirt, torn, blood-streaked, damp with sweat. His muscles strain beneath my touch, the tremble of his body unmistakable.

The air hums, a low roar that fades into a final, searing pulse. The room falls into a heavy silence, thick with the scent of burnt timber and the acrid remnants of what just happened. The Corestone's glow is gone. Zye lowers his shield, his shoulders rigid, his body heavy with exertion. Silvered currents coil tightly around him, swirls of liquid light, responding to the tension pulsing through his frame. That effort took a toll; it's written all over him.

The room is dim once more, the once-glowing stone is now nothing but shattered fragments, scattered across the floor, its energy pulsing faintly in the air. The magic inside me surges again a raw, chaotic force, more powerful than I've ever felt.

From the fractured Corestone, smoke begins to rise, curling upward in a slow, deliberate spiral that thickens the air and pulls every sound from the room into silence. Zye tenses beside me, his breath shifting as he braces again.

Then the glow deepens—gold and blue threading together, pulling inward. The shards that shattered moments ago lift from the floor, weightless, spinning slowly in the space between us.

"It answers to you now. Take it." Alara says.

The light flares and from its centre, a sword emerges. The hilt is carved with symbols that shift and pulse. My fingers close around it as energy rushes up my arm, into my chest, locking into place like it's part of me.

"This is not just to end him," Alara's voice presses hard into my mind. *"It's what you need to protect everything else."*

Dark smoke swirls in the centre of the room, twisting into a vision of an army clad in black armour, their march shaking the earth. The sound of war drums builds, a low, rhythmic thunder that rattles the walls. Zye's breath catches. The steady calm he wears falters, his jaw locks and for the first time, there's something close to fear in his eyes.

The Academy is under attack.

But before he can say or do anything, Myles calls out from across the room, confusion apparent. "Rae?"

Instinctively, I start to move toward him as the doors explode open.

"What the hell did you do?"

Ethan's eyes are wide, locked on where his father lies sprawled across the floor, blood streaked down his temple, barely conscious and before I realise what is happening, he lunges, his fist connecting with Zye's jaw with a sickening crack.

Zye stumbles, spitting blood, but he doesn't fall. His stance is steady, controlled, his silver tendrils shifting. I race between them before Zye can react, Felix and Annie moving swiftly behind Ethan. Zye is a single thought away from unleashing hell.

And Ethan isn't backing down either. His stance is rigid, wild with rage, his breath coming in sharp, uneven bursts.

"You piece of—"

But he doesn't finish the sentence.

He looks at the sword, then to me, and finally to Zye. His gaze narrows.

"Rae?"

"Has got to go. *Now.*" Before I can respond, Zye grabs my elbow, pulling me toward the door, but Ethan's hand snaps out, yanking me back.

"You aren't taking her anywhere."

"Ethan, it's okay!" My voice breaks. "He won't hurt me, but I need to go. Now. My friends are in danger. I will explain. I promise, one day I will explain everything. "

Felix is still trying to wrestle Ethan back, his hands gripping his arms but Ethan doesn't hear him, his rage is all-consuming. His eyes are locked on Zye and filled with nothing but fury.

"Ethan, look at me!"

I grab his face, forcing him to meet my eyes, his skin hot beneath my fingertips.

"Zye is not the enemy," I whisper, willing him to listen, to understand. "We have to go. Please, trust me. I'm fine. Felix and Annie will explain everything. I'm so sorry. So, so sorry. They will tell you the truth. All of it. And when I get back, I'll explain. Your dad is going to be—"

"YOU DID THAT TO HIM!"

Before I can react, Ethan shoves me aside and I stumble back as he launches himself at Zye.

But he is no match and Zye is in no mood. His hand snaps up, and a blast of magic erupts, hurling Ethan backward. The impact is brutal and I cry out.

He crashes against the floor, his body hitting hard, the sound almost unbearable. For the first time, his fury falters, his breath coming in sharp, pained gasps as confusion, fear, flashes behind his eyes.

Zye turns to me, his grip tight.

"Rae, please." He pleads. "Kail, Ember, and Thane are in trouble. We need to get Alara and leave. I won't risk their lives," he looks to where Ethan and Myles are now sprawled on the floor, "for theirs."

Felix is already kneeling beside Ethan, trying to help him up, but Ethan is still reeling, his face caught between shock and betrayal.

Annie grips my hand tightly. "I've got them," she says. She glances at Myles, whose expression is now one of pure confusion, the blood from a cut above his brow dripping down his face. "You two go. Now."

Her fingers dig into my arm. "Rae, be safe. You hear me?" She pulls me into a tight hug, and I hold on for half a second longer. Then I turn and run.

The corridor is eerily empty, our footsteps the only sound in the suffocating quiet.

"ALARA!" I shout, my voice hoarse as I swipe at a rogue tear that falls down my cheek.

We burst into the cold night, the air hitting me like a slap. My parents' car is the only thing in the loading dock, other than Dad, who is pacing frantically, his face drawn, anxious.

"She went mad," he blurts, running a hand through his hair.

"Raced down the stairs with the book and wouldn't stop barking until we got in the car."

Mum's hands shake as she reaches for me, eyes darting between me, Zye, and Alara.

"Are you all okay?"

I nod. "Yes," I manage, "but we have to go, now. Our friends are in danger."

Tears well up in Mum's eyes as she looks at Zye and Alara. "Please… look after our girl."

"We will." Zye's voice is steady as he turns to Alara. And with that, he unlocks the hold over Alara and lets them see her in all her glory.

Alara rises from the shadows, her white fur glowing in the streetlight. She bows to my parents, her deep green eyes holding their gaze. My parents stand frozen, awe and recognition dawning on their faces as they see her for all she is and what she is capable of. I launch into Mum and Dad's arms, clinging to them tightly..

"We love you, Rae. We love you so much."

"I'll be back. I promise. I'll be back soon."

My voice cracks as I squeeze them tighter. With trembling fingers I reach beneath my dress and pull the Baslithe free. The crystal thrums against my palm, heat rolling through it like a live current.

Light erupts, searing the night. The air splits with a low roar as a vortex blooms behind us, trees bowing toward the pull. Wind tears at my hair, the ground trembling beneath our feet.

Zye steps forward to embrace my parents, his touch brief but meaningful. I turn back one final time, holding their gaze.

"I love you more." And with that, we step into the portal.

We arrive to find Athyria already breaking..

The skies above us, once endless and bright, are now choked with swirling clouds of black and gray, churning and writhing like a beast in agony. The sharp, acrid scent of smoke and ash stings my nostrils. Above, lightning rips through the roiling clouds, illuminating the destruction below in jagged flashes that reveal the devastation in eerie, fragmented light.

The sword at my side trembles, sending a shiver through the hilt. The Corestone's magic surges through it, through me, and I feel the pull. Like joy. It's home.

We land on the edge of The Academy. The sound of shouting and the clash of steel fills the air as Ember emerges from the chaos. She's dressed in dark armor, hair pulled back into two tight braids, eyes burning with an intensity that matches the storm overhead. I see her for what she is—a force unto herself.

She rushes to us and, without hesitation, pulls us into a fierce embrace. "You're here," she says, her voice thick with relief. "By the stars! You're really here."

"I'm so sorry. We did all we could," Ember continues. "They hit us fast. Hard. We had to pull the line back to protect as many as possible. Most of the wounded are safe inside, but…" Her voice tightens. "The villages near the ridge didn't stand a chance.

We got who we could out—families, elders, anyone who couldn't fight—but not all of them made it."

"Kail and Thane are holding the west wall. Puk and Eko have moved to the outer ridge trying to buy us time. They sent word you were back." She glances at Alara. "Your pack's on the flanks. They left the valley when the first ward buckled." Her voice hardens. "Their army's been hitting them for days. What's left is holding, but barely." She draws a rough breath. "The Terralyns not with the wounded are reinforcing the wards. If the Vaulturians get through that... well, it would've made one hell of a showdown against me."

Her mouth twitches, the faintest hint of a smile. "And now you three. Not that I need you."

Zye's mouth tilts into a dry smile. "I missed having you to boss me around."

"Missed you more," she fires back, pulling him into a quick, fierce hug. "Even in whatever that is you're wearing. You look ridiculous."

Zye chuckles softly, but his eyes remain sharp, scanning the battlefield beyond her shoulder. Ember turns to me, her expression softening further. "Gods, I missed you just as much. You on the other hand look incredible." She pulls me into a tight embrace, and I feel the damp warmth of a tear on my shoulder.

The yips of Kail and Thane cresting the hill break the moment. They crash into us like a freight train, mud streaking their faces, trailing down bare chests slick with rain and battle grime. They look like they clawed their way back from hell.

Zye grips Kail's shoulder, regret written across his face. "I wish we'd gotten back sooner."

"No time for what-ifs, boss. Let's do this."

Zye's eyes darken, his fury clear. He glances toward the Wolves assembling at the frontline, their howls echoing through the thickened air as the storm itself seems to pause. The wind dies, the distant rumble of thunder fades, and an eerie stillness takes hold.

Kail's gaze flicks to the sword in my hand, its glow alive under the clouds. "Oh, someone's daggers got an upgrade," he muses with a wink, throwing an arm around my shoulders and squeezing me in. "Welcome home, Stingray."

Three simple words that ignite something in me I didn't expect. I'm home.

Zye steps forward. "Today, we release these lands from the shadows of the past and the clutches of Vaulturia. We have trained for this. Fought for this. Bled for this. And now, our time has come and so, too, has theirs. We stand against a force that outnumbers us, but they underestimate us. They always have. When they attacked us as kids, they thought fear, panic, and terror would break us. They were wrong. Instead, they forged us. They didn't destroy us, they united us. They empowered us. Every scar they gave us only made us stronger. We are not weak. We are warriors. Centuries ago, a battle was fought on these very grounds. They fought for something greater than power. They fought for protection. They fought so we could see today. Now, it's our time to step onto that battlefield so everyone out there can see a much brighter tomorrow. So, I guess there's only one thing left to do."

His hands clench into fists at his sides, the storm's winds tugging at his soaked hair. "Let's honor the wings, the wolves, and the Athyrian warriors. Let's end them."

The storm roars in response, lightning flashing across the sky as rain begins to hammer the earth and every part of me ignites with the fury of his resolve.

Kail and Thane yip as they begin to shift but this time, they don't rush the transformation. They embrace it, savor it. Muscles elongate, forms rippling with raw power as each cell surrenders to the primal essence of the wolves within. Fur sprouts as their human features melt away until they stand tall and ferocious.

Thane lets out a low, guttural growl that ripples through the charged air, sending chills racing down my spine. Then, as one, they throw their heads back and release a howl that is immediately answered from every flank.

Ember steps forward, fiery eyes now streaked with a silver glint. She leaps toward Zye, pulling him into a brief, fierce embrace before stepping back. "We go on your word." She gives him a single, resolute nod and then, like a rogue spark in the wind, she is gone.

Zye turns to me, his torn shirt clinging to his frame, blood smeared across fabric and skin. His hand closes over my wrist, grip firm but steadying, his throat works hard to swallow.

"Rae, you get on Alara's back, and you don't leave her. You don't dismount. You don't let go. And when it comes to it, you use that sword and fight with everything you've got." His voice softens, but his gaze holds me. "I promised your parents I'd keep you safe, and I intend to keep that promise."

Alara releases a powerful, soul-stirring growl, the sound ripping through the storm-laden air, reverberating off the mountains. It's met by a chorus of howls with Aric, Soraya, and the Wolves answering the call.

I force a smile to mask the turmoil inside me. I nod and turn away. But I don't make it a step before his grip tightens, pulling me back.

The motion is swift and deliberate. Our eyes meet as his other hand moves to my cheek, fingers rough as they trace the curve of my face. His thumb sweeps my cheekbone and then his lips are on mine, a moment pulled from the brink. A moment that shouldn't exist here, shouldn't exist now, but does, because it has to. Because this might be the last.

The storm howls, wind tearing through the battlefield as Zye turns to Alara, his fingers still tangled in mine. "If this starts to go bad, you go. You get her out of here. To her home. To safety."

Alara lowers her head, her green eyes flashing, understanding.

His eyes find mine again. His grip doesn't loosen. "And you don't come back."

"No!" The word tears from me as I slam my palm against his chest, shoving him back. "Don't you dare make this a goodbye. I'm here to fight with you, not watch you throw yourself at the dark alone. There was is no way you get to do that," I gesture to my lips, "say all of that, and then say that. I promised to fight with you, and I intend to keep that promise!"

He exhales sharply, jaw clenching. "I mean it, damn it. This is a battle you should never have been dragged into, Rae. That's my burden to wear. Not yours."

His voice wavers, betraying the fear he's trying to hide, before he kisses me again, this time it's hard and desperate. When he pulls back, his forehead rests against mine, breath hot, uneven, trembling.

"And yet, here I am." I grit my teeth. "You heard her. You were there. Dammit, I've got this thing now." I shove the hilt of the sword against his chest, my hand trembling but resolute. "So stop your noble high-horse shit and let's win this damn thing."

I press my palm to his face, thumb brushing along his jaw. His hands cup my cheeks; a thousand unspoken emotions flash across his face. He leans down, pressing a kiss to my forehead.

"Be safe, please."

Then, before I can respond, he turns and is gone.

I stand, staring at the space where he stood. Alara nudges me with her nose, eyes blazing with a fire I've never seen before.

"You can rekindle your love triangle when this is done. Get your armor on. We have a war to win."

I meet her gaze, fire in my own eyes. *"And if you even think about considering his command—"*

"I answer only to you."

I'm changed in a heartbeat. The daggers slip into their sheaths at my ribs; the sword settles heavy across my back. Magic hums through the leather of my armor, reverberating through bone. My hands tremble but I force them to still, drawing in a deep, shaky breath. The sword pulses in response.

I swing onto Alara's back. She doesn't hesitate before bolting to the front line where Aric and Soraya wait. Kail and Thane are already beside them, their forms rigid with tension. Around them, the wolves pace, restless, ready. Between them are all the people from The Academy. They look too young to be here, we all do, and that thought alone ignites a roaring fire in my veins.

"Simmer, Rae, we will protect them. As many of them as possible."

As she speaks, I turn my attention toward the Vaulturian fighters. We are grossly outnumbered. I curse under my breath.

"They may be many, but each one stands alone. Today, we hunt as a pack."

The words settle like a charge in my blood. I press a hand to Alara's back, feeling her power rise up my palm. She stands strong and my fear burns clean.

"Alara, I need to go."

"Rae, it's going—"

"No. I mean, I can't fight from here." I point to a nearby peak. *"I can't do this from your back. Not the way I need to. Take me to that ridge. From there, I can reach them all."*

"I will not leave you."

"You're going to have to. Trust me."

She hesitates for a beat, then a growl shakes the air. She pivots, body turning in a seamless motion as we race toward the peak.

Rain lashes against us, sharp as needles, wind screaming in my ears. I cling to her, burying my face in her sodden fur as her powerful strides eat the distance.

"This is reckless."

"Yep, maybe," I admit, swiping wet strands of hair from my face. *"But it might be our only chance."*

The storm claws at us as we climb higher. *"Drop me here,"* I say, sliding off her back. *"I'll climb the last stretch. You return to the others."*

"The second I sense trouble—"

"You'll be back," I finish. *"I know."* I meet her eyes, resting my forehead against hers. *"Thank you."*

She releases a puff of air that swirls around me, hiding her departure. I wipe a stray tear from my cheek and whisper, *"Be safe."*

When I look down, my signet pulses with a new, almost feral energy. I feel it deep in my core—a wild, untamable force flowing through me. It's her. The bond is alive, deeper than I ever imagined. The sword hums as though recognizing the shift. The weight of it feels right, a natural extension of the power coursing my veins.

I move farther up the peak, the rock slick with rain. From the summit, the battle spreads below in stark clarity. I thought I was ready. But as the storm rages around me and the battle unfurls below, I realize with chilling certainty: nothing could have prepared me for this. The chaos is overwhelming. I try to wield my power, but there's too much at once. The lines blur into a frenzy of violence. Panic sets in.

Wolves, winged Vaulturians, blades and bursts of magic collide in a roiling storm of motion.

I scramble down the rocky ledge for a clearer view. My gaze locks onto Ember, caught in a fierce fight with several men. She moves like a deadly flame but she's outnumbered. Kail fights beside her, a whirlwind of fury, but even he falters under the press.

I lurch forward, desperate to help.

"NO!"

Alara's voice slams into me like a physical blow. I slip, catch myself, glance back as her roar splits the air.

Above, shadows darken the sky. The wings have arrived.

Their massive figures descend as the Vaulturians retaliate with a barrage of fireballs, but they bank effortlessly, avoiding the assault. One dives, a blur of power and grace, and rips through the enemy ranks with merciless precision. It's Zye. His talons slash through armor and enemy lines as he lands beside Ember and Kail, immediately shifting, sword drawn. His movements are lethal, careening through their forces, leaving nothing but carnage in his wake.

An earth-shaking roar jolts me back to the present, rocking the mountain and the grounds below. It was enough to make everyone brace and clearly divide the forces. It is Alara. And it is just enough.

This is my chance. Possibly my only.

I close my eyes, grounding myself, pulling power from deep within. The storm is no longer raging. It's waiting. It moves with me. For me. When I unleash it, the world responds. Obsidian energy ripples outward. The Wind is a raging tempest that cleaves through the enemy lines, barreling the oncoming

Vaulturians back. Kail, Thane and their forces advance, but just as quickly, the Vaulturians rise and re-mount. Rain becomes a weapon, twisting into a monstrous wave that crashes through the Vaulturian lines, scattering them.

It's working, but the cost is brutal. My arms tremble at the power required to be effective.

"Manage your Power, Rae," Alara warns.

I glance down as more Vaulturians are already advancing, undeterred. Thane and Aric are locked in battle, Aric's side slick with blood. I anchor to the earth, ignoring the warnings, and call the storm down like a weapon. Lightning splits the sky, each bolt striking with surgical fury, vaporising winged Vaulturians and turning soldiers to ash.

"Manage. Your. Power," Alara growls.

Before I can respond, a blinding light catches my attention and, through a hole in the world, Puk and Eko arrive, their golden armor blazing. Even in a war, they are extra, and I love them even more for it.

My gaze shifts back to the battlefield, to Zye. He's running. Towards Alara. A riderless Alara. He knows I defied his command. "Sorry, it was the only way," I whisper, hoping it might carry in the wind down to him.

Movement flashes on a far ridge, a lone figure, high above the battlefield, a blackened staff raised like a conductor's baton. Every sweep of his arm sends waves of Vaulturians flooding forward, as if he's pulling them from the shadows themselves. I brace, instinct surging, but the distance is too great. My power won't reach him. Not without cost. Or precision.

My attention snaps back to Alara as she slams into a creature unlike I have ever seen before. Four legs but wrong in every way, shoulders too broad, spine hunched like a broken ridge. Patches of matted fur cling to skin stretched over jutting bone, tufts torn and filthy. Its head is a brutal mash of muzzle and malformed jaw, teeth like broken knives jutting at uneven angles. I know immediately, this is something created by the Vaulturians. Created to kill.

Alara is larger but overwhelmed, being attacked from both sides as one climbs onto her back. "ALARA!" I scream it out loud this time.

"Fight! You have to fight!"

Zye and Thane rush to her aid as Soraya's roar shakes the earth. I look up to see the man with the staff still orchestrating the chaos below. I look down to see Alara on her hind legs, surrounded by the bodies of the fallen. She is okay. For now.

"Are you hurt?"

"I'll be fine."

"Alara, there is a man. I can see him. I can get—"

"Rae, you do not leave that spot. You DO NOT!"

"He's on that peak to your left."

Alara's head lifts, locking onto the distant peak where the figure stands, wreathed in smoke and power, the staff raised. She races.

"No, Alara!"

My protest is swallowed by the storm as Alara charges toward the figure, she doesn't hesitate, doesn't look back. She leaps full-force, toward the distant peak, magic erupts as she collides with the figure, a clash of claw and darkness, their silhouettes barely visible through the storm.

Zye transforms mid-stride, his hawk form bursting into the sky like a missile, wings slashing through rain and smoke as he dives after her. I have seconds. One breath. One tether.

I slam my hands into the earth and drag the storm through me like a current. The lightning above answers, holding tight, waiting for release. Three... two... Now.

I lift my arms, and the skies rupture. Rain rips downward, forming a torrent that crashes through the battlefield like a tidal wave, swallowing Vaulturian soldiers in its path. Magic rips through the air, tearing into the ground. The ones left standing are dragged beneath the weight of it, their shrieks lost to the roar.

My vision blurs, the toll of the last blast drained me almost entirely. But after a few deep breaths Alara comes into focus, bloodied but upright, Zye at her side. Relief breaks through me so sharply it's almost pain. For the first time since we landed, my chest eases. They're safe.

But I am not.

Stone tears skin as my face hits the ground, grit grinding into my cheek. A force drives between my shoulder blades, pinning me flat.

"Well, well, well…" A woman's voice hisses in a serpentine manner, her breath hot against my ear. "Look who it is."

Her knee presses harder into my back. "Haven't you just saved the day for the good guys? All that new-found power put on quite the show," she mocks. "But now, look at you. Weak and alone. You saved them, but who's going to save you, Rae?" she challenges as she drives her knee deeper and I wince.

"Who…" My mouth is so dry I can barely speak. "Who are you?" I grit out.

"Has my high and mighty baby brother not talked about me?" She laughs.

My blood drains from my body.

"*Lyria.*"

Panic surges through me, but I force it down. I need to think, but Lyria's grip only tightens.

"Zye said—" Her knee drives hard into my neck. "You were—"

"Dead?" She finishes my sentence with a cruel laugh. "He wouldn't know. He never cared to find out. He ran and never turned back.

"He tri—"

"Don't you dare defend him. He didn't try. He didn't come for us. Not once!"

"Eight. He was eight," I cough out, the pressure suffocating.

"Was." She spits the word out like its poison. "He was then, but not now. Not for a long time. I was a kid, too, and I fought for our family. For years, I watched our parents cry for him, the boy who didn't fight, the one who ran. They were mad at me for not listening. For not staying to protect him. They didn't see that I risked everything to protect them."

"Alara."

Her name tears through my mind, not as a whisper but a desperate cry through the bond. I reach for her, across the storm, across the distance, feel the pulse of her magic like a fading heartbeat.

I turn my head, straining to see, but the downpour blinds me, turning the world into fractured silver and shadow.

My lips part. I breathe her name again, a silent scream lost in the chaos. Please. Let her be alive.

"The Vaulturians took us in, but they didn't treat me like the rest. They saw me. They saw me for what I was. They saw what I was capable of. They saw my loyalty." She grinds her knee down harder and I cry out in pain.

"Lord Erian raised me like his own. My parents were weak. Like Zye." Another force of pressure through her knee "They died of a broken heart. A broken heart he could have healed. Gods I tried, but I was never enough. When Lord Erian became too ill and weak to lead, I knew it was my calling. I knew I had to finish what he started."

She peels me off the ground with brutal force and throws me against a tree. The impact knocks the air from my lungs and pain screams through my body.

"You," I sneer. "This whole time, it has been you against your brother."

"No, Rae. Against you."

Lyria's cold laughter echoes off the mountain as she moves closer. "It's your blood that must spill to cement my rule," she hisses.

The weight of her words sinks in, but beneath it, something stirs within me. Power. I can feel it returning. Every second counts. *Patience, Rae.*

"*Alara.*" I push harder through the bond. Silence.

No answer. No flicker. Just the rain, which pounds down on us, like shards of glass tearing through the skies. I close my eyes, reaching deeper, past the noise, past the fear. "Please be okay."

"This cursed blood of mine will not spill for you. Not today. Not ever." I grit out

A flash of satisfaction flares in her eyes and then she strikes. Power bursts from her palm, but I draw the sword just in time, the force of it rattling through my arms. I twist, thrusting upward, forcing her to spring back or lose a hand.

She stumbles a step, surprise flickering in her gaze but it's gone in an instant, replaced by that cold, razor smile.

I lunge, driving her back with a flurry of strikes. The sword hums in my grip, magic coiling up my arm like a living thing. Each swing is sharper, faster, guided by the Corestone. Steel meets steel, the clash sparking in the rain. Each strike aimed with everything I have left. But Lyria moves like smoke, dodging, twisting, parrying each blow. Her eyes gleam with cold amusement, she's already decided this isn't a fight, it's a lesson.

My arms ache.

My body burns.

Her snarl widens as she presses me harder. She knows I'm exhausted. And she's waiting for it. I need to buy time, so I use everything I have to push her back. I force her to yield ground, stepping in hard, turning each strike into a shove meant to drive her toward the drop instead of me.

The amusement in her face is gone now. Then, with merciless precision, she strikes. Each blow lands like a battering ram, driving me back toward the cliff's edge.

The shock of her strength shudders down my arm. I shove back, teeth gritted, our swords screaming as they slide apart. I pivot low, slashing for her thigh, but she's already moving, coming around behind me with impossible speed.

"Alara."

A sharp crack of pain explodes across my back as she lands a blow with the hilt, the force sending me stumbling sideways. I catch myself, spin, and bring the sword up just in time to deflect a killing strike. Sparks shower between us.

She's faster now, relentless, each blow heavier, sharper, driving my guard toward collapse. My arms burn, the muscles in my shoulders locking tight, every breath a rasp. I keep swinging, forcing her back a step, even as the slick stone shifts under my boots, sliding me closer to the cliff's edge.

Her eyes narrow. She feels it. Smiles. And drives harder. One, two, three strikes, each impact like a hammer on the bones of my arms. The Corestone flares. White-hot light rips through the sword, searing up my arms, bursting from the etched steel in jagged arcs that split the air. Power floods me in a rush so violent it feels alive, hungry. The blade's glow blazes brighter than lightning, the force whipping the wind into a spiraling vortex that howls around us.

Lyria braces, but the surge slams into her chest like a physical wall, hurling her back but the sheer force of driving the power forward buckles my stance, my boots skid on the slick stone, the ground giving way beneath my heels.

I'm in free fall.

My fingers claw at empty air as my body twists midair, I'm weightless and helpless with the Corestone sword gripped tight in my hand. The hilt digs into my palm, carving a line of fire through my palm, even that isn't enough to save me now. *I failed you, I'm sorry.*

The sky wheels above me, torn open by lightning as the cliff drops away. Wind tears at my body as the earth drags me down. I have one hope left.

I press the words into the storm, my grip locking around the sword.

Please. Not yet. Not until they're safe. Not until I finish what I need to do. It isn't prayer. It's a vow.

Then a shadow splits the storm.

Talons.

His hawk form dives hard, wings cutting the sky apart as he barrels toward me. His claws catch me with brutal precision, slamming tight around my waist. The jolt knocks the air from my lungs, but I'm no longer falling, I'm flying. Zye's eyes lock on mine, burning gold, wild and sharp. The storm howls around us, brutal and blind, but his wings power through it, cutting the air in hard, controlled beats.

I glance down, rock and ruin falling away beneath us, as he banks toward the ridge. Alara is there, bloodied but standing, her white coat streaked with mud and ash. She doesn't move, just watches as we close in.

Zye descends fast and shifts faster. One second hawk, the next, he's human, soaked and heaving as he lands hard and pulls me into his arms. "Rae," he breathes. His hands are everywhere, checking, steadying, smoothing back my wet hair as his eyes rake over me.

"I'm good. I'm okay," I force out, though every word is a struggle. My legs buckle when I try to stand. "Help me."

Without hesitation, he pulls me upright, bracing my weight against his chest.

"Where is she?" I ask.

Alara steps closer, her shadow swallowing mine. Her eyes pin me and the words rip out before I can stop them. *"I thought you were—"*

Her growl cuts me off vibrating through my chest. *"I heard you, I felt every fracture of your fear. But something pressed against the bond, dulling it. I got us here as soon as I felt it. They're playing with new magic."*

She pauses, the rumble in her chest simmering. *"Without our bond, we should be weaker."* Her gaze flicks to the sword burning in my hand, the Corestone's light spilling between us. *"But with that... she won't be able to sever it completely."*

At that, Alara pauses, her eyes burn. *"What you're about to reveal will break him."*

I tighten my grip on the sword as I look from her to Zye, but there is no time to deliver this gently.

"I'm sorry, Zye."

"Sorry? Why are you so-"

"Not for what I did, but what she did, and what I have to do."

Alara lowers her head until her eyes burn level with mine, the Corestone's light flaring between us, threads of power winding into her massive frame. She bares her teeth, a sound like thunder rolling low in her chest. *"That is a kill I won't let you wear. It will destroy you both."*

Her heartbeat drums against mine, steadying my hands and my heart rate until I am in time with her. I reach for her without hesitation, burying my fingers in the thick fur at her jaw as Zye stiffens at my side.

"Rae," he demands. "Rae, what is going on?"

I meet his eyes, throat raw, no more strength left to soften it. "It's not him, Zye. It's her. It's Lyria."

"Lyria?" He stumbles back, his face draining of color. His eyes flare with disbelief, then rage. He stills. Blinks once, twice. Then his head shakes, a sharp, almost violent movement. "No. Don't say that. Don't—"

"She's alive," I rasp.

"That's impossible." His voice is hoarse. "I went to the village. I saw what was left. I—" He swallows hard, eyes flashing between me and some far-off memory. "I tried, Rae. I tried to knock down the doors of their damn castle to get them back." His jaw trembles, rage threading through the disbelief. "It isn't her."

A harrowing roar, laced with pain, erupts from the forest. Zye's head snaps toward the treeline. His gaze flickers between me and the forest, between the truth I've just given him and the loyalty that has defined him all his life.

"We need to move," I say, forcing strength into my voice. My legs threaten to buckle again, but Zye steadies me before I fall.

Alara lowers her head, her muzzle brushing my shoulder. *"Get on."*

My fingers fist into the thick fur at her neck, and with a desperate surge I haul myself onto her back. Her muscles bunch beneath me, pent-up power ready to tear the world apart. The Corestone thrums against my palm, answering her heartbeat as if the two are one.

Zye's jaw locks, his eyes burning, but he doesn't argue. He shifts with a snap of silver light, hawk wings unfurling wide enough to scatter the ash in the air. Then Alara bolts.

The forest blurs into streaks of stormlight and shadow as she carves a path through the trees, every stride shaking the earth. Branches whip past, snapping against her coat but never slowing her. I cling to her, pressed flat against her powerful frame,

A Vaulturian shadow darts out from the undergrowth, but Alara doesn't swerve, she doesn't so much as flinch, she tears straight through him in one motion. I lean tighter into her fur and feel the sword pulse under my grip.

The trees break as we explode into the ruins of a long-fallen kingdom, stone walls jutting like broken ribs, vines and ash draping them in decay. At its center is absolute chaos.

Puk is a blur of steel and defiance, his bright silks torn and bloodied as he spins, cutting down enemies with brutal grace. Eko fights at his back, shadow and blade moving as one, every strike clean, every Vaulturian that lunges at them falling in pieces.

And between them, Thane.

He's on his knees, shackled, blood pouring down his jaw.

Even broken, even bound, he radiates menace. His gaze is locked on the shadow striding through the smoke with all the patience of a predator who knows the kill is hers. Lyria.

Blood glistens down his jaw, his eyes burning feral as he rips a soldier apart with nothing but his hands.

Zye lands beside me, hawk form collapsing into human, his chest heaving. Alara plants her paws hard into the earth, teeth bared, every muscle in her frame straining to leap.

The battlefield stills for a breath as Zye locks eyes on his sister.

"Hello brother" Lyria sneers.

The fighting stops and from behind it all, I see Puk and Eko pull Thane into a portal and disappear.

"You were supposed to come for us." Her voice cuts through the air, sharp and full of venom. "You never came," she spits, stepping forward, her silhouette shaped in rage and sorrow. "And I'll never forgive you for it."

Before he can respond, a surge of power tears from her hand, a bolt of pure energy, fast and furious. It screams toward Zye, but he anticipates it, sliding beneath the strike and rising to one knee, flaring his hands as twin blasts of energy erupt from his palms instinctively, and he recoils almost immediately. And so does Lyria.

Lyria catches the first with her shield, the barrier rippling like shattered glass, and she releases an evil laugh. Zye's eyes are locked on her. Pain carved into every line of his face.

I barely register what happens next as I spin to where Kail and Ember have arrived in the forest behind me.

My heart lurches.

Ember gasps at the realization. The sudden motion draws the attention of Lyria and Zye.

Zye turns first, like he's been yanked on a tether. Lyria

follows, her expression is menacing. Her laughter rings out as she shifts her attention fully to me.

"Of course," she spits. "He rushed to save you. The pretty little distraction keeping his bed warm while the rest of us burn."

The air thickens around us, a static charge pulsing through the storm clouds overhead. Thunder cracks, low and furious, and I feel it hum through my bones, burning out the pain, steadying what's left of me.

Alara meets my eyes. *"Not yet, Rae. Not yet."*

"I can help."

"And when the time comes you will. We won't allow her the upper hand."

Kail shifts with a ripple of muscle and fur, his massive frame hitting the ground. The earth trembles under his weight as he moves to flank Zye, teeth bared, eyes bright with feral fire.

Alara growls, low and guttural, as she steps forward and suddenly a line of Vaulturian fighters and beasts appear out of the forest from behind Lyria. "Let's see how tough your dogs are now the sides are even."

Then the treeline ruptures. Vaulturian fighters spill from the shadows, armored and twisted, beasts snarling at their sides. Lyria stands tall, her dark hair plastered to her face by the storm, her eyes gleaming like a predator scenting blood.

"Kill the white one," she commands. "Break the bond, and the girl dies with it."

The words lance through me like a blade. My heart seizes. Alara only snarls louder, defiant, pressing forward with her head high. The Vaulturians surge.

Kail launches first, a streak of shadow against the flood. He collides with a beast twice his size, his jaws snapping bone, his claws raking deep, tearing through the first wave, until a fighter spears him from the side.

"No—" My scream tears raw from my throat as steel flashes and plunges into Kail's flank.

His roar ricochets through the trees. Blood sprays hot across the mud, and he crumples under the weight of the strike.

The world narrows, my vision burning white. Alara bellows, her rage echoing through the bond, she wheels toward me, eyes flashing with fury and promise both. *"Stay behind me. No matter what."*

But my hands are already tightening around the hilt of the sword, the Corestone burning in my veins, demanding, screaming, to answer.

Kail's human again as blood pools around him, soaking into the mud. Deep gashes crisscross his torso, and his chest barely rises.

The scream that rips from Ember's throat is sickening. Fire erupts from her hands, roaring toward the Vaulturians. They scatter, but not quickly enough. Flames devour armor, weapons, and flesh. Lyria throws up a shield, her teeth bared, but Ember's attack is pure rage as she advances forward.

In one fluid motion, Ember pulls a flaming sword from her back. She swings wide, the blade cutting through anyone still standing. Her movements are wild, vengeful. There is nothing but flames and hate in her vision.

"I will end you!" she roars again, charging at Lyria.

Ember lands a brutal strike that knocks Lyria's sword from her grasp. Lyria counters immediately, summoning a shard of white light and hurling it straight at Ember. The shard lodges deep in her side. Ember doesn't falter. Gritting her teeth, she yanks it free with a pained cry, blood dripping from the jagged edges.

She doesn't stop. Using the bloodied shard, she cuts down two Vaulturians in a single, merciless motion.

Zye is a blur in the chaos, overcome by enemies, his movements precise, lethal, Alara and Aric race to his side, picking them off like fleas.

Out of nowhere, Puk and Eko reappear beside me, they take one look and draw their swords, diving back into the fray without a word.

Electricity shifts through the clouds, igniting a searing pulse of power that explodes from my chest, radiating through every fiber of my being. It pours down my arm and into the hilt of the sword, the blade hums, its edge glowing fiercely, pulsing with the magic that now surges through me.

"Not yet," Alara warns. Pain burns through my body. The clouds above churn, electricity snapping between them almost impatiently.

Lyria stumbles. Her footwork slows, the toll of her magic finally catching her. But her eyes lock on mine. Malice radiates from her. She breaks from the fight, her steps slow and deliberate, power gathering at her fingertips.

Alara lunges, her jaws snapping shut on the back of my leathers, hurling me sideways with terrifying force. The blast hits where I stood not a second earlier, leaving a scorched crater behind.

Another blast comes, faster, harder, and Zye intercepts it, throwing up a wall of wind. It holds, but just barely. The impact rocks him, dragging him to one knee, his arms trembling under the weight of it.

Lyria screams out in frustration as her composure shatters. Rage spills from her as she prepares to strike again.

In that split second, I see the exhaustion in Zye's shoulders, the strain in Alara's form. The wolves, bloodied and panting. Ember somewhere behind me, still standing, but barely and then Kail, his body lifeless in the grass and that's all it takes.

The sky roils above us, a vortex of shadow and light. Lightning fractures the clouds, wild and volatile, tearing down in jagged forks that crackle with warning. But it's not just in the sky. It's in me.

I grip the hilt of the sword tighter. And that's when the blade responds, its pulse syncing to mine, building until it rings with the storm's fury. I raise it high, toward the clouds and they split wide open. A bolt of lightning, pure and blinding, strikes the sword's tip. The force rips through me, casting a light so fierce it scorches the battlefield. The air quakes. Time slows.

Thunder cracks open the heavens. Purple and white light arcs across the field, snapping through the Vaulturian ranks with precision. Some vaporize where they stand. Others turn and run, screaming as the earth splits beneath them.

Lyria's head snaps toward me, eyes wide with rage. "I will kill you!" she shrieks as she surges forward, all fury and flame.

But she never reaches me.

Aric bursts from the wreckage, slamming into her with the weight of a landslide. Her body is thrown like a ragdoll, straight toward Alara.

She meets Lyria mid-air, a strike with so much force I collapse to the ground and cover my head. I don't know if it's seconds or minutes, but eventually I look up to see Ember kneeling beside Kail, struggling to drag him back, her trembling arms unable to lift him and too weak to teleport them both.

Tears stream down her cheeks as she presses her forehead to his.

"You do not get to die on me. Not today. Fight, dammit. Fight."

Kail lifts a trembling hand, fingers brushing her face.

Ember sobs, her forehead pressing against his chest, her shoulders shaking with grief. His fingers tangle in her hair.

Puk and Eko appear beside her. "Ember," Puk says. "We'll take him. We'll get him to the Healer."

They shield Kail's body with theirs just as a portal crackles to life, pulling Kail through it with brutal force. His scream of pain rips through the air, raw and gut-wrenching, a sound that claws at my chest. I gasp, the sheer agony in his voice is one I'll never forget.

"It's done, Rae. It's over," Alara says.

A soft caress of air swirls around my waist, wrapping me in an unexpected tenderness, circling me with a warmth that steadies the tremor in my limbs. I glance up—Zye's eyes lock on mine, the storm in them quieted just enough for a flicker of tenderness to break through. He doesn't speak, but the wind does for him.

Alara steps closer, a fresh gash scoring across her shoulder where blood still runs. One ear is torn, her muzzle dark with the spray of someone else's fight. But her eyes hold mine as she presses her head to me, my hands curl into her blood-warm fur and the dam inside me breaks. I sob into her neck.

"You did it," Alara murmurs. And I sink further into her embrace.

Ember limps toward us, each step dragging with exhaustion. Her armor, once polished and vibrant, is now dented and scorched, the metal blackened and cracked. Blood seeps through the rents in the plating as she attempts to apply pressure to the gash in her abdomen. Her hair, once tightly bound, is loose now, cascading in wild, tangled waves around her shoulders. The fiery red that always seemed to smolder with life is gone, replaced by black. She looks like a burnt out wick.

When she reaches me, she uses her spare arm to wrap me in an embrace charged with everything that just unfolded—adrenaline, grief, relief.

"I need to get to Kail," she whispers, her voice full of emotion. "But you did it, Rae. You saved it. All of it. And hopefully, all of us." She winces, readjusting the pressure on her wound.

She pulls back, her eyes locking onto mine. "He's going to need you, Rae. Now more than ever." She gives my shoulder a squeeze before she turns and limps toward where Puk and Eko have re-appeared, the portal hums once more.

Zye sits alone on a jagged rock, head bowed, fingers pressed against his temples. He doesn't move, doesn't even seem to breathe. His hollow stare is fixed on Lyria. The sister he mourned for almost a decade. The sister he lost again today.

Puk and Eko wave frantically. "We need to go! Now! There are critically wounded people who walk among us!" Puk shouts, his voice sharp. "Now is not the time to die, Rae. Not after all of that. *Choppity-chop*, people!"

The portal swirls as Aric strides toward it, Alara close behind. She pauses; her emerald eyes meet mine, knowingly.

"You go. Ask them to keep it open for a few more minutes."

She hesitates but nods. A soft puff of air swirls from her nostrils, brushing against Zye like a fleeting caress. He looks up, acknowledging her with the faintest broken smile. Then she steps into the portal and disappears.

I cross the broken ground in silence and lower myself onto the stone beside him. He doesn't look at me but his hand finds mine, fingers cold and trembling.

His pain is raw and unfiltered, stripped of pride, stripped of control, just sorrow. And when the tears finally dry, when the shaking stills, I shift closer, wrapping my arms around him and pulling him to me. His head finds the curve of my shoulder and I press my lips to his hair. "Let's go home."

We step out of the portal to where the others wait at the edge of The Academy walls, which show faint traces of the battle. Scorch marks streak the stone near the eastern gate, dark smudges interrupting the clean lines. A thin crack splinters across the base of a column, and small fragments of chipped stone are scattered along the courtyard's edge. An axe is lodged in the wall by the main entrance. Above, one of the windows is missing a pane.

A rush of emotion washes over me as the Healer and Horo race toward us, their faces etched with urgency. In their wake are a flock of Terralyns at the ready.

"Oh, I knew it. I knew you could do it, all of you!" the Healer's voice rings out. Her relief is undeniable and she wastes no time.

"Come, come," she urges. Assessing us with a practiced eye, she immediately begins allocating fairies based on the severity of our injuries, her movements swift and decisive.

The Academy grounds are coming alive as people start to seep out of the building, their eyes darting between us. Whispers ripple through the crowd, rising into a crescendo of murmured questions and muted cheers. A few clap hesitantly, unsure yet if celebration or mourning is appropriate.

The Healer floats to Alara, resting a gentle hand on her blood-soaked fur. "Let's get you inside, Rae. Alara, you need to rest. I'll send Horo to tend to you; he has something that will dull the pain. For now, lie down. She's in good hands."

She turns to Zye, her tone softening. "Can you rift walk?"

Zye nods, though his exhaustion is evident in his unsteady stance. "I think so, yes."

"Follow me. You're going to need some taking care of, too."

She takes my hand. "This will hurt," she says, matter-of-factly, and before I can brace myself, the world twists.

We reappear in the makeshift wards. Pain flares through me, and I bite down on my lip to stifle a scream.

"You're going to be okay," she says, holding a small glass jar to my lips. "Here, sip this." A single drop of a blue liquid touches my tongue; its foul taste makes me gag, but the effect is immediate.

"I need to check on Kail. I'll come back for you in a second," the Healer says, her hand lingering briefly on my cheek before disappearing into the chaos. I hear a cry, raw and broken, but I can't tell who it belongs to.

Zye stumbles into the hallway a second later, pale and trembling. One of the Terralyns catches him before he collapses, slinging his arm over their shoulder to guide him to a bed.

Amid the flurry of healers and Terralyns, my eyes land on a familiar figure—Thane. He's propped against a cot, his torso tightly bound in bloodied bandages. A smaller one wraps around his head, blood seeping through the edges. He manages a faint, crooked smile.

"Rae." His voice is hoarse but steady. "You sure put on one hell of a show today."

"Thane!" I say with a breath of relief. "I thought you were—" I can't bring myself to finish the sentence.

"For a hot minute, so did I," he cuts in with a weak chuckle, grimacing as it jostles his wounds.

The Healer is back at my side, her hands hovering over me, glowing faintly as she assesses my injuries. Her brow furrows with concentration as she works. "Superficial cuts, broken arm, plenty of bruising," she lists clinically. "And possibly a couple of ribs fractured." She smiles brightly. "The good news is, you'll live."

"Kail. How is Kail?"

"Alive. Alive for now."

She presses a small vial into my good hand, the yellow liquid swirling ominously inside. "Sip this. It'll take the edge off."

I eye the concoction warily. "Is that optional?"

"Nope," she replies, already moving to the end of the bed.

Resigned, I pinch my nose, tilt my head back, and gulp it down in one go. It burns like fire, and I gag; pain jolts through my ribs, folding me over.

"Definitely broken ribs. Rest now. Your human-ness might mean you won't heal as quickly as the others, so you're on lockdown until you do, do you hear me?"

My tongue feels heavy, my words slurring as the potion takes hold. "Yis. Izz Alara n Zi ggooing t'b okay?"

"Yes, dear, yes," she whispers as the world slips away.

\#

When I wake, I'm in another room of The Academy. The walls are stone and timber, worn and familiar, and the high ceilings arch overhead like the ribs of a cathedral. Light spills in through tall windows. Alara lies curled at the foot of my bed. As I stir, she rises, her movements steady and careful, an unusual stiffness in her limbs.

"Nice of you to rejoin us in the land of the living, Rae."

I stretch like a cat in the sun. The muscles across my back argue in defiance at the movement. *"How long was I out?"*

"Three days," she replies. *"The Healer moved you here yesterday when your arm finally healed. This was the only room big enough for the both of us."*

The faint sunlight filtering through the window catches on her fur or the several missing patches of it. *"How are you feeling? You don't look great."*

"Let me fetch you a mirror," she quips, earning a small laugh from me. *"Stiff, but improving. I'll make a full recovery."*

"Thank you, Alara," I say quietly. *"For everything. You saved my life and risked yours more than once."*

"As did you," she counters.

I hesitate. *"And Zye?"*

"Still upset. You defied his orders… twice."

I wince. *"Eek."*

"Calm your racing heart, young one," she reassures me. *"He'll be here soon. He's been by your side for two days straight; he only just left to check on Kail."* Her knowing glance makes my cheeks burn.

"I'll get the Healer," Alara adds, moving to the door. She pushes it open with a soft growl that shakes through the room, it was a little more force than strictly necessary.

As my eyes wander around the room, I notice a table beside my bed piled high with flowers and a small mountain of chocolates. A glass of water sits precariously on the edge, and I reach for it just as the doors burst open.

Ember storms in, crossing the room in two strides before pulling me into a fierce hug. The sharpness of her embrace makes me wince, but I don't stop her and if she notices, she doesn't let on.

"Our Rae of sunshine!"

Alara huffs from the doorway as Ember waves her off with a dramatic flourish. "Oh, shoosh, you!" she teases. Turning back to me, she adds, "It's good to see you up. Well, almost up."

I gesture weakly at the glass of water. "Do you mind? My mouth feels like I've been eating sand."

Her puzzled look is almost comical as she hands me the glass. I drain it in one go. "Thanks," I mutter.

"Want anything to eat? I can grab—" Ember starts, but her words are cut short as the doors swing open again.

Thane limps in, leaning heavily on a crutch. Even through his black shirt, I can see thick bandages wrapped around his torso. He greets me with a lopsided grin, leaning down to kiss my forehead.

"How are you feeling?" I ask.

"Better. Much better. I'll have a nice big scar… another one," he lifts his shirt to reveal the bandaging, "but nothing that time and patience won't heal. And as I lack the latter, hopefully my wolf blood kicks in and it's not a long time!"

Horo enters next, the Healer at his side, followed by a small flock of Terralyns, including Nyxie. Horo heads straight to Alara, murmuring, while Nyxie and the Healer approach my bed.

Nyxie waves a hand over me, and I instantly feel cleaner, my hair falling smooth over my shoulder with the faint scent of florals. "There you go," she says, fussing with the sheets.

"Nyxie, I've missed you and your efficiency," I say with a smile. Her presence alone takes ten percent of my pain away.

The Healer places a cool hand on my shoulder. "You've been through a lot, Rae. You'll be sore for days, but you'll recover. I'd prefer you stay here another night, but I doubt you'll listen." Her eyes narrow onto Ember and Thane. "None of the others have. Although, you sustained injuries that most humans wouldn't survive. If you defy me, I'll force you to rest. Do you hear me?"

She says it with a smile, but the way she raises her brows tells me not to test it.

"I hear you."

Satisfied, she smiles and gently touches my cheek before vanishing in a puff of spice-scented smoke. When I look down, the glass of water beside my bed is miraculously full again. Nyxie hands it to me, and I drain it again.

"There she is," Horo says with a wide grin, clapping his hands together, his small frame filling the room with an energetic presence. His robes, too big for him, drag on the floor, and his bushy beard nearly sweeps the ground as he leans in to peer over the bed. "Your wolf's something else, kiddo." He waves a hand at Alara, who watches him from her corner, tail wagging lazily. "She's lucky to be here; you're lucky. She was in bad shape, Rae. Round-the-clock care, but she'll be back to full health soon. Just like you."

"*He's being dramatic,*" Alara interjects, the flick of her tail almost taking out a Terralyn.

I manage a faint smile. "Thank you, Horo. For looking after her and everyone else."

"No, Rae," he says as he steps closer. "It's us who should be thanking you." He exhales. "That was a lot. All of it. At once. A lot," he repeats, hands fidgeting at his sleeves before settling at his sides.

I swallow hard, his words pressing into places I didn't know were bruised. "Horo... my blood. The Vaulturians. What does it mean?"

He cuts me off gently. "Nothing. It means nothing. Causality contributes to but doesn't equal consequence. You don't need to worry about that. Not now. If you're worrying whether good or bad blood runs through you, you already know the answer to that, my dear. You need not question it."

There's a pause before he lowers his voice. "But as long as Vaulturian blood runs in your veins, their law stands. And inevitably, someone else is already vying to take—" He clears his throat, glancing toward the others. "Her place."

A shiver runs through me, but Horo presses on. "Horrible places breed horrible things, Rae. But the Vaulturians have a long road ahead. We did more damage than they ever expected, and this time, we have the upper hand. This wasn't just a battle won; it unearthed generations of lies, hidden truths, broken legacies and that fancy new sword of yours."

He straightens, his small frame unexpectedly commanding as he steps back, tone shifting. "And unfortunately for them, that's only the beginning. The Vaulturians are wounded, but wounded beasts are the most dangerous. So guard that sword, Rae. And be very careful who sees you carry it."

Then the storm breaks in his eyes, replaced by mischief. He grins as he leans in. "But none of that's your concern. Not tonight." He gestures to the side table with a tilt of his head. "Your only mission now is to eat those chocolates before the boys do. I tested one earlier, strictly for poison. You're welcome. And safe to consume," he adds with a hearty chuckle.

Horo gives a mock bow, then flashes a smile as he heads for the door, four Terralyns trailing behind him. "Alara, rest up. Be a good wolf." With that, he exits, his presence lingering even as he leaves.

I barely have time to process his words when I glance at Ember and Thane, deep in conversation by the armchair. "Kail," I ask, my voice tentative. "Is Kail... okay?"

They exchange a look, and Ember steps forward. "Kail is..."

The doors creak open, cutting her off. Zye steps in, supporting Kail, who, like Thane, leans heavily on a crutch. His face is bruised, a patchwork of yellow and black, and his veins spiderweb in sickly dark lines up his arm and neck. I can't hide the shock on my face.

"Poison," Kail says, simply. "The Healer thinks she countered it. Her so-called cure was twice as vile and three times more potent. That woman scares me but do not tell her I said that." He attempts a grin, wincing slightly as Zye helps him to the chair Ember pulls closer to my bedside.

Kail's eyes land on the chocolates instantly. "Oh, hello," he mutters, snatching a piece and tossing another to Thane before starting on a second.

"I thought chocolate was bad for dogs," I tease weakly, finding Zye at the edge of my bed, close enough that his arm brushes my knee.

"When your veins pump black, Rae," Kail quips, licking chocolate from his thumb, "what's a little more poison?"

The sharpness of my laughter pulls at my ribs, making me wince. Zye's hand rests on my knee, and even through the layers of sheets, his touch is electric. I swallow hard, suddenly aware of his proximity. His eyes hold mine, and the conversations around us fade into a distant hum.

"Hey," he says. It's all he has to say. I really hope the Healer can't feel what that single word did to my heart rate.

"Zye, I'm so sorry. About, um, everything. I mean, how are you? Oh, gods..." I squeeze my eyes shut.

I hear him smile. "I'm okay, Rae." He squeezes my knee, and I open my eyes.

"There's something I want to show you later, if you're up for it," he says.

"Does it involve cliff diving?" I ask, trying to lighten the moment and hide the sound of my heart pounding against my ribs.

His lips twitch into a slow, teasing smile. "Not this time."

"Anything that might get me knocked out for another week by the Healer? I just promised her I won't do anything reckless." My tone wavers between sarcasm and genuine concern.

Zye's eyebrow arches. "And since when have you followed a direct order?" He tilts his head, lifting a brow. "But no."

I hesitate, biting down on my lower lip. "I... I'm really sorry about that, but I knew it was... Wait." I hold up a hand, halting my own line of questioning as realization hits. "Is whatever this is punishment for defying your order?"

A wry smile tugs at the corner of his lips. "Orders. Plural. But no. But that will come."

"For now," he says, his tone rough and low, "let's get you settled back into your room and give you some time to rest. I'll check with Nyxie and come by this evening to pick you up."

"It's a date!" I blurt the words out before I can stop them. My eyes widen as I realize how loaded they are. "I mean, not a date, date. A da— I'll... I'll be there. I'm not expecting it to be a date. Just..." I throw my hands up to my face, trying to hide the heat rising in my cheeks.

"It's a date," he says, and I can feel his smile without needing to look up from my palms.

And then, just like that, he's gone.

"I've missed you, Nyxie," I whisper to the air. It's the first time I've been back in my room since my return to Athyria, and even in my haze, I can see her magical touch all over my room, fresh blooms everywhere and a steaming bath.

After a few hours of rest, a hot soak, and a chance to catch Nyxie up on everything that's unfolded, I find myself pacing, the thrum of my footsteps matching the frantic beat of my heart. I've never been on a date before. I run a hand through my hair and glance at the pile of outfits on my bed. I'm running out of options and patience.

It's not long before Nyxie arrives, a whirlwind of energy and enthusiasm. She doesn't waste a second, and before I know it I'm a canvas. She works on my hair, my makeup, and helps pick an outfit. She steps back, surveying her work with a critical eye. Her lips press together, then break into a satisfied grin.

"There," Nyxie announces, hands on her hips. "You look beautiful… and if he doesn't say it within the first thirty seconds, you turn around and shut the door in his face. Again."

"Where have you been my whole life?" I laugh, glancing into the mirror.

Just then, the Tome on my desk begins to hum softly, rocking side to side.

"I might leave you to that. Don't be long, Zye will be here any minute," she giggles, blowing me a kiss before fading into a soft puff of smoke.

I make my way to the Tome. I haven't heard from it in days, and after everything that's happened, I wasn't sure I ever would again. I reach for it carefully, sit on the bed, and lean back against the headboard as the pages begin to turn. I feel it, the change. It's different. I swallow hard as the words appear, one by one:

Because of you,
I am no longer held between realms, watching as the world
carried on without me, helpless to reach for what mattered most.
And you gave me what I have longed for most—Agatha.

Rae, tell them I was not a legend. Not a warrior. Just a man who
never once gave up hoping that the Corestone would one day
return home and bring peace to these lands.

If the winds shift, if the stars lean too close, you may still feel me,
a whisper steadying your grip when the weight grows too much.
You are not alone.

Wield the Corestone with mercy when you can, with fire when
you must. You don't need to be perfect. You just need to be true.

You are the storm we never dared to summon. Fight only for
what is worth protecting. And when the fear or doubt returns,
and it will, remember what it cost to get here.
Remember who it cost. And rise anyway.

For her. For me. For all of them.

—Ira

I clutch the Tome, my fingers pressing deep into the worn leather in an effort to steady the storm unraveling inside me. Before I can process it, there's a knock at the door. My heart skips.

"Coming!" I call, brushing my hands down my purple dress. Breathe, Rae. Breathe.

When I open the door, he's standing there. A crooked grin lifts at his mouth as he steps forward and holds out a flower, simple, a little wild, perfect. "You look beautiful," he says.

I can't help the smile that breaks across my face. Around us, wisps of Terralyn smoke swirl in bright, playful colors, their soft giggles echoing through the hallway.

My cheeks flush, warm all the way to my ears, and Zye sees it. His laugh is low and easy as he offers me his elbow.

"Shall we? Maybe somewhere a little more… private." He lifts a brow.

"You're answerable to the Healer if this goes badly," I murmur, trying not to grin.

"It won't," he says without missing a beat. "I promise. And unlike some… I keep mine."

I slide my arm through his, and together, we vanish.

#

We arrive on the roof of The Academy. I've been here before with Nyxie, but never like this. Tonight, Athyria glows.

I walk to the edge, taking it all in, then spin at what's been set up—a small, elegant dinner. Flowers. Fine linens. Candles floating in the evening breeze.

"This. All of this. It's…" I can't find the words.

"Rendered you speechless! Not what I was expecting." His voice is teasing.

I scoff but can't hide my smile. He gestures to the sky, his voice softer now.

"This is one of my favourite places to come and think. Or find peace and quiet. But tonight...it's also the perfect vantage for a once-in-a-decade meteor shower. It won't start for a few hours." He smiles. "Come, sit and eat."

We settle into the chairs. The soft clink of cutlery fills the space between us. Zye's eyes never leave mine as hours of endless conversation come easy.

The night is still as the stars begin to prick the dark.

He stands and moves to the edge and I can't help but notice the tight grip he has on the railing, his gaze locked somewhere on the horizon.

"I know what she meant to you, Zye."

He exhales sharply, squeezing the rail until it creaks. I cross the space before I can overthink it. He doesn't move, he doesn't so much as acknowledge me at first.

"I don't want to think of her as the villain," he finally says.

"I can't think of her as the villain. And I know she was, and what she did was wrong. Gods, she almost killed you." He slowly turns to face me and takes my hands. "But, Rae, before she was the villain, she was the victim."

He looks back to the forest that is now a sea of black. "What if I could've stopped it, Rae?" he asks quietly. "What if I could've saved her?"

"You did everything you could. You don't get to shoulder that burden," I whisper. "But I know you. And I know you'll do it anyway."

His lips part like he wants to argue, but no words come. Instead, he lifts his gaze to the stars.

"The night of the battle, everything changed. Not just below. Up there too." He points skyward, tracing shapes with a finger. "The Cup burned brighter than I've ever seen it, it was almost overflowing. And the Wolf stretched higher, standing guard."

He points beyond the Milky band. "And there…there was my family. Three stars I've looked to every night since they were taken. And that night, they were gone. All of them. Wiped from the sky like they never existed."

His jaw clenches.

"It felt like losing them all over again." I find the dark patch he means, a hollow where the three stars he showed me that night at the cabin were.

Then, without warning, a burst of light erupts from the void. It arcs outward in a sweep of fire, the blaze shaping itself into wings that stretch wide across the night. Zye jerks, breath caught, eyes wide.

The wings flare once, scattering into the first meteor that tears across the heavens, silver fire trailing. Then another. And another. Until the whole sky is alight, meteors raining in a cascade born from the place he thought was empty.

He holds my hand as I lean closer. "They didn't abandon you, Zye. They grew their wings and so did you. You're not the boy searching for their light anymore. You're it."

He turns to me, slowly, his lips brushing mine in a kiss that's soft, careful and then it deepens. Everything we've survived, everything we still don't have words for, pours into it. It speaks of redemption. Of second chances. Of things broken and still somehow beautiful. A kiss that makes everything else fall away.

Above us, the sky burns. Streaks of silver and violet arc across the dark. Meteors leave trails of fire in their wake, each one a promise, a wish.

Breaking the kiss, I lean back slightly, my forehead against his.

"Hey, Zye."

His lips tug into a faint smile. "Hm?"

I pull back just enough to meet his gaze. "For so long I was afraid. Of who I was. Of what I carried. Of where this was all going. But now… I'm not."

His hand tightens over mine. I glance once more at the sky, blazing with light, then back at him. "Where I am from, whenever we see a shooting star, we make a wish."

He raises a brow. "Thats a lot of wishes, Rae."

"Yup, it is." I say, lifting my eyes to the falling stars.

"But I want to do more than just wish on them. I'm ready to rewrite them."

THE END

"We don't want balance. We never did.
And now that we have your power, Athyria will burn"

A NEW THREAT. A DARK SECRET.
A WORLD ON FIRE.

RAE & ZYE WILL RETURN
IN BOOK TWO:

Ardence

ACKNOWLEDGEMENTS

Sometimes, when I'm hooked on a really good book, I flick to the acknowledgements to get a feel for the author. I'm guilty of doing it mid-way through a movie or TV show too. I want to know the who, the what, the why. I love details.

I don't know why I'm telling you this—maybe it's nervous energy, because writing this part is proving harder than writing any of the words before it—but whether you've read all of those or just flicked to the back to figure out more about me...

Thank you.

Turns out that writing a book is not for the faint of heart. I was humbled, quickly.

I embarked on this journey wide-eyed and eager, punched out a bunch of words, and, boom, wrote a book. *And it was awful.*

So I went back to it. And I kept reading, listening, learning, failing, and trying. If I'm being honest, I even threw in the towel a few times too. But for whatever reason, I kept at it. I absorbed everything I could from as many people as possible and kept writing, because I didn't want this dream to die.

Throughout all of that, I had a small circle of people who kept me moving forward—especially on the days (weeks, months...) I felt like I'd only gone back.

To Simon, you've tolerated more than your fair share of wild ideas and adventures in our marriage, and I wake up grateful every day for everything you've supported, encouraged, and, let's be honest, been dragged into fixing over the years.

To my kids, Harper, Quinn and Ari, you've inspired so much of this story and shown nothing but excitement and support through the entire experience. Blind faith is an incredible thing.

There's something that shifts in your soul when you're on the verge of quitting and your seven-year-old stands up and says, "But Mum…"

So I wrote on.

There's a remarkable woman in this story—the Healer—who was inspired by one of the smartest, most selfless, and incredible women I've ever known. Bróna, without you, this book would never have happened. You've been there every step of the way, through every typo, tense shift (legitimately whiplash-worthy), and tantrum—and you never wavered. Even at its worst, you encouraged me to keep writing, and to this day, I can't quite understand why. No words will ever be enough to thank you.

To my editors, Kaitlyn Katsoupis of Strictly Textual (she had me at the title!) and Dean Koorey, thank you. Kaitlyn was instrumental in guiding the plot and restructuring key moments to drive the story forward. Dean came in at what I thought was the very end to help with a few last-minute line edits and ended up sparking almost an entire rewrite. I look forward to working with both of you again in the (near!) future.

To Esther Maria, for the cover design, thank you. I'd consider myself creative, but your ability to pull this vision from a sketch that looked like it had been done by my dog was nothing short of incredible. And at the time of writing, I am in the initial stages of an audio book which is just wild – I am looking forward to sharing more on that soon.

And to everyone who beta read, made suggestions, tweaked, and navigated through the early versions right up until what you've just read—thank you. There were many of you, and I'm endlessly grateful for your time, opinions, and honesty.

I guess it's time to finish book two: *Ardence*, coming later in 2026!

If you enjoyed *Emergence*,
be sure to check out the website
and subscribe to the newsletter for
exclusive news and bonus content.

www.courtneybeaton.com.au

Instagram: @courtneybeatonwrites

Courtney Beaton is an Australian author and the founder of Kao Kreative, a marketing, event and creative agency. Through the chaos, one thing has always stayed constant — words.

Whether she's drafting client campaigns or content, reading late into the night or writing in stolen moments between deadlines and family life, storytelling is where she is most comfortable. It's the thread that's followed her through every career pivot and creative risk.

Courtney lives on the NSW South Coast, on Dharawal Country, with her husband, three children, a dog, and a suspicious number of chickens. Life is loud, wild and lived mostly outdoors. Which is where you'll find her if not at her desk (or phone) working on her next project.

Emergence is her debut novel.